A VOICE OF REASON

JOE CARGILE

SEVERN RIVER PUBLISHING

Severn River Publishing
www.SevernRiverBooks.com

This is a work of fiction. Names, characters, businesses, places, events and incidents are either the products of the author's imagination or used in a fictitious manner. Any resemblance to actual persons, living or dead, or actual events is purely coincidental.

ISBN: 978-1-64875-614-6 (Paperback)

ALSO BY JOE CARGILE

Blake County Legal Thrillers

Legacy on Trial

In Defense of Charlotte

The Wiregrass Witness

The Burden of Power

A Voice of Reason

To find out more about Joe Cargile and his books, visit

severnriverbooks.com

AUTHOR'S NOTE

A Voice of Reason is a work of fiction. Although I've pushed hard to make the characters in it feel authentic, none of them are based on real people. There are certain elements of Georgia law that are in fact real, but that information is meant only to lend more credibility to the scenes I've invented for this novel, and to arguably add some level of logic, maybe even trustworthiness, to the decisions that the characters make as the story unfolds. Lawyers in places all over the world do important work for their communities, and many of them come across very interesting cases while in service of their client and vocation. But trust me when I say that there is another side to the work that can be quite tedious at times, not to mention rather dry. For that reason, I've taken more than a few liberties in how I've gone about applying any of the real law found throughout this book. It's all for the story, friends, but I'm sure you understand.

Now, with that truly warmhearted disclaimer in mind, I do hope you enjoy *A Voice of Reason,* the fifth novel from my series of Blake County Legal Thrillers.

Until next time,
Joe

For my father, the best man I'll ever know.

PART I

THE HEIR

"Good wishes alone will not ensure peace."
—Alfred Nobel

1

He had his eyes on the screen when the message came in. It was from an unknown number, but the type that bore a not-so-random 706 area code, the kind that his father relied on whenever he had to make use of a cell phone. Such occasions were certainly rare, though, which was something the man liked to make known to nearly everyone he dealt with. *No personal matters over email or phone.* That was how it was for anyone who dealt with the Great Man. And there were no exceptions, not even for family.

Art Mortlake stopped his scrolling and waited for a moment until the notification banner disappeared from the screen on his cell phone.

In the time since Art had been away for college, some three and a half years now, he'd only been contacted by the man a handful of times over the phone. That's because whenever possible, his father preferred to send all personal communication the old-fashioned way—through the actual mail.

Not that the letters themselves included anything of substance. Most were just simple notes that read like business correspondence, the kind meant to function as a sort of paper trail. His father used the letters to confirm the quarterly bank deposits he made into Art's personal account, to request updated copies of Art's academic transcript, and sometimes even to schedule the rare in-person meeting between father and son.

Whenever Art and his father spoke directly, an event that only happened about twice a year, the two men almost always did so face-to-face. This had as much to do with his father's dislike for chitchat, particularly the kind that took place through the phone, as it did the man's concerns over the cell phones themselves. Art's father had strong opinions on data collection and the monitoring of phone conversations that bordered on paranoia. But somehow, the man wore his wariness of modern technology as if it were yet another stamp of the Mortlake Family's immense privilege.

Their life wasn't anything like that of a provincial, he'd say, and everyday people weren't the ones who needed to worry about their personal affairs coming under any real scrutiny. *But a Mortlake did*. And this was how the Great Man made his case to anyone who tried to argue he should act differently.

Not that this tin-hat stance on cell phone use really affected that many people. Art's father—Clive Mortlake—maintained very few friends, and he only allowed direct contact from a handful of trustworthy names. Keeping his tight-knit network allowed for him to live and work from the shadows (i.e. a compound in North Georgia, of all places), where he oversaw all the family's investments and businesses from a secure space, and from where he delegated to others nearly everything that didn't require *his* time and attention.

The man had more money than a person could spend in five lifetimes, so, of course the eldest Mortlake's gaze continually rested on the finite resources that couldn't be bought. And *time*, being the most precious among them, was something the Great Man didn't spend over the phone. He insisted it be spent instead on what mattered most to him: Mortlake business, his causes, and the people he still believed in.

This was how Clive Mortlake spent his life—*his* time.

But he didn't have much left.

Art Mortlake took in a deep breath, set his eyes on the screen of his cell phone, then mashed the message icon with his thumb. As expected, the text message from the unknown 706 number was in fact from his father. And per usual, the words from the man were cryptic, curt:

Art, I believe the time has come for us to talk about your future. I'll expect you tomorrow, Saturday, December 14, by 4:00 p.m. We can discuss any questions you may have after your arrival. Declan will be in touch with regard to any travel arrangements. Expect his call before 10:00 p.m. tonight. Do not ignore this message. No need to reply.

-Dad

A smirk crept onto Art's face when his eyes met the last line in his father's message. The word *Dad* looked out of place, like a foreign term among the other carefully assembled words that comprised that unexpected note.

Clive Mortlake was a great man who invariably appeared each year on the Forbes 400, usually somewhere in the top half of its well-heeled midfield. He'd served on the boards of several publicly traded corporations and was the soon-to-retire chief executive officer for their family's multi-national mining company. And he was also, as one might expect, seated at the head of Mortlake Ventures, their SFO (i.e. single-family office), which served as the primary investment vehicle for the family's $10 billion or so they claimed in assets, as well as the philanthropic arm for the family's *many* charitable activities.

The Great Man wasn't much of a *Dad*, though, Art thought. But maybe he was getting sentimental in his final months, or maybe this was him wanting to finally open up some kind of dialogue, a discussion of sorts that might allow for father and son to finally make amends. That's what a lot of people probably felt they needed to do at the end of their life, maybe even someone like Clive Mortlake.

Although Art's father was only fifty-seven, the man had an aggressive form of cancer spreading from his colon, the kind that even a Mortlake couldn't pay to make go away. And news of this diagnosis some three months earlier had come as a terrible shock. Because how could it not, right? No one *really* walked into their doctor's office for a yearly physical with the expectation that they might leave only days later with a newly inked death warrant—yet that's what happened to him.

Now, most knew that Art's father maintained a fairly demanding schedule, but few probably appreciated how hard the man worked to keep himself trim and fit. Clive Mortlake ate right, made sound decisions, and never overindulged in alcohol or drugs. In fact, even with the dark clouds bearing down on him, he looked healthy, certainly healthier than the majority of men his age. *But that's cancer.* It doesn't discriminate, as they say, and the dull pain that Art's father had dealt with off and on was something he should've asked his doctors about sooner.

Art still struggled with the idea, with the fact that his father had let the cancer come in and take him by surprise. The man was tough, and he was smart, too, and for as long as Art could remember, his father had never been the type of person to stick his head in the sand when it came to a problem. But *this*, he'd been stupid about. He'd let the exact things that made him a force in the world of business—his toughness, his grit, his capacity to persist—prevent early detection. He'd let himself explain away the weight loss, the fatigue, even the blood in his stool. He'd let himself wait and see, until it was too late.

He'd let himself make the mistake.

Art read his father's words over once more, set the message to memory, then deleted it all from his phone. He wasn't really surprised by the message. Nor was he frustrated by the man's heavy-handedness, his expectation that Art simply needed to accept this less than twenty-four-hour notice and drop everything before their meeting.

No, none of that bothered him. Not really.

But what did frustrate Art was the fact that his father still couldn't even bring himself to call with more details about his health and give Art just a little hint as to why he really needed his son to be there so soon.

What a prideful, selfish father to grow up with, Art thought.

But what an incredible man for the world to soon be without.

2

Art placed his phone on the bar in front of him, then picked up his beer and finished it. He knew he needed to get himself better prepared for what would eventually come—for whatever terrible news his father wanted to share with him during their meeting tomorrow—but Art was much too sober to deal with all of that at the moment.

He decided it would be best to first get himself into the right headspace, a process that would entail at least two more drinks, possibly three, and maybe a bit of what he had tucked inside the front pocket of his jacket. Then, once he had his mind right, Art planned on breaking his father's little rule on cell phone use.

He had to.

After all, Art was the man's only son, and he felt he deserved to know how much time they had left. Because only three months ago, the prognosis sounded grim: the patient had between six months and a year, *maybe*, although the oncologist couldn't be sure.

So, what were the doctors saying now? Art wanted to know. Had the timeline shifted? If so, by how much? Days? Weeks? Months? Frustrated, he shoved the empty beer bottle away.

Art and his father had a complicated history, but he still couldn't figure out why the man wasn't willing to tell him more about the cancer. If Clive

Mortlake felt the need to reach out on such short notice, needed to plan a face-to-face just a day in advance, then something was clearly wrong. And if the man had even an inkling that tomorrow might be their last in-person meeting between father and son, then Art felt he deserved to know that ahead of time.

That's why Art was going to need to call his father up directly, why he was going to need to find out exactly what was in store for their little sit-down tomorrow. The man might refuse to tell him *everything* over the phone, which was fine, but Art wanted to at least know if *this* was likely the end.

Because if it was—the end, that is—then Art was on the verge of being the last Mortlake left.

Art turned and spoke in the direction of a nearby pool table. "I need to head out back, boys."

Art and some of his old teammates had spent the last hour or so catching up around the main bar area inside *The Blue,* a little two-story college dive that held tight to the corner of West Peabody and South Gregson. Their unofficial pre-party had all but broken up, though, and most from the group had already decided to move on up the road for the night's main event—an engagement party, of all things.

But a few of the guys still remained, and Walker Boyd, one of the stragglers, was who called back a response: "Don't forget we're all supposed to be over there by eight."

"It's only seven-forty, Boyd. There's still plenty of time."

"Then let's be early."

"The Peach Basket is literally two blocks over from here."

"I know where we're going." Boyd said this as he shifted his attention back to the game he had going on the pool table. It was with some Zetas who were still in school. Both looked well out of the big man's league. "It hasn't been *that* long since I graduated."

"Let's not start rehashing your glory days. We all know you spent most of them at the far end of the pine."

"I'm not." Boyd's tone couldn't hide the fact that he didn't like the comment about his playing time, or lack thereof. "I'm just reminding you what direction you should be headed, *good buddy*."

"Oh, is that what we are?" Art asked. "You want us to be tight now?"

"Don't start getting all testy with me." Boyd smiled when he said this, as did the pair of blondes who were with him. "Nobody here wants to see you jump this table and come after me like some tough guy. Besides, that's your only move, Mortlake, and we're all tired of it."

"Don't start with that."

"I'm not starting anything..." Boyd put both hands up, did the mock protest thing. "I've put all that mess in the past."

"I doubt that."

"Well, I plan to, at least while we're helping out with this wedding."

Art couldn't help but notice how the chatter in the barroom had quieted down a bit, how a few more faces had turned to look over his way. He had a reputation, one that people expected he live up to. And although Art knew that tonight *probably* wasn't the best one for him to risk adding anything more to his public record, he also knew his old teammate pretty well, and Walker Boyd rarely stopped this kind of self-righteous banter until there was real pushback.

"Well, that's really good of you, Boyd." Art flexed both hands, felt a familiar stiffness in his left wrist. "I'll be sure you get your participation award framed after the wedding."

"Keep being an asshole if you like, but it's Tom who asked us to bury the hatchet, remember?" Boyd's voice had a condescending tone to it now, one that matched his dated metaphors and whole scolding-older-brother routine. "Now, I know you're not too big on sticking with your commitments and all—"

Art was about to take a step toward Boyd when he noticed, out of the corner of his eye, the redhead who was standing off to the other side of the pool table. She had her cell phone pointed in Art's direction, and she wasn't being all that discreet about it. He guessed she was probably filming, just in case.

"I remember what we agreed to." Art spoke slowly now. "And besides, you know I put the past in the past a long time ago. I had to."

"Good," Boyd said with a wink. "I guess as long as you can think about someone other than yourself for a change, then we'll all be just fine."

Art let the comment pass as he turned around to face the sticky, oak bar that had been at his back. He caught the attention of his favorite bartender, ordered another beer for himself, then added a few more shots for good measure.

"Hey Boyd, how about you have one of these with me?" Art turned in his place so that he could still lean with his back against the bar. His eyes went to the opposite end of the pool table, where his old teammate stood. "It's been way too long since we got rowdy together."

"You're damn right it's been too long." Boyd leaned over the table, lined his pool cue up for the next shot. "But I told Tom we'd all keep things relaxed tonight, at least until Zoe's family decides to take off. That's what they asked us *all* to do."

"Right." Art took a sip of his beer, smiled. This wasn't the first he was hearing about such mandate. The newly engaged pair—Tom and Zoe— claimed that a quasi-teetotal vibe was exactly what they wanted for the night's festivities, but Art doubted that this was really the case. He knew Tom's family well, and he'd heard plenty about Zoe's people, so his gut told him that this little suggestion to go light on the booze had little to do with creating a family-friendly atmosphere. *No*, what it had to do with was appearances, and when it came to the bride-to-be, Zoe Mitchell, nothing mattered more than how things appeared to be.

Art understood this side to her better than most.

Boyd paused his shot to ask his question. "You are planning to behave, right Mortlake?"

"It'll be fine. You handle any brown-nosing with the Bible-beating in-laws. I'll keep on living my life."

"No surprise there." Boyd then let the pool cue rip, showboated a bit as one of the striped balls slid smoothly into a corner pocket. He didn't look at Art as he stalked around to the other side of the table, lined up another shot. "It's your world and we're all just living in it..."

Art shook his head. "You think I'd try and screw up Tom's engagement party?"

"Did I say that?" Boyd asked this as he hammered the last striped ball on the table, sending it back in Art's direction like a rocket. The ball made a loud *clang* after it met the inside of the pocket. "I don't think I said anything of the sort. I'm just making sure you show up, Art."

"Just get off your high horse and have one of these with me." Art picked up two of the small plastic cups from the bar, held one out to his old Duke teammate. He had enough problems to think and drink about that night. He didn't care to collect any new ones. "We'll drink to whatever you like, Boyd."

"Fine." Boyd was shaking his head, but at least he was starting to walk over to accept the drink. "Remember, though, I'm not the guy who's supposed to be keeping an eye on everything. That's something you—one of the *groomsmen*—is tasked with doing."

"Oh, I disagree." Art handed Boyd one of the shots of brown liquor. "When a friend is dumb enough to be getting married at twenty-two, then it's on his boys, especially the ones who he's asked to be groomsmen, to make sure that his last days as a free man are spent in *good company*."

Boyd downed his shot, coughed. "And you think you're in that good company?"

Art knew his old teammate was just trying to needle him now. It was the way Boyd was. It was the way he went about getting under a person's skin, and the approach wasn't all that different from how Walker Boyd once liked to play ball. A shove here, an elbow there, a grab of the jersey whenever he got behind you on the block. It was his way. He chipped and chipped at you, until he forced a mistake.

"Hell, I'm the best of company," Art said. He paused a moment so that he could knock back his own shot of bourbon. "That's why people like having me around. There's always that potential for a great time..."

Boyd only nodded at this. The six-eight Tennessee boy had left the Duke program after graduating two years earlier, but he'd been a rising junior the year that Art came to Durham. Boyd went on to finish his college career as a four-year letterman, although the minutes he'd received throughout his years were the kind that came during garbage time, or when a coach needed to send a message, needed a player who could do a little dirty work in the paint. Still, Boyd could have been a starter at a lot of other schools. He was big and thick and surprisingly fast, especially for someone who talked with a slow, Southern drawl such as his.

Except here's the thing, Boyd had wanted to play ball in Durham, just like Art.

And although Walker Boyd had that swooped hair look of a guy who'd learned to hoop in the parking lot of his old man's country club, he was anything but soft. He'd made his reputation as someone who worked hard, as someone who made the most of the opportunities given to him, which was precisely why Boyd had always harbored a dislike for the other athletes who chose to squander their own opportunities.

People just like Art.

"Well, you're right about that potential," Boyd finally said, turning back to the pool table. "There's always been plenty of that with you."

Art turned and picked up his cell phone from the bar, grabbed the bottle of beer beside it. Behind him, he could hear Boyd starting to sum up his little fireside chat.

"I won't go lecturing you about all the promise and potential and success you pissed away, though." Boyd spoke loud enough for most in the room to probably hear. "I'm not your daddy, Mortlake..."

Art considered the weight of the bottle in his hand, even pictured it smashing against the side of Boyd's skull, spraying beer and glass throughout much of the room. He took in a deep breath, though, and paused long enough to remind himself that it was best to just leave the comment alone. Besides, Boyd didn't know the first thing about what he was talking about. He just wanted to chip and chip and chip until he got some kind of reaction, like he'd been able to get from Art in the past.

But things were different now, Art thought. He couldn't afford to be that person anymore.

Boyd leaned over the green felt surface of the pool table, lined up his last shot. "Let me know when you're done just trying to have a good time." Boyd spoke with his head turned so that he could look at Art, then let the shot fly on the table. It caught the edge of the eight ball, pushed it into one of the table's side pockets. *Thump.*

Art held the big man's gaze. "You didn't call your shot, *good buddy*."

Boyd seemed to ignore the weak comment. "Let's all get going," he said, placing his pool cue on the empty table. "This thing starts in about fifteen, right?"

"Always good catching up." Art said this as he started walking away, angling himself toward the back of the bar. "I'll see you later on at the party. If you make it there before I do, tell Tom he needs a drink."

"Come on, Art, we can all just roll up there together."

Art didn't say anything. He knew he was in the wrong, so he just waved a hand.

"Fine, go ahead and be selfish," Boyd called out, his voice at full volume. "Just don't go disappearing on us tonight."

"I'll show up, Boyd." Art didn't look back. "You know I always do."

3

Art made his way along the edge of the bar. As he did so, he stole a glance at the wall behind it, at the line of jerseys that hung high in a row of shadowboxes. The Blue was the kind of bar that looked from the outside like it was just another run-of-the-mill college watering hole, but the place was a favorite among a certain group of students who were there for school in Durham, mainly the partiers and athletes. And because of this, the bar owners had been gifted dozens of jerseys from big-name basketball players who'd come through there during the past couple of decades. The jerseys were all signed, too, and the boxes each had a picture of its star player in action.

The names on those jerseys were of legends, at least most of them were.

There were also a few on that wall who were considered, well, more obscure players. The names on those jerseys weren't the guys who'd made it to the NBA, not even for a cup of coffee, but they were still players who'd all found their own unique place in the program's history.

And on that wall of old Duke players—among them, previous lottery picks, all-conference studs, and former All-Americans—was also *his* jersey: a ripped, blue-and-white #20 from a season three years earlier. This jersey's story was different from all the rest on that wall, as evidenced by the faded splatter of blood across the front of it and the wild picture and caption selected for the box. The copper plaque on it read:

The Tallahassee Tussle – January 18, 2022

Art Mortlake got his first real minutes during a Monday night home game, a non-conference matchup against the South's most prestigious military college. The Citadel's starting five didn't offer much of a test for the Duke squad that night, but the game still provided a valuable opportunity for the home team to get reps in at full speed, and for the coaching staff to evaluate the quality of any young talent they had waiting near the bottom of the depth chart.

The decision to play Art and the other freshmen was probably made well before tip-off. The coaches needed to keep minutes down on the team's everyday starters, keep them healthy before things opened up the following week with conference play. And they probably needed to find out who they could trust coming off the bench. So, during the team's first thirty-second timeout, the coaches finally decided to give Art and a few others the nod.

He still remembered everything about the moment. The boys were all gathered together, getting coached up on the sideline, when one of the assistants called it out from the other side of the huddle: *Mortlake, get ready, you're taking Silva's spot at the two.*

Art entered the game with twelve minutes left in the first half. He put in a good shift, too, racking up four dimes, three steals, and fifteen points.

This debut performance came as a surprise to those who followed the team closely from the stands. Not many expected Art Mortlake—a freshman shooting guard billed at an ambitious six-two, one-eighty-five in the program—to be much of a factor that season. This was because most people didn't quite trust the idea that Art deserved his spot on the team, deserved his opportunity to take the floor and hoop with the best in the country. Their lack of trust had to do, in part, with what Art looked like: another fair-haired, undersized product out of the lilywhite prep leagues along the East Coast, *which he was.* And it had even more to do with *who* he was: heir to one of the country's largest fortunes.

Not that it wasn't right for the fans and sportswriters to harbor suspicions. The roster spot that Art occupied as a freshman—for a short time, at least—placed him on a team that was filled end-to-end with *the* best college basketball players in the country, a line-up packed with the bluest of the blue-chip prospects. So, when it became news that Art Mortlake, a three-star wing who most considered a mid-tier prospect, might soon join the side in Durham, the selection raised eyebrows.

Lots of them.

To be fair, though, the scouts and local sports journalists did at least acknowledge Art's impressive toolset: elite speed, above-average skill on the defensive end, a light touch from pretty much anywhere inside twenty-five feet. Those same insiders just also pointed to the fact that he was outside the top-tier rankings put together by the national services. And *every single one of them* questioned his ability to compete, at least in terms of guard play, with the other players who'd made their way to the highest summit of college basketball.

But Art's last name—and the wealth his family commanded—was really what made things messy.

The accusations began rolling in as soon as the school announced Art's commitment to play ball in Durham. They got ugly, too, as did the conspiracy theories that followed, but it all sort of became part of the legend that surrounded Art's very short-lived time on the hardwood: Mortlake money paid for the roster spot, number 20's daddy applied pressure to somewhere high above, nasty people blackmailed a decision-maker to secure Art's spot at Duke, etc., etc.

No one could ever deny what happened, though. Not before. Not after.

And it was that Monday night home game against the cadets from Charleston that really started it all. It gave fans a glimpse of something special. People outside the program started to question the assumptions they'd first made about Art, about his place on the team. Their suspicions fell to the wayside over the course of the ten games that followed, too, because every single time Art stepped out onto that court, everyone watched him go to work.

They watched him do what he once did best: *shoot the lights out.*

Art followed up his solid debut performance with another fifteen-point night, this time against Gonzaga. Then he scored eighteen points when they went to Columbus to visit Ohio State and had twenty-three more when they hosted South Carolina State at Cameron Indoor.

Although Art never cracked the starting five that season, he continued to come off the bench night after night and thrash teams from beyond the arc. He posted valuable minutes and kept hitting big shots in their games against App State, Elon, both of the Techs, Miami, Wake, and at the end— Florida State.

The game in Tallahassee was Art's last. He posted a modest stat line: 9 points, 2 rebounds, 2 assists, 2 steals, 0 blocks—*1 technical foul.*

The announcement was swift. The school suspended Art, pending an ongoing investigation, which didn't come as much of a surprise to anyone who'd witnessed the Tallahassee incident live.

Then, the video soon started making the rounds, a clip from the fight that spread across social media like wildfire.

The recording captured everything in incredible detail: Art diving into the second row of the stands, his fists pummeling the faces of not one, but two unsuspecting fans, then players from both teams, along with security staff, finally jumping into the mix, pulling Art back out of the stands by his arms and ripped jersey.

The bizarre scene looked outrageous, unimaginable, and quickly became the hottest, most delicious story for the talking heads of sports media.

The team flew back to Durham that night, leaving Art behind at one of the area hospitals, where he was a patient who was also *technically* in the custody of the Leon County Sheriff's Office. And while he waited on news as to his official criminal charges, the doctors handed over a crushing update of their own: scans of Art's left hand and wrist revealed a scaphoid fracture, which wasn't good, along with significant damage to both the fourth and fifth metacarpal of that same hand.

Art caught two charges for aggravated battery, posted bail the next day, then headed for Louisiana to undergo surgery.

The following week, he officially parted ways with the team.

Now, Art doesn't admit this to anyone, but he still thinks about that night in Tallahassee almost every day.

After the game ended, while he waited in the hospital, Art's father came down from Georgia to see him. The man stood right next to his hospital bed, the one Art's good wrist remained handcuffed to, and he explained to Art exactly how everything would work going forward: the best hand specialist had already been lined up to perform the surgery, the best physical therapists were ready to handle his rehab, their all-world attorney would be there within the hour, and another well-known local lawyer had already been engaged to assist in Art's defense of the criminal case.

Art was a Mortlake, *dammit,* and on that night, Clive Mortlake assured his son that he would certainly receive the best care, best counsel, and *best* results possible.

But that would be it.

Nothing more.

That night, Art's father made it clear that their relationship—what little of it remained at that point between father and son—essentially ended there. Art was a liability who couldn't be trusted. It was the conclusion being drawn at that very moment by every sportswriter in the country, and it was a fact being brought into existence by every newsperson given the opportunity to comment on the fight.

Above all, though, Art's recklessness had tarnished the public's perception of the Mortlake men.

Which is why Clive Mortlake, then and there, made it known that he would *not,* under any circumstances, bring Art into the family business. Not for as long as he lived.

It was what was best for the family. It was the way things had to be.

Except now his father was dying.

4

With the pool tables and main bar area to his back, Art started down a long corridor that led him toward the rear of the building. People littered the hallway, leaning against the walls, talking and laughing, while others chatted up strangers as they waited in long lines for the bathrooms. Art nodded as he passed a few of the familiar faces along the way, said a quick hello to an old girlfriend who still texted him late at night, even caught an invite to another bar sometime later on into the evening.

Everyone was young. No one was in a rush. It was just another Friday night.

Art loved college. And he knew a lot of the faces in and around campus, especially those of the other upperclassmen who liked hitting the bars on weekdays. Sure, there were still plenty of people around the school who looked at him and saw three things: a short-lived basketball career, an unproven commodity on the court, a cocky, absurdly privileged guy who once exhibited the recklessness of a should-be two-time felon. But there were *also* people around campus who saw Art in a slightly better light: still cocky, although arguably a decent guy, who had the dependable reputation of a charming, somewhat lovable fuck-up.

Art knew things needed to change, though. He was now in his senior year at Duke, which, to be fair, he'd only arrived at by some strange miracle (i.e. a sizable donation), because even he agreed that the school's administration probably should've kicked him out after the fight in Tallahassee.

Except that's not what happened in the end. The charges brought against him in Florida evaporated when the two victims decided not to prosecute, and Art's lawyers, of course, put on an impressive case when they sat for his hearing before the CB, Duke's conduct board. One decision *shouldn't* cause a promising young man to lose everything, his attorneys had argued, certainly not one with Art Mortlake's level of potential.

It helped that Art was a good student, as did the fact that Clive Mortlake wanted to hand over a no-strings donation that was somewhere in the millions.

So eventually, things worked themselves out. The powers that be latched onto Art's contributions in the classroom in justifying their decision *not* to expel him at the end of his freshman year. And Art's privilege to remain on campus, as *just* a student, remained in place, conditioned upon his maintenance of a certain GPA. The school also quietly accepted the donation from Mortlake Enterprises, a contribution they deemed *wholly unrelated to Art's continued enrollment at Duke*. Then everyone officially put the matter to rest.

Except money wasn't able to change everything. It couldn't get the NCAA's two-year ban lifted, nor could it accelerate the healing of the bones in Art's left hand. Both eventually caused him to dispense with any illusions of returning to the basketball court, and, with time, Art turned his sights to enjoying all the things his college years had to offer.

Although it's true that Art no longer enjoyed the perks of being a ballplayer on campus, he still had plenty to like about being a student at Duke. With his more than three years living there in the Piedmont, he'd fallen into a routine that made the region feel like home, and for some strange reason, he'd come to develop a sort of interest in some of the names forever tied to the history of Durham.

No, Art couldn't go back and change anything about the fight in Tallahassee. Nor would he—even if he could—go back and change what had defined his last few years: the partying, the girls, the days that started in the afternoon. But if the words in his father's rather vague text message—specifically: *I believe the time has come for us to talk about your future—*

meant Art would soon be tasked with managing the billions of dollars that were under his father's command, then that meant a lot of things for Art. The first being the most obvious: that Art needed to be ready to shift course.

Durham had taught him about other men who'd done such things before.

There is an argument that James B. Duke did with tobacco what Rockefeller did with oil, and Carnegie with steel. But the sound of the bull whistle blowing from one of Duke's factories isn't what continues to reverberate throughout his old North Carolina town, nor is his legacy anchored to the sweetish odor of tonka bean, the pungent scent of the tobacco stemmeries that once wafted over the streets of Durham. In fact, today, the average person probably doesn't draw any kind of connection between Duke and the American Tobacco Company, the warehouses along Morgan, or the things of the past that once made his city the center of the bright-leaf belt.

But that's because in December of 1924, Mr. Duke made a decision that would forever shape the family's name. An endowment of $40 million—the modern equivalent of $75 million—was established for several benefactions, but a strong focus was placed on those programs that would aid in growing a hospital on the campus of the city's little university, a school once founded by Quakers and Methodists. And not long after that, when Mr. Duke died the following year, his last will and testament provided that an increase be made to the endowment, bringing the total sum to somewhere around $80 million—which amounts to roughly $150 million in today's monies.

In 1925 this was the largest endowment that'd ever come out of the South. It was made to a city in a region that was already struggling, and it was made in a time when the country was nearing the worst economic downturn in its history. Mr. Duke's decision to make this end-of-life bequest not only survived the Great Depression, but it also ensured his family's name would endure long after the fall of the institutions that had defined the South during his time: textile mills, tobacco, and the white man's segregated, blatant mistreatment of others.

So, nowadays, the connection between Duke and Durham and North Carolina isn't really about tobacco or the past. Duke is more so tied to those beautiful campuses that lie to the northwest of Durham's city center, their handsome stone buildings and gothic architecture. The Duke name is on those world-class research facilities, the hospital, and on the diplomas of every student who graduates from any one of the school's top-ranked undergraduate or professional programs. And Duke is a name that's synonymous with basketball, because it's found on that sacred hardwood inside Cameron Indoor Stadium.

For someone like young Art Mortlake, a child who grew up with an almost unfathomable amount of wealth, the stories that surrounded the great families—those with surnames like Duke, Vanderbilt, Rockefeller, Carnegie, Ford, etc.—they weren't just part of history. Those names didn't just pop up when high school teachers taught lessons about the rise of industrialism in America. Young Art didn't see those families, the people in them, as mythical beings, nor did he view their stories as cautionary tales about the consolidation of wealth, a reimagined version of aristocracy in America, or the root cause of the countless inequities that existed throughout the world.

He just viewed their stories as the history of people like him.

He knew first-hand what their privilege really meant. He knew that their wealth and status certainly made things so much *easier*. But he also appreciated the fact that the birth lottery didn't fix everything, didn't make *everything* easy. So, despite all of Art's faults, his *many* mistakes, he still had his whole life ahead of him to do something worthy of respect, maybe even self-respect. And he held great admiration for the men and women who chose to do important things with their own vast wealth. Art saw in their stories the power that money had when it came to shaping a family's legacy.

The choice had to be made, though. It was almost like a fact of life, at least for people like him, and it carried with it a decision that wasn't easy for anyone to make. *How much should a person give away?* It was a question he was beginning to think about more and more, especially in the wake of his father's recent diagnosis. *How much is enough?*

Art knew that his family had given away quite a lot during his father's lifetime, certainly more than some of Clive Mortlake's peers, but Art also knew that their family's wealth had continued to grow at an exponential rate during that same span of time.

Clive Mortlake would be remembered differently by those people who didn't *really* know him, people who saw him for only his businesses and charitable efforts, just as Art might one day be remembered in a way he didn't yet understand. Art had started to wonder, though, if it mattered at all what he or his father did in their personal lives. Or if all of it, even the false steps, would eventually be glossed over once enough money went to the right causes.

Art wasn't yet sure—but he planned to have a good time until he found his answer.

5

It's important to note that the Mortlake name isn't up there with the most recognizable surnames found in 20th Century American History. It's certainly old money, though, at least by American standards.

Although Art didn't know everything about the earliest origins of his family's wealth, he learned at an early age that it was his namesake—Arthur E. Mortlake—who the Mortlake Family considered responsible for elevating their station to America's upper-crust. *Big Arthur*—as Art liked to call him—amassed several million dollars in the years leading up to the First World War, then left it all behind when German machine gun fire cut him down during the final weeks of the Battle of Passchendaele, a ferocious and difficult campaign that left thousands buried in the fields of Flanders.

That was 1917.

With the death of Big Arthur, the family at that time was essentially the newly widowed Helen Mortlake, and her young child, Art's great-grandfather. Although times were much different then, Helen still managed to take control of the stakes they had in a number of companies. Two of them mined and cut timber in the central parts of Appalachia. Another prospected in places on the West Coast. And three others ran short-line railroads along the East Coast. Helen chose to remarry after some years, but her subsequent marriage never produced another child. The family all moved onto an estate in coastal Connecticut, a four-hundred-forty-acre *farm* that has remained with the Mortlake family to this day, and the rest is, as they say, history.

Now, it's Art's understanding that in the years that followed, it was Helen who made the shrewd decisions that led to shifting a large portion of the family's investments to the banks on Wall Street. The US economy had hit its stride, and Helen got in on the markets at a time that allowed the family to take full advantage of the boom that occurred during the 1920s. Westinghouse Electric. American Telephone and Telegraph. General Motors. On and on.

The Mortlake assets ballooned.

But as the Roaring Twenties began to draw to a close, Helen, almost prophetically, began to concern herself with protecting the family's assets. Her only son, Art's great-grandfather, was easing into his early teenage years then, so she made the decision during the early summer of 1929 to cash out eighty percent of the family's holdings that'd been invested in the stock market. The sum was somewhere north of $30 million. Helen divvied the spoils up among the industries that her late husband, Big Arthur, once valued, those like mining, timber, and rail, then stuffed the lion's share of it into the sectors that she'd kept her eye on, those like real estate, foreign banks, and aviation manufacturing.

Black Tuesday hit Wall Street in October of 1929. The Mortlake fortune, thanks to Helen, was left relatively unscathed, and the family didn't just survive the Great Depression and the years that followed, it thrived.

It was 1937 when Helen lost her second husband, and 1939 when her own health suddenly began to fail. Walter F. Mortlake—Art's great-grandfather—was just twenty-four when he and his new wife were forced to go about the business of burying Helen.

Walter took his mother's place at the helm of their little empire during the summer of 1939.

The Nazis marched into Poland not long after that.

Art remembers the first time his father spoke to him in earnest about the string of early deaths that'd plagued their family. Little Art wasn't much older than ten. The Great Man directed his son to attend the meeting—by way of a handwritten letter—and the two sat down together in the home office, at the appointed time, like adversaries: each positioned on opposite sides of a large mahogany desk. And from there, Art's father spent an hour or so talking about the meaning of sacrifice, about their family's commitment to military service.

Their meeting took place a few weeks after Art lost his mother to a car wreck.

Clive Mortlake told his son that *their* recent tragedy—the gruesome wreck that took his mother's life on a hilly two-lane in North Georgia—wasn't all that different from the ones that Art's grandmother had to deal with some years ago. He said that *their* tragedy also wasn't all that different from the grief that Art's great-grandmother had dealt with.

The comparisons confused Art at the time, but looking back, he could understand the line his father was trying to walk.

Military service. Car accidents. Health scares. They had little in common, but they still fit neatly into the only explanation his father could muster, one meant to describe the pain a person feels when they lose someone they love.

He explained that Walter F. Mortlake—Art's great-grandfather—served in the US Army, Second Ranger Battalion. He'd been running the family's companies and investment strategy for only a couple of years, those that followed the death of Helen Mortlake, when war broke out on multiple fronts. Walter joined up to fight in 1942, then shipped out the following year. When he lost his life during the offensive on Omaha Beach, he left behind a young wife, Pauline Mortlake, and a two-year-old son, Charles.

Young Charles Mortlake, Art's grandfather, grew up without a father of his own, but that didn't stop him from enlisting in the US Navy when the conflict in Southeast Asia escalated to an all-out war. At the age of twenty-six, Charles shipped out to Vietnam, where he served on a twelve-man platoon, one tasked with carrying out missions in parts of South Vietnam. In December of 1968, Charles went missing in the Mekong Delta. And just as his father had before him, Charles Mortlake left behind a young wife, Judith Mortlake, and a young son, *Clive*.

That conversation between Art and his father was one of the few times Clive Mortlake ever spoke about his own upbringing. He tried to explain how his years growing up without a father had made him more resilient, more purposeful. He tried to lay out how Art, in growing up without a mother, might also benefit in some of the ways that he had.

It was a heart-wrenching, somewhat disgusting interpretation by Art's father, but it was his best attempt at verbalizing how the tragedies of youth had affected him. It was his pre-apology for the years and years ahead, his justification for why he'd end up leaving Art mostly on his own, and it was a glimpse into how a family saddled itself with unnecessary burdens.

Being a Mortlake wasn't just about having immense privilege, he'd said.

It was also about surviving.

<u>**Exhibit "A"**</u>

Mortlake Family Tree

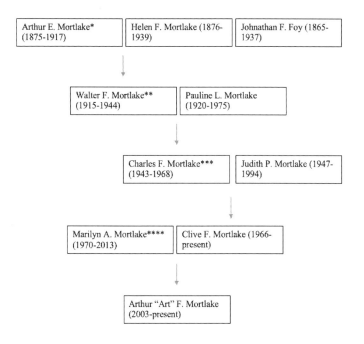

*KIA – West Flanders, Belgium, November 1, 1917
**KIA – Normandy, France, Omaha Beach, June 7, 1944
***MIA, presumed KIA – Mekong Delta, Vietnam, December 20, 1968
****MVA – Gilmer County, Georgia, United States of America, June 7, 2013

6

Art reached for the metal door at the far end of the hallway, gave it a shove, then left the crowded, noisy corridor behind him. There was an *Employees Only* sign plastered to the outside of the swinging door, one probably meant to deter random college kids from wandering into the kitchen area, but Art sauntered past the sign in his snaffle-trim loafers. He wore a black custom suit, sans tie, and with the wad of cash in one pocket, and an eight ball at the ready, he felt like Henry Hill from *Goodfellas,* kind of favored him, too.

Art glanced around the room and saw that no one manned the kitchen at the moment, so he dipped his hand inside the front pocket of his jacket and pulled the tight little baggie out. He began tapping it against the palm of his opposite hand, feeling the weight of the small, pebbly rocks that were inside it. He didn't usually do the stuff, unless it was a special occasion. *Which tonight was,* he told himself, starting to rub the bag between his fingers, breaking the rocks up until everything inside the plastic started to feel more like a fine powder.

And besides, he needed a little help, needed a little something to spur some action, especially given all that was on his mind: his father's cancer, the whole groomsman thing, the responsibility and billions that awaited him...

But what was the name of *that* club? Art asked himself, thinking back to that old mob movie. He was well aware that his mind was straying from what was important.

Art knew the place popped up in one of those early scenes from the 90s Oscar-winner, maybe thirty minutes into the film. He could picture it in his head: Henry rolls up to *that* club. It's his first date out with Karen, and when they pull up to where they're going for dinner, Henry just leaves his Cadillac at the curb, right out front, then walks Karen inside, taking her in through the kitchen. The guy starts handing out twenty-dollar bills to everyone he sees, and then the pair strolls right up to a table that's within feet of the stage—a place for the VIPs among VIPs.

Art shook his head. He tended to lock onto a thought, a question—especially a problem he couldn't yet figure out—and sometimes it took everything in his power just to leave the thought alone. And it didn't matter how trivial the question was, he often had to go back to it, over and over, until an answer finally came to mind.

He took another glance around the kitchen, searching for his roommate. Art knew that his friend would know the answer.

"Hey, Frank!" Art shouted. "Where you at?"

He waited for a long moment, heard no response. Then he noticed the door at the other end of the room. It was open, swung out wide, and from where Art stood, he could see out through the open doorway to the narrow alleyway that ran behind the bar. It looked cold out there.

"Frank, my boy!" he called out, this time louder. "You out back?"

The Blue itself was just another college bar at the edge of West Campus, but plenty of students preferred it over the other options that were available, and hordes of young people poured through its doors nearly every night of the week. Very few came there because of the food, though, and the owners knew this.

In fact, Todd and Brad, the couple who ran The Blue, had an incredibly clear vision for what they wanted their bar to be about. And the guys often proclaimed that they made their bacon by way of the realtor's mantra—

location, location, location—and The Blue certainly had all three: proximity to campus, proximity to ballplayers, and, of course, proximity to all the best-looking co-eds who liked to party.

So, the owners didn't give a rip about the food. And on most nights, the bartenders and bouncers rarely bothered even coming back to check on the kitchen, at least not until after eleven o'clock, when the drunk orders finally started rolling in. Because it didn't matter how busy the place was, the bartenders were instructed to tell everyone who ordered from the menu that it would be a long, long wait on the food. The owners wanted their young patrons filling their tabs with over-priced shots and cheap beer, not food, so they kept their kitchen a slow, one-man show.

Which is precisely why Art's friend and roommate, Frank King, had decided to apply for the open back-of-house position when one came available at The Blue.

"My goodness, man." Art muttered this as he tried to decide whether it was worth it to wait around for his friend. "It's hot as hell in here."

From where Art stood, he could already feel the kitchen's heat beginning to surround him, seeping into the fabric of his suit. It was that steamy, oily, thick kind of heat, the kind you only came across when inside a working kitchen. The room smelled of fried everything, too, which tracked, because the bar only sold four menu items: hushpuppies, tater-tots, chicken wings, and smashburgers.

Art saw that the little industrial kitchen did have a large fan in the opposite corner, one propped up near the dish pit area, but it was hard to tell whether the old Honeywell was actually running. Not that it looked like the dusty box fan could compete much with the heat that leapt from the kitchen's old flattop grill, or the smells that bubbled from its massive double-fryer, or the sound of the music blaring from the kitchen's speakers.

Yet, even amongst all that heat and noise, Art still felt like he could almost hear his own arteries backing up while he waited there in the room. He took the last swig of his beer, washed the sensation down, then slowly took a few more steps into the belly of that greasy sauna.

Art soon hollered, "Health inspector here! Who in the hell is running this place?"

Finally, the deep house music that poured from the speakers dropped in volume, and the lone cook stuck his head inside the kitchen's only other doorway.

The familiar face of Frank King had a brief look of panic on it. The expression was soon replaced with a broad smile, though, once the cook recognized who was calling out to him from inside the kitchen. And with Frank's appearance, even in the opposite doorway, came a potent combination of cologne and marijuana, a mixture loud enough to put up a fair fight with the other smells wafting about inside that grease pit.

"What's happening, Art?" Frank asked.

The chef took a few steps back inside the kitchen, leaving the door behind him open to the alleyway. Frank was a gangly dude, maybe a few inches taller than Art, and his long hair was tied up behind his head into a tight manbun. He held a big plastic cup, one that looked like it doubled as a soup container of sorts, and it was filled to the brim with his favorite red drink, Hawaiian Punch. He also had what looked like a joint tucked behind his ear, one he'd slipped just under the edge of his hairnet. And, as always, the guy carried himself with the ease of a young man who didn't appear to have a care in the world. "Didn't expect to see you come through here tonight," he added.

"I won't be here long," Art said, hoping no one else was going to come through the doorway with his friend. No one did. "I'm about to head over to that engagement thing for Palomino."

"I thought I heard you mention something like that." Frank placed his cup on a countertop, then picked up a can of body spray. He spoke as he doused himself with a long, fragrant blast, one that covered his six-four frame from head to toe. "When's the party starting up?" he asked.

Art glanced at the watch on his wrist, tried not to cough as his nostrils took in the newest scent in the room. The kitchen suddenly smelled like his old high school locker room, which was still an improvement. "Well, it's actually supposed to be starting right now..."

Frank didn't say anything, only nodded. He was a good friend, good roommate, the kind you could hang out with for hours, talk about life with, party with, and do all of it without judgment.

"Can you believe Palomino is getting hitched?" Art finally added, although he meant it more as a rhetorical question. "That crazy son of a—"

"Hell yeah, I can see it, especially when it's putting a ring on Zoe Mitchell." Frank let out a low whistle as he reached over and grabbed a white apron that hung from a peg on the nearby wall. He threw the top of the apron over his neck, then started tying the cords behind his back. "She's as *fine* as fine gets. And don't tell me you don't agree."

Art didn't say anything.

Frank continued. "Plus, she was like freaking runner-up for Miss Georgia, right? There's no way you're convincing me that Tom Palomino is making the wrong call."

"Yeah, but come on, Frank, I doubt you'd be making that decision if you were heading for the pros next year."

"I don't know," Frank said, offering a shrug and a glassy-eyed smile. He was obviously stoned. "Where am I going? Hopefully not somewhere that's going to stick me in the G-League."

Art laughed. "How about, say, somewhere in the first round? Maybe the fifth or sixth pick overall." Which is exactly where most analysts projected Tom Palomino would come off the board in the upcoming NBA draft.

Frank paused for a long moment. "So, that means I'm going to a city like—"

"It doesn't matter," Art said, cutting him off. "Small-market team. Big-market team. It's all still the NBA however you look at it."

"And *she's* still a total smoke show, however you look at it."

"Yeah, maybe," Art said. "But that's not enough, especially when you're about to essentially be a made man."

Frank was the one to laugh now. "He's already got it made, Art, and most people don't have the cards you boys have. We don't already have our spot waiting for us at the table, don't already know the things you know about—"

Art waved a hand. "I don't want to get into all that."

"All right, all right."

Art paused. "Appreciate it, brother."

"Don't mention it," Frank said with a flip of the hand. "We all have the right to keep our personal shit on the low, right?"

———————

The truth was, Art, just like his father, didn't really like getting into his own private business with anyone. But on those rare occasions when he did, he couldn't go to his old teammate, Tom Palomino, the all-conference megastar, the guy who'd asked Art to stand up there as part of his wedding party.

Not anymore.

No, Art usually went to Frank King these days. Which was kind of strange when he thought about it, because Art didn't really see his roommate all that often.

Although Frank looked to most like he was just another stoner, the guy was at the top of their class, and he insisted on working at least five nights a week. Sure, Art and Frank shared a great party house in Old West Durham, one that Art didn't let his friend pay rent at, but Frank still had plenty of other bills: food, gas, books, his extracurriculars. And Frank's upbringing wasn't anything close to the one Art had experienced, nor had he come there to Durham to just be an athlete.

Frank was there at Duke on a merit scholarship, one that took him away from the King Family's little hometown in rural West Virginia. Frank came from a life in a place that was very different from where Art grew up, which was good, because the contrasts in their lives played a big part in why the two young men worked well as friends. And those same differences actually made it easier for Art to shoot straight with his friend, to confide in him, at least when it came to certain things.

"By the way, how's your old man doing?" Frank asked.

"I'm still not too sure." Art paused for a long moment, then added: "But I'll actually be heading out to see him tomorrow."

"Yeah?"

Art nodded. "But I doubt I'll be gone more than a day or two."

"He's still in North Georgia, right? Hope he's not in the hospital."

Art sort of grinned to himself, mostly at the thought of his father stepping inside any kind of healthcare facility that wasn't at some discreet address hidden somewhere on the Upper East Side. "He's still in Georgia, at least as far as I know," Art said. "I doubt he's in the hospital, though. There's sort of a family friend of ours, Declan, who's my father's right-hand man, and he stays with my father twenty-four-seven. I think he'd have called me sooner if that was the case."

"Well, I guess that's good." Frank took a sip of his red drink. "At least there's someone around to check in on him."

Art chuckled. "Yeah, except good old Uncle Declan is only around because of his background in special operations. I doubt he knows much about caring for someone with a late-stage diagnosis."

"Might be surprised," Frank said. "Either way, he's probably still a good friend to have."

Art nodded again. "Especially for *my* father. He gets a little paranoid."

"Then you need to bring this to him," Frank said, pulling the joint from behind his ear. "I'm sure it'll calm his nerves."

"Believe me, I've tried that before."

"Okay, but this is the best bud I've gotten from my guy in a while." Frank slid his offering into a pocket on the front of his apron. "I mean, just now, when I was hanging out back, this stuff had me thinking I could almost speak French. I might be some kind of polyglot and not even know it."

Art just smiled, shook his head.

"I swear it." Frank laughed. "I was just there in the alley, minding my own business, when I realized that I'd been listening to a whole damn conversation in French. I'm pretty sure I even understood most of it."

"Then you should've invited whoever those exchange students were to come over and join you, Frank. That would've been some good, American hospitality on your part."

"Nah, these guys were probably too old to be students. And besides, they didn't give me the right vibe. Know what I mean?"

Art absorbed this. There was something about the way Frank said those words. It triggered something in Art's mind, made him think for a moment about some of the things Declan had once told him to keep an eye out for. "Are they still out there?" Art asked.

"No. I saw them strut away a few minutes before you came in here. You could tell they had that uptight look to them, though. Wouldn't have surprised me if they were former cops or serious military types."

"Right," Art said.

"I know you think I'm just messing around, but I have a real eye for these things."

"I'm sure their uniforms probably helped."

"Nope. No uniforms, just—" Frank paused.

"What?" Art asked. "You too blitzed now to remember what they were wearing?"

"Nah." Frank grinned. "Both of them had on a suit, just like your ass."

Art thought about this as he glanced down at the three-piece wool he had on. It was something he'd picked up from a haberdasher near Vanchiglia, a little university neighborhood in Turin.

"So, where's this one from?" Frank continued, pointing to Art's clothes. "It's slick."

"I'm really not too sure, actually. It might be from that—"

"Don't do the whole I-might-have-picked-it-up-at-Banana-Republic crap." Frank laughed as he said this. "I mean, maybe those two grunts outside had on something like that, but I know you, Art, and you *always* have to bring a little something different to the party."

He was certainly ribbing Art, but it wasn't being done in the way Walker Boyd had earlier that evening. There wasn't any sting behind these words. It was just two friends cutting up because they could.

"And look," Frank went on. "I know I'm from the woods, as you say, but even I can tell that your suit isn't the kind of thing you pick up at good old JCPenney."

Art played along. "Come to think of it, I got this one from that Jos. A Banks near the mall."

"Wrong." Frank made a buzzer sound after he said it. "Come on, blank check, where's it from?"

Art shook his head, smiled. "It's Italian."

"So, that's like an Armani or something?"

"This one I found at a place I came across in Northern Italy. It's from a little clothier that does bespoke—"

"Woah, woah, Richie Rich." Frank was still smiling as he started dusting crumbs from his greasy white apron. "I get it, the suit is custom as hell."

Art held up his hands. "You asked."

"And look at that." Frank pointed to the plastic bag in Art's hand. "What's all this talk about hospitality? I don't see you offering anything up."

"This?" Art began tossing the bag up and down, like it was a golf ball. "Let's break it out and see."

"All right, bet."

Art made a showing of glancing all around the room. "You think we can find a spot on any of these countertops that's not a potential health code violation?"

"Lock the door." Frank pointed to the one behind Art. "I'll make us up a place here quick."

"What about the one to the alleyway?" Art asked.

Frank smiled as he waved a hand. "I'm not worried about those Frenchmen charging in here. Are you?"

7

Art pulled the lock on the door, then turned and started walking along the side of the kitchen that ran opposite the fryers and flattop grill.

There were several waist-high coolers that commanded this side of the room, each with a jumble of messy dishes and knives left out on top of them. At the far end sat a large white cutting board, and beside it lay a mound of chopped vegetables and several half-filled containers with what looked like date stickers tagged to the outside. Ten more just like them had already been placed inside one of the open coolers, positioned there on the kitchen line and covered in saranwrap. And a dozen or so plastic bottles also sat out on one of the countertops. These looked like they contained all the sauces a person could ever need: bar-b-que, ketchup, mayonnaise, mustard, some kind of Siracha Ranch.

Art noticed that gobs of the stuff had dripped out onto the counters, and some of it had even made its way onto the floor.

"Chef, remind me again why anyone eats here." Art said this as he stepped his way, carefully, toward the edge of the door that led out to the alleyway. When he reached the exit, he peeked out into the little brick cut-through. It was empty, quiet, so he just waited there at the threshold, enjoying the cool December air that swept in from the outside. Art could tell that a cold front was making its way over the Piedmont that night.

"You've eaten here plenty of times," Frank shot back. "I'm sure of it."

Art saw that Frank was quickly wiping down an open surface and he tried not to look too closely at the grimy looking towel his friend had selected for the job.

"You know as well as I do that around ten-thirty," Frank continued, still defending his food service, "those orders just start flying in here. All these people get hungry once they get a few pitchers of beer in them. And that includes you, Mr. Germaphobe."

"You might be right, Frank, but you also know that I don't usually try and defend any of the decisions I make after midnight."

"Oh, I'm rarely wrong." Frank stepped back to admire the glistening surface in front of him. "I wouldn't be featured on the Dean's List every semester if I was."

"You'll be right at home in medical school, my boy. That ego is everything I want in a doctor."

"Don't forget I have a few six-figure job offers." Frank offered a wink. "Although that salary is probably a paltry sum to a Mortlake man."

Art laughed. "Then quit working here."

Frank shook his head. "I like working, young prince, and at least while I'm here, I get to have a good time doing it."

Art knew that his friend would graduate at the end of next semester with a dual degree in biomedical engineering and computational media, and that he would probably finish with something close to a flawless GPA. The guy was the son of a truckdriver and a teacher. And in about six months, he'd be out of this kitchen, and hopefully on to medical school, or on to working in some lab where they were aiming to find the cure for a life-threatening illness or syndrome. The twenty-two-year-old Marlinton native had the dogged work ethic of a coal miner and an IQ that was well above the ninetieth percentile. Frank was certainly going to go far, and he wasn't long for his current place in the world.

But Frank also really liked getting high, which was where Art usually came into the picture.

"This spot should work fine," Frank said. "Now, let me see what you have for us."

"Beats the hell of that bathroom down the hall." Art tossed the bag onto the newly cleaned area, then took another glance at his watch. It was now almost eight fifteen. "I only have time for a couple, though. I need to get out the door soon."

Frank nodded and got to work. "Yes sir, Mr. Mortlake."

"You know what, I'll just do it," Art said, stepping toward the waist-high countertop. "I don't like all that yes sir—"

"No, no." Frank put up a hand. "This is free for me, so I don't mind."

Art stepped back. His friend tipped the bag over and dumped a small mound of white powder onto the surface. He then took one of the smaller, flatter kitchen knives, and started chopping up the coke. Art was used to people doing things for him: cooking, cleaning, training, anything he needed, really. And old habits were certainly hard to break, even with friends.

"Hey Frank, do you remember that scene from *Goodfellas* where Henry —you know, Ray Liotta's character—takes Karen in through the kitchen when they go out for their first date? They go to that dinner club."

"Of course." Frank pulled a card from his back pocket, his student ID. He used it to flatten the mound out, then divvyed the powder up into four tidy rows. "Karen was played by Lorraine Bracco, who, by the way, is *also* very fine."

"No, I know all that."

"But I do love that scene." Frank started going through his pockets, searching for something. "And I'd probably give my left nut to take her out like that."

Art saw that his friend had come up empty in searching both pockets, so he handed over a crisp, hundred-dollar bill. "Here," Art said. "But do you remember the name of the club they went to? It's been bothering me."

"Well, hello there, Silence Dogood..." Frank grinned as he took the bill, seemingly oblivious to Art's question while he rolled the Ben Franklin into a short tube. He held it back out for Art. "You want to do the honors?"

Art shook his head. "After you."

"All right." Frank leaned over the countertop, took in one of the lines, coughed. He then shot back up to his full height, straight as a rail. "Okay, Mortlake, you're not messing around tonight!"

"Never." Art refocused his friend. "The dinner club, man, what was it called?"

Frank handed over the rolled-up hundred. "It was the Copacabana."

"That's right." Art snapped his fingers. "The Copacabana."

"Why'd you want to know?"

Art leaned over the surface, hoovered a rail of his own. "It was just bothering me, you know. I've seen the film at least a dozen times, and I couldn't pull the name of the club from my mind."

Frank knew all about Art's tendency to obsess over an unsolved problem. "You're like a dog with a bone, man. Why not just pull it up on your cell phone? That's what everyone else does. Hell, that's why we all have those things!"

"No, that's for the weak minded." Art realized he sounded a little like his father as he said this. "And besides, I have you, Frankie boy, and you really do have a wealth of information tucked away inside that brain."

"What can I say? It's a gift."

Art handed the bill back over to his friend. "It's just too bad you're burning half of it up..."

"You know, you're a pistol, Art." Frank put on an accent that he probably thought fit the kind you heard on the streets of New York. "I mean, you're really, really funny."

Art knew this bit from the film. "What do you mean, I'm funny? Funny how?"

"It's funny, you know. I mean, you made a good joke."

"Let me understand this, *Frankie*. You saying I'm funny like a clown?" Art added a bit of the Bronx cadence to his own words. "You think I'm a clown?"

He and Frank laughed as they went back and forth like this, reenacting some of their favorite dialogue from the old mob film. Neither of them knew the words by heart, but it didn't matter. They had their whole lives ahead of them to get things right.

"You know, *Frankie*, you're a good guy, a *good* fella." Art said this as he slipped his little stash back inside the front pocket of his suit jacket. He felt charged up, ready to roll. "But I've got to get going, got to get out of here."

"Go ahead, then, get out of here!" Frank hollered, still using his accent. "We'll hang out sometime next week."

"Yeah, sounds good." Frank patted Art on the back. "And look, in all seriousness, I hope your dad's okay. Make sure you give him my best."

"Appreciate that," Art said. "I'll probably call him tonight and make sure."

"That's a *good* son."

"I don't know about all that..."

"I do," Frank replied. There was real sincerity to his words. "You're a good guy, Art. Don't forget that, okay?"

Art didn't say anything more as he slipped out the kitchen's back door and stepped into the cold night air that filled the alleyway behind the bar.

He glanced to his left, toward the space where the alleyway opened onto West Peabody. He saw no one passing by along the edge of the dark sidewalk, which wasn't uncommon at that time of night, mainly because the streets which stretched in that direction led toward a semi-industrial pocket of town, a row of decaying buildings that ran along the edges of the railroad tracks, and a bridge they called the Can Opener. Places the students didn't usually go to at night.

Je ne sais pas, Art thought, grinning as he turned to start walking in the opposite direction.

He felt good as he headed toward West Main. He could see ahead, at this other end of the alleyway, that the well-lit sidewalk bustled with students: twenty-somethings talking and laughing, young people just enjoying another Friday night.

Art felt his mind had kicked into a higher gear, and everything appeared faster, clearer, sharper. It was the blow, he knew this, but it was a sensation he could chase all night. It was like being wrapped in a Kevlar-like confidence, one that made Art feel like he could do anything, be anything, see anything.

But as Art headed toward his old teammate's engagement party, he didn't notice the pair of men who stood on the other side of the dumpsters, watching him from the shadows.

He didn't see what waited for him.

8

It was the bride-to-be who first saw Art come through the front doors of The Peach Basket. She stood just inside the venue's main entrance, with a somewhat older couple at her side. All three of them wore wide smiles and seemed genuinely happy, wholesome. Art had to admit, Zoe's all-white, backless minidress, coupled with those long, perfectly sculpted legs of hers, certainly made for a welcome sight to any guest arriving late to the party.

Art glanced down at his wristwatch as he left the doors behind, knowing good and well that Zoe had already spotted him. Maybe eight thirty-two is a little late, he thought, but at least I'm here for the party.

Art lifted his eyes and offered a smile, not to Zoe, but to the striking, age-resistant blonde who stood next to her. "I take it you're Mrs. Mitchell?" Art asked as he eased closer to the mother-daughter side of the Mitchell Family trio. "I'm Art Mortlake, one of Tom's friends from school."

The woman nodded. "Hello, Art." Her voice sounded as rich and smooth as buttermilk pie.

"I know I'm running a few minutes late." Art added some more wattage to his smile. "I hope that's not too much of a problem."

"More than a few minutes," Zoe chirped, jumping in before her mother could say another word. "But I'm sure you have an excuse of some kind, right Art?"

Zoe's mother politely cleared her throat, then offered a rather coy smile of her own, one that Art took to mean one thing: Mrs. Mitchell knew more than enough about him already. "As you suggested, Art, which you Northern boys should understand is something you're not really supposed to do, I am Zoe's mother."

"It wasn't meant to—" Art said, beginning to form an apology.

She winked. "Not to worry, you're forgiven." She then held up a well-manicured nail. "However, I will have to ask you to excuse my daughter. See, planning a wedding can often be more stressful than it is fun, and I've encouraged her to remember that."

"Well, I don't know a thing about planning weddings, ma'am." Art dropped his voice to a conspirator's tone. "But I do know a little bit about having fun..."

She seemed to like this. "Just call me Coco. Everyone does."

"Yes, ma'am." Art knew that as long as the mother of the bride liked him, he could do little wrong. "I take it that's short for Colette?" he asked.

"Careful," replied the woman. "There you go again."

Art nodded dutifully.

"But yes, Art, you're correct. My mother, who grew up in Montmartre, insisted I carry a French name. She and my father met after the war in Europe. The Army had him stationed in Germany, but the two of them crossed paths while he was on leave for a weekend in Paris."

"Ah, well, Coco is *très chic*," Art said. "And Montmartre is one of those magical places you'll only find on the Right Bank. Hopefully some of your family is around tonight. I'd love to meet them."

"I'll point out a couple of my cousins who—" she started to say.

"That's enough, Mom." It was Zoe who interrupted. "I just need Art to go join the rest of the *potential* groomsmen by the bar. He's the only one we've been waiting on, remember?"

"Zoe, there's no need for—"

"No, that's okay," Art said. "I'll keep on moving toward the bar area." He leaned in and pecked Zoe's mother on the cheek. "It was wonderful to meet you, Coco. It's such a privilege to be a part of all this."

"And it was lovely to meet you, Art." She offered him that same smile from before. "Go have some fun tonight."

Zoe's father, Bedford Mitchell, was a man who Art was familiar with only by reputation. Pastor Mitchell was the face of one of the largest megachurches in the South, and he was also a strong candidate in the upcoming race for the governor's mansion in Georgia. The man's stare found Art from a few feet away, and his twangy, pulpit ready voice soon followed.

"Good evening, young man." He extended a smallish hand for Art to shake. "The party started a little while ago, so I'm glad you could finally make it." The good pastor's words made him seem perfectly happy to take up his daughter's cause.

"Evening." Art gripped the hand. "Art Mortlake, sir. I'm a friend of Tom's."

"Right, yes. And I'm Bedford Mitchell." There would be no offer to call this man by his first name.

"That's right. I knew I recognized you, sir." Art knew the game. "Didn't you submit your bid recently for governor? For the race come twenty twenty-six."

"I see you've done your homework, young fella."

Zoe huffed from nearby.

Art ignored her. "You know, last time I was in Georgia visiting my father —" Art felt the man's grip loosen, just a bit, and watched him quickly morph from pastor into politician. He was obviously familiar with the Mortlake name, at least by reputation. "I saw you were getting a lot of favorable press in your race for governor," Art said. "I even caught a few of your ads on television. I understand that politics can be a tough business, Mr. Mitchell, so it's nice to meet someone who's still willing to get in there and risk it."

Pastor Mitchell had obviously been keeping one eye on his little girl, and probably the other on his wife, but now he was being forced to set his sights on the thing politicians needed more than anything else: campaign dollars.

"It's a *very* tough business these days," he said, a ruefulness in his voice. "And it's getting harder and harder for the good guys. I mean, just look at all the fundraising being done for my opponent. Most of it is coming in from those intolerants out there on the Left Coast." He chuckled as he said this, but his eyes were fixed on Art's face, probably watching for a reaction that might provide a clue as to Art's political persuasion.

"I'd really like to hear more about that, sir." Art almost felt sorry for the man. "I don't have much of a nose for politics—" Art sniffed, tapped a nostril. "But I'm doing my part in developing a sense for these things. As you may be aware, my father, Clive Mortlake, has been known to involve himself in a number of worthy causes over the years, and he expects me to do the same."

"Well, I've spent my life in service of worthy causes." The good pastor side of the Jekyll-and-Hyde combo had suddenly worked its way back into the mix. "Doing good works is part of what the Lord has called me to do, son. It's all I know."

Zoe inserted herself more forcefully now. "Daddy, please, Art really needs to go." She sounded even more frustrated than before. "I'm sure you two could talk about your campaign later." She then turned to look at Art. "Hopefully before things get too rowdy at the bar, right?"

Art ignored her and kept his eyes on the politicking evangelist. "Like I just mentioned to your lovely wife, sir, it's a real privilege to be a part of all this."

"Well, it's our pleasure, son." The politician's smile told Art that he didn't really care about all that right now. He was ready to have that conversation about the Mortlake Family's support, and their vote of confidence that would never come. "How about we talk later this evening?" the man prodded.

Zoe didn't allow Art to respond. Her hands just shooed him toward the next room, the mass of faces and well-dressed bodies that looked to be swirling around inside it. "Just go!"

Art nodded to the man, smiled. "I better do what she says."

"I certainly would if I were you." He laughed. "It was *very* nice to meet you, young man."

Art started for the party.

And Zoe followed.

9

Much to Art's surprise, Zoe proceeded to tuck her hand inside the crook of his elbow. She guided him, ever so slightly, as they walked together in the direction of the other partygoers. Although the former pageant star kept a smile plastered to her face, Art could tell from the way her hand gripped the inside of his arm that she was just waiting for an opportunity to lay into him.

"What do you think you're playing at?" she hissed, once they reached a small anteroom that divided the venue's foyer from its main party area. "I specifically told you to steer clear of my family, especially my parents."

"Come on, Zoe." Art started to pull his arm away from her hand, but she held tight to his bicep. "What was I supposed to do?" he asked. "Walk right by them without saying a word? I'd have looked like a real jackass."

"Just avoid them, okay? That's all I'm asking." There was a hint of what sounded like pleading in her voice. "It'll keep things from getting, well, even more complicated."

"Your dad's a politician," Art scoffed. "I wasn't going to get very far without him talking about his campaign. It's part of the game."

"This isn't a game to me!" Zoe snapped. "Besides, I shouldn't have to remind you how important this night is to Tom and I."

"Tom and me," Art quipped.

"Now you're being a jackass."

"No, I'm just being—"

"*Yes*, you are." She paused. "You know you don't have to be a jerk, Art. Even with all that's happened between you and—"

He cut her off. "You're right, I'm sorry."

Zoe only nodded.

When they made it to the edge of the party room, Art could tell that Zoe had obviously gone to great lengths in her quest to ensure that everything looked perfect for that night. Although he would never admit this to her, Zoe Mitchell certainly had a knack for making the difficult appear easy.

The party itself was being held only four weeks after the couple's engagement, so the event felt timely, fresh, and relevant to their big announcement. And because the party wasn't scheduled too close to the actual wedding itself, there was a different kind of energy in the room, one that felt lighter, and purely celebratory.

Everything was customary, too, even down to the invitations for that night, which made clear that gifts were not expected, only attendance. Art could see once they were further inside the large room that it was almost completely full, although he felt certain Zoe had made sure to include all of the important people, as well as friends and family members from their respective families, especially those persons who'd be invited to the official wedding weekend. And the arrangements, he had to admit, blended just enough modern with the traditional, a style that she and the planners had incorporated beautifully into the historic, old-Durham venue that was The Peach Basket.

Zoe slowed her pace, then released his arm as they started to make their way toward the bar. The bartenders were all positioned along the left side of the room, and behind them ran a row of glass cases, each filled with an array of items that helped tell the story of basketball: photos, jerseys, old game balls, peach baskets once used as basketball hoops.

Art saw a waiter come by with a tray full of drinks. Perfect timing, he thought, lifting a cocktail and a glass of champagne from the man's tray.

"Quite the event," Art said, holding the glass of bubbles out for Zoe. "I've only been inside this place during the day, when it's a museum for the greatest game in the world."

Zoe waved off the offer. "I'm not thirsty."

"Suit yourself," Art said. He knocked the bubbles back with ease, then flagged down another waiter who passed by with a tray of canapés and hors d'oeuvres. Art handed the man the empty champagne coupe. "Thank you."

"Take it easy, please." Zoe said this with a practiced sigh. "I have my entire family here, along with most of my friends from back home. The same goes for Tom. Just keep all that in mind tonight."

"Noted," Art said. He took a sip of bourbon cocktail. "You're the one who asked us all to be here, Zoe, so try and at least enjoy it. Maybe even act like *you* want to be here."

"Tom and I *both* want to be here, understood?" Her tone had that special, sweet bite to it, the kind that only Southern women seemed to know how to use properly.

"I know Tom wants this." Art grinned as he shook his head. "But I don't know who else you're trying to convince..."

Zoe looked like she was about to add something more, then stopped at the sound of a loud, familiar voice beginning a speech at the opposite end of the room. She hustled Art along and the two of them made their way to the edge of the bar, where the first person to spot them was Art's least favorite teammate, Walker Boyd.

Boyd offered a hug to Zoe and a few words of admonishment for Art. Then Zoe quickly left the bar area and disappeared into the crowd ahead. Art shot Boyd the finger once she was gone.

"Typical Mortlake—" began Boyd.

But the clinking sound of silver on glass cut his old teammate short, then sliced its way through the other muffled noises scattered throughout the room.

"If I could please have everyone's attention." The owner of the booming voice was Luca Palomino, Tom's father. "I'd just like a moment of your time, so that I can say a few words about my son and his gorgeous fiancée, Zoe."

The buzz of conversation in the room soon quieted.

"And I promise that once I'm done," Luca continued, "I'll let you all get back to the task of putting a dent in all my liquor that's behind the bar."

Healthy laughter erupted from the large crowd. Art turned and tried to find Zoe's parents. He spotted them near the back of the party room. As expected, Coco wore that same little foxy grin, while the good pastor looked unamused.

"It's open bar, right?" yelled someone buried among the well-dressed guests. An idiot cousin, Art guessed.

"That's right," said the man at the head of the room. "But it's the Mitchells, Bedford and Coco, who've been kind enough to allow me to pick up the tab tonight. It seems I might've made a grave mistake, though, given all you 'heathens' who're in attendance." Luca Palomino smiled and pointed toward the bar with his champagne glass. "I'd like for your people to put all my nephews on a pitch count, okay?"

More laugher ensued. It was obvious that the Palomino guests looked to be the liveliest of those in attendance. These were mostly Catholics with some blend of Italian or Portuguese heritage, but they seemed even more, well, red-blooded, when compared to the stuffier, more Baptist-like guests who had been invited from the Mitchell side of the engagement.

"All jokes aside, though." Luca Palomino quieted the crowd with his strong, deep voice that didn't require a microphone. "It's an incredible honor to get to stand up here tonight, celebrating my youngest child getting engaged." He paused for a long moment. "I'm just so, so happy—"

Luca trailed off.

It was then that Art caught the first glimpse of his friend that night. The crowd clapped and cheered when Tom Palomino—the six-seven, do-it-all wing, an unquestionable NBA talent—walked over to give his father a hug. It was a heartwarming scene. And although Luca Palomino was considerably shorter than his baby boy, the father still made for an imposing figure. The elder Palomino had spent twelve years as a catcher for the Baltimore Orioles, and looked, even in his late sixties, like he could probably still protect home plate.

"Now, I want to thank everyone for being here tonight." Luca pulled a handkerchief from his coat pocket, wiped his face, eyes. "Because when I look out at all these wonderful, beautiful faces, people I've known for a long, long time, I can't help but think how far this family has come. How far my little Tomaso has come..."

There was no question where Luca Palomino came from. The same went for Tom. The Palomino Family was like proletariat royalty for those who called home to Long Island, and Luca had earned the respect of his neighbors by putting his own blood, sweat, and hard-earned dollars back into the communities that stretched along that little isle in southeastern New York. It was where Luca owned a string of restaurants, body shops, pawn brokers, and everyman insurance companies. And it was where the youngest in that family, Tomaso Cristoforo Palomino, had grown into an intense person, and an even better basketball player.

"I know we're here to celebrate Tom and Zoe, but I do wish that my late wife, Giulia, was here to share in this with us." Luca turned to look at his son. "Because I know she would've loved your little Zoe, right Tom?"

Zoe appeared beside Tom and his father, looking every bit like the perfect, angelic addition to their family. The extended family and friends in the crowd all seemed to enjoy the sentiment, and everyone leaned into that brief moment of reflection.

"Zoe, I'm so happy for you and my son." Luca put his arm around the bride-to-be, kissed her on the cheek. "I'll be looking forward to the day you officially join the family."

From where Art stood, he could see that Tom was now scanning the crowd for the faces of those he wanted to acknowledge. He had lots of teammates in the room, his sports agent, and plenty of people he might call friends of the family. When his eyes made their way over to Art, he nodded and smiled.

I shouldn't be here... Art thought, lifting his drink, smiling back at his friend. I shouldn't have even come tonight.

10

It wouldn't be fair to say that Art Mortlake and Tom Palomino were the unlikeliest of friends.

In fact, the two of them had a hell of a lot in common. They both enjoyed a unique kind of privilege, both loved playing the game of basketball, and the boys had both grown up in the same region of the country. They just came up on opposite sides of the Long Island Sound, in places that sat at a distance of maybe twenty, twenty-five miles from the other.

Places that were very different from the other.

Still, when Art and Tom arrived in Durham for their freshman year, it was only natural that the two of them found common ground during summer camp. They trained together, fought hard for one another, and thrived in an environment that was chock full of main-character energy and big egos. They were the kings of campus, even riding the bench during their first games as freshmen. And in those early days of bonding, they made a vow to one another that they would always have the other's back.

No matter what.

And although Tom Palomino went on to start more than a hundred games for the Blue Devils, Art was the one who got the minutes first. Art was the one who got his playing time on the hardwood, his moment in the spotlight, long before Tom had a chance to get his.

The rush and excitement that Art experienced during his playing time as a freshman was unlike anything he'd ever felt before. The roar of the crowd. The stares of opposing players after he knocked down another big-time shot. The elation he felt after each win.

All of it came first for Art, not his friend.

Art sipped his drink and watched the partygoers mill about the room. The Peach Basket paid homage to the game that Art would never play again, the one Tom Palomino would certainly go on to play at the professional level.

Art looked around at all the faces of former players, and he tried not to think about *his* last game, the one against Florida State. He and Tom had sat next to each other on the bench that night, like they did during most games. And both were commenting on the crowd, the dancers, and the opposing team while they waited for their opportunity to enter the game. The two were staying loose, cutting up, watching their teammates take care of business, when Art pointed something out to his friend.

Art had recognized, at least he thought he had, one of the people seated on the opposite side of the court. Art only knew this man because of an old picture, but it was an image that had been seared in his mind since childhood. Because how could it not?

That's the man who killed my mom.

Art thought about those words now, and he could still almost hear the matter-of-fact tone in his own voice, the one he'd used while pointing the man out.

See him there, Tom. He's sitting just off the court, in that middle section, second row up. The white guy who's wearing the gold polo and black baseball cap. You see him?

Tom's first question: *You're sure?* Because Tom knew already that Art had lost his mother to a car wreck, a tragic accident somewhere along the roads that swept through the mountains of North Georgia.

I'm certain, Tom. That's George McRae. I've never seen the man in person, but I know that's him.

Then that's real messed up, Art. You think he knows he's here watching you play?

That, I'm not sure about. I hope like hell he doesn't because—

He should know. There'd been no hesitation in Tom's voice when he uttered those words. *That piece of trash shouldn't be allowed to ever forget what he did to your family.*

Everyone knows what happened after Art checked into the game that night. It's all on film, at least most of it is.

Art played furiously for a stretch of about three or four minutes. He was like a wild man out there on the court: running down loose balls, busting through picks, calling for the rock as soon as he crossed half-court.

Then, the Seminoles called a thirty-second timeout, and Art made his way back over to the bench. He was doing his best to play the game of his life that night, to leave it all out there on the court. But with the opportunity to rest, Art found himself staring over at the man who'd killed his mother. George McRae had been convicted of second-degree vehicular homicide after the car accident with Marilyn Mortlake, and he'd gone on to spend a year in the Gilmer County Adult Detention Center for his sins. But on that January night in Tallahassee, McRae came roaring back into Art's life, and he sat within spitting distance of where Art had just hit his last three-pointer.

Hey Art, it looks like he might be leaving already... Tom had apparently kept his eyes on the man while Art was out on the hardwood, and he said the man had started to look uncomfortable after staring down at his cell phone for a long moment.

Art took another sip of bourbon. He could still remember how everything looked on the opposite side of the court that night. The way McRae seemed as he got up from his seat, collected his jacket, empty beer, and popcorn container.

Too bad we can't just go catch him in the parking lot... Tom had whispered this in Art's ear while they watched the man start to leave that night. *I'd make sure he never forgot the Mortlake name.*

Except on that night, in that particular moment, something clicked in Art's mind, and he decided then and there that he didn't really need to wait for a dark parking lot. He had George McRae right there inside a well-lit coliseum, and it was as fine a place as any to confront the man. So, after the timeout, when Art stepped back out onto the court, he was really just making a beeline toward the opposite side of the hardwood, where he beat the hell out of McRae and the man who'd come with him.

It was a mistake, Art knew this now. But George McRae had also made a mistake when he let his Ford F-150 drift over the centerline after a long day of fishing. Art's mistake took his own college basketball career away. McRae's mistake took the life of Marilyn Mortlake, the most wonderful woman Art had ever known. So, as far as Art was concerned, the decision he made that night in Tallahassee, *his* mistake, was worth it, even given all that followed after it.

But Tom Palomino never said a word to anyone after the fight that night, and Tom stuck close when Art caught his criminal charges down in Florida. It was Tom who showed up to check on Art when he was down and out, rehabbing his wrist and hand after surgery. It was Tom who stuck up for Art, even argued on his behalf, when the time came to discuss whether Art might be allowed to rejoin the men's basketball team. And it was Tom who appealed to his own father, Luca Palomino, when a discussion needed to be had with McRae, an off-the-record conversation about whether Art should be prosecuted for the assault.

McRae came to see things more favorably after that visit from the Palomino crew.

Art had to admit, though, he'd known few people like Tom and those who made up the Palomino Family. Tom was a person who'd shown Art true devotion to a pact, one made between two people who weren't even related by blood. And it was Tom who insisted that he and Art make that pact—the promise to always have the other's back, *no matter what*. And it was Tom who told Art that as long as they stayed in this thing together, whether it be at Duke, or in the NBA, then both of them would always have someone there to solve a problem, whenever they needed it.

Sure, both of them had money—although the Mortlake Family had much, much more—and both of them knew that money solved *most* problems. But Art's family and Tom's family were very different when it came to the issues of loyalty and respect. Art's father, Clive Mortlake, had the respect of others because of the responsible ways in which the man wielded their family's enormous wealth. While Tom's father, Luca Palomino, had the respect of others because of the way he wielded the power that wealth afforded his family. And loyalty in Art's family came down to the Flag, then after that, to paying someone what they deserved for their work, treating *them* with respect. While loyalty in Tom's family came down to a code.

And it was a code they all lived by.

Art knew that all someone had to do was look around that large party room, at the people in it, and a few ideas would probably come to mind as to what that code might be. It was unwritten, sure, but their code was like any other in life: there were rules, and there were consequences. And for most of their people, it didn't matter whether you were connected or not. If a person violated the code, then a penance had to be met.

Art didn't know exactly what the consequences were when someone violated the Palomino Family's code, but he wasn't stupid. He also knew that once you owed someone a favor, like he probably owed Luca, then it was best to understand the rules of the game they liked to play. And Art was willing to bet that one of those rules was very, very simple.

It didn't matter who you were, no one fucked around behind a Palomino's back and got away with it.

Art knew this. He just hoped like hell that Zoe did as well.

_____

11

Art was standing near the front of the room, smiling alongside the rest of the soon-to-be bridal party, when his cell phone started buzzing. He pulled it out of his pocket, checked the screen. It was Declan, his father's security specialist.

"You in the back, dark suit, I need you looking at the camera." It was the voice of the event photographer. "And no phones, please."

Art had already been subjected to more photos than the newly engaged couple would ever need to remember that night's party, so he held up his cell phone and begged off with the excuse that he had a family emergency. Which wasn't a complete lie, he decided.

"Can't it wait?" cried the photographer. "I only have a few more shots planned for this room, then we have the big one out front if we can beat the winter weather."

"Sorry," Art said, walking away from the group. "This can't wait."

Art heard the event planner beginning her discussion with Zoe and the photographer, one about potentially resuming the photo session later in the evening. But Art was well out of earshot before he could hear anyone place blame on him for the delay.

He made a quick pit-stop at the bar, just to grab another drink, and felt the cell phone start buzzing again in his pocket. It was the second call from

Declan. He knew the calls would just continue, back-to-back, until Art eventually answered.

"Bourbon and ginger ale," Art said in the direction of the nearest bartender. "And don't be shy. Make it a heavy pour."

Art answered the fourth call from his father's bodyguard.

"What's good, Declan?" Art spoke as he pushed through a door at the back of the venue's large party room. The oak door had a *Staff Only* sign on the outside of it, one that Art ignored. "I hear my father has you handling travel packages these days. What's that about?"

"It's all part of the job, Mr. Mortlake." Declan Tao had an accent that came from somewhere in the Pacific Northwest, and it always had a smooth, relaxed tone to it whenever the ex-soldier spoke about his work. "How are you doing?" he added.

"Oh, you know me—" Art said, letting the heavy door close behind him. He stared down a long, quiet hallway, one lined with small offices that most likely belonged to the museum's employees. "I'm always good, Declan."

Declan passed on any additional small talk. "Okay, let's get into the game plan for tomorrow."

"Hold on." Art started trying knobs on the office doors until he found one that opened. "What happened with Callie?" he asked, intentionally ignoring Declan's agenda for the conversation. "I liked her. She's who usually handles things like this for us."

"Nothing happened to her." Declan didn't offer anything more.

"Come on, Declan, don't tell me my father had her fired." Art stepped inside one of the depressing little office spaces, then closed the door behind him. "Because if he did, I'm hiring her tonight, just to spite him."

"All I can tell you is that he didn't let her go." Declan paused for a moment. "Now, should I give you the details on the special one-day vacation package I have for you?" The question almost sounded like an attempt at humor, a thing that was completely out of character for the ever-professional Declan Tao.

Maybe something really was wrong, Art thought, taking in the small, cluttered office space before him. There were books and folders stacked on the floor, two metal filing cabinets, and a rather small, paper-laden desk with an old leather office chair behind it.

"Art, did you hear me?"

"Yeah," Art said, although he couldn't help but wonder if his father was already making some unsettling end-of-life arrangements. "It's just, well, Callie has been handling things for my father for almost—"

"Twenty years," Declan said, finishing the sentence. "And I assure you she plans to keep doing so for as long as she's needed."

"That's good to know. How's my father doing?" Art asked as he walked around to the other side of the desk and took a seat in the faded leather chair. There, he waited to hear something other than silence on the other end of the line.

Declan cleared his throat. "Ask your father when you get here tomorrow." There was some hesitation in his voice. "I'm only authorized to discuss your wellbeing and travel."

"That's bullshit, Declan. I just want to know how he's doing."

Silence returned to the other end of the line.

Art placed his mixed drink on the desk, then pulled the plastic bag out from inside the front pocket of his jacket. My wellbeing, he thought, pushing aside the paperwork that was on his side of the desk, then dumping some of the coke out onto the wood surface. He knew there wasn't much use arguing with Declan. The former Green Beret was his father's closest confidant, the right-hand man, and it was Declan's job to keep a watchful eye over Clive Mortlake. So, Declan absolutely knew how the man was doing, he just wasn't going to say a word about any of it until Clive Mortlake gave him the go ahead.

Art repeated the words out loud: "My wellbeing and travel…"

Declan spoke now. "That's all I can discuss at the moment."

"Well, like I said, I'm doing good."

Declan's tone stayed even. "And I'm glad to hear it, Mr. Mortlake."

"You don't need to call me that, Declan."

He ignored the offer, like always. "That's very kind, Mr. Mortlake. Now, should I tell you about the schedule for tomorrow?"

Art didn't say anything for a moment as he picked up a business card from the unknown person's desk, one that read: *Gerald T. Barnes, Curator for Basketball History, Culture, and Media,* which Art actually thought sounded like an interesting job, albeit one that came with some very sad looking office space.

Art used Mr. Barnes's card to line up a few rails on the desk.

"Yeah, let's hear it," Art finally said. "But I hope you have something hot and tropical in mind. I think they're calling for snow tonight in Durham—" Art pressed the mute button on his cell phone, then leaned over the desk and ripped a line from the wood surface.

"Well—" Declan paused. "That depends on your definition of hot and tropical."

Art unmuted the phone. "Anything that'll put me on a beach. How about St. Kitts? I'd even take BVI as a back-up." Art felt that wonderful rush hitting him, the kind that made his mind climb the rollercoaster. "Come on, *D.T.,* I know you could use some R&R. Convince the Great Man to meet me on an island somewhere."

Declan never laughed, but his easygoing nature was something he didn't try and hide. "Maybe next time, Mr. Mortlake. Your father wants you in Georgia tomorrow. He'll meet you here, at the compound, to discuss his health, along with a few family matters."

"Fine. Give me the details," Art said, muting the phone again. He leaned over the desk and snorted another rail.

"I have a team that'll be heading to get you first thing tomorrow morning. They'll be landing at IGX. We'll be monitoring the weather throughout the night, but I don't expect the pilots will have a problem with any of it. The G650, as I'm sure you know, is fit to endure quite severe weather-related conditions."

Art unmuted the phone. "Things might get a little sporty, yeah?"

"Right." Declan sounded like he was working through a checklist. "An SUV will come by your house in Old West Durham at oh-seven-thirty. It'll be a contractor, but I know the service, and they'll make sure to get you over to the airport without issue. The driver will be in a black GMC Yukon Denali, one bearing North Carolina plates. I want you to check the license plate number before you get in."

"Copy that."

"It'll be 5GEBLX. That's Five, Golf, Echo, Bravo, Lima—"

"Declan, relax. If you're comfortable with it, I'm comfortable with it."

Art mashed the mute button on the cell phone once more, then leaned over to snort the remaining line from the desk. When he sat back up, he ran a finger over the wood surface, swiped up the last grains of powder, then rubbed the coke remnants onto his gums. He felt like his night was about to make the jump to another level, one reserved for the likes of Dominique Wilkins and Vince Carter, the greatest dunkers of all time.

"Okay, well, I need to switch our call to FaceTime." Declan's voice kept that same even tone to it. "This is just to confirm you're secure, Mr. Mortlake. Is that fine by you?"

Art unmuted the phone as the device notified him that there was an incoming video request. When he accepted the call, Declan's face and chiseled, Eastern features came into view on the screen.

"Okay," Declan continued. "I know you know the drill, but let's walk through the standard questions. Where are you right now?"

Art sighed. "I'm at a museum that's also an event venue here in Durham. That's North Carolina. The place is called The Peach Basket."

"Are you in any danger at the moment?"

Art laughed. "There's probably fifteen or so Italians packing heat in the next room over, but they're all friendly." Art could see from his own video image on the screen that there was a bit of white powder just below his nose. He used a hand to wipe his nostrils clean.

"Okay, good." Declan gave an almost imperceptible shake of the head. "You're at the Palomino function tonight, right?"

Art wasn't even surprised that the man knew his whereabouts already. "Yeah, it's an engagement party for some friends."

"Any threats you've received in the last forty-eight hours?" asked the bodyguard.

"None."

"How about anything out of the ordinary?"

"Look, everything's cake, Declan." As Art said this, he thought about Frank King's comments from earlier that night, the ones his friend had made about the pair of Frenchmen in the alleyway. Art had already decided not to mention this to Declan, because the men were probably just related to Coco Mitchell, a couple of cousins who were in town for Zoe's party.

"You're sure?" Declan asked.

"Positive." Art smiled. "There's nothing to worry about."

"Good," the man said. "Then that's all I have for you at the moment. You'll get the flight information first thing tomorrow."

Art paused. "But that's not all I have for you."

Declan gave away little. "Is there something else?" he asked. The bodyguard's stoic expression stared back at Art from the phone screen.

"I want to know how my father's doing, Declan, how he's *really* doing. And I want to know tonight, so tell him I need to speak with him."

"Anything else?"

Art felt like a short fuse had just been lit inside his brain. "Yeah, there is. Make sure and tell him that I'm not coming tomorrow until he agrees to take my call."

There was a long pause, then the video went dark on the other end. Declan remained on the line, though.

Art raised his voice. "Did you hear me?"

"I heard you, Mr. Mortlake."

"Then go do what I've asked. Go get him. Now."

"He's not available right now."

Art wondered if his father was sitting there in the same room as Declan, listening to every word from the call. Art pictured the two men smiling about this together, enjoying their little game of keep-away.

"You think this is funny?" Art slapped the desk in front of him. "I told you to go get him. You work for the Mortlake Family, dammit! That includes me."

Declan didn't sound the least bit frustrated when he responded. "He's not available, Mr. Mortlake. However, I will tell him that—"

"What the hell?" Art shouted this toward the phone's screen. "If he's sleeping, then go wake him up. If he's in a meeting, then go pull him out. Do you understand where I'm going with this?"

"I do, Mr. Mortlake."

"Good," Art spat. "Then I'll wait."

There was another long pause before Declan spoke again. "Unfortunately, sir, like I said earlier, he's just not available at the moment."

"Then tell me where he is, Declan. Explain to me why my father's *not available,* as you say."

"I'm not authorized to tell you."

Art exploded. "You know what, I don't give a shit what you're authorized to do. I want to speak with him tonight. He's dying and I deserve to know if tomorrow is it for us."

"I don't know what else to tell you." Declan still sounded calm, relaxed. It was as if he was practicing some kind of Zen-like meditation on the other end of the line. "I'll make sure to let him know that you're frustrated."

"Oh, don't just tell him I'm frustrated, Declan. Tell him I'm fucking livid, you hear me? And tell him I'm not coming tomorrow."

Silence filled the other end of the line.

"Do you understand me?" Art yelled. "He's dying and won't even tell me how long he has, so that selfish son of a bitch can die alone for all I care."

"Is there anything else, Mr. Mortlake?"

Art paused for a long moment. He could tell that Declan was letting him get it all out. "Just tell him…" Art started to say. No other words seemed to come to mind.

"Good night, Mr. Mortlake." Declan spoke slowly, forcefully. "I know your father is really looking forward to seeing you tomorrow."

Art was about to say something more when the phone beeped twice in his ear.

The call went dead.

12

Art looked up from the desk when he heard a knock on the office door. Then it opened, and Zoe Mitchell appeared alone in the doorway. She seemed to consider him for a moment, her lower lip tucked between her teeth, her deep, brown eyes fixed on him.

The first thing Art thought wasn't how beautiful she looked that night, although she certainly looked stunning. Nor was it how frustrated she probably was that he'd cut her photo session short, or how he'd probably sounded like an entitled little prick during his call with Declan. No, in that moment, the only thing that came to mind was how good it was just to see her.

"Hey there, Mortlake." Zoe stood at the edge of the doorway, teetering on the threshold of the ill-advised. "I've been looking for you. Everything okay?"

Art stared back at her for another long moment, then remembered his manners. He started to stand from the chair. "Look, I'm sorry I ran out on the photos. If you need me to come out there and finish, then I'm happy to go right now. I just had a family issue that needed—"

Zoe interrupted him as she took a step inside the office. "I asked you a question." She then closed the door behind her.

Art continued taking in that stare of hers, those unblinking, gold speckled eyes that had him cornered. Although Zoe cared a bit too much about the way things appeared to be, she wasn't the one who usually ended up having to conform herself to the expectations of others. In fact, it often seemed to be the other way around in her world.

See, Zoe had a way of bending most things, and people, so that they suited her own liking, her own expectations for how life was supposed to be. And the on-again, off-again fling she'd kept going with Art wasn't the kind of thing that fit neatly with her vision for the future. Which was saying something, because Art hadn't met many girls who weren't at least willing to make a run at him and his family's wealth.

"Don't worry about me, *Zoh*." Art picked up his glass, then finished what liquid remained in it. "Like they say back in your home state, everything's just peachy."

"No, it's not." She offered him a sweet smile, the one he liked best. "You didn't tell me about your dad."

"Right, that..." Art paused for a long moment. "In all fairness, though, not very many people know."

"Not even Frank?" she asked.

Art grinned. "Frank does know."

Art and Zoe only stood a few feet from each other now, but it felt like there was an invisible barrier between them, the kind of wall that slowly went up between two people who left things unsaid.

"I assume—" she began, glancing down at a space on the floor where Art's cell phone now lay smashed at their feet. "At least given what little I overheard, that you're no longer expecting your dad to call you back..."

"Someone likes to eavesdrop."

"Maybe," she said, using one of her red-bottomed heels to scoot the smashed device aside. "But you were the one yelling loud enough for people to hear you out in the hall."

"People?" Art asked.

"Just me," she quickly amended. "But don't try and change the subject. I want to know what's going on with your dad."

"There's not a whole lot to say, Zoh. He's just sick."

"How bad is it?" she asked, scrunching her face up into a look of concern. It was an elegant face, but a face that also had sharp edges to it.

"I mean..." Art looked away from her. All of a sudden, he felt his own face stiffen, like he might cry. "It's cancer, you know. And it's the bad kind."

"They're all bad, Art."

"Yeah." Art cleared his throat. "Well, it's all in his colon now, and I guess it's spreading fast, so he apparently has the kind you don't ever get to celebrate going into remission."

Zoe took the first step through their invisible boundary, then reached out to put her arms around his waist. She pulled him close so that she could lean her head against his chest. "I'm so sorry," she whispered. "I know this must be awful for the both of you."

Art hesitated, then put his arms around her. Although his face felt as if it was frozen in place, his insides were beginning to melt with Zoe's body pressed against his. He could smell the shampoo in her hair, the sandalwood and vanilla on her skin, and this brought back memories of her coming over to his house, always late at night. It made him think about the two of them wrapped up in his bed sheets, talking and laughing and enjoying one another.

"Do you know how long he has left?" she asked, prodding him away from his thoughts.

"I'm not sure," Art finally said. "I think he might have a few months more, but who really knows. The man won't tell me anything."

"Why?" She sounded surprised.

"He and I just don't have a great relationship." As Art said this, he realized how little he'd told her about his past, and how little she'd asked about it. "But I guess it's been that way for some time now."

Art felt Zoe nodding her head up and down against his chest. "I know how that can be," she said, although she didn't offer anything more on the matter.

"I take it growing up with the good pastor wasn't always easy?" he asked.

"Let's not talk about my family," she replied. "I just wanted you to know that I understand how hard it can be when parents keep secrets."

"Right, secrets," Art murmured, rubbing a hand across Zoe's shoulders and bare back. "I thought we were done with those."

Zoe smiled up at him, then lifted onto her tiptoes, kissed him. "I think we may have room for one more secret," she whispered.

"Yeah?"

She nodded. "But we don't have long."

Art knew he wasn't thinking straight, but he still didn't hesitate at snapping up the offer. He picked Zoe up and placed her on the cluttered desk that was beside them. He began kissing her neck, and she started working at the belt on his pants. He pulled his arms from inside his jacket and tossed the coat into a corner of the office, then put his hands to work on Zoe's seemingly eager, lithe body. His hands soon made their way under her dress, where his fingers began playing at the edges of her panties.

"I missed this," she said, not even waiting for him to pull down her white, lacy underwear. "I can tell you did."

Art grinned. "I might be warming up to the idea."

"Come on." Zoe grinned back at him. "We need to hurry."

Art pulled her close. "You know I'm not going back to the party."

"Shut up," Zoe whispered, grinding her hips into his. "And don't you dare stop."

13

Art watched Zoe head toward the door that led to the venue's large party room, toward the life that she wanted, then he turned and started walking in the opposite direction. He was on his way to another night out with casual friends, another blackout, and another tomorrow he might spend with his father.

As he passed the doors to the other offices along the corridor, Art tucked his shirt tail back into his pants, fixed his belt. His time for self-loathing would come later, he told himself, eyes fixed on the outline of the green *EXIT* sign that glowed at the end of the hallway—the door that might allow him to leave the building undetected.

He knew he shouldn't have come that night, shouldn't have done what he did, but Art was certain no one else knew he was leaving the party early.

No one other than Zoe.

Art pushed through the metal exterior door, then stepped out into what looked like a narrow alleyway. Although he'd never been behind The Peach Basket before, Art felt certain that this little cut-through would lead him to one of the main downtown thoroughfares, back toward his favorite little dive bar that was only a few blocks over.

Art glanced up and down the alleyway, blew warm air into his cupped hands. He could tell the temperature had dropped quite a bit in the last couple of hours, and he even saw that the first signs of a dusting were beginning to cover the ground. They were calling for snow all across the Piedmont, which meant most of the Southerners would be staying close to home that night, where they would wait anxiously for any snowflakes to fall.

Although a few inches of snow meant little to the boy who hailed from New England, he decided it'd still be best to check the weather, so Art instinctively reached a hand inside his pocket for a cell phone that wasn't there. "Oh, you've got to be freaking kidding me," he muttered, realizing he'd left his shattered phone inside that sad little office that belonged to Mr. Gerald T. Barnes, The Peach Basket's curator for basketball history, culture, and something else.

With a heavy sigh, he turned to walk back toward the metal door, the one he'd just left through. It was locked, though, which meant he'd probably need to go back through the front door of the building if he wanted to get his phone. And that would involve walking back by all those people who were probably still inside: Coco the Fox, Pastor Mitchell, the always judgmental Walker Boyd, and all those Long Island royals (i.e. the Palomino Family).

Art considered this.

He figured that if he was lucky, he might be able to avoid most of the faces who were left inside. But he knew he wouldn't be able to completely bypass Tom and Zoe. And he knew there was an off chance that his reappearance at the party would look, well, suspicious, especially if Zoe had already come up with some kind of an excuse that was meant to justify Art's absence.

No, Art decided, pulling the collar up on his suit jacket, I'm not going back inside.

Art knew when the chauffeur would be at his house tomorrow morning, and he knew he could just have another phone delivered to him at the mountain house in North Georgia. Most of all, though, Art knew he didn't really need his phone that night. His father wasn't going to call.

Art turned and started walking toward the lights of a nearby street. The Blue was no more than a few blocks away.

———————

Art didn't see the man step out from behind the dumpster, but he heard the rustling of what sounded like movement from somewhere behind him. And when Art turned to see what it was, he took his eyes off the shadows in front of him, which is where the second man waited for him.

While glancing over one shoulder, Art assumed the noise had come from a raccoon or a cat. What he saw looked like a man, though, someone Art didn't have pegged as being one of the homeless. Art slowly turned to face the man, tried to quickly recall some of the training he'd received over the years from Declan Tao. The acronym *L.B.A.* came to mind.

L—Declan always began—is for *Look*: Look around, Art, evaluate your surroundings.

Art could see that the man stood about twenty or so feet away, which was about how far it was between the basket and three-point line on a basketball court, a distance Art could cover in around two seconds. And Art could see the man wasn't much bigger than he was, although it was hard to tell given the man's dark suit and balaclava. What was crucial, though, was that Art could see no weapon in the man's hands.

B—Declan would harp—is for *Breathe*: Remember to breathe, Art, and stay calm.

Art still had his eyes on the first man when he felt something being shoved into his lower back area. Whoever held the item pressed it hard into the space between Art's spine and lower ribcage. It wasn't a knife, that much Art was sure, but it was a blunt, metal object of some kind, one that Art decided was most likely a handgun.

"Arrgh!" Art grunted, trying his best to breathe. He could feel every bit of the object as his assailant dug it deeper into his lower back area, apparently trying to crush Art's right kidney. "What do you want from—"

"Don't say a word!" It was a man who growled into Art's ear, and the voice had an accent to it, one that Art couldn't place. "I promise I'll kill you if you scream," the man added. He spoke in English, but that wasn't the man's first language.

A—Declan usually hesitated here—is for *Act*: If you act, Art, it's best to be early.

Although it's possible this was due to the large amount of booze in Art's system, or the Kevlar-like confidence that'd literally gone to his head, but Art decided in that moment that he needed to act, that he needed to try to defend himself. So, Art made like he was trying to readjust the position of the weapon at his back, then drove an elbow into the unknown animal who stood behind him.

The elbow caught the man right in his gut, and Art heard a coughing sound as the wind *whooshed* out of his attacker. After that, it was the sound of metal hitting the pavement at their feet, which was right when Art shook himself free from the man's grasp. He then turned and began yelling as loud as he could, like some kind of wild banshee from a wildlife film. Art saw the object that'd been at his back, a black handgun, and it was now on the ground, so Art gave it a swift kick that sent the weapon skittering away.

Then, Art turned back around and sprinted straight for the first masked man. Art could see that the man was fumbling for something inside his jacket, but Art knew it was too late for the guy. He'd already closed the distance on the man in the mask, and the guy was still groping for his weapon when Art collided with the assailant's chest. Art was leaning forward, right shoulder square with the man's sternum, when they made contact. The shot blew the man off of his spot, and Art kept his feet churning, driving his shoulder straight through the man until he barreled him over.

Art didn't stop to appreciate his luck. He just kept on running, all the while hollering like he was a close cousin of Tarzan. "Oh-oo-ee-oo-oh-oo-ee-oo!" Art yelled, breathing hard as he closed the distance to the well-lit street ahead.

It was the nearest exit from the alley, and he wasn't more than thirty feet from the corner. Art wasn't sure, but he figured if these men were really planning to shoot him, then they'd do it right now, while they had a clear shot at his back.

Then one of the men screamed something in a language Art didn't recognize, one that sounded like it came from somewhere in Eastern Europe. Although Art didn't understand the words, he felt pretty confident that the man had just yelled out a fairly simple command:

Don't shoot him!

14

Art made it to the corner without a bullet in his back, then he turned onto the sidewalk and kicked it into high gear. He'd been a basketball player by choice, but that didn't mean he hadn't spent a fair amount of time training on the track. And three plus years ago, before the beer and bourbon and clouds of smoke, Art had been a pretty strong four-hundred-meter guy, a sub-fifty runner on a good day.

Art never ran on a track when it was wet and below freezing, though.

So, when Art took his first steps onto the street, at an angle that would allow him to cut between two parked cars, his snaffle-trim loafers found a thin sheet of ice. He lost his footing and went down hard, his face smacking the trunk on one of the Toyotas parked on that downtown street.

"Faaaack," Art moaned, feeling something pop at the bridge of his nose.

Still dazed, he picked himself up from the wet pavement, then stumbled out into the roadway, working himself toward the opposite side of the street, where he thought he might find a string of student apartment buildings, maybe even a rent-a-cop watching the door.

"Arthur!" yelled someone behind him. "Stop running!"

Why in the hell do they know my name? Art wondered, trying to regain the rhythm in his feet, struggling to get back up to speed. His nose and face had started to throb, and Art winced at the sharp pain that followed each deep breath.

"Stop, we're friends!" called another voice. This one also had a heavy accent to his English, but it came with a more Slavic bent to it than the one his partner had. "Arthur, we want to help you!"

Art didn't look back as he cut across a half-empty parking lot. He then hopped over a chain-link fence, one that backed up to a popular student apartment complex.

Snow was falling now, that sleety, wet kind, and Art hoped the weather might draw a few college students outside their doors, just to take a look. Maybe one of them would see him running for his life and take an interest.

Maybe someone would call the police.

Art saw the car parked near the back of the next parking lot, a good distance still from the edge of the apartment buildings. It was a little beater Honda Civic that had its running lights engaged. On top of it, there was a half-lit sign that read: *Pearson's Security Professionals.*

"Help, help!" Art yelled, feet sliding on the asphalt as he approached the trunk of the little car. "Come on, get out!"

Although Art hadn't yet looked back at his pursuers, he soon heard the chain-link rattle on the fence behind him, so he figured the masked duo wasn't far off. Art was banking on these guys not wanting to deal with any potential witnesses, so he hoped the sight of the rent-a-cop might at least cause them to reverse course. Because robbing a rich little punk wasn't worth a ten-year stretch in prison, right?

"Yo!" Art hollered out, beating his hands on the trunk and side of the vehicle as he made his way around to the driver's side door. "Call 9-1-1! Now!"

When Art came around to the driver's side window, he could half see his own reflection on the outside of the glass. He had blood running from his nose and mouth and smudges of dirt and grime on his clothes. And with Art's crazy, flipped-up hair, he looked every bit like an urban wildling.

Art went for the handle on the door and found it was locked. "Get out, man! I need your help."

The man appeared to be middle-aged and was seated alone inside the vehicle. He didn't look like your stereotypical, wanna-be cop, but the expression on the man's face told Art everything he needed to know about this hourly Barney's appetite for danger.

"Come on!" Art shouted, jiggling the door handle. "Do something!"

Art looked to his right and saw that both men had stopped their pursuit. They waited together at the edge of the parking lot, a distance of about thirty yards away, where they remained somewhat hidden in the shadows of several large trees. Art still couldn't see their faces.

"Okay, okay," began a startled voice from inside the vehicle. "I'm calling someone now."

Art turned his attention back to the man inside the car and saw the glow from the screen of a cell phone. The rent-a-cop held the phone out cautiously while he found the courage to dial for backup.

"Thank God..." Art muttered, more to himself than the man seated in the driver's seat.

The door on the Honda unlocked, then out stepped the rent-a-cop, his cell phone pressed to the side of his face. "Yeah, it's Dale," he said, speaking with familiarity to whoever was on the other end of the line. "I'm over at the downtown complex tonight, the one on Callaway, and I've got some kid here who looks wasted. He's pretty banged up, maybe from a bar fight, and he's asking for the police."

"Is that not the police on the phone?" Art exclaimed. He then realized he needed to lower his voice. "I told you to—"

The man covered the bottom-half of his cell phone. "It's my boss," he said, interrupting Art. "He's retired D-P-D, and he'll know what to do about—"

"I said to call 9-1-1," Art growled, reaching for the man's cell phone. "I didn't say call your boss and ask permission for anything. Just give me the dang phone, I'll call them myself."

The man spun away like he was afraid of even being touched by Art. "No way," he whined, "I'll decide how this investigation is—"

But then the sounds of gunshots interrupted the rent-a-cop mid-sentence.

Pop! Pop! Pop!

15

Art ducked for cover at the first sounds of gunfire. Then he heard what sounded like a gurgling, chortling cough from the rent-a-cop, one that was soon followed by a stillness that Art was unfamiliar with. When Art turned his head to look over at the man, to check and see if he was okay, Art came eye to eye with the security guard. There was a disturbing blankness in those eyes, and a gaping hole where the hairline had long receded from the man's pale forehead.

"Holy shit..." Art muttered, pressing himself flat to the pavement and starting to work his way around to the other side of the rusted-out Honda. From there, Art thought he might be able to make a break for the apartment buildings.

When Art had nearly reached the other side of the Honda, he stopped crawling. His hands were wet. His suit was soaked. His face was covered in something that felt too thick to be slush or snow. And he was trying to keep his eyes, his attention, on where he wanted to go. But as he prepared to lift himself off the ground to make a miracle dash across the parking lot, Art stopped at the sound of his own name.

"Arthur!" began a voice. It sounded like it was coming from the trunk side of the vehicle. "I'll give you one more chance to stop running."

Art froze in place but tried to quickly walk himself through the progression that Declan had taught him. L-B-A, he reminded himself, taking long, deep breaths. What's the move?

"You are very, very fast," the voice continued. "Like cheetah. But now it's time for you to come with us."

"Who are you?" Art shouted this toward the other side of the vehicle.

"I told you earlier," the man said. "We're your friends."

Art laughed. "You expect me to believe you guys are my friends?"

"We can be your friends—" the man stopped his threat, as if searching for the right words. "So long as you don't make us your enemies."

Art heard the crunching sound of boots walking on slushy pavement. He figured the men were making their way around to him from opposite sides of the vehicle. He knew that even crouched down low, there at the hood of the car, he wouldn't be able to hide from them much longer.

"I'm standing up," Art said, surprised at the relative calm in his own voice. "I'm not making a run for it."

The men both grunted their approval.

"See," Art said, slowly, "everything's good, everything's fine."

"Good," one of the men said.

Once Art was on his feet, he could see that both men weren't taking any chances. They were keeping their guns trained on him. They also still wore masks, although both had their balaclavas rolled up to their noses, probably just to get some more airflow into their lungs after their little footrace from earlier.

"I need to try and help this man get to a—" Art stopped when he leaned over to get a better look at the rent-a-cop's body. The man had fallen awkwardly onto his side, and his head was angled toward the front of the vehicle. The arms were both splayed out in unnatural positions, and there was now a puddle of blood creeping its way outward from the man's neck and head area.

The shorter of the two men spoke: "There's nothing that you can do for this man."

Art was about to say something more when a pair of headlights swept over the parking lot. His heart leapt, only for a moment, as he turned to get a better look at the vehicle.

Not good, he told himself, watching the van and headlights as they approached.

Not good at all...

16

The large white van whipped in close to the rent-a-cop's Honda Civic, then a tall, dark-haired man quickly hopped out of the passenger side door. Another man stayed inside the vehicle, where he waited behind the wheel.

"Good evening, Arthur," began the tall, wide-shouldered man who'd just arrived in the van. "I hope you're doing well."

Art didn't say anything. He just watched as the large man took a few steps closer to the body that lay some ten feet away. For a few seconds, the man sort of squinted down at the lifeless security guard, almost like he was trying to appraise the value of his operation's little indiscretion. The big man sucked at his teeth as he did this, making the issue seem even more like an unfortunate inconvenience to all who were involved.

"I'm Petrut," the man finally said, his eyes shifting their attention back over to where Art stood. His face appeared relaxed, but the eyes had an intensity that issued a warning of danger. "And on your left and right are my colleagues, Jarek and Marko."

Art cut his eyes back to the two men who'd assaulted him only ten minutes earlier. Both had now removed their head coverings, which Art felt like wasn't a good sign. The two grunts simply nodded back when Art met their eyes, so he shifted his attention back to Petrut, the man who was obviously the leader of this little gang's criminal enterprise.

Petrut spread his hands out wide, like he was prepared to ask but a simple favor. "Now, I understand you may not want to, Arthur, but I'm going to need you to get inside the van that's behind me."

"What do you want from me?" Art asked. "It's money, I presume."

"We can talk about what it is I need from you later," Petrut said. "Besides, it's too cold out here to talk right now."

Art ignored him. "If it's money, then I can get you money. I don't have to go in the van with you. All I need is a cell phone."

The big man smiled. "We'll get to that."

Without waiting for an answer, the man called Petrut turned to his partners and started handing out directions. He spoke in French while he directed them to dispose of the car and the body, and he was adamant that they do it all quickly, discreetly. Then he told them to make their way back *home* once they were done. There was an orderly, military-like cadence in the brief exchanges between the men, which led Art to believe that this was no rag-tag group of criminals.

"It's Petrut, right?" Art asked, once he noticed there was a natural break in the issuance of commands.

Petrut turned his gaze back to Art. "Yes. You're welcome to call me Peter, if you prefer it."

"Thanks, *Pete*." Art was trying his best to appear confident, cool, in control. "But all I need is a phone, yeah? I can get money to you tonight. I assure you I have it."

He smiled. "I know you do, Arthur."

Art didn't like the way the man said this. It sounded too disinterested, too statement-of-fact like, especially given the violent situation at hand. Art was the sole heir to a billion-dollar fortune, and his lot in life was essentially common knowledge due to the interest that ultrawealthy families garnered in places all over the globe. And the potential for kidnappings was like a part of life, at least for families like his. But concerns were usually highest when traveling to places outside of the US—not while here on American soil.

"I'm not going to say a thing, okay." Art tried to dig inside himself, tried to pull out that reliable charm of his. "We'll get you and your guys the money, and that'll be the end of it. It's a modern world, man, as I'm sure you know. So there's no need to kidnap me."

"We're not kidnapping you," the man said. "We're helping you."

Art shook his head. He didn't like the sound of this at all.

"Look, Pete, I've been told how to handle these kinds of situations." Art tried not to shake as he spoke. He could feel his hands trembling, but his guess was that it was just a combination of adrenaline leaving his body, and the cold night air finally settling in. Although he was terrified, Art didn't want these men to interpret any of his movements as fear. "I know exactly how my family will handle your demands," Art added. "I've known the protocol since I was a child."

Petrut seemed like he wanted to hear more.

"I know that if you take me..." Art leveled his gaze with the big man's eyes. "Then my father will be forced to get law enforcement involved. The FBI, the SBI, anyone who he thinks needs to be involved. There's an insurance policy and all that crap, but we'd have to get the police involved if—"

"I understand this." Petrut put a hand up. "I don't care about the insurance policy. I don't care about the police."

Art looked around at the other men, hoping one of them might see this as a simple misunderstanding. "Insurance pays out on the kidnapping policy. That's where the money often comes from. But you don't care where the money comes from, right?"

Petrut nodded.

"Because money is money, yeah?" Art continued. "We don't need to get insurance and the police, and all those other people involved. I can just get you the money tonight."

Petrut smiled.

"Yeah?" Art asked. "It's good, right?"

"It must be nice," the man said. "You, Arthur, being just a young man, yet you already have all these vast resources available to you."

"I just want to make this easy," Art pressed. "For you. For me. For everyone."

"Right."

"We're good then?" Art said, not waiting for confirmation. "Fine. I just need the phone."

Petrut nodded. "Get in the van."

"Excuse me?"

"Get—" Petrut pointed to the Mercedes Sprinter that still had its engine running. "In the van."

Art felt a hand on his shoulder. It didn't grab at him, but it told Art what he needed to know. He turned and looked at the man—a youngish guy who was either Jarek or Marko, Art wasn't sure. Art offered the man a nod. He wanted to make sure that all these people knew that he was planning to comply, at least for now.

"I'm going," Art said, his eyes back on Petrut. "Can you tell your man to get his hand off of me?"

Petrut pointed at the man. "Marko, please be careful with our friend Arthur."

"We'll see how tough he is," Marko said, still following close behind. "At least, I hope we get to."

A sliding door opened on the white panel van, revealing little inside its dimly lit interior. When Art took his seat in a captain's chair, he was taken off guard when a bag came over the back of his head. He tried not to wince when the material caught his injured nose, or when he felt the strap being tightened around the bag, fastening the black sack to the base of Art's neck.

"*Allez!*" shouted a voice from outside the van.

Then the doors all closed, the van shifted into gear, and off they went.

17

Art tried to stay awake, tried desperately to map the route out in his head as they drove. It was impossible, though, and he soon found himself getting confused the longer they travelled over those icy, North Carolina roads. Once the initial shock of being kidnapped started to wear off, the late-night road trip became just another something that he couldn't control. So eventually, Art had little choice but to let the rumble of the van's tires on the highway lull him to sleep.

When Art woke up, the van was no longer moving, and all was quiet. He still couldn't see any light through the material that covered his head, but he could tell they weren't sitting in traffic, weren't waiting at an intersection somewhere. *No*, they were parked now, which meant they'd arrived at a place where the kidnappers felt somewhat out of sight.

Art tried not to move much while he listened to his surroundings. He could hear at least one other person breathing, so Art knew that someone else was seated there inside the van with him. And it seemed like a window was rolled down on the vehicle, because Art recognized the sounds of birds squawking outside, the smell of smoke from a cigarette burning nearby. From time to time, Art heard a beeping sound, one that carried from a place off in the distance. It reminded Art of that sound large trucks made when they shifted into reverse, so Art figured they were somewhere near a construction site, maybe a warehouse of some kind. There was no way to know.

A door soon opened on the van and the weight of a body jarred the vehicle as it stepped inside. The door slammed shut once the person was comfortable and seated. Art figured this was Petrut, the largest of their sordid bunch, so he waited to hear if the man had anything to say to whomever was tasked with keeping watch over Art, their sleeping hostage.

"*Il fait très beau,*" began the voice of Petrut. "*Il n'y a pas un nuage dans le ciel. Il n'y a pas, non plus, de vent. L'eau est bleue, calme.*"

"*Oui,*" said the other man. "*Mais on est encore loin...*"

Art listened as the two men continued to talk about the weather, specifically its impact on the sea. He noted that the French they spoke didn't sound like it was their native tongue, although both men seemed to speak the language with ease. Art didn't understand everything they said, but he picked up on most things from the discussion, and it sounded like the men were pleased with the conditions outside, with the calm waters that lay ahead. And although it had been some years since Art had been forced to make use of *le langue française,* he was confident that he was at least gathering the larger points from this conversation between his captors.

The passenger side door opened once more on the van, and the large man stepped out, slammed the door shut. In the quiet that returned to the vehicle, Art's thoughts drifted to his mother, who often took him on trips abroad, even when he was just a small child.

Art had fond memories of the summers they enjoyed together. Those were the days when Art's father still liked to spend time with his son, with his lovely wife. The family spent summer after summer in the South of France, and Art's parents always encouraged their son to spend his mornings learning the local language. When Art finished with his tutor, usually sometime around lunch, the family would then spend the afternoons together on the beach, where Art and his father would build sandcastles together, and where Art's mother would take her only boy for long walks at the edge of the surf, hunting shells and sea glass and wandering intentionally all the way. Then, the family would often ride their bikes into town for an early dinner, maybe an ice cream by the sea.

But those days were long gone, Art thought, as was any real command he'd ever had of the French language.

Still, Art understood most of what Petrut had discussed with the other man, and he'd taken away a rather concerning piece of information: the group planned on taking Art away from the good old US of A.

And the gang planned to use a ship to do it.

18

Once again, Art heard one of the panel doors slide open on the van. He felt something nudge the side of his ribcage.

"Get up, Arthur." The owner of the voice placed a hand on Art's shoulder, then started undoing the cord around his neck. "It's time to get out and stretch your legs."

When the black sack came off Art's head, he didn't have any trouble acting as if he was just waking up. The bright morning sun—at least, Art assumed it was morning—forced him to squint as he adjusted to the sudden burst of daylight. He leaned forward in his seat, stretched a bit to loosen up his stiff neck, and all the while tried to get his first glimpses of the place that waited for him outside of the van.

Art turned and examined the smiling face of the short, thirty-something man who stood nearby. He was dark-haired like Petrut, had a big nose, stubbled jawline, and wore a thick flannel shirt. But this man was much smaller than his boss, smaller than the men who'd assaulted Art the night before, and Art decided this new face had to belong to the driver of the van.

"Good morning," the man said. "My name's Jetmir."

Art still wasn't sure how to deal with these men. The way they blended common courtesy with passive threats of violence made his stomach uneasy, which Art could only assume was what they were going for in all this. It had to be part of their strategy for dealing with a hostage.

"We met last night," Jetmir added. "I'm the wheelman."

"Right," Art grunted. His entire body felt stiff, sore, and his head was killing him. "Thanks for not wrecking the van, I guess."

"You're quite welcome." Jetmir had what sounded like pride in his voice, and the accent on his English was the least noticeable in the bunch. "How'd you sleep, Arthur?"

"Well, *Jet*, that's a downright ridiculous question—" Art cleared his throat some more, feigned the thick grogginess of having just woken up. "But if you really want to know, then I'd say that was the worst I've slept in my entire life."

Jetmir looked a little unsure of himself. "Oh."

"Look, Jet—" Art let his eyes drift over to the grassy bank that wasn't far from the door of the van. "I need to take a leak. Mind if I do that now?"

"Of course," the man said, reaching over in an attempt to help Art undo the seatbelt at his chest.

"I've got it, man. I can manage it all from here."

Art stepped out into the cool morning air. He could smell the ocean, and he could see what looked like seagulls hovering somewhere off in the distance, so Art knew they weren't far from the coast. His guess was they'd made about a six- or seven-hour drive from Durham, one that brought them to some place along the Atlantic Coast, which meant they could be anywhere between Wilmington and Myrtle Beach, if they were even still inside the state.

"Where are we?" Art asked, stepping closer to a grassy space he had picked out.

"We're near the beach," Jetmir said. "Too bad it's winter, right?"

"I like being at the coast during any season," Art said, glancing down to unzip the fly on his pants. He realized his clothes were still damp from the night before; that his shirtfront and jacket were still caked in dirt and blood. The sight of this on his clothes made him nauseous.

"By the way—" Art continued, trying not to think too much about whose blood had been splattered across his suit jacket. "Any chance I can get a change of clothes?"

"We have a set for you in the van."

Art glanced over his shoulder. He saw that Jetmir had a handgun tucked inside the front waistband of his pants. Although the man didn't seem too concerned about losing his hostage, it was obvious he didn't plan on fetching those clothes until Art finished irrigating that bank of cordgrass.

"Okay," Art said, his eyes turning back to the stream in front of him. "Well, do you know how long we're going to be out here?"

"Not long."

"And how long is *not long*?"

The man didn't respond.

"You know—" Art paused, considered his words. "If you get me a cell phone, then I'll be able to get this handled a lot quicker. That way we can all just go home."

"I'll let you talk to Petrut about that."

"Right, the big man," Art said. "Where is he?"

"He'll be back soon."

Art started to zip his pants. "Look, I'm trying to be patient here, Jet, but I don't know what the game is if you don't want me to work on getting you some money."

"This isn't a game, Arthur."

"All right, well, call it what you want to call it." Art turned back around to face the man. "I just want to get out of here, you understand?"

Jetmir smiled. "I'm glad to hear it, because I think we'll be leaving soon."

Art shook his head at this. He knew the longer he went without getting close to a phone, the likelier it was he'd be leaving the country with these guys.

"Everything okay?" Jetmir asked.

"No, Jet, not at all. But let me see those dry clothes you have for me."

———

Art got his first look at the suitcase the men had packed for him. Inside of it were several sets of boxers, shirts, socks, and pants, and all of it seemed to be sized to fit Art's frame. There was also a pair of sneakers, and a pair of leather boots to choose from. The Dopp kit tucked inside one of the inner compartments of the suitcase had all of the essentials that Art might need for a month, and in the external pocket, Art found two plain ballcaps, a pair of sunglasses, and a few unusual looking paperbacks.

"Should I change clothes here?" Art asked.

Jetmir nodded.

Art stood at the back of the van, which was parked on a gravel road. He could see that the road seemed to follow the bank of the nearby river, one that probably fed into the Atlantic several miles to the east. Although Art couldn't see any houses along this little stretch of waterfront, he had a feeling that other people weren't very far away.

"Hurry up," Jetmir soon said. "I don't want someone to come driving up behind us on this road."

"All right, take it easy." Art began removing his jacket and shirt. As he did so, he remembered the plastic bag that was in the front pocket of his jacket, and Art had himself an idea. "Hey Jet, are you much of a coffee man?"

"Of course." The man offered another smile as he said this. "I believe Petrut will be back soon with some coffee."

Standing there, shirtless, Art dug his hand inside the pockets of his soiled jacket. "You care for a little pick-me-up before the big guy gets back?" Art asked. "I have a little sweetener for us..."

"I don't know," Jetmir replied, eyes on the bag that was now in Art's hand. "We have a pretty long day ahead of us."

"That's even more of a reason to make the morning enjoyable."

Art got the impression that Jetmir was considering the offer because the wheelman did a quick survey of the deserted space that surrounded them. No one was around.

"Come on..." Art went with his most charismatic smile, one that caught the man right as he was about to respond. "It's just a couple of lines, Jet. What's the big deal?"

Jetmir finally nodded, then held out his hand. "Let me see it."

Art grinned when he heard this, then handed the man what was left of the coke. Although Art wasn't yet sure how to deal with his kidnappers, he figured befriending one of them might be the first step to splintering any loyalties among their group.

"This looks like it's good quality," the man said, inspecting the bag. He dipped a finger into the powder, tasted it. "I bet it's not cheap."

"It's the best around." Art knew he had his captor convinced. "Where should we line up some rails? I was thinking we could use the center console inside the van."

The man paused for a long moment, then asked: "How much did this cost, Arthur?"

Art was a little surprised at the strange question. "I don't remember exactly, but my guy probably charged me around two-fifty."

"And by your *guy*, you mean your drug dealer?" His tone sounded a tad self-righteous.

"Yeah." Art was confused now. "Look, do you want to use the van or what—"

"Do you know the name of that river?" the man asked, cutting Art off.

Art pointed to the water that ran alongside the road. "You mean this one?"

Jetmir nodded.

Art was more than a little confused now. Still, he walked over to the edge of the gravel road and looked at the brackish water that swept by. Along the edges of the bank, broomsedge and switchgrass billowed in the breeze. And off in the distance, Art could make out the outlines of what looked like tall cranes and several large container ships.

Art turned his eyes back to the man. "No idea, Jet."

This seemed to be the response that the short man expected. "See, Arthur, I was looking at the map earlier, while you were trying to act like you were sleeping in the van—"

Art didn't say anything.

"And I saw that this body of water is called the Cape Fear River—" he paused. "Which I think is perfect. Do you know why?"

Art didn't hesitate with a smartass remark: "Oh, I don't know, maybe because your little gang of wanna-be Eurotrash picked me up last night and scared the shit out of me? Or, how about because you're holding me against my will and won't tell me—"

"No—" Jetmir held up a hand, gave his words a thoughtful pause. "I think the Cape Fear River is a perfect place for you to begin your journey because it's the fear that's holding you back. It's the fear that keeps you from doing what's right."

Art responded with a heavy sigh. "Thanks for the geography lesson. But how about you keep your damn lectures on my life journey to yourself, yeah?"

Jetmir seemed to ignore Art's words as he reared back with the plastic bag in one hand. Art watched as the man threw the bag high into the air, where it sailed out over the river, then disappeared somewhere among the waters of that rising tide.

"Finish getting into your new clothes," Jetmir said. "Petrut wants me to burn everything you had on last night."

"Fine." Art bent over and stuck his hands inside the jacket, started going through the pockets to pull out what remained inside of it. Pretty much his keys and a wad of cash was all he had left. "I just need to get the rest of this money out."

"You don't need it."

Art stopped, looked over at the man. "It's a thousand dollars, *cash*."

"Leave it, Arthur. You won't need it."

"You don't want it?" Art asked. The Mortlake in him wasn't accustomed to someone not being interested in the world's most alluring asset.

"I don't want it," the man said. "It'll be burned along with everything else."

19

On December 14th, Art Mortlake was set to board a German-owned freighter bound for the second-largest port city in Europe.

In the suitcase set aside for Art was the passport of one Andrew Neilson Gibbs, a young man who was only a year older than Art, and who for reasons unspecified, had already been accounted for on the ship's manifest. It seemed Mr. Gibbs had been hand selected by Petrut and his band of Merry Men because he'd recently graduated from the University of North Carolina at Chapel Hill, and was supposed to be travelling back to his hometown of Bristol, the one in South West England.

It was a long post-graduation trip, but the young man's family and friends expected to hear little from Mr. Gibbs throughout his trans-Atlantic voyage. And that was because the recent college graduate intended to make productive use of the roughly fifteen-day journey ahead. As an aspiring novelist, the twenty-three-year-old man saw the ship and antiquated form of ocean travel as an opportunity to get a jump-start on writing his first work of fiction.

Except, unfortunately for Mr. Gibbs, Art's kidnappers decided that his story was one that would need to go on to write itself.

Of the four men who were directly involved in the kidnapping, only two of them held tickets to board the ship: Jetmir Miličević Babić, a thirty-three-year-old Croatian-born French national, and Petrut Noica, a forty-one-year-old Romanian-born French national. The two men carried French passports in their own names, and both were booked into the same interior cabin, one that was conveniently situated right next door to the one reserved in Mr. Andrew Gibbs's name.

The kidnappers approached the German-owned freighter about an hour before the ship was scheduled to set sail, and both men wore muted clothing and broad smiles as they carried their luggage up to the long line at security. Among their suitcases was an unusually large instrument case, one that pretended to hold a high-end, six-foot double bass, an instrument that boasted an approximate value of seventy-five thousand dollars.

But what was really crammed inside that case was Art Mortlake, an instrument that was worth much, much more to Petrut and his group of thugs.

From inside the case, Art strained to hear as much as possible, especially any of the conversations taking place nearby. Art could hear just about everything that was said when the men strolled up together to one of the security checkpoints at the Port of Wilmington.

"Good morning, gentlemen," began a woman with a distinctly Southern accent, one of the hillier varieties. "Where is it that y'all are heading today?"

Art tried to yell, tried to make any kind of sound that might be heard from outside of the case, but he could barely breathe with the two rolls of duct tape wrapped around his mouth, hands, and feet. The more he strained himself, the more he worried about exhausting the small amount of air he had available inside the case.

"We're going all the way to the Port of Antwerp," began Petrut's deep voice. The man's accent sounded even thicker now, and Art wondered if this was intentional, maybe a little something to make the big man sound even more European.

"That's a long time on a boat, sugar." The woman sounded well-caffeinated, chipper as she said this. "What's the purpose of your trip?"

"I don't like to fly," Petrut replied, rather congenially. "But I must return home to France where I live and work. Once we arrive at the port in Belgium, I'll go on to take a train home to Paris."

"Shoo, honey, I don't much like flying either," the woman said. "All these planes and helicopters crashing has only made me more nervous, too. You have the right idea using these boats and trains, certainly a whole lot safer."

Petrut murmured a knowing reply of some kind.

"I see that you were in the US for about a month," the woman said, obviously flipping through the man's passport. "Was your trip over here for business or pleasure?"

"I do admit, I always love coming to America..." Petrut seemed to be patting the case while he spoke. "This trip was for business, though."

Art groaned as he tried to reposition his six-foot-plus frame inside the case. He couldn't believe the naiveté of this woman at passport control who was just chatting it up with his kidnappers. Art wanted to scream: *Hey lady! He has a body inside of the case. Just open the damn case!* He knew she couldn't hear his murmurings, though. And why would she even suspect there was a man inside an instrument case? Weren't people just screaming about all the people illegally coming *into* the country?

"What line of work are you in?" the woman asked.

"Oh, I don't do anything too exciting for work," Petrut said. "I'm just a musician and member of the Paris Orchestra, or *l'Orchestre de Paris*. I came over to America to purchase a few new instruments for our string section."

"You don't say?" the woman squealed. "You're with the people who play the violins and all that, right?"

"Very good," Petrut chuckled. "I'm impressed with your knowledge of the orchestra."

"My daddy played the fiddle," the woman replied. "I'm from the Mountains, that's the western part of the state, and Bluegrass is a part of life back home."

"I enjoy the great American Bluegrass artists," Petrut said. "Do you play?"

"Oh, heavens no. My mother made me learn the piano."

"My mother wanted the same for me!" he exclaimed.

The two of them continued jabbering until Art heard the voice of what sounded like another customs or security officer. This new voice was that of a man who sounded very blasé, but he at least asked Petrut what was inside the instrument case.

"This is an Upton double bass," Petrut replied, continuing to *tap tap tap* his fingers on top of the case. "It's a near perfect replica of the *Giacinto Santagiuliana,* a 19th Century—"

"We call it an upright bass, sweetie," interrupted the bubbly woman who had started the conversation with Petrut. It sounded like her comments were being directed more to her colleague, though. "This gentleman here is from *Paris,* and he plays music over there with the symphony."

"Do you have any paperwork for the instrument?" asked the man who sounded barely awake. "Then I'll ask that you put it on the belt over there, just to run it through the machine."

Art could hear Petrut murmur something while he exchanged the necessary documents with this newer voice from security. "This here is for the instrument's authenticity," Petrut said. "I also have here a certificate from the seller that denotes all taxes have been paid in full."

"Fine," the man said. "Let's give it a quick run through the baggage scanner, then I'll have you on your way."

There was a pause, then Petrut said: "If I may say, sir, this is a very fine, American made instrument. I want to make sure the machine doesn't harm the delicate components and craftsmanship that the luthiers—"

"I assure you, it won't," the man said.

Art felt his heartrate pick up. He couldn't believe what he was hearing. It seemed pretty clear that Petrut didn't want them to put the instrument case through the baggage scanner, and it sounded like this man at security wasn't going to let Petrut pass without doing so. Art moaned and groaned against the duct tape: "*Put it through the machine! Come on, do it!*"

"I know you're the expert here—" Petrut appeared to be laying it on thick. "I did, however, read an article not that long ago about these machines. And I believe they use low levels of ionizing radiation, no?"

"That's correct, sir."

"I knew *you* would know. I just worry about how that may affect the instrument itself as it—"

"Let this man go ahead!" It was the same woman's voice from earlier, urging her colleague to move it along. "I've got a whole lot of people waiting behind this nice man. We don't have all day to get these folks onto the ship."

Unbelievable, Art thought. Why not peek inside the case? Or just put it through the machine. I thought we had the Patriot Act, dammit!

"You're right," the man finally said, although it sounded as if he just didn't want to argue with his colleague. "I don't want to damage this nice instrument."

"That's very, very kind," Petrut said. "Thank you so much."

"Do you need a hand with the case?"

"No, it's precious cargo," Petrut quickly said. "I'll take care of it."

"I understand," the man said. "You're free to move along."

"Have a nice trip!" shouted the woman. "My daddy will just be tickled to find out I met a famous string man from France."

"I'm sure your father won't be too impressed." Petrut sounded as if he was trying to show true modesty with regard to his distinguished, albeit fake career as a renowned concert bassist. "I'll think of North Carolina next time I hear a Bluegrass number."

"Please do," she added. "Bye-bye now."

Art felt like he was going to be sick. He also had another vicious cramp setting in on one of his legs. He tried to breathe in and out through his nose as Petrut or Jetmir began rolling the instrument case over the ground. The case rumbled along, bouncing down steps, knocking into walls, and even seemed close to falling over on a few occasions.

Soon, the case slowed, a door unlocked, and the case was then rolled inside what Art could only assume was one of the ship's cabins. After that, Art heard what sounded like a door slam shut.

All was quiet.

They were on the ship.

20

From the edge of the bottom mattress on his new bunkbed, Art took stock of his little cabin. His guess was that the room was probably close to a couple hundred square feet in total. Based on the lack of windows, as well as the room's spartan furnishings, he figured the cabin had to be on the lower end of the container ship's offerings.

Still, Art reminded himself that his *holding cell* had to be far better than what most hostages ever saw. There was the bunkbed at one end of the room, a corner sofa that sat no more than ten feet away, and a door to a tiny ensuite bathroom, one that Art could stick out an arm and almost reach from the edge of the bed. He also had a very basic looking television mounted to the wall, a small fridge, and a scratched-up desk with a simple wooden chair beside it. The room looked like it once had a phone mounted to the opposite wall, but Art's guess was that Petrut had removed it before releasing his hostage from the instrument case.

Art stood up from the bed. He rubbed his wrists, then his face, as he stepped toward a mirror that hung on the cabin wall. The duct tape restraints had ripped hair and skin from his body, but he could see from his reflection in the mirror that most of the damage had been caused by the events from the night before. Art's nose looked badly bruised, and was probably broken, and much of the right half of his face was covered in scrapes and cuts.

At least I have all my teeth, Art thought, staring at a beaten image of himself. And at least I'm still alive, right?

There was a knock on the cabin door, then it opened as Petrut stepped inside. The big man wore a thick sweater and dark slacks, and he smelled of cigar smoke, most likely the celebratory kind.

"I've brought you some dinner," Petrut said. He held what looked like a to-go bag in one hand. "It's a chicken schnitzel with potatoes."

Art could already smell the warm food in the bag. He suddenly felt like he was the hungriest he'd ever been. Art was about to offer a word of appreciation for the food but caught himself just in time. "Put it on the table over there," Art said, pointing to the little banquette eating area, one that doubled as the living room sofa.

"You need to eat, Arthur."

"I'll eat later," Art said. "Once you leave."

Petrut pulled a large bottle of water from inside the bag. He took a few steps closer to where Art sat on the bed. "Here," he said. "I at least want you to get some water in you."

Art was exhausted, but he put everything he had into glaring back at the man. "You trying to keep me alive or something?"

Petrut sighed. "We talked about this earlier when—"

"When you pulled me out of that death trap of a case," Art said, finishing the man's sentence.

"That was the only way I could get you onto the ship."

"Here's an idea—" Art finally reached out and snatched the water bottle from Petrut's grasp. "How about you just not carry my ass across the Atlantic? I mean, come on, man, why the hell is any of this necessary?"

Petrut took a few steps back. He turned and reached for the wooden chair that was beside the desk, then placed it at the center of the room, where he eventually took a seat. "I can tell you why we're doing this," Petrut said, folding his hands so that they lay across his stomach. "It might take some time, though."

Art shook his head. "If everything you have to say leads to making a demand for a ransom, then just skip to the end and tell me how much it's going to cost."

Petrut smirked. "You keep saying things like that to me."

"Things like what?" Art unscrewed the cap on the water bottle, took a sip. The liquid was cold, delicious.

Petrut actually tried a little comedy as he mimicked the words of his hostage. "Just tell me how much money you want so I can go home." It was just an exaggerated impression of a whiny, petulant child. "My father will pay whatever you want if you just give me a phone," he continued. "I just need a cell phone. *Wah, Wah, Wah...*"

"Okay." Art actually grinned. "What's your point, *Pete*?"

"My point is this—" Petrut leaned forward in the chair, placed his elbows on his knees. "You haven't been listening to anything I've said to you. This isn't *just* about money."

"I'm listening right now," Art said, taking another gulp of water. It did feel good to get some fluids back in his system. "Tell me what you want and let's figure this thing out."

Petrut took in a deep breath, then said: "We're here to help you, Arthur. We're here to help you understand—"

"Just stop with that, Pete, because it's a tired line that means nothing to me—"

Petrut put up a hand to stop him. "You told me you were listening."

"All right, fine," Art said. He took another swig of water. "I'm all ears."

Petrut pulled a folded piece of paper from one of the pockets on his slacks. As he unfolded it, he cleared his throat like he was preparing to make some kind of formal address to a committee.

"This is a copy of a letter," Petrut began. "You'll see that it's quite old, at least based off of the date at the top of the letter, but I assure you we have the original, and I assure you the letter is quite real."

Art placed his bottle of water on the floor, then reached out to take the paperwork from Petrut. "What kind of letter is this?" Art asked.

"Read it," Petrut said. "I'll wait."

Art could tell that fatigue was beginning to set in now. He was starting to feel his eyelids get heavy, and his body felt weakened, like it was in serious need of sustenance and sleep.

"Okay," Art muttered, having to focus so he could read the typewritten note.

The letter looked like the kind of document you skipped past at a museum. It was addressed to Messrs. Mortlake and Hambledon, and it appeared to be little more than a summary of some kind, one that had to do with a business deal that took place during the spring of 1911. Art did the rough math in his head, which led him to question whether the Mr. Mortlake being referred to in the letter could be his great-*great*-grandfather—*Big Arthur*.

"Sounds like this fellow named Mortlake borrowed a bit of money," Art said. "Is that what this is all really about? Are you kidnapping people to collect on a more than hundred-year-old debt?"

Petrut pointed to the paper in Art's hand. "You see the amount that was borrowed?"

"Two million," Art said. The tone in his voice made this seem like it was but a meager sum.

"That was a lot of money in those days."

"And it's still a lot of money." Art lowered the paper. "But it's not worth all this, right?"

Petrut shrugged. "We'll see."

Art's eyes went back to the letter, and he slowly reread everything on the page. "Who's this Hambledon?" Art asked.

"Lester T. Hambledon was a lawyer. You'll notice in the letter that there's a reference to a contract, one that this Mr. Hambledon probably advised on."

"It would still be a very, very old contract," Art said, carefully choosing his words.

Petrut nodded. "It's a contract, nonetheless."

Art acted as if he were weighing Petrut's words, but his gut told him this was all just part of the game, part of whatever scheme the big man was cooking up. Art had grown up with a father who continually dealt with people and organizations who had their hands out. Clive Mortlake was a man who paid his debts and gave lots of money to worthy causes. But he was also a shrewd businessperson, and the man rarely ever let people take advantage of his family's status and wealth. So at least in that regard, Art planned to be just like his father.

"Well," Art said, handing the letter back to Petrut. "I may have missed the bus to law school, but I'm pretty sure you've already broken a shit ton of laws to collect on whatever it is that this contract says."

Petrut took the paper back without a word.

"Is it two million you're after?" Art pressed. "That's the number?"

Petrut nodded. "I work for someone who would like to collect on what they are owed pursuant to the contract."

"I see—" Art said. "And who would that person be?"

"I can't tell you, Arthur. Not right now."

"Well, are they going to relay the demand for two million to my father?"

"We will make a demand eventually," he said. "But it's going to be for more than two million US dollars."

Art absorbed this. He didn't feel like arguing semantics with the big man, but collecting on a dusty old debt didn't make what they were doing any less of a pay-the-ransom type scenario. And besides, all Art really cared about was whether their collection tactics might involve actually trying to maim, abuse, even kill their hostage.

"I have a copy of the contract here," Petrut said, pulling another folded up sheet of paper from his pocket. "The original version is not on the ship, if you must know, but I'll let you keep this one."

Art took the single piece of paper that was handed to him. "This is it?"

Petrut nodded.

Art winked. "Looks kind of light, yeah?"

"Just read it," Petrut said, smirking. "I'll wait."

21

The simple contract ran the entire length of the page, and the black letters all had that old typeface look to them, the kind that people liked to use nowadays to try and make their social media content look like it came off an old Underwood. And a quick glance over the page revealed that the words were mostly that boring, unnecessary legalese that all lawyers felt compelled to use, which meant the core of the agreement was likely hidden somewhere amongst all those whereofs, heretofores, and hereinbefores.

Art lifted his eyes to Petrut, as if to say: What in the hell is this? But the man was just seated there in his chair, quietly waiting for his hostage to wade through the copy of this old legal document. Art rubbed his eyes as he trained his focus back on the page.

The contract read:

State of Georgia

County of Gilmer

*This Agreement made and entered into this 11th day of May, 1911, by and between Arthur E. Mortlake, hereinafter referred to as "**First Party**," and Amerikaanse Liefdadigheid Stichting, hereinafter referred to as "**Second Party**."*

There's no way in hell I'm ever going to law school—Art thought, skipping the paragraph that followed. He was doing his best to speed read as he searched for what was supposed to be the meat and potatoes of the Agreement.

*Now therefore, for and in consideration of any and all of First Party's future trust interests, hereinafter referred to as the "**Extraordinary Guaranty**," and the promises, covenants, and agreements contained herein, Second Party agrees to lend First Party the sum of TWO MILLION AND NO/100 US DOLLARS ($2,000,000.00), as a charitable investment, so long as any and all paperwork required for said Extraordinary Guaranty is executed within the defined period of time.*

Art couldn't seem to stop rubbing his eyes as he worked his way down the page. "It's like you said," Art murmured, bringing his attention back to Petrut. "It's just a loan for the two mil, and a bunch of unnecessary legal jargon."

Petrut nodded. "Read the fourth paragraph on the page."

Art shook his head as he skipped down to the next paragraph, kept reading.

Second Party shall have the right and option to demand repayment at any time, so long as the demand for such repayment is served directly upon First Party, its heirs, successors, and or assigns. The principal sum of Second Party's charitable investment shall be recuperable, in full, along with any and all interest and/or profit accrued thereon—

Art chuckled as he read this last sentence. "Any and all profits can be recouped?"

"Is that what it says?" Petrut asked.

"Now I know this is a joke."

Petrut leaned forward again. "Do you see me laughing?"

This more aggressive stance from Petrut was probably supposed to make Art feel uneasy, anxious, but it really just made Art feel like the night was starting to push him a little too far. "Look, I'm pretty beat," Art said. "I'm all for hashing this thing out, but I think I may need to hit the rack and start again tomorrow."

"You're not that tired," Petrut said.

"I think I know how my body's feeling right now—"

Petrut interrupted him. "It's the scopolamine, Arthur, the Devil's Breath.

I've combined it with a very, very small amount of sodium thiopental, and both are slowly working their way into your system, so this is making you feel—" Petrut paused, obviously searching for the word. "This is making you feel loopy."

Art was confused. "The devil's what?" he demanded, glancing down at the half-empty bottle of water that rested on the floor. Art tried to remember whether that cap had seemed sealed on the bottle, tried to remain calm as he lifted his eyes back to his kidnapper. His mind started to run through what possible reasons lay behind Petrut's decision to slip a tasteless, odorless substance into his hostage's drink: *none were good.*

"Let me see the paper." Petrut made a motion with his hand. "I have a few questions about this agreement."

"You dosed me?" Art cracked back. His temper felt even sharper, and he wielded it quick as a whip. "What the hell is this stuff going to do to me?"

Petrut laughed. "You've been drugging yourself for the past three years, Arthur. What's one more night?"

Art glanced around the small cabin and saw that the lights were beginning to look fuzzy. He wasn't above trying whatever the latest party drug *du jour* was, but Art wasn't into the downers. Those drugs took their toll on a person, and Art had spent a month on opioids after his freshman injury. The painkillers provided relief, but it was a feeling he liked too much, mostly because it gave him a lovely, blissful high, one he probably could've lived in for another five years, which is why the Oxy had to go as soon as Art could force himself to dump his pills into the toilet.

Art began standing up, intent on moving himself away from the bed.

"Sit down," Petrut said.

"How about you go—" Art started to say. But he didn't get far into his verbal rebuke because a backhand caught him across the good side of his face. "Faaack," Art groaned, falling back onto the bunkbed. As he went down, he smacked the back of his head against the railing that ran along the top bunk.

"This is what we're going to do." Petrut was already back in his seat. The big man was smooth, yet incredibly quick for his size. "I'm going to need you to sit there nicely while I walk you through some questions."

Art watched as Petrut pulled a cell phone from his pocket.

"And you're going to answer my questions," the man continued. "Every. Single. One."

The big man placed the cell phone on the floor, face up, then pressed the red button on the screen to record their conversation.

"Are you ready, Arthur?"

22

Petrut nudged the phone a few more inches across the floor, then left the device there, only a foot or so from where Art's feet touched the ground. The big man had his hostage cornered and drugged, and he claimed he only wanted to ask a series of questions.

This guy's the worst friend I've ever had, Art thought, glancing down at his own hands. He saw that they weren't even shaking, which surprised him, because Art's heart felt like it was about to beat its way out of his chest. Whatever was in his system wasn't a pleasant experience, and the drugs were somehow keeping him physically stable, while also allowing his mind to experience the tell-tale symptoms of a near panic attack.

"Is this the first time you've ever heard about this old contract?" Petrut asked.

Art ran a hand across his forehead. Although the room still felt cool, he suddenly realized his face was pouring sweat. "Yes," Art said. "It's the first I've ever seen it—"

"Or heard of it?"

"Right," Art added. "This is also the first I've ever heard about some old contract to borrow two million dollars."

"Do you believe the paper is authentic?"

Art felt like he couldn't slow his words down and was quick with his response: "Absolutely not. It's a crap forgery and it's all part of whatever grift you and your boys have going on."

Petrut smiled. "I see the dosage is working nicely."

"*Va te faire foutre*," Art spat.

"Language, Arthur..." Petrut made a face as he said this. "But I must say, your accent isn't bad, and I do appreciate you volunteering that nice little nugget of extra information for me. I assumed your privileged upbringing had afforded you a wider, *easier* understanding of the world. I just wasn't sure which parts of the globe might be included."

"Kind of funny how being privileged just makes everything so easy, right?" Art felt like he was about to slide down some kind of angry, trippy rabbit hole. "I mean, it's all just sunshine and daises and unicorns when you have *beaucoup* money, right?"

Petrut leaned back in his chair, folded his thick arms across his chest.

"But yeah, I guess you could say my French isn't all that bad, Pete." The filter in Art's mind was gone, and he couldn't seem to stop his yapping. "It's not like I went and downloaded that stuff into my brain, though. My parents had me sit through hours and hours and hours of tutoring as a young kid."

Petrut only shrugged at this benign revelation.

"Not like I actually had to work for any of it, right?" Art felt the fire being stoked with every word. "I mean, I was just a little rich kid of eight, nine, ten years old. I *loved* getting to spend half my summer days indoors, seated at a desk, with a demanding tutor who had zero sense of humor."

Petrut seemed to be trying his best to appear bored. "I speak several languages, Arthur."

"Of course you do," Art shot back. "You're some kind of European, which means you probably think the only sport out there in the world is the one where you kick a soccer ball into a net—"

"A football," Petrut quickly corrected.

"*Right*, a football," Art said. "But I came up playing another sport, one you probably care nothing about. See, you shoot the ball up in the air, try and put it through a rim that's ten feet above the ground. It's called basketball and—"

"I know what basketball is."

"Yeah?" Art laughed. "Did you spend four-plus hours in a gym just about every single day from age ten until age nineteen?"

"Of course not."

"But I bet you once thought you were pretty good at football or rugby or—"

"Handball was my preferred sport."

"Whatever that is," Art scoffed. "But you know what, big guy?"

Petrut continued to appear disinterested.

"I know you weren't as good a player at *grabbing* balls with your hands as I was at playing basketball. And you know why?"

Petrut sat up straighter. This little comment seemed to have struck a chord.

Art kept going. "Because even if you thought you were good, which I'm sure you did at some point, I'm still ninety-nine percent sure you never worked at it as hard as I worked at my craft."

"I didn't get to play with my toys all day," the man said.

"Wrong." Art made the same buzzer sound that Frank King had made only the day before. "I was better than you because I was the guy who was willing to do the hard work. I was the one willing to—"

"*No,*" Petrut said, his feathers clearly ruffled. "It was because you had everything you needed to succeed, and all those little training sessions were paid for by your father who—"

"My father wasn't around!" Art yelled. "*I* lifted the weights. *I* ran the sprints. *I* shot basket after basket after basket. It was me, not him!"

Petrut shrugged, then offered a pouty, condescending expression. "Should I tell you about my childhood now?"

"I don't give a shit about what your life was like as a kid." Art spit at the ground between their feet, then kicked the water bottle aside. "Whatever hell hole you came from turned you into a piece of garbage who—"

"Careful, Arthur."

Art could feel himself spinning out of control. He just couldn't stop it. "What? You think just because you're extorting money from my family that you know what my life is like? You think you get to tell me how easy everything is? You kidnapped me because of my life!"

Petrut sighed. "Don't pretend you're not living a very privileged and easy life."

"Oh, it's easy alright. It's so easy that nothing I do even takes any real skill or talent or persistence. In fact, everything is just handed over on a silver fucking platter. It's amazing how easy life is with just a few extra zeros in a bank account."

"Well, I'm sorry for your troubles," Petrut said without any hint of concern. "Now, how about we just get back to my questions about the contract?"

"Nope." Art felt like something had been unearthed inside of him now. "I want to know what you think, Pete, so go ahead and tell me everything is just easy as pie once you have a bunch of money. You seem to know a lot about these things."

"It doesn't matter what I think," Petrut said, his second attempt at slowing Art's little diatribe. "I'm here to help you decide what to do with—"

"Yeah, yeah, yeah," Art said, smiling. "You've already told me plenty. You're here to help me see the light or some crap."

Petrut was beginning to look frustrated by the interruptions, so he returned to his more aggressive stance. "If you will listen, *Arthur*, then I'll tell you what I intend to do."

"Who are you to even think you understand my life?" Art demanded. "Who are you to try and teach me anything? Just tell me how much I need to pay and let me go home."

Petrut paused for a long moment. He flexed his hands while he appeared to consider his response. "I know you must feel angry," he finally said. "I imagine you might even carry some of that anger with you because of the guilt that rests on your shoulders."

There was something in the way the man said those words. "Do you expect me to confess or something?" Art asked.

"I do," he said.

"Oh, I didn't realize this was a mission from God you were on. Why didn't you tell me, Pete? I probably should feel a little guilty now."

Petrut ignored the provocation. "Tell me about your mother, Arthur."

"What does my mother have to do with your little kidnap-for-ransom scheme?"

"Tell me about Marilyn Mort—"

"Don't say her name," Art growled. "I'm not getting into it."

Petrut paused again for a long moment, then asked: "Do you feel guilty, Arthur?" His voice had taken on a serious, somber tone. "Do you feel bad about being the one left behind?"

"All the time!" Art shouted back. "It's what this life is about."

"Keep your voice down," Petrut warned.

"All the fricking time," Art said again, this time through gritted teeth. He wiped a hand over his face. He knew that what continued to run down his cheeks wasn't just sweat from his brow.

"Arthur, there's still things you can do that would make her proud. I imagine she wanted something different for you. You probably know that better than anyone."

"I'm not talking about her, you understand?" Art spoke with his eyes glued to the floor as he tried to calm himself. He couldn't seem to hold onto any one emotion. He felt all over the place, and he vowed that once he had the chance, he would take the control back.

"Fine," Petrut said. "Then let's talk about doing something great for yourself."

"Listen, Pete, I'm one of the most selfish people you'll ever meet." Art couldn't deny the fact that his own words had that unmistakable tinge of honesty to them. Maybe it was the drugs in his system, or maybe it was just the fatigue and stress finally wearing him down, but there was no denying who he was. "I do everything for my own benefit, and I've fucked around and ruined almost every good relationship in my life. And I doubt there's much hope for me anymore."

"Well..." Petrut paused. He obviously wasn't there to massage his hostage's ego. "I have an idea for you to consider."

Art laughed. "Now you're the one who's not listening, man. See, if I go on to do anything in this world, and I mean anything, it'll be because of the money. Everything else means nothing. Nada. Zip."

Petrut seemed to be driving toward a point of some kind. "But it's still better than someone who does nothing with their money, right?"

"Right," Art said. He could feel his heartrate finally beginning to slow. He wanted to quit talking, but he just couldn't bring himself to stop baring his soul. "Because if I do nothing, Pete, then that's an even bigger disappointment. I mean, who accomplishes nothing when they have my kind of privilege?"

"A loser," Petrut replied, quietly. "A quitter. A coward. A person who doesn't show up."

"That's the burden," Art said as he looked up from the floor. "And while I may be a lot of things I'm not proud of, I'm still always the guy who shows up."

Petrut nodded. "What if I told you I could help you with this burden?"

"No," Art said. "This is about whatever ransom amount your boss has in mind. Call it a contract if you want to, but let's stick to that. Let's stick to the money."

"I told you, Arthur, my work here is more than just about the money." Petrut leaned down and picked up the phone, then he held it out so that it was closer to Art's face. It was still recording as he spoke. "But if I'm going to help you, then I need you to tell me everything you know about your family's history, and I need to know everything about your father."

"I'm a Mortlake," Art replied, surprised at the sudden calm in his own voice. "We don't talk about the family's personal business. Ever."

"Interesting..." Petrut said after a long moment.

Art could tell that the man was trying to weigh his options. He'd obviously gathered enough about their family's history to know *why* Art's mother was on the road the day she died, but he didn't seem to know much about where things were with his father, more specifically *his* health.

"Let's try this again," Petrut said. "I need you to tell me everything you know about your father."

I'm not the person to ask, Art thought. He shook his head, grinned as he realized his father's paranoia was actually paying off for once.

"Do you find my question amusing, Arthur?"

"Look, you can ask me as many times as you want." Art sat up straighter as he spoke. "I'm not close to the man, so my answer won't change. I don't know what else to tell you."

The backhand caught Art across the side of the face. And this time the knuckles crashed against the injured parts of Art's cheekbone and nose.

"That's where you're wrong, Arthur." Petrut was standing now, leaning forward with one hand against the top rail of the bunkbed. "You can tell me now or you can tell me later. But your answer will change, because eventually you'll tell me what I want to know."

"*Va te faire foutre,*" Art murmured, one hand trying to plug the blood that trickled from his nose.

"What's that?" Petrut growled.

"You heard me," Art said, pulling his blood-soaked hand away from his face to offer the man his middle finger.

Petrut looked as if he might strike again. He lifted a hand, but it was only to bring the phone up to where it was close to his own mouth. He glared at Art as he spoke: "I've completed my first interview with Arthur Mortlake," he said. "Hostage has reviewed the agreement but has been uncooperative on matters regarding his family tree."

Without another word, Petrut turned and started for the room's only exterior door. Art could hear the big man continuing to add additional notes to the recording on the cell phone. Art could only assume this was some kind of digital record that would eventually be sent back to whoever Petrut and his gang worked for.

"Fourteen days remain on our voyage," Petrut continued. "I will resume my interrogation of Mr. Mortlake tomorrow morning."

Petrut then slammed the door.

Art was all alone.

He needed help. He needed advice.

PART II

THE ADVOCATE

"Failure is simply the opportunity to begin again, this time more intelligently."
—Henry Ford

23

The practice of law can be many things. It can be a profession in the highest sense, just as it can be a job like any other. But the privilege to engage in the practice of law comes with a strict statutory framework, one with high expectations and ethical considerations. And while these rules that apply to the conduct of lawyers are often viewed as unwavering, they are also what cast a long, grey shadow over this profession, as they are what sometimes provide refuge and protection for the law's most nimble practitioners.

But what's also true is that the law itself can be much like a fiery, jealous lover. It offers a purpose, a pursuit, a passionate quest for those who court it, and yet the law can be as brutal as a scorned ex, one who senselessly tramples on the heart of its most loyal. *Yes*, the law changes with time, with precedent, and it's even malleable to a point, depending on the facts. But the essence of the law never *really* changes, and only those lawyers who stay inside the bar long enough know what this means.

Lawyers come and go over time, most of their own accord. But for the ones who get forced out—especially the ones who truly love the law, blemishes and all—they are the ones who're subjected to the law in its most cruel form. Because once the law turns its back on one of its own, and an attorney loses the privilege to practice their craft, then it's the lawyer who must begin the most painful process of all: reckoning with the fact that they may love a vocation that will never truly love them back.

Maggie Reynolds sat alone at a large mahogany table, one at the center of a handsome conference space that belonged to *her* lawyer. In front of her lay the manila envelope that contained all of the final paperwork from her disciplinary action. It was thick, sealed, and would probably remain that way for the foreseeable future.

For thirteen years Maggie had practiced law in places all over Georgia, and not once had she ever needed another lawyer to handle anything more than a few real estate closings on her behalf. And for thirteen years she'd been advising clients in conference rooms just like the one she sat in now: helping them, advocating for them, preparing them for trials and hearings in courtrooms all over the state. And for thirteen years she'd scrapped and fought and won a lot of cases for the people she represented, people who needed her.

Except none of that really mattered anymore. The highest court in the state had rendered its decision.

"Everything I worked for..." Maggie whispered, her fingers playing at the corners of that large manila envelope. She shook her head. "It's gone, all of it."

The door opened to the conference room and in came Eddie Crabtree, one of the most well-respected legal malpractice and professional misconduct lawyers in the state. Eddie was one of the best at what he did, was certainly the most expensive, and always handled the defense side of things.

"I apologize for being late," Eddie said. He eased the door closed behind him with one hand, balanced a legal pad, newspaper, and coffee mug in the other.

"Not to worry, Eddie." Maggie said this while she rose from her seat and accepted a handshake from her busy lawyer. "You know I'm not in a hurry, at least not for another six months..."

Eddie acknowledged the bit of gallows humor with a warmhearted wink, then set his mug and other items down as he took a seat on the opposite side of the conference table. He was an older member of the bar, probably closing in on seventy, but Eddie was still considered by most to be the go-to guy when it came to this niche area of practice—which was essentially the representation of naughty lawyers, doctors, and any other licensed professional who could afford to pay Eddie's hourly rate.

"I had to shake myself loose from a conference call with Judge Winbolt," Eddie said, obviously trying to warm things up before they discussed Maggie's six-month suspension. "She's the new judge down in Laurens. Have you dealt with her yet?"

Maggie smiled at the question. Everything about their discussion felt routine, but there was also a strange, unfamiliar tinge of discomfort to it now. Lawyers who argued cases before judges often engaged in chitchat, even gossip, when it came to the jurists they encountered across the state. Unfortunately, Maggie didn't feel like she belonged in that kind of conversation anymore.

"No, I don't know of her," Maggie finally said. "I've only had to go over to Laurens County for a few cases. I seem to recall it being Judge Fenland who handled those for me."

Eddie nodded with gusto. "I know Carlton well," he said. "Been dealing with him for years and years without a problem. Knew him long before he took the bench, back when he and his daddy still had their little practice over in Twiggs."

There were one-hundred-fifty-nine counties scattered across Georgia, and the State's trial lawyers were famous for quite a number of things, one of which being their deep knowledge and command of their state's geography. Seasoned courtroom brawlers knew a great deal about the regions they practiced in, and most could rattle off the names of the towns, circuits, and important players in them, and the best trial lawyers knew everything about their judges, especially the peculiar ticks and preferences of those who sat atop the bench like heads of a fiefdom. Few lawyers, though, even those who had what they liked to call a *state-wide practice*, handled such a diverse caseload that they could actually mark all one-hundred-fifty-nine counties off on their bingo card. But Eddie Crabtree had been around for a long time, and he was probably one of the few among the old bar who was still vying for such a feat.

"Being in Blake County—" Maggie paused at the sudden need to talk about her work in the past tense, to talk about her home in southwest Georgia like it was a place she used to be. "I've not had to go over to Dublin for much. There were a couple of sizeable cases that came in the door a few years back, all of them car wrecks along I-16, but it's always been hard for me to justify the drive over, especially for anything run-of-the-mill. Sometimes I'll get a call about a DUI case in that area, but I usually send those over to Kathy Preston."

"I like Kathy," Eddie said. The older lawyer certainly had a sharp memory, and he was always able to quickly pull any name from his large, mental rolodex. "Her uncle, Rick Preston, had himself a fine bankruptcy practice several years back, then he went and got himself into a bit of trouble with the feds." Eddie rubbed his index fingers together, smiled. "I helped him out as much as I could, got him a real nice deal, but you know how those federales can be..."

Maggie nodded.

"But Rick still sends a Christmas card every year," Eddie rambled on. "Has himself a new wife and a farm over in Hancock County, says he hasn't missed practicing law for even one day. Tells me he's been growing turmeric, or something other."

Eddie was originally from the little town of Ocilla, but he'd been an Atlanta lawyer since he'd finished law school some four decades ago. He liked to act like he was still just a boy from Irwin County, but his high-end office, suntan in the middle of winter, and custom suit made his connection to rural Georgia seem more like a distant memory.

"Well, I don't plan on doing any farming," Maggie said, although she had considered trying her hand at a bit of gardening. "After these six months are over, I just hope to go back to doing what I know..."

As if on cue, Eddie turned his attention to his legal pad that sat on the table. A sweeping, blue-ink scrawl looked to cover many of the lined yellow pages, and Eddie took a moment to flip through his notes until he found the ones that corresponded to Maggie's case. He then placed his hand, rather cautiously, on the newspaper he'd brought with him into the room.

"I had my secretary walk across the street and grab a copy of the paper for me this morning." Eddie slid the folded-up newspaper across the table. "You made the front page today, above-the-fold."

Maggie pulled the newspaper close, then opened it. On its front page was a picture of her, along with several columns of text that probably covered a third of Page One. Maggie had stayed off her cell phone that morning, mostly because she anticipated a number of well-meaning, somewhat awkward messages might start rolling in. A part of her hoped that her friends and former colleagues would feel the need to show their support, especially once news of her suspension became public knowledge, and a part of her just wanted to go hide somewhere far, far away.

People will certainly know the final outcome now, Maggie thought, staring down at the newspaper. It all felt very official with her own picture staring back at her from that day's copy of the *Atlanta Journal-Constitution*.

"It's a tacky article, no question," Eddie added. "There's no way around it. But we got ourselves a good outcome, regardless of how the media views it. And I'd even say things probably shook out better than we expected, right?"

Maggie swallowed hard as she stared down at the words on the page. "Give me just a moment to read this, okay?"

"Of course," Eddie said. "You just take your time."

Maggie could see from the byline on the article that it'd been written by one of her most outspoken critics.

Although Maggie and her lawyer had discussed the barrage of negative articles that had openly criticized her over the past few months, Eddie had never once asked any questions he didn't need to know the answers to. And Eddie Crabtree didn't need to know why this one journalist—Ben Moss—a late twenty-something reporter and Blake County native, a newspaperman who'd already made his way to the big leagues, simply refused to quit writing hit pieces about Maggie.

And this latest article read like all those that'd come before it.

EXHIBIT "B"

THE ARTICLE

SUPREME COURT OF GEORGIA SUSPENDS MAGGIE REYNOLDS, SPECIAL PROSECUTOR IN BOTCHED CASE AGAINST US SENATOR BILL COLLINS.

By: Ben Moss
December 18, 2024

When Bill Collins, United States Senator for Georgia, first left his hometown of Blakeston for the wide, stately halls of Washington, D.C., he was a much younger man, but one whom the voters had called to represent them on the national stage.

Until, some thirty years on, in the twilight of Senator Collins's career on Capitol Hill, the 68-year-old was finally called back to his hometown in South Georgia. Except this time, it was to stand before his voters in a new role—that of a criminal defendant charged with the unthinkable: Murder.

State of Georgia v. William H. Collins was a trial that was billed as the first of its kind, as no sitting US senator had ever been formally accused of such a heinous act. But the speculation and accusations that tried to attach themselves to this man's illustrious career were short-lived. And by the end of Collins's first week of trial in Blake County Superior Court, the region's beloved senator was walking out of the courthouse doors a free man. This was after the special prosecutor's shaky case all but unraveled, and the judge assigned to handle Senator Collins's trial committed suicide in his own chambers.

When proceedings finally resumed months later, the newly assigned trial judge found that the State had intentionally withheld evidence in the case against Collins, and that Maggie Reynolds, the special prosecutor appointed to spearhead this unprecedented matter, had likely taken payments from non-state actors who sought a conviction against the long-time US senator. The flimsy criminal case brought against the senator was dismissed, with prejudice, once these developments were officially released to the public.

But yesterday, on Tuesday, December 17, 2024, the Georgia Supreme Court made their opinion public with regard to a state disciplinary matter brought against Margaret A. Reynolds, and justice was finally served when Reynolds—a Blake County lawyer who once made a career specializing in both criminal defense and personal injury lawsuits—received a temporary suspension of her law license for violations of Georgia Rules of Professional Conduct. Her six-month suspension is said to now be in effect.

Although the swift unraveling of the case against Senator Bill Collins came as a surprise to very few legal observers, most agree that the decision to suspend Reynolds from the practice of law was all but inevitable. What has puzzled some in Georgia's legal community is the fact that Reynolds did not suffer complete disbarment.

Top legal pundits already consider State v. Collins to be one of the most botched prosecutions in America's legal history, and a number of these same observers believe that the case will likely be taught in law schools as an example of how not to bring a criminal prosecution against a private citizen.

Senator Collins is said to have applauded the justices' decision but has declined any further comment on his involvement in the matter. It's been reported previously that the senator sought to offer mitigating evidence in support of Reynolds

—*the now disgraced Georgia lawyer—but said reports have not been confirmed by the senator's office.*

It should be noted that members from the local family who are believed to have privately funded the prosecution efforts, as well as Reynolds herself, have all refused to provide any comment whatsoever on the matter.

24

Maggie stared down at the article. The words stung worse than anything she'd ever seen written about her. And that was telling, because as a female trial lawyer, one who'd handled her fair share of higher-profile cases, she'd been on the receiving end of some pretty nasty remarks—things that no person should ever say about another human being.

But this wasn't some troll on social media, nor was it some angsty backwoods bubba who was making lewd comments about what she was wearing or where her place was *supposed* to be in the world. *No*, this was a front-page article in one of the South's most reputable newspapers, and it was a scathing, *very* public indictment that would overshadow everything she'd accomplished in her career up to that point.

One of the most botched prosecutions in America's legal history. Maggie turned those words over again in her mind. *The case will likely be taught in law schools as an example of how not to bring a criminal prosecution against a private citizen.*

Harsh.

All Maggie felt she could do in that moment was wait for the storm to pass. "Everything I worked for," she murmured again. "It's gone, all of it."

When Maggie refolded the newspaper, she turned it over and left it there on the conference table in front of her.

A different photo stared back at her now, one from another article. It was a story about the disappearance of a college student, a kid with the last name *Mortlake* who'd apparently gone missing in North Carolina the weekend before. Maggie's eyes rested on the young man's face for a moment. He looked like a nice kid.

"I told you the article was tacky," Eddie finally said, pulling Maggie's attention away from the picture of the missing Duke student. "Still, I can't even imagine how you must feel having to deal with this trash."

"I'm a big girl, Eddie." Maggie didn't want anyone feeling sorry for her. She'd made her decision to take the big case, to step onto the big stage, and things just didn't go as planned. That happens sometimes. It didn't mean she wouldn't try again someday. "I can take most anything they have to say about me. I've told you that before."

"I have no doubt..." Eddie seemed like he was trying to get one last read on his client, something she'd done many times with the people she'd gone about representing over the years. "But that doesn't mean it's easy, Maggie. No one likes getting dragged through the mud, no matter how tough they are."

"Oink, oink," Maggie replied, doing her best to put on a good face. Even if Maggie did feel like she might go through an entire box of Kleenex during her four-hour drive back home to Blakeston, she wasn't going to shed a tear while seated inside another lawyer's office.

Eddie Crabtree smiled. He'd been holding these kinds of exit consultations for a long time, and it was obvious to Maggie that the old lawyer knew how to handle the more delicate issues a person faced when they were preparing to confront the world with a professional reputation that lay in ruins.

"I'm probably not supposed to tell you something like this," Eddie began. "But I don't like most of my clients." He said this with a warm, grandfather-like calm. "That's because a lot of them are just drunks or addicts or thieves, and usually by the time they come to see me they've already been caught with their hand inside the cookie jar. They may be saying they're sorry once they get jammed up, but most of them have been sorry for quite some time."

Maggie nodded. "That's the work, Eddie, you know that. Besides, I always liked to think I had job security, because I knew there wouldn't ever be a shortage of dumbos out there walking around. I just didn't think I'd end up being one of them."

"But you ain't one of them," Eddie said, really leaning into his Irwin County roots. "You probably don't need anyone to tell you that, but I'm telling you anyway. You just ain't one of them lost causes, okay?"

Maggie sighed. "What's done is done, Eddie."

He nodded back. "This is true."

A moment passed, then Maggie asked: "I take it you need to walk me through the *dos* and *don'ts* of any unauthorized practice of law?" She already knew she wouldn't be allowed to give legal advice, go to court for a client, or do any of the actual legal work she'd handled over the past thirteen plus years.

"Once a lawyer, always a lawyer," Eddie said. "But *UPL* shouldn't be much of a problem for you, Maggie, as long as you have someone who can handle your caseload, someone who can get you and your practice through the next six months without another bar complaint."

She did have such a person. "I should have that covered," Maggie said. "She's supposed to start later this week."

"Good." Eddie paused. "Anyone I know?"

Maggie laughed. "I think you already have the name of everyone there is to know in this state."

"Try me," he said.

Maggie studied the man's gaze. "Oh, I just have an out-of-state lawyer who's willing to come in and manage the firm for me. She's actually a local girl, so I hope she'll at least be familiar with some of the players around town. That's half the battle right there."

"And *that's* what we call a non-answer, Maggie." Eddie leaned back in his chair, shot her a grin. "What makes you think you all of a sudden need to be coy with me? I know where the bodies are buried, remember?"

"Not all of them." Maggie winked.

"Okay, fair enough," he said. "But if you find yourself in a sticky situation, then you should know I'm not the kind of man who says no to repeat business."

"I'll call you if I have a problem."

"That's what they all say, counselor."

"Anything else?" Maggie quickly asked.

Eddie paused for another moment. "I do have one more question."

"Tick, tock," Maggie said. "I know the meter's always running here at Crabtree & Associates."

He ignored the comment. "*The letter*, Maggie."

Maggie half-expected this. "What about it?" she asked.

"Do you really think the senator had a hand in filing that letter on your behalf?" Eddie asked.

Maggie started to answer. "I'm almost sure he—"

Eddie put up a hand to stop her. "And if you do, Maggie, then why do you think he would go and do that? Why the hell would he go to bat for you?"

The ethics complaint that'd been brought against Maggie included a number of potential violations. And although the Georgia Supreme Court justices who were involved in her case found little merit in *most* of the allegations levied against Maggie, they did decide her lack of candor with respect to the trial court was certainly enough to warrant a severe slap on the wrist.

But then the aggrieved party (i.e. the senator) went and did something that Eddie Crabtree had apparently never seen happen before. Senator Collins stepped in with a written request of his own, one that implored the justices to not take away Maggie's license to practice law, and to instead suspend her for a reasonable period of time. His letter had even suggested the six-month punishment as one that fit *his* expectations, because that's what someone does when they have *real* power.

"We've been round and round on this letter," Maggie eventually said. "I'm tired of talking about it, and I really don't know why he did what he did."

"But do you have a theory?"

Maggie did, of course. "I might."

Eddie was still leaned back in his chair. There was real curiosity in his face, which made the older lawyer seem much younger than his age. It was that spark, that fascination, that made many a lawyer stay in the business well into their retirement years. "And what would that theory be?" the man asked.

Maggie considered her words for a moment, then said: "I think the senator has been a politician for a long time, and I imagine he understands the value in being owed a favor."

Eddie seemed to be trying to absorb this, seemed like he was working to make it fit with the outcome of her case. "As you know, Maggie, I've also been doing this kind of work for a long time, and I can't remember something like this ever happening. I can't remember anyone ever facing the kind of steep climb that you had, only to then walk away with your kind of deal."

Maggie laughed. "I'm glad I could bring something new to the table, then."

"I'm serious, Maggie." Eddie had obviously struggled with this question. "It makes me think there's something I missed in all this..."

"You're who put this deal together for me," Maggie said, although she knew her lawyer was too experienced when it came to these kinds of things. Eddie had to know that the deal she received—her six months on the sidelines—was *really* just based off the letter in question. "You helped save my license, Eddie. Say what you want, but I wouldn't have gotten this short of a suspension without your help."

"Maybe not," he finally said. "I usually don't care how things get done, so I know this is a good outcome, regardless as to who made it happen."

"You're still the best around," she said. "I'll tell all my friends to call you if they have a problem."

"Only tell your country club friends," Eddie said with a smile. He was the kind of man who seemed to recover quickly from anything that bruised his ego.

"Fair enough." Maggie offered another smile of her own. "Anything else?"

Eddie took one more glance at the notes in front of him. There appeared to be nothing else on his mind, or his notepad. Nothing except what prompted that letter from the senator. "I don't believe so," he said.

"Then I assume that means I'm free to go?" Maggie asked.

"Go forth and sin no more," Eddie said, now pointing to the conference room door. "Just promise me you'll steer clear of any *potential* trouble."

Maggie reached over the table to shake her lawyer's hand one last time. "You know I'll do nothing of the sort."

25

Clive Mortlake spent his fifty-eighth birthday in the foothills of Appalachia, wading in the shallows of cool mountain streams and their branches, where he hid in places that were tucked deep in the woods of North Georgia. It wasn't a region he was from—that place would always be somewhere in the North—but Clive Mortlake had spent much of the last twenty years or so feeling quite at home while spending time in the Blue Ridge Mountains. And although he would always be a Yankee in that area of the country, Clive knew the seasons of northernmost Georgia, its waters, its foreign landscape, better than most who called home to the counties that stretched over those foothills and well-hidden terrain.

Where does the time go? Clive asked himself. He shook his head as he picked up his rod case, threw his pack over a shoulder. Fifty-eight years was certainly a good ride in this life, *no question*, but he'd not expected things to end this way.

He'd not expected his only son—Art—to be the Mortlake they'd end up coming for in the end.

The weary fisherman took one last glance toward the stream below, toward what remained of the golden light from that December day, then he tightened his pack and turned for the trail home. Long cuts of the day's last light slashed through the tall, pine canopy above, and those final sunrays provided Clive with just enough daylight to navigate the path in front of him. It was a steady climb back up to the house, but it was one he always made after a day of fishing, and one he made every year without fail on December 18th, *his birthday.*

"Not happening this year..." Clive muttered, already feeling the first twinges of that burning sensation in his tired legs. It was hard for him to ignore the newfound weakness that the cancer meds had brought to his muscles, the added strain they caused to his voice, but that didn't mean he couldn't try and do his best to disregard both. "All the way to the top," he continued, urging his legs to keep pushing. "Come on, you pair of legs, let's go."

Breathing hard, Mortlake kept his eyes on the trail ahead as he read-justed the strap on his shoulder. The sweat from his hands made the leather slick, and he felt every bit his age as he switched the weight of the field bag to his opposite shoulder. The muscles in his calves started to cramp, screaming at him to stop and rest, but the man ignored their protests. It was his birthday climb, *dammit*, the same one he'd made for twenty years straight, and cancer or not, he didn't plan on his twenty-first attempt being the one that ended that simple tradition of his.

Clive felt one of his boots slip on a spot of slick, red clay. "Whoa!" he belted out, throwing a hand down to steady himself. He pushed off from the ground, kept his legs churning. "Not far to go, old boy..."

He could see that new light shone through the trees ahead now, pouring out from the large windows at the back of the Mortlake Family's mountain house. Clive knew he didn't have but fifty yards or so. He'd soon see the edge of the wooden steps come into view, the ones that led up to the porch, and that would be the final stretch of this year's little birthday challenge.

His last birthday, most likely.

As Clive made the turn at the top of the trail, he felt his legs wobble on him. "Come on, Clive," the man said to himself. He was smiling as he tried to coach his body up, painfully aware that this challenge was but a steep hike, a rutted-up, half-mile trek that a younger person, someone like his son, Art, might tackle at a much cockier pace.

"Twenty steps up to the porch—" Clive said once he reached the bottom of the stairs. He stared up at the wide, wooden deck that ran along the back of the house. He could see the windows were cracked open at the rear of the kitchen, could smell the first hints of potatoes and bacon and whatever else was already cooking for dinner inside the house.

Clive went to take the first step on the stairs, then felt his knee buckle as his foot met the first wooden plank.

He heard the sound before he felt himself hit the railing.

Thud.

Then it all went black.

26

It was Declan Tao who Clive Mortlake first heard as he came to. Declan was singing in that hazy moment, riffing along with whatever song played from the nearby sound system. It was something he only did while he worked in the kitchen. The man held the position of head chef whenever Clive needed to work from the compound in North Georgia, which was quite often, but Declan Tao's exceptional cooking was only secondary to the man's primary assignment: *physical protection*.

The Oregon native was former United States Army, a special operations man with deployments that took him on hundreds of classified missions, most of them to places that led deep into the unknowns of the human capacity for violence, cruelty, and sheer perseverance. Then after his exit from the service, Declan had made the transition into the shadowy world of executive security, where he made enough of a name for himself to come highly recommended when Clive Mortlake—the quintessential white whale for those involved in this very specific area of the security industry—came looking for a new close protection officer (i.e. a CPO).

The day that Clive hired his do-it-all CPO was more than ten years ago, and Declan Tao had rarely left his boss's side ever since.

Clive let his eyes continue to adjust, his ears continue to take in the sounds that surrounded him, and he soon came to the realization that he lay on the floor of his own kitchen. He heard what sounded like a grungy, nineties rock song pouring from the home's premium speaker system. It was an old Soundgarden track, he was almost certain, and what clipped in and out at times between the driving guitar solos, the hard-hitting lyrics, was the sound of a knife chopping and working away over one of the kitchen's wooden cutting boards.

"I have to say, it's quite the haul, sir." The familiar voice of Declan Tao easily overrode whatever song it was that carried on from the speakers. Clive didn't turn his head to look, but his guess was that his man probably stood somewhere on the other side of the kitchen's large, marble island. "I counted eight rainbows, four stripes, and one fifty-eight-year-old American shad, the old-money variety."

"Throw that last one back," Clive said with some effort. His throat felt dry, clogged up, and he could hear a weakened sort of raspiness to his own voice. "Nobody wants to eat that Nutmegger trash."

"It's too late, sir."

In that moment, Clive suddenly realized there was a pillow at his neck, and when he placed his palms flat to the floor, readying himself to push up off it, he felt what were probably grains of clay and dirt strewn around him. "Don't tell me you had to drag my ass into the kitchen, Declan."

"I had to, sir." Declan said this like it was just another part of the job, then continued chopping away over the countertop. "You didn't give me much of an option," he added. "You weren't in any shape to walk."

Clive sat up slowly from his place on the floor, a spot that wasn't very far from the kitchen's rear door. He looked toward the kitchen's center island, where he could see only the top half of Declan Tao. The large man wore a black apron over a black T-shirt and, with a fillet knife in one hand, seemed to be carefully working his way through the stack of fish that'd been caught earlier that day.

"I've been in worse shape before," Clive finally said, glowering at his forty-four-year-old CPO. "You should know that better than most."

"That you have, sir." The six-four security specialist had a dish towel slung over one shoulder. He wiped the thin blade of the knife across it, then moved on for another one of the glistening, pink and green fish that lay in front of him. "But I decided it was best to bring you inside. It was starting to rain, and I just saw no reason to leave you out in it."

Clive smiled. "You could've let me salvage whatever shred of pride I might've had left. Besides, I'm sure I would've woken up eventually."

"I guess so, sir." Declan looked over just as Clive started to make his first efforts to stand up from the floor. The bodyguard could get around the island within seconds, but he seemed to only be readying himself for the move should it be necessary. "But if I'd left you out there soaking in the rain, sir, then I don't think the doctor would've been too happy with me."

"Nope, I won't have it." Clive kept his eyes on the man, daring his CPO to move even an inch toward helping get the boss fully onto his feet. "I'm not going to the hospital, Declan. I've already told you that's out of the question."

Declan remained silent for another moment, then turned his eyes back to the knife and cutting board before him.

"*Tao*, did you call an ambulance?" Clive took a couple of steps forward, felt dizzy, so he reached out and placed a hand on the edge of a nearby table. He knew it was at least a thirty-minute ride for a car in town to make it up to the Mortlake property, even one with speeding privileges. "Don't tell me you called this in without my permission. This is a complete breach of—"

"I followed your instructions, sir." It was a rare interruption from Declan. "I did everything like we discussed. *All of it*." The man just kept his head down, kept on carefully cleaning the fish.

Clive narrowed his eyes. Declan Tao had been protecting the eldest Mortlake for more than a decade now, and the two men had an understanding on how things needed to be done. Although Tao was originally from Oregon's rural coastline, he was about as buttoned-up and respectful as any person that came from his generation. And he'd seen a portion of the world during his time in the military, then gone on to see a hell of a lot more of it while in Clive Mortlake's employ, so Declan had an extremely polished, professional, and somewhat cultured approach to the way he interacted with others. But Tao still didn't have a problem following orders, even if he was the kind of man who disliked being told how to do anything more than one time.

"Which doctor did you call?" Clive finally asked. "And how long do I have before—"

Clive stopped at the sound that carried from the front of the house: *ding-dong!*

Tao set the knife down as the doorbell rang. He wiped his palms on the towel that was still draped over his shoulder, then he tossed it toward one of the kitchen's large, single-basin sinks.

"I called Dr. Thompson." Tao said this over his shoulder as he turned and walked toward the front of the house. "And I've already invited her to stay for dinner, so please don't make a big thing about it, sir."

Clive didn't say anything more. He just stood there, alone in the room now, still steadying himself at the edge of his kitchen table. He heard the clanking sound of the deadbolt on the front door, then the creaking and groaning of heavy oak in the mountain house's main foyer.

"Is he awake yet?" started the familiar voice of Dr. Sarah Thompson.

"Yes, ma'am. But he's only been up for a few minutes."

"Where is he?"

"In the kitchen, ma'am. I'll take you to him."

27

No Mortlake had ever been born south of Philadelphia, and few in their family—aside from Clive's great-grandfather, Arthur E. Mortlake—had ever really expressed much of an interest in holding property in any of the places that comprised the American South. Clive had always been intrigued by the stories about his great-grandfather, though, so much so in fact that Clive ended up naming his only son after the man. So maybe that's why Clive ended up taking such an interest in his family's forgotten mountain house in North Georgia. It was a little one-hundred-and-twenty-two-acre spot that Clive's great-grandfather had staked out himself during the summer of 1912, mostly for fishing and hunting. And it was a property that the man had specifically ordered never be sold.

"Hey there, Clive," began the voice of Dr. Sarah Thompson. The local physician had appeared in a doorway at the opposite end of the kitchen and was heading straight for him. She wore a yellow rain slicker, and her mussed, greying hair looked damp from the heavy rain shower that was still coming down outside. "It's good to see you—"

"And it's good to see you," Clive said, releasing his hand from the table that steadied him. He straightened his back, evened up his posture. Although he'd been coming to stay in North Georgia for years and years,

Sarah Thompson was one of only a few locals who Clive had ever come to know personally.

"I was going to say it's good to see you're up on your feet." The doctor smiled at him while she seemed to take stock of his appearance. "Declan told me over the phone that you took a little tumble outside."

"Right." Clive coughed to clear his throat some more. "Well, I'm sure Declan was just being cautious. I'd spent the day out in the woods and just had a little fall after coming up the slope this evening. Must've missed a stair on the porch steps. Nothing serious."

"Uh-huh," she said, placing her bag on the kitchen table. She opened it and began rummaging through its interior. "Declan told me you were out cold but said that he didn't feel any lumps or cuts on your scalp, didn't see any noticeable markings on your face or neck."

Clive didn't like the tinge of concern that colored her voice, didn't like the idea of Declan being forced to frantically evaluate his boss's unconscious condition. "I should've taken more water with me when I left the house this morning—" Clive began.

"Just have a seat in that chair," Sarah said, stopping his excuses. The doctor was in now. "Let me have a look at you first."

Dr. Sarah Thompson was a local girl who'd gone away for college and medical school, then returned home to Gilmer County to work as a family practice doctor in her hometown of Ellijay. Her people all had long, respectable ties to the area, and she was just another fine example of what it meant for a person to show commitment to the success and wellbeing of their own community.

"Take in a deep breath for me," she said, holding her stethoscope flat against Clive's back. The cool metal instrument remained in place for a few seconds, then the doctor slid it over to his opposite shoulder blade. "Give me another one," she continued. "Try to take long, deep breaths, okay?"

While Clive followed each of her instructions, his mind drifted back to the first time that the two of them met. It was something he always did whenever he saw the woman, he couldn't help it, and it was because that memory—the one from the day of their first meeting—was part of a flash-back that often played in his mind.

"Open your eyes wide for me," Sarah said, now holding a slit lamp in one hand. "I need to take a look at your pupil size and their responsiveness, okay?"

Clive did as he was told and shifted his gaze until it was level with the small beam of light from her tool, and his eyes came squarely in line with the familiar face of his beautiful, fifty-something doctor.

"It's been a while," Clive said in a low voice. Sarah was now only a few feet from his face. "You look good."

"It has been a long while," she replied, evading his compliment. "It seems we're back to only seeing one another on the not-so-good days."

Clive only nodded. There was a lot of truth to those words because the first time the two of them met was also the day that Clive Mortlake lost his first and only wife, Marilyn. And although Sarah Thompson had been wonderful and attentive on that day, it was a hard memory that he still asso-ciated with the good doctor's face, even some twelve years later.

"But I hope there have been some good days peppered in between our meetings," she said, lowering the tool with its tiny light and microscope.

"There have been plenty of good days, Sarah." Clive couldn't help but wonder if his local doctor was tiptoeing around the mention of their short-lived fling, one that fell apart quickly a few years back. "You know that better than most," he added.

"Can you tilt your head back for me?" she asked, ignoring her patient's last comment. "I need to take a look at your neck."

"Of course," Clive said, easing his head back so that the doctor could place her hands on his neck and traps. She felt along both sides of his throat, then examined the area that ran along the base of his skull. "But I guess you don't get to see too many of your patients on their best days, right?" Clive asked.

Sarah smiled as she took a step back. "That is very true," she said. "The bad days do come with the work, but I still get to see plenty of people getting better."

A silence fell between them for a brief moment, and Clive looked away from the doctor's gaze because he could almost still see those same lines in her face, those same creases of concern that had been there in that moment when she stepped out into the hospital waiting room all those years ago. It was that face of hers that had made things hard when the two of them woke up next to one another. It was part of their connection, their bond, but it was also part of a terrible memory that remained frozen in time.

My Marilyn never got better, he wanted to say. She never had a chance.

Dr. Sarah Thompson was also a rural physician, so working in the local hospital's emergency room was something she had to do on occasion. And on that awful summer day, some twelve years ago, she'd been the physician in charge when a number of car crash victims came through the hospital doors. Clive's late wife—Art's mother—had been the driver of one of the vehicles involved, and had come into the ER on a stretcher, barely hanging on when the EMTs handed her off to Dr. Sarah Thompson.

Clive finally broke the silence. "Well, how do I look, Doc?"

"Not bad for fifty-eight." Sarah grinned. "I'd say you're a little tired, birthday boy, maybe a little worn down from the cancer meds, but I don't think I'll have to make Declan tie you up and carry you down the mountain to the hospital."

"That's good," Clive replied. The CPO wasn't in the kitchen with them, but Clive knew his man was probably standing just outside the doorway, listening. "I'd hate to have to whoop Declan's ass again—"

"I would hate that too, sir." It was the voice of Declan Tao. He popped his head inside the door to the kitchen.

"Men..." Sarah added, shaking her head.

Clive waved his bodyguard inside. He knew Declan needed to continue working on their dinner.

"But I do think this fall can probably be attributed to a combination of things, Clive." Sarah obviously wasn't done with her work up just yet. "I'll need to take a blood sample with me, maybe a urine sample, too, and I'll drop them with my lab first thing tomorrow morning."

"They can't be in my name," Clive responded. "I don't want your system to have me logged in anywhere with—"

"I know, Clive." Her voice sounded serious, stern. "You've explained to me once already your expectations as far as discretion, and *I'm* the one doing *you* a favor by keeping these consultations off the books."

Clive nodded. "Fair enough."

"My gut tells me that today's episode has to do with something more than just blood work, though." Sarah turned for her bag on the table, then started putting her tools back inside it. "I think it probably has to do with the stress."

Clive didn't say anything. He knew where she was going with this.

"I saw the news today about your son's disappearance." Sarah spoke slowly as she pulled what looked like a newspaper out of her bag. "I watched you tragically lose someone you loved once, and I know you must be worried about that happening a second time."

Clive wasn't sure he wanted to talk to her about this. He wasn't sure he wanted to talk with anyone about this. Hell, Sarah had been the first person to deliver the news to him that his wife was dead, that she'd never be coming back home. There was something cruel in him having to see her face again as they now discussed the prospect of Art, his and Marilyn's only son, maybe suffering a similar fate.

"We don't know anything for certain," Clive finally said, although he wasn't sure who his use of the word *we* really encompassed. "Art's a young, carefree guy, certainly one with a bit of a wild streak, and I'm not jumping to conclusions yet."

"I'm just saying, Clive, that it's natural to be concerned. Any parent in your position would be worried sick. And piling it on top of your diagnosis is even more—"

"Let's not," Clive said, carefully taking the newspaper from her hands. He turned the paper over and placed it on the nearby kitchen table. As he did so, he saw there was a story about some lawyer on the front page, a woman who'd been suspended for going after a US senator. Clive stared at the picture for another moment. The woman had an alluring face, and he'd always liked people who tried to buck the status quo.

"I'm telling you, Clive," pressed the doctor. "I know I'm not your oncologist, but there's a lot of moving parts to a terminal diagnosis and I think you have to consider—"

"Please—" Clive lifted a hand to stop her. "I'd rather talk about something nice this evening."

Sarah paused, then glanced over her shoulder at Declan who was back working away over the marble island, diligently preparing their dinner. "It is his birthday, right?"

"Yes, ma'am."

"And we're *really* going to celebrate it?" There was a playfulness to her question.

"I have to, ma'am. He tells me he doesn't like celebrations, but I worry he'll fire me if we don't make an effort."

Clive laughed. "Oh, come on, you two—"

"And is there a cake?" Sarah asked, holding up a finger of her own.

"He prefers pie," Declan said. "I do have some candles, though."

"Pie, huh?" Sarah finally turned back around to face her patient. "What's your favorite?"

"This is the apple capital of Georgia." Clive grinned. "I've never tasted anything better than what's grown right here."

Sarah shook her head. "Slow down, birthday boy."

"I'll try," he replied. "But as my doctor, you should know I don't have many birthdays left."

"Don't let him use any of those lines on you, ma'am." Declan couldn't help but add his dry sense of humor to the moment. "He'll start thinking that just because he's a widower, a cancer patient, and a worried father, that he's entitled to our sympathies."

"We can't have that." Sarah kept her eyes on Clive. "But are you sure you don't want to talk about your son?"

Clive glanced down again at the newspaper. He knew what the reports were saying: blood at the scene of an apartment complex shooting, Art's house in Old West Durham ransacked by unknown burglars, and a dozen or so friends who hadn't seen or heard from Art in five days. Yet, all he could see as he stared down at the newspaper was the face of that suspended lawyer, a woman with the last name *Reynolds*.

"We're working on finding him," Clive said, shifting his attention back to Sarah. "But maybe we can talk about it later?"

"Okay." Sarah slowly nodded as she spoke. "I guess we'll just have to see about that."

28

On Friday morning, Maggie Reynolds left home early with a thermos full of coffee. She was headed for her law firm—*Reynolds Law*—a fine set of offices that occupied one of the historic, downtown buildings that fronted the brick cobbled streets of Blakeston. Her firm sat only two blocks from the town's historic courthouse, and the business's very visible, smartly appointed office building had become a point of pride for Maggie ever since she purchased it several years earlier with settlement proceeds from her first, big personal injury case.

The building itself had come to be featured in several design magazines that covered the culture and happenings of the New South, and her invest-ment in the community had not gone unnoticed at the local level. But in Maggie's mind, her ownership and added level of care for the downtown building was more than just tasteful preservation of Blakeston's historic downtown, it was also an extension of her brand, and it told her clients and colleagues that Maggie Reynolds was committed to remaining a staying power in the important affairs that touched her region of the state.

Except now, given Maggie's six-month suspension and newfound standing in Georgia's legal community, she felt as if she needed to avoid her own law firm, the streets that surrounded it, the merchants and business owners who'd come to be her supporters.

But on that morning, she needed to be back in the office. She had one more meeting to get out of the way.

It was seven-thirty when Maggie pulled into a parking space on the street that ran behind her office building. She grabbed her thermos, along with a few casefiles she'd been studying back at the house, then stepped quickly out of her vehicle, hoping to avoid any chance encounters with a friendly passerby.

Every little street in downtown Blakeston had its own story, every building a business and an owner who'd contributed something to the town's history. Maggie would never be from Blakeston, would never be someone the locals truly accepted as their own, but she was slowly coming to terms with this immutable fact, slowly starting to come to the realization that it was the outsiders in this town—people like her—who often ended up getting the most done. And Maggie knew her neighbors would be watching her with interest throughout her suspension. She knew that some of them would even be quietly praying for her, hoping her place in the history of Blake County might continue to build once the storm passed.

Making her way around to the front of the building, Maggie caught sight of the early morning sun. It warmed the dewy, brick streets of Blakeston, and its soft rays came through the strings of Christmas lights that crisscrossed above the glistening roadway. It was unseasonably cool that morning, even for December in Blakeston, the county seat for Blake County. It was an area of the Deep South that one found in the southwestern corner of Georgia, a place that hugged the Chattahoochee River and the Alabama line. But it was almost Christmas there, so the remarkably cool weather felt more like a treat for the Southerners of that little town, a gift that seemed to match the wreaths and other holiday decorations that were out on beautiful display.

Blakeston was deep in Bible country, so the town had subtle nods to verses of scripture pinned on downtown lamp posts, angels positioned at the corners of the busiest streets, and a live nativity scene that ran streetside reenactments in the nights leading up to Christmas Eve. Although Maggie certainly wasn't the most devout of those believers in her community, she still very much loved the holiday season, and she thought it was one of the best times of the year to be in Blakeston. She also knew that it was almost considered a sin for any shop owner not to have decorations that matched those of their quaint little downtown.

While unlocking the front door to her law firm, Maggie saw that the office Christmas tree stood handsomely in the building's front window. At the base of the tree was a collection of law books and varying treatises, each of them wrapped with red bows so that they were made to look like presents. A sign above the window read: *Naughty or Nice? Call Santa cLaws at Reynolds Law!*

Maggie shook her head. "Might need to take that down..." she murmured, stepping inside the building.

She locked the door behind her once she was inside and left the small flip sign on the door's window in its place.

The little sign read: *Closed.*

Come nine o'clock, Maggie sat in her office's main conference room. Seated across from her was the young lawyer who'd agreed to take over the responsibilities that came with running Maggie's law firm.

Reynolds Law operated in a fashion that was typical among many a small-town law firm. Maggie was a solo-practitioner who handled all of the courtroom appearances herself but relied on her staff of paralegals and admins to support her with much of the in-office legal work. And although Maggie had certainly found more success in private practice than the other ham-and-eggers across her circuit, that didn't mean her practice was all that different from the other lawyers in her area, nor did it mean her path to becoming a capable small-town attorney was necessarily unique when compared to the road taken by her competition.

That's because there were *really* only three ways for a young lawyer to get their start in Blake County: through a family connection with someone who already had their own law firm, as a prosecutor in the district attorney's office, or as a criminal defense attorney in the public defender's office. Through each of these three routes, young lawyers developed their contacts in the local legal community, got to know the judges, and learned valuable lessons from early skirmishes with other lawyers in the area. Then, after a young lawyer's informal apprenticeship ended, they usually went on to hang out a shingle of their own—like Maggie had—or they partnered up with other lawyers in the area.

But Maggie's temporary replacement—Charlotte Acker—would be very different. Although she certainly wasn't coming into Blake County blind, she also wasn't exactly coming into small-town practice with the kind of experience that resembled that of the other lawyers around town. Which was good, because Charlotte would be far better prepared than any young lawyer who'd come before her.

She just didn't know it yet.

"Did you have a chance to look over the firm's current case list?" Maggie asked, once they had coffee arranged and covered the usual topics that came with the chitchat of catching up. "I sent it over by email the other night."

Charlotte nodded. "I skimmed over the spreadsheet as soon as I got it. Looks like you've been keeping to about a 50-50 split between the criminal and civil casework."

"That's right," Maggie said. "I seem to recall there being about two-hundred or so open cases, give or take."

"That's a lot for one person, Maggie."

Maggie took a sip of coffee. It was her third that morning. "It's not just me," she said. "There's the whole team here at the firm, and I'll introduce you to everyone later this morning."

"Then it's a lot of cases for one lawyer," Charlotte added, amending her comment. "And way more criminal work than I expected."

"You're right," Maggie replied. "But most of the criminal work is misdemeanor stuff, okay? You'll see that once you go digging through the files. There are some weed cases, lots of DUIs, and about a dozen or so family violence matters that have probably already worked themselves out through a break-up or divorce filing."

"What about the more serious cases?" Charlotte asked. "I saw a few felony matters that looked pretty nasty, and I don't think I'm ready for that yet."

"The heavy stuff can be farmed out, Charlotte, especially if you or the client wants that done."

"Okay, that's good I guess..." Charlotte gave a noticeable exhale. "I'm sure I'll end up taking you up on that offer."

There was obviously a lot of hesitation on young Charlotte's part, which made perfect sense. Maggie had been sworn in during the fall of 2012—when Charlotte was probably still in middle school—and Maggie had gone on to spend *her* first five years in practice as a vaunted member of the Southwest Circuit's Public Defender's Office. There, Maggie handled misdemeanor and felony cases, and she learned on the job while she guided her clients through all levels of the criminal justice system. Her clients were poor, usually somewhat disenfranchised, and were often dead-to-rights guilty. But Maggie still came away from her time in indigent defense with a strong track record in the courtroom and a thorough understanding of what was required of those who practiced the art of defending the accused.

"You're forgetting that the other half of my client list—*your* client list, that is—has nothing to do with criminal defense work." Maggie shot a reassuring grin across the table. "And you don't have to worry about anyone going to jail while you work on the civil litigation side of the equation."

"I like the sound of that," Charlotte replied, her spirits seeming to lift as they shifted away from discussing the gloom of criminal work.

Although Maggie continued taking on private criminal defense cases (i.e. the kind for clients who could afford to pay her flat-rate fee), her years as a public defender sat squarely in the rear-view mirror. In fact, what Maggie really focused on now, through her advertising and contacts and ever-growing caseload, was improving her standing as a civil litigator, specifically in the arenas that dealt with tort and injury work (e.g. auto accidents, slip-and-falls, tractor-trailer wrecks, defective products, workers compensation claims, and other similar cases). It was where the money was made.

"How do you feel about working on those cases?" Maggie asked. She needed Charlotte to feel comfortable with something on her plate. If not, the practice would start hemorrhaging cash, *quick*.

"It's a little more in line with where I'm headed in my career..." Charlotte still didn't sound too enthused, but her voice had at least regained its usual confidence. "But you know I'll do what I need to do, right? That's what I'm here for, Maggie. I'll figure it out."

"Thank you, Charlotte."

Charlotte Acker was coming in from a big, DC law firm, one with a brand of practice that was certainly more prestigious and highbrow, so Maggie was interested to see how those skills would fit in with the more practical aspects of rural South Georgia lawyering. And although Charlotte was a friend, and much more of a local than Maggie would ever be, it was hard for Maggie not to feel like she was playing the role of country mouse in their meeting today, that Charlotte had been cast in what was obviously the more glamorous role: mouse from the city.

"I still don't think I really want to be involved in much of the personal injury work," Charlotte said. "Down the road, that is...I just see myself better suited for the transactional work, the dealmaking, the M&A side of things."

"That's why you're headed for the big leagues, Charlotte." Maggie smiled. "But while you're here, slumming it in Blakeston, don't forget what you already know about courtroom work."

Charlotte nodded.

"Because you already know a lot," Maggie said, pressing on. "You have a kind of real-life experience with this work, certainly more so than most of the clients you'll have a chance to work with."

"I know that, Maggie." Charlotte offered back what looked like a half-hearted smile. "I guess there aren't too many lawyers out there who've had to experience being put on trial for murder."

"Not many at all." Maggie couldn't help but grin. "And you know what?"

"What's that, Maggie?"

"There's nobody out there who could've beaten that case like you did."

"Like *we* did," she replied.

"That's right." Maggie paused for a moment and tried to squeeze just a bit of pride from that memory of her representing Charlotte at trial. "Like *we* did."

29

Charlotte Acker was under no obligation to leave her job as a new associate at the big Washington firm that hired her out of law school. But now that she was back home in Blake County, at least for the next six months or so, the young attorney needed to prepare herself for a crash-course in small-town lawyering. Although Maggie knew plenty when it came to the ins and outs of this kind of work, Charlotte had to be ready to learn some hard lessons on her own. Because once the holidays were over, Charlotte was going to be thrown straight into the proverbial frying pan.

"Let's talk about the work," Maggie said. "I know you've seen some of it in action, but things are going to be a little different now that you're the one running point on matters in the courtroom."

"Things are going to be *very* different. I'm not a trial lawyer, Maggie, and you should probably know I don't really plan on becoming one."

Maggie knew all of this already.

"In fact," Charlotte continued. "I've steered clear of courtrooms ever since my own trial ended."

Maggie couldn't blame Charlotte for wanting to stay away.

"You were with your firm in DC for a little over a year, right?" Maggie asked. "Didn't they try and rotate you through the litigation section to at least get you some exposure to courtroom procedure?"

"Nope." Charlotte shook her head. "The hiring committee knew where my focus was when they brought me on, and I never tried to get anywhere near the litigation side of things. The class of new associates I came in with was full of hard-charging, soon-to-be highflyers, so I wasn't among those trying to cozy up to the partners who handled the trial work."

"Maybe that'll change, Charlotte."

"Maybe so," she replied. "But I don't have a whole lot of interest in carrying someone else's briefcase."

Maggie smiled. She wouldn't have faulted her old client for choosing to stick with the job in DC. It was a position with a silk-stocking, K Street firm that offered Charlotte the typical big-firm experience, one that came with a hefty six-figure salary, a barely reachable number of billable hours for each year, and what was no doubt a very enticing bonus structure.

"You'll only carry your own briefcase while you're here," Maggie said. "I can at least promise you that."

"That's part of the reason I'm here."

The firm that Charlotte left behind was the kind of opportunity that suited the young woman's long-term goals, but it was also the kind of law firm that kept all of its *baby lawyers* very, very far from the courtroom. It was a place that had an army of capable attorneys, and they had an effective model for weeding through the crop of fresh-faced, top tier associates they brought on board each year (i.e. T14 grads like Charlotte Acker). And although the firm's powerhouse training model allowed for young lawyers to prove their mettle, it also required them to take on years of grueling, not-so-glamorous work, the kind that eventually churned out attorneys who specialized in mind-numbingly specific areas of the law. So, Maggie hoped that while Charlotte was in Blakeston, she might come to realize that there are advantages to not becoming another well-paid, one-trick pony at some hoity-toity law firm.

"I understand you don't plan on making a career out of being a trial lawyer—" Maggie began.

"Don't worry about it, Maggie." Charlotte's sense of loyalty seemed unshakable. "I'm here to help *you* get through this. It's the least I can do, given what you've done for my family."

"No." Maggie held up a hand. She wanted the new lawyer to at least feel like she'd be able to tread water while she was here doing Maggie this favor. "Courtroom experience really is my selling point, okay? Although I really do appreciate you being here, I also think the time here in Blakeston will help make you a better lawyer."

Charlotte didn't seem totally convinced. Still, she was there, and that's all that mattered. "Then let's get to it," she said. "Tell me about the work."

"Things will be slow around here during the Christmas holidays," Maggie said, cautiously. "The courts won't be doing much. The judges and prosecutors will all be enjoying their time off, and many of the clerks will be working to get everything organized before the New Year."

"Good," Charlotte said. "That'll give me a chance to get settled in, maybe even prepare for the January docket."

"But that doesn't mean there won't be some phone calls coming in," Maggie added. "The holidays can be all over the place at times. Things can even get a little crazy around here."

Charlotte nodded along as she fired up a tablet that she'd brought with her to their meeting. She started taking notes.

Maggie kept going. "As you probably know, people get hurt around the holidays, people get arrested, and I don't expect anyone to stop calling the firm just because I'm not here."

Maggie paused for a moment. She wasn't yet sure how the community would respond to news of her suspension. Although the marketing campaigns that ran advertising slots on television and radio had all been paused for the time being, there was still a whole network of referrals that came to Maggie just on a word-of-mouth basis. There was also a certain amount of *street cred* that Maggie would probably gain from all of this, a strange respect that she might garner for simply having to take it on the chin, something that actually could endear her to the underdog clients she typically represented.

"What should I do about new cases?" Charlotte asked, head still down. "Should I be taking on any new clients for you?"

Maggie considered the issue for a moment. Profits were usually pretty far downstream with her personal injury work, so Maggie didn't want to completely cut the flow of new clients off for a whole six months. "Technically, Charlotte, you'll be the one deciding what clients need to be signed up. These are *your* new clients, okay? I'm really not supposed to direct anything here—"

"It's just us, Maggie." Charlotte looked up from where she took notes on the tablet. "You've known me long enough to trust that I won't say a thing."

"I know," Maggie replied. "And I do trust you. But what I really care most about is finishing my suspension up without an issue, okay?"

"Fine."

Maggie grinned. "However, if I were here with you on a daily basis, then I would tell you *not* to take on any new criminal work. It's time consuming, it can be frustrating to learn the racket, and I'm quite sure the current client list will give you enough grief to go on."

Charlotte smiled back. "Did I give you any grief?" she asked. Charlotte knew she had, no question.

Maggie shook her head. "You don't want to know, Charlotte."

"Fair enough," she replied, laughing a bit now, which was a good sign. "Anything I should do with new clients who have a civil issue?"

"That's simple." Maggie leaned forward and placed her elbows at the edge of the conference table. "Only take new personal injury cases and *only* take on the ones that the staff believe have real merit."

Charlotte looked a little confused. "You want me to run all potential cases by the staff for their approval?"

"Yes." Maggie didn't see any reason to sugarcoat things for young Charlotte. A law degree and license got young lawyers into a courtroom, but the day-to-day business of a law firm wasn't necessarily handled by the people who carried the title of esquire. "Look, my team already knows more about this kind of work than you'll be able to learn in the coming six months. You'll soon find that out. And if you treat the group well, Charlotte, they'll back you on any problem that pops up. I promise you that."

Charlotte wasn't writing this down.

Maggie pressed on. "I won't be here to tell you not to take a case, Charlotte, but it's best to trust my paralegal to—"

"No, I get it," Charlotte said. Maggie loved how her old client always seemed to easily adjust and move past anything that threatened her sense of autonomy. "I'll work closely with the team, you know I will."

"I do," Maggie said. "But whatever you decide, Charlotte, *do not* take anything but injury work, okay? No tedious property line disputes. No Lemon Law cases. No small-business problems. And absolutely no will contests, understood?"

"Understood," Charlotte said. She was back scribbling away on her tablet. "Can I get my own billboard out beside the highway? I was thinking we might put a banana peel on it…"

30

The truth was, Maggie wasn't sure how much Charlotte really needed to know about going inside of a courtroom. Maggie came to represent Charlotte a little over three years ago, while the young woman was still a student in law school, and the murder case brought against Charlotte had probably taught the young attorney things about the law that Maggie would never know herself.

"Listen, Charlotte, you're smart, and you have enough of a handle on how to find the answer when it comes to the questions of law." Maggie took another sip of her coffee. It was cold now. "But most of the work that happens around here is going to come down to the people you deal with, okay?"

"Okay."

"Every judge is going to be a little bit different, every prosecutor is going to have their own preferences, and every lawyer you have as opposing counsel will have certain quirks."

"Of course, Maggie. This is a people business."

"That's right," Maggie said. "These people all have a seat at the table, too, just like you will."

Charlotte kept scribbling.

"I'll try to give you the names of people who're in what I like to call deck chairs."

"Deck chairs?" Charlotte asked, glancing up from her notes.

Maggie nodded. "Those are the lawyers who fold under pressure, at least when you negotiate hard with them."

"I like that."

"And you'll notice my files sometimes have a *WB* or a *BA* beside the name of opposing counsel—"

Charlotte turned her attention back to taking notes.

"*BA* is for *Broken Arrow*, and you'll usually see that acronym in the civil files. These are lawyers who don't work but never get fired, okay? The insurance adjusters they work with eventually wise up, but it takes time."

"And what about *WB*?" Charlotte asked.

"Those are for the *Wheelbarrows*," Maggie replied. "They are the lawyers who only work when you push them."

"Got it."

Maggie paused. She wasn't exactly sure how Charlotte would take this next bit of advice, but she wanted the young lawyer to hear it anyway. "But you're going to have one big advantage, okay? And it's one that I haven't had myself for years and years."

Charlotte looked up from her notes, a student ready to absorb whatever wisdom the teacher had for her.

"You're not going to have a label. You're going to be *new*, okay?" Maggie really wanted to hammer this point home. She wanted the young woman to accept it, maybe even use it to her advantage. "And there's going to be an extra bit of courtesy given to you. It's just the way it works around here."

Charlotte rolled her eyes. "I grew up here, remember? I know I went away for school, but I still know more about Blake County than most people do. It's my home, even if I don't live here for—"

Maggie stopped her. "Don't ever use those kinds of words in a courtroom."

"Why?" Charlotte sat up a little straighter and placed the tablet on the conference table. There was a fair amount of that Southern, blue bloodedness in her raising that might prove to be problematic for her if she didn't tread carefully. "My family has been in this town for more than a century. Even if I never say a word about any of it, people will know who I am, who Mom is, who Dad *was*..." Charlotte's voice trailed off at the mention of her father—Lee Acker—another client who Maggie once represented on a murder charge some years ago.

"That's why it's important you never mention any of it, Charlotte." Maggie made sure her voice remained even, calm. "You don't ever acknowledge your family's place in the community, okay? You're just another new lawyer who's trying to learn as you go, and one who's doing me a favor in the process."

"What's next?" Charlotte demanded, shaking her head. "I just never talk about the fact I was put on trial here?"

"Actually, Charlotte, I wouldn't mention that either. *Ever.*"

"What if someone brings it up?" she shot back. "What if—"

"No one will." Maggie cleared her throat. "But if someone does, then just dismiss the subject with class, all right?"

"What does me ignoring my past do for me?" Charlotte asked. "What does me acting like an idiot accomplish in any—"

"First," Maggie interrupted, "I didn't say for you to go and act like an idiot."

"You want me to play everything like I'm naïve and new and dumb—"

"New, *yes*, but that's it." Maggie smiled. "I'm recommending you do this because being new to the courtroom process will give you a lot of wiggle room on things. Think of this as an asset, nothing more."

"An asset?" Charlotte chuckled. "You going to tell me the combination of being young and single is my second-best asset?"

Maggie sighed. "If you want to have that conversation, then let's have it, okay?"

Charlotte folded her arms across her chest.

"I can tell you that your looks are probably going to turn heads in a small town like this." Maggie pressed on. "I can tell you how sometimes it's best just to wear a conservative skirt and blazer instead of a full-on pantsuit because there's still a handful of judges in our area who're old-school misogynists. I can tell you that the occasional flirting with a sheriff's deputy or police officer will sometimes get you *way* more information about a client's case than any open records request can provide you. Hell, I can tell you that just being nice is going to help catch more flies than—"

"I'm nice." Charlotte smiled. "But would you be telling some male attorney to come in here and act all *nice*?"

Maggie quickly replied. "I would certainly tell them something similar."

Charlotte huffed. "Right."

"Look, I'm not advocating for some of the behind-the-times crap that I deal with every now and then. But I'm also a realist, okay? And I want you to recognize where you can manipulate the system, where you can use it to your advantage."

"Things like *this*, conversations like this, are part of why I left Blake County—" Charlotte started.

"But you're back!" Maggie added a bit more firmness to her voice. "And sure, while you're here, you may see why a lot of smart, funny, and awesome women who're just like you decide to go live and work elsewhere. But you know what?"

Charlotte sighed and looked away.

"What we don't know about other people isn't what gets us in trouble, Charlotte, it's what we *think* we know about other—"

"I know plenty about this place, Maggie."

"But you still might be surprised by what you learn, okay?" Maggie paused. "Because I know for a fact that there are some lawyers and judges and police officers around here who're going to teach you some things about this work. And many of them are going to surprise you, all right? I can all but guarantee it."

"I hope you're right," Charlotte said, turning her eyes back to Maggie. "You've certainly followed through on your promises before."

When Maggie finished covering the rest of Charlotte's questions about the law firm, she asked her replacement if there was anything else she needed from Maggie that day. It felt strange going through the process of handing the practice off to someone else, even someone like Charlotte.

"What else can I do for you?" Maggie asked.

From across the table, it seemed like Charlotte was getting more and more comfortable by the minute. There was probably something freeing in knowing that the assignment was confined to a six-month window. It was just enough time for Charlotte to get her feet wet, yet not enough for her to run the risk of becoming stuck in the ways of her hometown.

"Maybe," Charlotte finally said. "I've been working up the nerve to ask because—"

"Come on, out with it," Maggie quickly said. "I'm giving you the keys to my business. The least I can do is help you out with something you need."

"It's more of a favor, actually."

Maggie raised an eyebrow. "Okay."

"Mom asked me to bring it up during our meeting today, just to see if it was something you were interested in. No pressure at all."

"What is it?"

"It's a job."

"What?" Maggie was the one who was confused now. "It's one thing to help direct some of the work here, and it's something altogether different to practice law while I'm suspended."

"It's a friend of the family who reached out." Charlotte had obviously waited until the end of their meeting to bring this up. "He knows you're suspended and all, so it's not like he's asking you to take a case or file anything with the court."

Maggie was the one to sigh now. "I don't know if there's *any* kind of legal work I feel comfortable doing right now."

"His son is missing, okay?" Charlotte was suddenly the one trying to bring Maggie around to another point of view. "At least, he's pretty sure his son is missing."

"I'm not a private investigator."

"And he knows that."

"Then, what is it that I can do?" Maggie asked.

"You can give advice, Maggie." Charlotte stood. "I think his son is missing, and I think he needs to talk to someone about it."

"It sounds like he needs a counselor."

"He needs you, *counselor*." Charlotte smiled.

Again, Maggie sighed. "I don't know about this."

"Mom asked that I just urge you to consider it." Charlotte grabbed her tablet from the table. "And that's what I'm doing."

"Advice is what the man needs?" Maggie asked. She couldn't ignore the feeling in her gut. It was the feeling of intrigue.

"That's right," Charlotte said with a nod. "A bit of advice—*a voice of reason.*"

PART III

THE DEAL

"The man who dies rich, dies disgraced."
—Andrew Carnegie

31

Four days after Christmas, the German-owned freighter carrying Art Mortlake docked at the Port of Antwerp. It'd taken fifteen days in total for the container ship to load and unload at various ports of call along the Eastern Seaboard and make its long journey across the Atlantic Ocean to the freighter's port of destination in Flanders. During the course of that journey, Art continued to meet briefly with his kidnappers and continued to study them as much as he could. Although the men never once allowed for Art to leave his cabin on the ship, Petrut Noica, along with his accomplice, Jetmir Milićević Babić, still arrived each morning with enough food and water for Art to manage the trip.

Art's first days on the ship were terrifying, but then he soon came to find his journey spent mostly in isolation to be an experience that was long, tiring, and very lonely. The roughly two-week voyage was the longest Art could remember going without a cell phone or internet access since his early teenage years, and with each day that passed in his state of solitary confinement, Art found himself waiting with a kind of strange anticipation for his kidnappers to return.

He first expected them to start interrogating him once again in that same manner as before, the one that was patient, methodical, and cruel. But the harsh questioning that Art had experienced on the first night of their journey together never resumed. They didn't physically abuse him, didn't drug him, didn't hardly speak to him. In fact, the kidnappers mostly just left their hostage alone without any new information to go on.

To pass the time, Art read through the paperbacks that'd been left for him in his suitcase, did push-ups and other bodyweight exercises, and turned the question of his escape over and over and over in his mind. And in those long hours alone, he eventually came to formulate a plan of his own. Art just needed an opening, and he needed to know exactly what it was that these men wanted from their hostage.

Because Art knew what he wanted. It was simple now.

He just wanted to live.

There was a loud knock on the cabin door, then it opened. In stepped Petrut and Jetmir, Art's captors. The men wore jackets and carried suitcases with them. It was clearly time for them to go. What was unclear was how Art might leave with them.

"We're going to disembark." It was Petrut, the leader, who said this. "Grab your things."

"Well, good morning, guys." Art spoke as he stood from the worn loveseat that occupied one corner of his cabin. Everything in the little room felt so familiar now, even the unannounced intrusion by the two men who were holding Art hostage. "Please, come on inside." The sarcasm in Art's voice was just another piece of the routine that they'd all grown accustomed to.

"Good morning, Arthur." Petrut's tone was cordial, as was typical. Hidden beneath the polite demeanor, though, was the man who'd directed his thugs to dispose of an innocent rent-a-cop's body, who'd directed his men to bag and kidnap another human being, and who'd happily slapped Art around while asking questions about some old agreement to repay two million dollars. "I hope you slept well," he added. "We have a full day of travel ahead of us."

"Where are we going?" Art asked.

"We'll get to that, Arthur."

Art considered Petrut's face, then shifted his gaze over to Jetmir. The second-in-command leaned against the only door to the cabin. Art assumed the man was blocking the door for a reason. Although he couldn't hear what was going on in the corridor outside, Art imagined there had to be more activity taking place than usual: passengers readying their things to leave, crew members making sure everyone was disembarking safely, cleaning crews getting ready to scour the ship.

"Here, I want you to take this." Petrut held out what looked like a navy-colored passport book. "You'll use it when we walk off the ship."

"Walk?" Art asked, making no attempt to hide his surprise as he took the booklet from Petrut. Art slowly turned the passport over in his hands, noticed the gold embossed words stamped on the outside: *United Kingdom of Great Britan and Northern Ireland.*

"Everything in the book is authentic," Petrut said. "Aside from the photograph, of course."

Art opened the small passport book to the first page. In the top left-hand corner was a recent photograph of Art, one from a student networking event he'd attended on Duke's campus some two months earlier. "Who is Andrew Gibbs?" he asked, eyes on the unfamiliar name, the purported owner of the British-issued booklet. To Art's untrained eye, everything else about the passport looked legit.

"Mr. Gibbs was a passenger on this ship."

Art glanced back up at Petrut. *Was?* he wanted to say, but Art kept the thought and other inquiries to himself. Gibbs was dead, no question.

"You've been staying in Mr. Gibbs's cabin for the past two weeks," Petrut continued. The way he said this almost made it seem like Art had a choice in the matter. "And you'll walk away from the ship with his passport today. After that, we'll all go together to meet the vehicle that's waiting for us in a nearby car park."

Art gripped the booklet tight in one hand. It felt like he was holding the golden ticket.

"But you need to promise us something," Petrut prodded on. "You need to swear you won't do anything stupid when you get outside today."

Art couldn't help but glance over once again toward the door to his little cabin. There wasn't much he wanted more in that moment than to step outside, to feel the sunshine on his face, the fresh air in his lungs. "I'm not planning to do anything crazy..." Art let the words hang in the air for a moment, unsure as to whether he even believed them himself. "But I'd also like to think you wouldn't have carried me all this way just to put a bullet in my head, certainly not right before you leave this ship."

Petrut seemed to be well prepared for this question as he pulled what looked like a kitchen knife from the pocket of his blazer. Petrut was a large, dangerous looking man, one with wide shoulders and a thick neck. Although the item of common cutlery in his hand didn't look like the most capable of murder weapons, Art had little doubt that Petrut could find a way to get the job done with whatever tool he had.

"Why not stick me back inside the case?" Art asked. He wasn't exactly sure why he wanted to know the answer to this question. In fact, his experience being smuggled onto the ship in a container fit to hold an upright bass was a trauma that Art was certainly in no hurry to relive. "Why not roll me back off the ship the same way I came on?"

Petrut looked somewhat amused at this. "Do you want to be stuffed back inside the instrument case?"

Art shook his head. "*No*, not particularly."

"Then why ask?"

Maybe Art thought he couldn't trust himself *not* to take a risk once they walked him outside. Maybe this was all just a form of self-preservation, part of some survival mechanism built into Art's psyche long ago. "I'm just curious is all," Art said. "Kind of seems like you're willing to trust me. Why the change of heart?"

"We do trust you." Petrut kept his face relaxed. "And if you do like we say, then we'll reward you at the end of the day."

"What kind of reward?" Art asked.

Petrut had the carrot ready to dangle in front of Art's face. "I'll allow you to start communicating with your father," he said. "My team will have final approval on the content of the message, but I'll at least be authorized to start the process with you."

Art gripped the passport book even tighter now. The words from Petrut's mouth were what Art had been waiting to hear for the past two weeks. "What's the catch?"

Petrut smiled back at Art, then turned his head to look over at his companion, Jetmir. The men exchanged glances with one another like they had some kind of wager playing out between them, like they had an inside joke that could only be enjoyed quietly.

"Tell me." Art wasn't angry, although he could feel his impatience growing.

Petrut turned his gaze back to Art. "The catch, as you say, is your father's life."

Art considered the big man's eyes. They looked serious, like they usually did, and Art knew he needed to decide a couple of things in that moment: whether the threat was real, and how he needed to go about handling things if it was. "You're going to try and take out my father?" Art asked. "That would bring your body count to at least three, right?"

Petrut kept his poker face. "At least."

"I should warn you," Art said. "My father isn't an easy man to find. He's even harder to kill."

At that moment, Jetmir stepped away from the cabin door and came over to stand in front of Art. The thirty-something-year-old, dark-haired man pulled a tablet from his suitcase, then held it out with one hand. He turned the tablet around so that Art could see the screen. On it was an image that Art felt certain he recognized.

"What the hell am I looking at?" Art demanded, hoping his own face didn't betray his words.

"I think you know..." Jetmir handed the tablet over to Art. "Look closely if you need to."

Art could just make out the backside of his family's North Georgia mountain house. Art liked to call the place his father's compound, which wasn't an unfair characterization. The property and house had cameras everywhere, and Declan Tao kept several other ex-soldiers patrolling the grounds at all hours. So, that meant whoever was filming this image was a person of considerable skill. They'd found a way to bypass Clive Mortlake's high-end, paranoia-like defenses, and they'd been able to get fairly close to the house in that process.

"It's still early there," Jetmir said as he glanced at the watch on his wrist.

"It's four-forty in the morning. The sun will be up soon, though, and so will your father."

It was possible the image wasn't actually from a live feed, but Art quickly decided this wasn't the issue that mattered right then. If the men had someone who could get past the security perimeter once, then they probably had someone on the payroll who had a decent shot at bypassing the compound's defenses on a second go-around.

"I understand what will happen if I fuck up," Art finally said, handing the tablet back over to Jetmir. Art didn't want to look at it anymore, didn't want to think about a first-person shooter game playing out at his father's compound. "But just to be clear..." Art paused to make sure his voice remained firm, his words unambiguous. "If I play along while we walk through security, then nothing happens to my father, right?"

The tactic was playing out perfectly for the kidnappers. Petrut had been the one to dangle the carrot and Jetmir had been the one to show the stick. And it seemed the only option that Art had in that moment was to blindly comply with whatever his captors wanted.

"He won't even know we were there," Petrut said, his tone cool, business-like. "He just keeps living his life."

In that moment, Art couldn't help but feel a bit of pride in being his father's son. The man had taken an extremely tight-lipped approach to the news of his terminal diagnosis. It was a strategy that Art had taken personally, and it was an approach by his father that Art initially chocked up to the man's self-centeredness, or possibly his paranoia, or maybe even some strong sense of embarrassment over being sick. But now it seemed to Art that his father's discretion was paying off. And this approach by Petrut—his smug negotiating with Clive Mortlake's life—might've just revealed the first avenue for Art's escape.

"When do we leave the ship?" Art asked.

Petrut smiled. "As soon as you're ready, Arthur."

32

Trying hard to act normal, Art Mortlake waited in a short line with the other passengers who were preparing to clear customs and immigration. The Port of Antwerp was a key entry point into Belgium, a member state of the European Union, so Art knew that if he made it past border control, then he would soon be in a country that formed part of a somewhat free-movement zone called the Schengen Area. And *this* was another potential problem for Art, mainly due to the fact that his kidnappers wouldn't need to worry any longer about having to hand Art a passport if they decided to shuttle him across one of the country's adjoining borders. Although Western Europe wasn't as large as the Continental United States, the much, much older cities that dotted this part of the world offered a bevy of hiding places. And with Europe's varying jurisdictions, customs, and languages, its cities had for centuries over been perfect places for those persons who suddenly needed to disappear.

Art took a few more steps forward, easing ahead with the line of people toward a row of guardhouses. Each tiny house acted as a little office space for the uniformed officers who worked the border. The customs and immigration officials were trained to do a number of things, but the bulk of their work involved asking questions of travelers, checking their passports, and ensuring all documentation was in order before authorizing admittance into the EU. Although Art wasn't proud of it, he was actually still weighing his options while he waited there in line to speak with one of those officers at the border. Could it be that easy to sell his own father out? he asked himself, watching the uniformed officials stamp the passports of the other passengers ahead. Art wanted to live, *sure*, but was the easy route something he could continue to live with?

Yes, he'd already assured Jetmir and Petrut that he would play along with their little charade, but that didn't mean he couldn't still go back on his word. He'd done it plenty of times before, right? Besides, what waited ahead was probably Art's one and only chance to have a face-to-face conversation with someone who held a badge, someone who could do something. It was that familiar selfishness in Art, the one that often plagued his thoughts, that was starting to tug his mind in directions he didn't need for it to go.

I mean, he's already dying, right? Art turned the question over in his mind, trying to convince himself that sacrificing his father's life might actually be okay in this situation. *It's possible the man might even want me to do this for the future of our family...*

Art took two more steps forward, still mulling things over in his mind. There were only a few people now between Art and the uniformed woman who was checking passports at the head of their line. Art wondered what his father would tell him to do, wondered what the man's advice would be in this situation. Although Art rarely spoke with his father anymore, he still coveted the little bit of time they spent together. He still valued the man's counsel.

Art was next up in the line now, and his thoughts suddenly turned back to the image of a sniper waiting in the woods behind his father's mountain house. It was a scenario that sickened Art, angered him, and the idea of it all suddenly caused the sole heir to the Mortlake fortune to focus on the strengths of his father, the positives that were still in him, in both of them.

What if he *actually* had good news to tell me? This was the question that really bothered Art. His father had summoned him to the compound for a meeting on December 14th, one that Art had not been able to make thanks to Petrut and his little gang of thieves. Art had assumed all along, rightfully maybe, that the meeting between father and son might be their last. But what if the meeting had been scheduled for another reason? What if the man meant to tell his only son that the cancer prognosis had improved?

What if Clive Mortlake wasn't *really* dying?

Art stepped to the edge of the guardhouse window and handed over the navy-colored passport book. The uniformed official on the other side of the glass opened the booklet in a very practiced manner, then flipped through it until she found whatever pages she needed to review.

Art didn't say anything to the woman while he waited for her to start with any questions. Although he'd traveled plenty to other countries, Art wasn't exactly sure what a customs and immigration official was usually looking for in these kinds of situations. He also didn't know a whole lot about how facial recognition software worked, or whether the photograph in his stolen passport booklet was going to be compared with any photographs taken of the now deceased Andrew Gibbs. Art could only assume photographs were taken during border crossings whenever Gibbs travelled back and forth to the United States. Maybe Petrut and his boys just didn't think of that?

"I see that you were recently in the US on a student visa?" the woman asked. She looked up from the passport and seemed to be comparing the photograph on the page to the face of the young man who stood before her.

"That's right," Art said. He made no attempt to hide his American accent.

"Were you there for university?" asked the customs official.

Art nodded. Thanks to Petrut, Art knew the basics now about the last weeks of Andrew Gibbs's life: where he was from, what he was doing in the US, and where he met his demise. "Yes," Art responded. "I was attending school in North Carolina."

"And what's the purpose of your visit to Belgium?"

"I'm on my way back home." When Art said this, he couldn't help but wonder how long it would take for Andrew Gibbs's family to find out their son wasn't ever going to come back to their home in Bristol.

"To the UK, Mr. Gibbs?"

"That's correct."

The officer's face didn't change. "You don't sound British." This wasn't a question.

"My father's American." Art smiled. He figured the more truthful his statements were, the more genuine he'd appear.

"Very well," the woman replied. "How long do you plan to be in Belgium?"

"Not long." Art knew there had to be something that sounded like hope in his voice. "A matter of days, maybe."

"And are you travelling with anyone else?"

Art paused a moment. He knew this might be his last chance to get himself out of this. He figured that if his father had already reported him missing, then his name and face had to be in whatever system Interpol maintained. It was a kidnapping, for God sakes, and the International Criminal Police Organization should at least have some kind of warning issued by now. There had to be agencies looking, right? If not, then that meant people believed he was already dead...

Except Art Mortlake, for the first time in a long while, wasn't thinking *only* about himself. He was also thinking about the shooter who was waiting in the woods behind their compound in North Georgia. He was thinking about the people and the resources that *might* already be in play, experts who were working hard to find him. And Art was thinking about his father's wellbeing.

"Mr. Gibbs." It was the voice of the uniformed officer. "I asked if there was anyone else travelling with you."

"No, I'm alone on this journey," Art finally said, offering the customs official a weak smile. "I'm looking forward to getting home, though. It's been a long trip."

The woman offered a quick nod, then stamped the passport. "Very good," she said, sliding the booklet back over to Art. "You're free to go."

The woman didn't even look twice at him as he took the passport book from her. As he stepped away from her elevated desk, then turned to walk for the exit, he couldn't help but recognize how proud he was of himself. He'd been tested by Petrut and Jetmir, by himself, by his father—although the man didn't know it—and Art had passed their test with flying colors.

"Very nice," Petrut said when Art got within earshot of the big man. "I wasn't sure you would show back up once we left you to your own devices."

Art stepped to within feet of the man. "I always show up, Petrut."

The large man reached out and took the navy-blue booklet from Art's grasp. He looked pleased with himself, pleased that everything seemed to be going according to plan. "I'm rather proud of you—" he began.

"I don't give a shit what you think." Art was whispering and feeling good as he spoke the words. "You just tell your gunman to stay away from my father, yeah?"

Petrut smiled at this. He seemed to like the fiery response from his hostage. The days on the ship were probably almost as long and boring for Petrut as they had been for Art, so a bit of excitement had to feel like a welcome change.

"How about we get a coffee and something to eat?" he asked.

Art ignored him. "Just know that when we get to wherever we're going tonight," he said, still keeping his voice low. "We're going to reach out to my father. Because that was the deal, right?"

Petrut nodded back. "That was the deal."

"Good."

"Let's have coffee, Arthur, then we'll go to the car."

"Where are you taking me?" Art asked. "You've been jerking me around for weeks, and it's time I know the—"

"Coffee first," Petrut interrupted. "Then we'll get to that."

33

After New Year's Day lunch, a traditional spread of ham and collard greens and black-eyed peas, Maggie Reynolds loaded her suitcase into her car, kissed her husband goodbye, then rolled out of Blake County.

The drive up to Ellijay would take four hours, more or less, if Maggie followed the shortest route on her cell phone's GPS. It was New Year's Day, though, a busy holiday, and she knew the roadways would be filled with lots of travelers who needed to make their way home from vacations and visits with family. People would be hurrying on the interstates, anxious to get back to their lives and jobs that started back up tomorrow, resolute and ready to get after whatever opportunities awaited them in the coming year.

Maggie, however, was in no such hurry. If she could avoid the traffic, the rumble of eighteen-wheelers, the massive SUVs and pick-up trucks tail-gating other drivers along I-75, then she would happily take the longer route up to the hills of North Georgia. The backroads were slower, *sure*, but Maggie had no plans to exceed the speed limits in any of the small, speed-trap towns along the way, nor did she have any reason to fuss about the spotty cell phone service she'd find while travelling off the beaten track. She had no client phone calls to make, no urgent messages to handle, and no one expecting much from her, especially while she sat behind the wheel that day. It was just her, an audiobook she'd been wanting to get to for some time, and the roads of rural Georgia.

When Maggie crossed the northernmost edge of the county line, she made a left onto US-27. The mostly four-lane highway would take her through Cuthbert, Lumpkin, then onto Cusseta, where she could then pick up SR-280 to keep on heading north for Columbus. It was thereabouts in Muscogee County where she would cross the Fall Line, leaving South Georgia and the Coastal Plain behind. And in this new part of the state, Georgia's Piedmont Region, the hills would begin to rise as the vast stretches of tall pine forest and farmland slowly dropped away. The seamless evolution of Georgia's landscape would continue in that part of the drive, shaping itself and moving with the roads that snaked through the counties of Harris, Troup, Coweta, and so on. Then, it was on to Atlanta, a city that was big and sprawling and urban, a contradiction of rural Georgia in almost every way.

But once Maggie was beyond Georgia's own Piedmont Region, and the masses of concrete and metal that comprised Metro Atlanta, she would once again be able to rejoin the quieter roads of this state. It was there around Pickens County, if enough light remained from the day, that Maggie would begin to see the Blue Ridge Mountains stretched out in the distance. It was there the air would get cooler, fresher, and the sightlines more elevated, and it was there in those mountains ahead that she would stop for the night.

Maggie had a meeting the following day.

It was already dark when Maggie pulled up to the address. She saw that a tall fence and wrought iron gate blocked the edge of the property. The headlights on Maggie's Saab 900 lit up the spindly, decorative bars at the edges of the gate, while casting long shadows that stretched out over the main driveway that ran opposite the iron barrier. Maggie rolled the window down on her car, then reached her hand out to press the button marked *Call* on a metal intercom device.

The potential client who Maggie was supposed to meet with tomorrow

morning was apparently a bit of a recluse. His conditions for their meeting
—a client consultation, really—were the kinds of things that Maggie would
normally never have agreed to. But the man was a friend of the Acker
Family, so Maggie was trying to do her best to accommodate the strange
demands of this nameless individual. And truth be told, Maggie also just
wanted to get out of Blake County for a few days, wanted to get away from
the shame that followed her each time she rode into town, the meaning-
lessness she now felt whenever she was there.

Maggie pressed the button on the intercom once more. "Hello?" she
called out. "Anyone there?"

The intercom beeped once, then a voice came from the device's small
speaker. "Is this Maggie Reynolds?" the voice asked.

"It is," Maggie replied. Her own voice seemed to disturb the quiet forest
that surrounded the gated property. "Who's this?"

"I'm Declan Tao. I run the security out here. Come on through the gate
and I'll make a proper introduction."

"That'll be fine," she agreed. "Do I just follow the driveway straight
ahead?"

"That's right," the man responded. His accent didn't sound local. "When
you come to the first fork in the road, hang a left and follow the drive until
you see the cabin on your right."

"Sure," Maggie said, glancing over to check the maps application that
was still pulled up on her cell phone. She noticed the entire area on the
screen, which was supposed to be a map of the property in front of her now,
didn't show any roads to speak of. As far as the GPS was concerned, Maggie
was about to drive straight into a dense wood. She repeated the directions
to the man on the intercom. "Left at the first fork in the road, then stop near
the cabin on the right."

"Yes, ma'am," replied the voice on the intercom. "You should find me
standing on the first parking pad you come to once you see the cabin. I'll be
there at the edge of the driveway."

Maggie rolled the window up, then eased her vehicle through the open
gate.

When Maggie saw the building through her front windshield, the first word that came to mind to describe it certainly wasn't *cabin*. The massive home was lit up end to end so that it burned bright in the darkness of night, and the structure looked like a beautifully designed mountain villa. A porch appeared to stretch around most of the home, and there were tall, wide windows that gave the dark-wooded forest mansion a very modern appeal. Maggie admired the home as she slowed her vehicle to a stop and couldn't wait to get a good look at the property during the light of day.

"The house is absolutely beautiful," Maggie said, stepping out of the Saab. She could see her breath now in the cold, mountain air. "I'm not sure I've come across anything like it, especially not hidden back in the woods like this."

The man who'd just directed Maggie into the parking space kept a safe distance. He wore a dark T-shirt, heavy-duty pants, and didn't seem to mind the cool temps of that January night. He was big and tall, but the build wasn't that of a man who spent much time in front of a mirror. The muscles all looked practical, sensible, and the voice of this man suited his appearance. "The home is something the family is very proud of," he said. "And I'm sure you'll have time to explore the grounds tomorrow."

"I'm Maggie Reynolds," she said, rubbing her palms together for warmth. She then extended one hand out for a handshake. "I hope I didn't put you into overtime with my late arrival tonight."

He took her hand with a steady grip. The palm felt dry, warm. "Declan Tao," he replied. "And don't worry about it. I'm always working."

Maggie smiled. "I know what that's like."

"I'll show you to your accommodations, ma'am." Declan obviously wasn't one for chitchat. "We've opened up the cottage for your visit, and I think you should have everything you need."

"Is the cottage bigger than the cabin?" Maggie asked.

Declan almost smiled at this. "No, ma'am, it's a *little* bit smaller.

"I'm sure it'll be fine."

"I'll grab your luggage, ma'am."

The *cottage* was within short walking distance of the exquisite mountain house. And it was a building of almost equal appeal, one that could've been the main attraction on any other piece of land for sale in the state. But true to its description, the cottage was certainly smaller, a little more charming. Still, the five-bedroom guest house would provide Maggie with plenty of room and privacy for her stay there on the property.

"If you need anything while you're here tonight, call this number." The man named Declan handed Maggie a business card. He'd just given her a short tour of the cottage's ground floor, having politely walked her through where all the bedrooms, bathrooms, and exterior doors were located. "This will get you to someone on staff at any time, day or night."

Maggie took the card. "I'm sure everything will be fine."

Declan nodded at this. He didn't seem like the kind of person who liked to speculate on matters of safety. "The alarm pad is right here," he said, pointing to a digital screen on a nearby wall. The security specialist and Maggie stood just inside the front door of the cottage. "The code is on the other side of the business card I just handed you. It changes daily, so someone from my team will provide you with a new access code tomorrow, should you need it."

"That'll work." Maggie flipped the card over in her hand, checked the six-digit code on the back. "It sounds like you have a state-of-the-art security system in place."

"We try."

Maggie smiled. "I thought most people around here just relied on a shotgun by the door?"

Declan actually grinned at this. "We also keep a few of those around, ma'am."

"I'm sure y'all do..." Maggie took one last glance around the beautiful guest space, wanting to make sure she didn't have any other questions about her stay there.

The man began again before Maggie could think of anything else. "Look," he said, "I can imagine that being out at a strange property, in a rural part of this state, isn't the ideal situation for most people." Although

Maggie didn't know it, there were cameras all over the place, sensors on every door, and guards patrolling the grounds at all hours. "But I assure you this property is secure, and there's nothing to be concerned with while staying here."

Maggie shrugged the comment off. "The accommodations here look *much* nicer than what the Best Western probably has to offer in town."

"I would certainly agree, ma'am." Declan then glanced down at the watch on his wrist, a basic Timex with a dark, cloth strap. "Breakfast will be at eight o'clock tomorrow, which is in about ten hours." He lifted his eyes back to Maggie's. "The food here will be the cherry on top of it all."

"Oh-eight-hundred, got it." Maggie didn't want to tell this man of obvious military bearing that she wasn't a morning person. "I'll be ready."

"And someone from my team will come by to escort you up to the main house."

Maggie almost saluted but thought better of it. "That'll be perfectly fine."

"Anything else you need from me?" he asked.

"At breakfast tomorrow, will I be meeting with Mr.—" Maggie stopped, then asked, "Can you help me out with this mystery person's name?"

Declan didn't even play along. "I'm sorry, ma'am. I can't tell you that information."

"But *he* will be at breakfast?"

"He will."

Maggie nodded. "I'll come ready to learn," she said. "All I know right now is that his son has been missing for quite a while."

Declan paused. He seemed like he wanted to say something more, but then he asked, "Anything else I can do for you?"

"I don't think so," she replied. "It was nice meeting you, and I hope you have a good night."

"Good night, ma'am." Declan said this as he was turning for the door, then clumsily stopped like he'd forgotten something. "There is one more thing..." he let the words hang there as if they were an invitation.

"What's that?" Maggie asked.

"How are you with motion sickness, ma'am?"

"Um...motion sickness?" Maggie paused at the question. "In what context?"

"Planes," he said, slowly. "How are you with small planes?"

"Why?" Maggie asked, although the question sought an answer that was patently obvious.

"Well, ma'am, I just need to know whether you'll require any Dramamine with your breakfast. If so, then I'll need to send someone out tonight to get some more from the pharmacy in Ellijay."

Maggie ignored the question. "But why would I be getting on a plane tomorrow? Isn't the meeting supposed to take place here?"

"You won't be required to get on a plane, of course not." Declan seemed to be trying to toe a line here. "*But*, if you were to end up working with the family, then my boss is going to want to fly you up to North Carolina. He's going to want you to start working immediately."

Maggie absorbed this. She realized now what the security specialist was doing. He couldn't tell her who the mystery person was, what the job itself was, but he was still trying to give her the pieces she needed to be able to put the puzzle together: son who recently disappeared, very wealthy family, and North Carolina.

"I'm not a big fan of small planes," Maggie finally said. "So, it wouldn't hurt to have something to take ahead of any *potential* flight, just to be safe."

"Very good." Declan began turning for the door. "Then, good night."

"Good night," she said again. "And thank you for the tip."

"I'm just doing my job, ma'am."

Maggie closed the door to the cottage, locked it, then armed the alarm using the nearby keypad.

She knew where she was now. This cottage, this property, was owned by the family of that college student who'd disappeared the week before Christmas. It was a story Maggie was familiar with because the media had jumped all over it. A twenty-two-year-old guy, the heir to a billion-dollar fortune, had disappeared into the dead of night without a word to anyone. And as far as anybody knew, not a single person had seen or heard from the young man since.

"Holy shit..." Maggie muttered. She couldn't be sure, but her guess was that she would probably be meeting with Clive Mortlake tomorrow. He was one of the richest people in the country, and also the father to Art Mort-lake, the college kid who most already believed was dead.

Maggie suddenly felt a tightness in her stomach. It was the kind of sensation that started whenever her anxiety kicked up a notch. It wasn't a pleasant feeling, but it was a signal she always took to mean she was about to push the limits of her own perceived abilities. That tightness, that sense of dread, was something she'd not expected to feel again for a long, long time—if ever again.

Maggie wasn't sure what kind of advice she could give a person who was still searching for a child who was most likely dead. That didn't matter, though. She was going to come prepared for their meeting tomorrow, prepared to help in any way she could.

It was the right thing to do.

34

Maggie woke earlier than usual, took a long shower, then started getting herself ready for the eight o'clock breakfast meeting. While she worked on her hair and put on a light touch of make-up, she listened to an hour-long podcast episode about the latest theories surrounding the disappearance of twenty-two-year-old Art Mortlake. There were lots of wild conspiracies out there (e.g. family members stricken with greed, mobster hits, scorned baby mamas, and so on), but the stories all seemed to rely on the same, simple motive: *money*.

The podcaster wasn't your typical true-crime enthusiast. She was a thoughtful, former policewoman turned crime journalist, and her opinions on how investigators should handle cases of national interest were often worthy of serious consideration. Although Maggie didn't always agree with the host's hard-liner solutions as to certain matters that involved criminal justice reform, she did like the woman's facts-based observations when it came to the effectiveness of modern policing, and her willingness to at least question the constitutionality of cutting-edge investigation techniques. And while her latest episode: *Neither Hide nor Heir: Who Killed Art Mortlake?* still seemed to take the usual out-of-the-box approach to the ongoing investigation, the former policewoman sounded noticeably frustrated whenever discussing the lack of evidence tied to the young man's disappearance.

Had the senior at Duke University in fact been murdered? That was most likely what happened, the true-crime podcaster thought, but only because the young man's blood had been discovered in the parking lot of a popular student apartment complex. *But was there any evidence that suggested Art Mortlake might still be alive?* Not really, the crime journalist lamented, but there was at least a sliver of hope. This optimism in the case stemmed from what North Carolina investigators had come across in the past week: the decomposing body of a rent-a-cop who'd gone missing the very same night that young Mortlake disappeared.

Why did the podcaster believe this new evidence meant that Mortlake might still be alive? Well, strangely enough, when investigators tested the rent-a-cop's remains for traces of foreign DNA—hoping, of course, that those samples might lead them to *his* killer—the lab came back with DNA matches for only one other person: Art Mortlake.

These latest findings in the case baffled the former policewoman. They were obviously even more troubling for all who were working the homicide investigation. But the discovery of the rent-a-cop's body came with more questions than answers, and this break in the case hadn't led investigators to uncover any additional human remains.

The body had been spotted by a pair of nineteen-year-olds, but the college couple only found *one* blood-stained corpse at the edge of the well-known forest area that wasn't far from West Campus. The news of the rent-a-cop's body had apparently been released to the public a full week ago, so that meant that key agencies had since spent countless hours scouring the nature trails, streams, and fields in that section of Durham County. Yet, over the course of the past week, it'd become clear that there was zero evidence to suggest that Art Mortlake's remains were also hidden somewhere inside Duke Forest.

So, where was Art Mortlake? Probably dead and buried somewhere else, the former policewoman argued, but her guess was that no investigator would find the young man's body anytime soon. The strange disappearance of Art Mortlake, the podcaster believed, would plague the minds of law enforcement experts for years and years to come.

Except Maggie wasn't ready to believe the young man was dead. Not yet. What she was ready to do was learn—more about Art, more about his father, and more about their family. Because *if* there was even still the remote possibility that this young man was still alive, and *if* everyone assumed the motive behind his sudden disappearance was tied to money, then that left only one logical explanation for all of this: *a kidnapping.*

35

Maggie Reynolds saw one person waiting for her at the table when she stepped inside the large, wood-paneled dining room. She immediately recognized the face of the late fifty-something man, thanks in large part to the images that accompanied most of the online articles about Clive Mortlake. But in the search engine research that Maggie undertook the night before, she found very few interviews where the man discussed anything beyond his role as chief executive officer for their family's multi-national mining company, a position he would soon be retiring from. Everything else about Clive Mortlake—his private life, his hobbies, *his son*—seemed to be very much off limits. And those were the things Maggie needed to know more about if the man really wanted her advice on anything to do with his life.

"Good morning," the man began, standing from his seat at the table. He was of decent height, maybe six-two, and his trim, toned frame looked to move comfortably for a man his age. "I'm Clive Mortlake," he added, coming around from the other side of the cherry-colored table. He wiped his hand with a cloth napkin before offering a handshake to Maggie. "You'll have to excuse my appearance. I just finished up a short five-miler through the woods. I'm training for a race next month in San Diego."

Maggie took the hand. It was still warm, a little moist. "Maggie

Reynolds," she said with a smile. "And don't worry about it one bit. I'm a runner myself, but I just can't seem to get myself into the habit of waking up early to knock out my runs."

"Ah, well, the early morning is *my* time." Clive shook her hand firmly, vigorously, then released it. "I tell my people that everything after nine o'clock is fair game for my attention, but the team knows not to bother me a minute before then. On a good day, I'll run, lift, then hop in the cold bath, all before seven-thirty."

Maggie kept smiling, although she wasn't sure why. Maybe it was because she felt a little silly standing there in one of her sharpest, best-cut dresses, while this billionaire stood before her in running shorts, a pair of Hoka blues, and a sweaty quarter-zip. He seemed to be keeping up with the high-powered CEO lifestyle, though, so her guess was that he was used to attending meetings in workout gear, probably even more so used to people feeling uncomfortable whenever he was in the room.

"Let's take a seat and have some coffee," the man continued. He sounded like he was already well into his day: quick words, sharp cadence, that mid-morning energy. "I'll also get Declan to whip us up some eggs and whatever else you like to start your day off with."

"Declan Tao?" she asked. "The man who welcomed me last night? Isn't he also the head of security around here?"

"Declan is my go-to guy, Maggie—" he stopped. "It's not a problem if I call you Maggie, right?"

She only nodded back. There wasn't space to slip in a reply.

"Good," he said, firing along. "I like to be on a first-name basis, so long as people aren't offended by it. But it makes me feel like I can better trust people when they break down all the formalities. Know what I mean?" He paused to take a breath. "Now, what was it I was saying earlier?"

"You were talking about your head of security being your go-to guy."

"Right!" He knocked the table twice with the knuckles on his left hand. "Declan is a man of many skills, Maggie, *many* skills. His team keeps every-thing secure around here, but the guy is also a top-notch chef. I'm surprised he didn't tell you. It's the only thing the man is capable of bragging about."

"I got the run-down last night on the property's security," Maggie said, a little curious now to see what the stoic bodyguard had in store for them. "And I guess he did make a small mention about the food, something about it being the cherry on top of my experience here at the property. He didn't say he would have a hand in cooking the meals, though."

"That's Declan." Clive offered a sharp wink. "I didn't know anything about it either, at least not until after I hired him. Then, one night my head chef came down with the flu, so Declan stepped into the role and made a few dishes that were damn good. And by good, I mean Michelin grade snow tires good."

"People just surprise us sometimes, right?"

He nodded along. "Yes, they certainly do, and that's precisely why I invited you here."

Maggie offered a wink of her own. "I'm not much of a chef."

"But you're apparently one hell of a good lawyer, Maggie Reynolds." Even Clive's stare from across the table was healthy, intense. "And you come highly recommended."

Maggie wasn't prepared for the immediate pivot toward professional matters. She should've been ready, though, just based off the man's energy and quick moving approach to their meeting. Clive Mortlake looked to be the healthiest, sharpest, and cockiest person she'd come across in quite some time.

Still, Maggie opted for humility. "Well, that's very kind of you to say, Mr. Mortlake—"

"It's Clive," he said. "Just Clive, okay?"

"Of course." Maggie was about to continue thanking the man, for what she wasn't exactly sure. "And thank you for the nice words. But I must say, *Clive*, I'm not so sure why I've been invited here. You probably already know that I've been suspended from the practice of law for the next six months—"

Clive held up an index finger, turned and looked toward an open doorway at the other end of the dining room. "Declan!" he hollered out. "Let's get a couple of coffees going—" he stopped, shifted his attention back to Maggie. "Unless you want a cappuccino or latte or—"

"A coffee will be just fine for me." Maggie got the impression that the billionaire wasn't in need of coffee, that he was usually running at top speed. It made her feel like she needed to be the one who took additional breaths for the man.

"That's two coffees!" Clive belted out.

"I heard what she said, sir." The newest voice poured from the same open doorway. It sounded like it belonged to the bodyguard of few words, the one Maggie met last night. "If you'll give me a moment, Mr. Mortlake, I'll be in there to get your breakfast orders."

"He calls you Mr. Mortlake?" she asked.

"That's my man Declan." Clive shook his head and grinned as he set his sights back on Maggie. "I hired him as my CPO over ten years ago, and yet he still refuses to call me Clive."

"Well, you've obviously been able to get past it." Maggie couldn't tell if this was going to somehow be a sensitive topic for the man. "I mean, he's head of your security, right? I know you must trust him completely."

"I do indeed, Maggie." Clive nodded along at this. "But there's an exception to every rule, right?"

"You're preaching to the choir," Maggie agreed. "I've actually made a living on the exceptions to rules. Obviously, there are times when it's backfired on me—"

Clive interrupted her once more. "Let's get your whole suspension talk out of the way, okay?"

"Sure, Clive." Maggie tried to focus on keeping her face relaxed, her voice calm. She'd come ready to answer questions about her little misstep. "What do you want to know?"

Clive folded his arms across his chest. He seemed to be preparing himself to judge the responses she might offer to his questions. "You prosecuted a US senator last year and lost the case, right?"

Maggie nodded. "That's probably the nicest way you could put things."

"Why did you do it?" he asked. "And don't worry about offending my political views. I don't give a damn about politics."

Maggie cleared her throat while she considered a response.

"And I don't want to hear some bullshit answer, okay?" Clive added. "I just want the truth."

"Right," she began. "Well, I went after him because he deserved to be brought to justice for—"

"No—" Clive said, holding up a hand to stop her. "I don't want to hear whatever response you had for the reporters or the judges or the Georgia Bar. I want to know what motivated you to do it."

Maggie leaned back in her chair, counted to five in her head before responding. She didn't need another person raking her over the coals for her past mistakes. And she certainly didn't need another person questioning the decisions she'd already made. The past was the past, as far as she was concerned.

"And before you respond, Maggie." Clive picked up a glass of water from the table, then sipped from it. "You should know I'm not trying to bust balls here. I'm just trying to get to know you, all right? And I think the best way for two people to do that is to just go ahead and cut through the shit."

"I can understand that approach..." Maggie spoke slowly. "But is this conversation going to be a two-way street? Are you going to answer these kinds of questions when they get turned around on you?"

"I invited you here because I need your help with something that's important to me."

"At least be straight with me," Maggie pushed back. "If you expect me to not sugarcoat things when it comes to my suspension, then I expect you to provide me with the same courtesy when it comes to questions I have about your son's disappearance."

He paused for a moment. "That seems fair enough."

"Okay," she said, taking in a deep breath. "Then you should know that I took the case that got me suspended for two reasons."

Clive waited patiently for her to continue.

"Money," she soon added. "And media exposure."

Clive seemed to appreciate this answer. "What about the Acker Family?" he asked. "They referred you to me because they've placed immense trust in you over the years."

"I took the case because of them, because of my relationship with the family, but I wouldn't have taken on that kind of risk at this stage in my career if—"

"If not for the money and potential benefit for your media profile," Clive said, finishing her sentence. "I understand."

"With all due respect," Maggie quickly replied. She was growing tired of the man's interruptions. "I'm not sure you would be able to understand."

Clive acknowledged her comment with the arch of an eyebrow, then soon carried on with his questions about her suspension. "And would you do anything differently if you had another crack at the case?"

Maggie shook her head. "I don't spend too much time thinking about what I can change about the past. I just try to move forward and make decisions—"

"*No*—" Clive stopped her with the firmness in his voice. "I'm not talking about what you can do to change the past. I'm asking about what you've learned from that mistake, what you can apply to the future."

Maggie sighed. This was a topic she wanted to avoid. "You want to know the truth?" she asked.

"Always."

"I'm not sure what it is I've learned from it all." The words felt true as she said them. "But I guess I'm not the best at the whole introspection thing."

Clive paused for a long moment. "And why is that?" he finally asked.

"Well, it's probably hard for you to even appreciate these kinds of things, but being a trial lawyer, at least for me, has been mostly about chasing money and notoriety." Maggie looked away from the man's gaze. These words didn't feel as true, she thought, trying to remember the time in her career when money and fame wasn't the focus. There *had* been a time, though, when her motives were purer, more noble. Maggie continued: "So, I guess I'm not sure what it means to be an attorney if I don't have those kinds of goals in front of me."

"I doubt there are many people who do truly spectacular work without an insatiable appetite for wealth and recognition..." His words trailed off in a way that made this point seem up for debate.

"But?" Maggie asked, turning her eyes back to the man on the other side of the table.

"*But*—" Clive smiled. "Those strong urges in any high-performer demand balance, purpose."

Maggie was listening.

"God knows I've made mistakes while chasing the goals I've had for my businesses," he added. "And maybe that's why I know how important it can be to find that balance, that purpose."

Maggie nodded. "People tell me the time away from my work might help with that."

"It won't," Clive replied. There was a certainty to those words. "But I know what will."

Maggie almost offered a smartass remark, but decided it was best not to be rude. She was a guest in this house. So instead, she said: "Clive, I think this would be a good time for you to tell me why I'm here."

Clive slid some papers across the table. "I'll need your word that no one ever hears anything I'm about to tell you."

Maggie didn't touch the paperwork at first. She just left them there beside her place setting. She could see from the heading on the top page that this was some kind of non-disclosure agreement. "What's this?" she asked.

"An NDA."

Maggie wasn't the least bit surprised. "What happened to this conversation being a two-way street?"

"It is," he replied. "And your willingness to be so forthcoming with me is what makes the next phase of our conversation possible."

Maggie stared down at the multi-page agreement. "Along with my signature, right?"

"Of course." Clive leaned back in his chair. "We're just going to have a discussion, Maggie. If you're interested in working with me, then we'll talk about next steps. If you're not interested, then you're still welcome to stay on the property to rest and recharge."

Maggie bit back the urge to ask about her compensation. That would come later. She knew the man was good for it. She also knew she was interested in finding out what this was all about. "Okay," she finally said. "I'll take a look at the agreement."

It was in that moment that Declan Tao came through a doorway on the opposite end of the dining room. He carried two mugs of coffee with him.

"Right on time, Declan." Clive was smiling again as he took a mug from the man. "Thank you for bringing these in for us."

"Yes, sir," Declan replied. He then directed his words toward Maggie. "Good morning, ma'am."

"Morning," Maggie replied, her eyes still down as she quickly scanned the NDA. From the looks of things, it all appeared to be fairly standard. "Can I get some milk for the coffee?" she asked.

"Of course, ma'am."

Maggie flipped a page on the agreement, kept scanning. "And Declan, it looks like I'll need a pen."

"Anything else?" he asked.

"And probably some of that Dramamine you bought last night."

"Coming right up, ma'am."

36

Maggie stood at the edge of the dock. She had her eyes fixed on the single-engine floatplane parked nearby, one that bobbed up and down with the gentle waves that rolled in from the lake. If anything, the small yellow plane had a simple, fairly unassuming look to it, one that certainly didn't scream billionaire boy's toy. But as far as Maggie could tell, everything about the aircraft still looked to be clean, sturdy, and in good working order. *Which was good*, Maggie thought, because this little yellow airplane would be her ride up to North Carolina.

"Climb on over, Maggie." Clive Mortlake said this from where he sat inside the aircraft. He'd just run through a pre-flight checklist of some kind, and his slow, methodical approach to each task on the list had at least put Maggie more at ease with the prospect of going up in the little plane. "Once you're strapped in, Declan will start untying the plane from the dock, and then he'll give us a good shove to get us well away from the bank."

Maggie stayed put where she was. "Are you sure this is the best way to go about this?" she asked, still weighing the idea of the trip itself, the appearance of her pilot. Although the billionaire's serious approach to readying the plane suggested to her that flying was more than just another hobby to this man, Maggie still wished she'd been offered the option to fly commercial. "I mean..." Maggie could feel herself stalling. "I know you have your reasons to keep a low profile, but there has to be a safer way for me to get up to the Duke campus, right?"

"We've already discussed all of this, Maggie." Clive didn't sound frustrated. Instead, he just sounded confident. "This is going to be the best route, okay? If you've changed your mind, or need to back out for whatever reason, then now is the time to tell me."

Maggie shook her head. "No, I'm good to go."

Declan Tao reached over and offered her a hand. She took hold of it while stepping away from the dock. When her feet hit the composite, buoy-like material that kept the plane afloat, the aircraft dipped a little deeper into the murky lake water. "I've got it from here," Maggie said, letting go of the bodyguard's grasp. She then took hold of a bar that ran under one of the wings on the aircraft, used it to pull herself up toward the cockpit area. "Nothing to it, boys."

"We'll take the Gulfstream next time," Clive said with a wink. "It at least comes with a nice set of stairs."

"But this little airboat still has in-flight service, right?" Maggie grinned as she asked this, now settling into the right-hand side of the airplane. She began to fiddle with the harness straps and buckles that were affixed to the little cockpit seat.

"Uh-huh," Clive answered. He seemed to be waiting for her to try and fail with the collection of straps, buckles, and harnesses that went with her seat on the plane.

"I might need that drink," Maggie muttered, feeling a bit foolish as she fussed with the straps. "So I'll just take that first glass of champagne whenever you're ready—"

"You clasp it right there," Clive interrupted. He was now pointing to where the harness met the buckles that lay on Maggie's lap. The man was obviously unwilling to joke around whenever matters of safety needed to be addressed. "Then you pull it there—" Clive actually reached over now to help pull at the harness straps. "May I?" he asked.

"By all means," Maggie replied. "Have at it."

The straps tightened over her shoulders, waist, then the two metal buckles clicked in a satisfying manner. "Good to go?" Clive asked.

Maggie actually felt safe and snug. "Yep."

Clive handed her an over-ear headset, then gave her a thumbs-up.

The engine started smoothly, then the sound of a radio sparked to life. It wasn't someone in a control tower on the other end of the radio, though, it was an unfamiliar voice from the Mortlake security team. Clive finished his pre-flight checklist as the plane floated farther away from the dock and waterfront, then the voice of Declan Tao eventually joined in with the radio chatter. Everything had checked out. All was quiet on the lake and the weather was good for flying.

They were clear for takeoff.

The small plane soon gathered speed as they headed for the opposite end of the lake, then Maggie felt the aircraft begin to lift slightly onto one of its floats. The plane kept moving forward over the water, gathering more and more speed like a slalom skier over the lake, then the sound of the water rushing under the aircraft fell away as the plane lifted completely off the lake surface. Maggie watched through her little side window as lakeside cabins, more docks, and multi-colored trees swept by below. They were almost into the northernmost part of the state, where farms, apple orchards, and cool, trout-filled waters skirted the fringes of Coal Country. They were leaving it all behind as they headed for the skyline that stretched over the Blue Ridge Mountains.

Maggie was on her way out of Georgia.

At five thousand feet, while they crossed the Georgia-Tennessee Line, Maggie felt herself finally beginning to relax. It was well past midday, the skies were January cool, and everything outside the aircraft looked calm, clear, and spectacular.

"First time in a small airplane?" Clive finally asked.

A gust of wind suddenly caught the airframe, causing Maggie to throw her hand against the metal door just to steady herself. "*Yes*, it is," she said, once the plane quit shaking from side to side. Maggie was doing her best to appear calm. "I must admit, though, I had slightly higher expectations for my first private flight."

Clive laughed at this. "What do you think so far?"

Maggie took another peek outside her window. There was something in her—in every person, probably—that just couldn't ever seem to get over the magic of flying. It was as if the body knew it wasn't supposed to be high above the clouds, soaring like a bird in the sky. "It's beautiful up here," she finally said. "Especially looking out over this part of Southern Appalachia."

Radio chatter popped in their headsets again as the voice of Declan Tao checked in with them. Clive then asked for another weather update—maybe just for Maggie's peace of mind, she wasn't sure—then the pilot signed off without even a hint of concern in his voice.

"We've got about three hours until we start our descent," Clive said, directing his words to Maggie. "And I never rush things when I'm the one at the controls, so you just sit back and enjoy the view."

Maggie took in a deep breath and tried to do just that. It didn't take long though for the questions to start swirling around in her mind, questions that had to do with how she would be expected to perform while on her trip to Durham. Maggie wanted to keep talking about the project, but it was Clive who beat her to the punch.

"I know we covered quite a bit in our discussion this morning," Clive said, his voice coming in clear through the headset. "But I think there are a few more things you should know about my son's situation."

While the sound of the small plane's engine continued to hum along, Maggie waited for the man to add to his statement. Her project—her role as a consultant, really—sounded pretty simple based on the conversation they'd had over breakfast. Maggie would spend a few days around the Duke University campus, chatting with friends who'd been close to Art, talking with the investigators who were still working the case, then she'd report back to Clive to discuss her impressions of all who were involved. *It was an easy gig*, at least that's what Maggie told herself, and it was the kind of thing that allowed her to pull in a bit of money as a consultant. *No*, it wasn't practicing law. But the gig at least kept her close to the game, which is where Maggie wanted to be.

She prodded the man along. "I need to know everything, Clive, so tell me more if you think it'll help."

"I've not told anyone with law enforcement..." Clive's words came with something that sounded like reluctance, maybe even wariness. "But it's important for you to know that I recently received a message from my son."

Maggie turned to look at the pilot. He suddenly looked older, more tired. "Okay…" was about all she could muster at first. If this man was about to start sharing crucial information, then it would be something the investigators needed to hear about. But if he was about to start spouting delusions, then her only option would be to listen, maybe even act like she was willing to seriously entertain the desperate theories of a father who just wanted his son to be found.

"And he's alive, Maggie. I'm certain of it."

Maggie wasn't sure what to say. She wasn't even sure whether she should believe what the man was telling her. She'd just spent half her morning talking with Clive about the unknowns still surrounding the investigation into his son's disappearance. Hell, once she signed the NDA at breakfast, Clive went on to explain her role as a consultant for the family, their *ears on the ground* so to speak. The man made it clear that her role was to help him get a better understanding of the investigation itself, said he needed her to help make heads or tails of things, said he thought the case might be going cold…

Except now, Clive seemed to be changing everything. He was bringing fresh information out about the project itself, information that investigators should've heard as soon as it came to light. Maggie wanted to know how the man could now be so sure his son was alive, wanted to know why he even brought her on board for this project in the first place. But what Maggie really wanted to know, at least in that moment, was this: "Why the hell didn't you tell me earlier, Clive?"

"Here—" Clive said, pulling a cell phone from the inside pocket of his jacket. "I think you should take a look. I think you should read the message, first."

Maggie and Clive sat within a few feet of one another, so she didn't need to reach very far for the cell phone. "You should've brought this up sooner…" she reiterated, taking the phone from the man's grasp. As she did this, Maggie noticed there was something about the way Clive Mortlake looked in that moment. It was a face she'd not expected to find on the man. It was the face of someone who was afraid.

"The passcode is eighty-five, twenty-one, thirty-four." Clive turned his eyes away from hers. "The message will be the first thing that pops up."

She typed the numbers onto the screen. "Is this the message?" Maggie asked. She turned the device so that the screen would be easier for the pilot to see.

Clive didn't even glance back over at the phone. "That's it."

37

Maggie could feel her brow furrow when she turned her eyes back to the screen on the cell phone. Holding the device in one hand, she used her other to massage the deep creases that'd started forming along her forehead. She knew her past thirteen years of practicing law were slowly beginning to show themselves on her face. She'd worked hard to build her career, her profile, but at the age of thirty-eight, she was now *also* working diligently to prevent the effects of aging: the breakdown of collagen, the deepening of wrinkles, the volume loss in her skin, the things her male adversaries didn't worry so much about.

Of course, the stress didn't help, and Maggie knew this. But there was little she could do to prevent the stressors that came with her chosen vocation. Just like there was little she could do to stop clients from lying to her about their real motivations. No client *ever* told the whole truth during their initial consultation, and it seemed that Clive Mortlake would be no exception to that rule.

The text message that sat open on the screen of the cell phone looked like a strange, short letter. The message read:

Father, I'm alive. I'll stay that way if we pay back the two million—plus interest. I'm told that LT Hambledon is dead, so get someone new to handle the exchange for my life. Tell whoever it is to go see Tom Palomino. And tell that person they will hear from me after the meeting. No one else can know about this message except the new advocate. No one else.

- Art

PS - Sorry I missed your birthday. Hope you didn't decide to wuss out on the birthday climb this year. Make sure Declan goes back and saves the footage for me. Tell him about the big camera at the top of the trailhead. It'll provide the best angle.

Maggie read the message over twice more, then handed the cell phone back to the pilot. Although the message looked too personal to be a prank of some kind, it also didn't prove to her that Art Mortlake was actually alive. People were beyond resourceful these days, and Maggie couldn't put it past some savvy criminal to add a few personal details to a bogus text message. It was a shameless, sickening angle for someone to be working, but it wasn't inconceivable, especially when it came to the cowards who inhabited the world of digital scam artists.

"*Again—*" Maggie started. "Why didn't you tell me about this message earlier, Clive?"

Clive lifted one hand from the aircraft's controls, used it to scratch at the line of stubble that was forming on his neck. "Why does that matter?" he asked, obviously disinterested with the question. "I'm telling you about it now, Maggie, and you're the *only* person I'm planning to tell."

Maggie shook her head. She felt like she was being jerked around. "What about your *go-to guy*," she chided. "You expect me to believe you haven't discussed this with Declan or anyone on your security team?"

Clive spoke firmly. "Declan doesn't know about the message, Maggie. He can't know about it."

Maggie thought about the words from the note, the specific directive regarding discretion: *No one else can know about this message except the new advocate.* There was a threat hidden behind those words, but she still found it hard to believe that Clive wouldn't at least tell his security team about this new development, about the arguable proof that his son was being held for ransom.

"Then, why tell me?" she asked. "You probably have an army of lawyers at your disposal, right?"

He nodded. "I do."

"Why not go to one of them?"

Clive sort of grinned as he started to speak. "Well, I'm not sure my primary lawyer would believe any of this about—"

"No surprise there," she interjected, trying to keep her tone even. "Because I'm not even sure I believe any of this is real." Maggie was doing her best to not get frustrated, to not let her ego get in the way, and she was trying to focus on the right thing to do in this situation. "*But—*" Maggie took another breath. "If the message from your son is authentic, then you need a specialist for this kind of work. You might even need a hostage negotiator."

"Absolutely not." Clive paused for a moment. "I don't need some high-paid, big-law schmuck to represent me, and my son doesn't need a hostage negotiator."

Maggie didn't say anything as she continued to mull over the absurdity of the man's approach.

"I haven't always been a good father," he added, "but I know what my son needs right now." Clive actually reached over and placed a hand on her shoulder. "He needs an advocate, Maggie, which is what *you* are, regardless of license status."

Maggie absorbed this. "I'm not sure I'll be the right person to deal with this..." Her words trailed off as she avoided using the term *kidnapping.*

"But I am, Maggie." Clive sounded calm, certain. "I just need you to be sure of yourself."

Maggie couldn't help but think about their conversation from earlier that morning: her acknowledgment of past missteps, and his beliefs around high-performers requiring balance and purpose. The non-disclosure agreement that she'd signed took the prospect of media attention mostly off the table, and the compensation structure that she and Clive had settled on was a *very* generous hourly rate, far higher than anything she'd ever charged a client for her time. So, Maggie found herself wondering: *What was the risk?*

Clive seemed to be trying to prod her along. "My son needs you, okay?"

Maggie knew what the risk was. It was clear to her now. And it didn't have one thing to do with her reputation or career aspirations. "If this message is real—"

"Maggie, it's as real as the wings on this aircraft."

"Then—" Maggie wasn't sure she wanted to say the words out loud. "You know what's at stake, right?"

He nodded. "But that's flying, and there's always going to be a risk when it comes to—"

"Clive, I'm not talking about flying."

"I know," he said. "You're talking about my son's life."

Maggie paused for a long moment, then said: "Okay, I'm still in this. But I need you to tell me *everything* this time."

38

Maggie tried to listen without judgment while Clive Mortlake walked her through a story about the message. It was a ransom note, *obviously*, one that he'd received four days earlier, on December 29th.

"How do you know this message isn't part of some twisted scam?" Maggie asked. "I mean, updates on your son's disappearance have been running on just about every major news outlet. Your family's wealth and situation would make for a perfect target, right?"

"It's no scam, Maggie." Clive reached a hand into his jacket pocket and pulled the cell phone out once more. "This phone has a number that shifts periodically, and the device isn't something you buy from your average retailer. It's military grade technology, the kind sold to the highest bidder, and it's virtually impossible to hack—"

"But it's not impossible," Maggie pushed back.

Clive shook his head. "I rarely speak in absolutes, Maggie, but I'm certain this isn't a fake message, just like I'm certain it came from my son. He's alive, okay?"

"Let me see the message again," Maggie said, reaching for the phone.

"Of course." Clive handed the medium-sized, brick-like device over. He repeated the passcode so she could unlock it.

While she scanned the message over another time, Maggie said: "It's obvious that the two million, plus interest, is the ransom demand."

"That's right."

"Do you know how the interest will be calculated?"

"I'm not sure, Maggie. I assume they'll tell you that amount once you make contact with the Palomino boy."

The podcast episode that Maggie had listened to that morning made mention of Tom Palomino. He was a college basketball star who played for the Duke Blue Devils, and he and Art Mortlake had been teammates for half a season during their freshman year at Duke. Although Art no longer played on the team, the two young men were apparently still close friends.

"Why go to this Palomino kid?" Maggie asked.

Clive offered a shrug. "Again, I'm not sure. But I imagine someone in his family will let you know why fairly soon."

Maggie nodded at this. The podcaster, as well as investigators involved in the case, hadn't highlighted Tom Palomino as a person-of-interest in the disappearance of Art Mortlake. But young Tom was, let's say, an interesting part of the equation.

"He's one of the last people to see your son alive, right?"

"There's a lot I don't know, Maggie." Clive kept his eyes on the expanse of sky that lay stretched out before them. "However, what I do know is that Tom had asked Art to be in his wedding—"

"That's right," Maggie interrupted. "Tom Palomino is marrying the daughter of that gubernatorial candidate from Georgia, the one who's also a megachurch preacher in Atlanta."

"Bedford Mitchell," Clive added. "And his daughter's name is Zoe, I believe."

Maggie now remembered all of this from the podcast episode. Art had been a guest at the Mitchell-Palomino engagement party on the night he disappeared. It was a large, fancy event, one attended by plenty of state-level politicos. Investigators had apparently interviewed hundreds of people from that night, and per the former policewoman turned podcaster: the list of potential witnesses included a *very* sketchy collection of individuals, namely the dozen or so well-known Long Island mafiosos who came to show respect for their boss, Luca Palomino, and his family.

"From the little I've heard," Maggie said, "this Tom Palomino is supposed to be a pretty clean kid. His family, though, is another story."

Clive nodded. "I had some people do some digging into them a few years ago, back when my son had a problem down in Florida."

"And?" Maggie asked. She tried to make a mental note about Florida while she waited for the man to respond.

"The Palomino Family is connected, *sure*, but they're still low-level mobsters, the kind who earn at a regional level by running all kinds of grifts and schemes."

"Kidnapping might just be the next step up," Maggie mused. "I'll have to just see what young Tom tells me, right?"

"He may not tell you anything at all, Maggie, at least not at first."

Maggie wasn't about to start twisting arms and busting kneecaps. But she had a way with people who had something to lose. And this Tom Palomino was slated as a high pick in the upcoming NBA Draft, which meant the young man had a lot to worry about when it came to matters of reputation. "I can be mighty persistent when I need to be, Clive."

Clive glanced over at the seat to his right. "Whoever kidnapped Art isn't playing around, Maggie. I'm sure you already appreciate this part of the problem."

Maggie didn't really want to think about the risk to her own life in that moment. She preferred to stick to the business of saving someone else's. "I'm aware," she said. "I'll let you know if I receive any threats while I'm there in Durham. And I'll be on a flight back home if someone gets too close for comfort."

"But you might not see the threat coming, Maggie." Clive reached over for the phone that was still in Maggie's hand, then took it. He swiped at the screen before handing the device back to her. "Because until I received the message from Art, I didn't even know about a threat that was waiting for me in my own backyard."

Maggie stared down at the screen on the device. There was a clear image of someone in tactical gear, and they held a long barrel rifle of some kind. "When did you receive this?" she asked.

"See, that's the thing," he replied. "I didn't receive the image from anyone. This is something Declan pulled from one of the cameras on my property. This was a critical breach that his team missed by a mile, something he's never once let happen before."

Maggie considered this for a moment. "Could the security breach be more than just an oversight? Could the kidnappers have someone on the inside who—"

"This was certainly a serious mistake on Declan's part, but that's *all* it was." Clive sounded firm in this belief. "And the hole in my compound's security has been addressed, so I'm satisfied with the response from Declan and his team."

Maggie wasn't satisfied, but she also didn't want to push too hard. Her thoughts turned back to the message from Art Mortlake. "So, did this image come from the camera that was mentioned in your son's note?" she asked. "*The big camera at the top of the trailhead.*"

Clive nodded. "And that's why I know this isn't a scam, Maggie." He then reached over and took the phone from her. "My son knows where that camera is positioned at the top of the trailhead, and he knows it doesn't cover a part of the property that he and I like to call *the climb.*"

"That's a good son right there," Maggie remarked. "And it was a smart way for him to go about warning you."

"And now I'm warning you, Maggie, so just be careful, okay?"

"You also need to be careful, Clive." Maggie was almost surprised by her words, by the genuine concern she felt. "Because I'm sure these people are going to continue watching you, at least until they get what they want."

Clive didn't add anything more to those concerns. Instead, he pointed toward the stretch of woods that covered the mountains below. "This is one of my favorite places in the country," he soon said. "It's where I used to take Art camping, back when he was still just a little boy."

Maggie turned her eyes to the window on her side of the aircraft. "Where are we?" she asked, looking down over the canopy of green treetops.

"We're at the southern edge of Pisgah National Forest," he replied. "It's a beautiful place to hike, fish, and camp, and I have some good memories that are left down there."

A strange kind of quiet filled the cockpit while the father seemed to think about those days spent with his son. Maggie felt the need to offer something light, encouraging. "You should go back one day, and you should plan to take Art with you. You two could add to those memories."

He nodded at this. "I plan to go back soon, Maggie."

There was something hollow in those words. It was a sound that Maggie couldn't ignore. "Good," she said, turning her gaze back to the pilot. He looked tired. "And I'll do anything I can to help make that happen."

"I know you will." He turned his eyes to hers, then offered a weak smile. "In fact, next time I go down there, I'll make sure to drop you a letter."

39

Of course, the story that he told her was only partially true. But the best of lies always held *just* enough of the truth, at least that's what Clive Mortlake had come to believe. It was the only way you could get a person to really believe any lie you told them.

See, people needed to hear a story, needed to take only what they wanted to from that story. And then it was up to the person to take the lies from that story and fit them in with their own personal narrative. Because once this happened, once a lie took root in the story of another, that's when a person could start to defend the lie all the way to the end. It was just how most people were.

In Clive's mind, the reason this worked came down to one simple truth: *most* people desperately needed their own story to be true. Because if their own story wasn't true, then that just meant they were the ones who were lying...

Clive Mortlake certainly hoped that Maggie Reynolds wasn't like *most* people.

Clive checked his heading, then cut his eyes west toward a sun that weighed heavy on the distant horizon. Behind him were the banks of Falls Lake, where he had safely deposited his passenger. There, a vehicle sat waiting for Maggie, one that would take her on to a hotel near the campuses of Duke University. She would be able to take things forward after that and would be able to contact the people who were responsible for holding Art hostage.

But Maggie would be alone from here on out—*they both would*.

While Clive made his way back over the mountains of Southern Appalachia, back toward the woods of North Georgia, he let his thoughts wander. He thought about Maggie, her perception of him, and he thought about what would come to pass once he was no longer around. Although Clive was thoroughly exhausted from playing the role of the healthy, exuberant billionaire, he felt confident in the way he'd performed throughout that day. He was convinced he'd not given the lawyer any reason to suspect there was something wrong with his health.

After all, only a handful of people knew about the cancer that continued to spread throughout his body. While the plane continued to soar somewhere above seven thousand feet, Clive made a mental note of those people he'd talked to about the diagnosis: Art, Declan, his oncologist in New York, and Sarah Thompson—his physician and occasional lover in Georgia.

It was a small group, *yes*, but there was still the off chance that a few other people might learn of his condition. There was little he could do about that, though. He'd been clear and stubborn with the people he'd already told, and now Clive just had to trust they would honor his wishes.

All of them.

Secrets were something that Clive had grown used to from an early age. They went hand in hand with the task of surviving life as a Mortlake. What was truly difficult about Art's kidnapping, though, was the fact that Clive wasn't the least bit surprised by it. For years and years, he'd known about the threats to the family, known about the *good* people who claimed the Mortlakes still owed them a large debt. And Clive had done his darndest to keep those people, *that secret*, far away from the ones he loved.

As Clive started to ease the controls forward, he thought more about the secret his family had carried over the course of several generations. It was a secret that started with a simple agreement, a one-time loan for two million dollars. With that agreement came certain responsibilities, some of which included a dogged commitment to peaceful, charitable endeavors. But what the agreement also required was full repayment, *at some point*, of the entire loan itself. And failing to repay the loan was never going to be an option, because once a demand for repayment was made—*which one had*—the Mortlake Family had only two paths available to them: pay with monies or pay with lives.

While he eased the throttle back to slow the little plane, he kept a close eye on things as the aircraft dipped below five thousand feet. "Easy now," he murmured, watching the altimeter's dial turn to forty-seven fifty, forty-five hundred, forty-two fifty, then four thousand.

He kept on like this.

Turning to the southwest, Clive looked out over what he knew to be the edges of Pisgah National Forest. Darkness had fallen outside, and the GPS receiver and other gauges were all that glowed inside the airplane's dimly lit cockpit. The aircraft was still an hour plus from any lake or airstrip near the mountain house in Gilmer County, but Clive had no plans of making it that far on his journey back.

At around forty miles east of Asheville, now cruising at fifteen hundred feet, Clive put in a call to the tower. The conditions couldn't have been much better that night, and the skies were cool and clear as the plane made its way over the dense woods that skirted to the northeast of Montreat. Clive eased the controls forward some more, keeping a close watch on the altimeter as the aircraft dipped below a thousand feet.

Clive knew just about everything there was to know about the topography below him. He'd studied it closely for several weeks, so even in the darkness of night, he could close his eyes and still see the streams, ridges, and hills of that wild North Carolina terrain.

Air traffic control finally popped in his headset. The voice was calm and ready to help.

It was time to go.

EXHIBIT "C"
THE CRASH

Pilot: Mayday! Mayday! This is November thirty-eight, seventy-two, Yankee. I just blew my engine, and I've lost all hydraulics.

Asheville Tower: Roger, November thirty-eight, seventy-two, Yankee. I understand you just lost engine power, and, ah, that you're flying without your hydraulic system.

Pilot: That's affirmative. I've almost got no rudder or elevator left either.

Asheville Tower: Roger that, sir. November thirty-eight, seventy-two, Yankee, your present track puts you about forty-two miles to the northeast of the airport.

Pilot: Say again—

Asheville Tower: You're forty-two miles northeast of the airport, sir.

Pilot: Tower control, my nose is coming down. I'm going to have to fly this to the ground.

Asheville Tower: November thirty-eight, seventy-two, Yankee, is all hydraulic quantity gone?

Pilot: Yes, dammit, all hydraulics are gone.

Asheville Tower: Copy, November thirty-eight, seventy-two, Yankee. Souls on board and fuel remaining?

Pilot: One soul on board.

Asheville Tower: Fuel?

Pilot: Uh, thirty-three.

Asheville Tower: November thirty-eight, seventy-two, Yankee, you're still five miles from the edge of Pisgah National Forest. The nearest highway is to your nine o'clock, at one zero miles out.

Pilot: Copy. I'm going to have to set it down. Can you give me the elevation?

Asheville Tower: Field elevation in your current position is two zero eight. That's two zero eight—

Pilot: Ahhh, shit. I can't see a thing—

[Sounds of pilot screaming. Tree limbs crack and break as airplane cuts through the forest canopy and slams into ground.]

Preliminary Notes – Crash Investigation

At roughly 8:08 p.m., on January 2, 2025, a small, single-engine aircraft (Tail No.: N3872Y) lost contact with the air traffic control tower at Asheville Regional Airport. Emergency services were notified immediately, and units were soon dispatched to a densely wooded area at the western edge of McDowell County, North Carolina. Attempts were made to obtain visible confirmation of the crash site, but the darkness of night, as well as the characteristics of that largely uninhabited area, greatly frustrated the search-and-rescue process.

Roundabout 5:30 a.m., on January 3, 2025, the charred remains of a small aircraft were spotted in western McDowell County, a half-mile from the waters of Big Creek. The yellow, single-engine airplane appeared to be owned by a company registered in the Cayman Islands. A call was placed with the FAA office in Taylorsville, North Carolina, requesting more information on the owner of the aircraft, and a forensics team was called in from the McDowell County Sheriff's Office to swab the scorched airplane for human remains.

As of 9:00 a.m., on January 3, 2025, the investigation into the cause of the crash, as well as the identity of any occupants who may have perished in the emergency landing, remains open and ongoing

PART IV

SHOWING UP

"If your only goal is to become rich, you will never achieve it."
—John D. Rockefeller

40

Maggie Reynolds stepped onto the front porch of a Craftsman-style bungalow, one belonging to an LLC that the Mortlake Family probably formed for liability purposes. It was Art Mortlake's last known address there in Old West Durham, and Maggie had gathered from a quick search of the public records database that young Mortlake had not lived there alone. Although it was Friday morning, Maggie understood that classes weren't yet back in session at the University, so her hope was to catch Art's roommate there at home, possibly nursing a hangover.

A rough-looking screen door covered the main entryway to the house. Maggie didn't see a doorbell anywhere, so she pulled the flimsy screen barrier back, then knocked twice on a front door that'd been painted Duke Blue. Maggie then stepped back from the doorway so she could wait for any movement from the other side.

All appeared to be quiet inside the home.

Maybe the roommate's still away for the holiday break, Maggie considered, glancing back toward the yard and quiet road that fronted the house. The little bungalow occupied one corner of the street, and the other houses around it all looked like nice rental properties for a college neighborhood. SUVs, base model luxury cars, and pick-up trucks lined the little residential street. At least half of the vehicles looked to have Greek letters stuck somewhere on their rear windows, while the rest had a Duke University sticker of some kind.

She turned her attention back to the porch on Art Mortlake's little Craftsman. Strewn about were the things one expected to find at a college student's house: two empty cases of beer, chairs with worn cushions on them, some questionable looking cigarette butts, stacks of empty pizza boxes, etc., etc. All of it was further evidence of college life at its finest.

Maggie shook her head. She couldn't help but think about the boys she'd known back in college. Of course, none of them were the sons of billionaires, and yet they'd all managed to keep their houses a little tidier than this one.

Pulling the screen door back, Maggie knocked two more times on the blue door. "Hello!" she hollered. "Anybody home?"

Hearing no response, Maggie let the thin screen door slap loudly against its doorframe, then turned to be on her way.

Maggie was two steps from the porch when she heard a door opening behind her. The squeaking sound of the springs on the screen door soon followed. A voice called to her before she could turn around to see who was in the doorway.

"Jesus, lady," began the groggy voice of Art's old roommate. "It's barely nine o'clock."

From just off the bottom step of the porch, Maggie considered the young man in the doorway. The tall, twenty-something college kid looked to be close to six-foot-four, but he was of the wiry variety, the kind who seemed to be made of mostly bone, sinew, and muscle. She could tell the young man had probably just woken up. His eyes were barely open, he wore only a pair of basketball shorts, and his long hair was tied up in a messy top-bun.

Maggie pulled her cell phone out and checked the time. "It's almost nine-thirty."

The young man sighed as he ran a hand across his face. He looked rough. Probably felt that way, too. "Whatever," he finally said. "I'm up, I'm here, so what do you want?"

"I'm looking for Art."

"Fucking hell," he said, shaking his head. "Everyone's looking for him. Come on, lady, how do you not know that already?"

Maggie smiled. "I do know that, *guy*, which is exactly why I'm here."

"Are you a reporter?" he asked. "I've dealt with so many of you people lately. I'm just tired of it, okay? I don't know what happened that night—"

"I'm not a reporter."

"Are you a—"

"I'm not a cop, either."

His face reported some relief at this fact. "Well, that's good," he eventually said. "I've had enough of that lately."

Maggie nodded. The brief snapshot she was being given of this young man's lifestyle made it pretty clear he wasn't a great candidate for sporadic visits from law enforcement. "I'm Maggie Reynolds," she said with a smile. "I've been hired by the Mortlake Family to do a little work on Art's disappearance."

"Who else have you talked to about Art?" he asked, still not looking too convinced she was worth his time.

"No one except his father."

He raised an eyebrow as he leaned a shoulder against the edge of the open doorway. "You met with Clive?"

"In the flesh."

"Interesting…"

"Now, usually when I tell people my name, they tell me theirs."

"I'm Frank," he replied. "Frank King."

"All right, Frank." Maggie took the few steps up to the porch, then put out her hand for a handshake. "It's nice to meet you."

Frank stared down at the hand that greeted him. "I'd shake your hand if I hadn't just been scratching my balls."

"*Gross.*" Maggie pulled the hand back. "Probably best we skip that."

"Come on inside," he said, holding the door open while offering her a broad smile. "I'll tell you anything you need to know about my boy."

Maggie shook her head again as she stepped inside the house. She was feeling more and more like she was back in college.

41

The house was a complete wreck on the inside. When Maggie stepped into the living room area, she could see that almost every open surface was stacked high with empty beer cans, red cups, or discarded take-out containers. Although there were two leather couches in the living room, one of them was almost completely covered in laundry.

"I hope those clothes are clean." Maggie wrinkled her nose as she made her way to the other couch, the one that wasn't already covered in clothing. "But I'll let you be the one to sit over there, just in case."

The shirtless Frank King grinned as he stepped closer to the other couch. He picked up a hooded sweatshirt from the stack, gave it the sniff test, then pulled it over his head. "I think these clothes are mostly clean," he said, taking a seat at one end of the cluttered sofa.

"Uh-huh, sure," Maggie said, still taking stock of the little college living space. On the walls were movie posters, a few black-and-white photos from some US national parks, and one beautifully framed image of Cameron Indoor Stadium, the basketball mecca that served as homecourt for the Duke Blue Devils. "Thanks for letting me come inside," Maggie finally added. She turned her attention back to young Frank.

"No problem," he said. "Can I get you anything? I have water and beer."

"It's a little early for a beer, at least it is for me."

"True." He paused a moment, then asked: "You smoke?"

Maggie shook her head, and this seemed like an unfortunate revelation for her host.

"Actually—" Frank began to stand. "I might have some orange juice in the fridge. I'll just need to check real quick—"

Maggie stopped him with as nice a voice possible. "Frank, it's okay. Let's just talk for a bit about Art."

"All right, well, let me get my head right." Frank then leaned to one side of the couch, where he rooted around for a few seconds until he found what appeared to be a water bong. After placing the glass looking cylinder on the floor between his feet, he proceeded to pick up a metal grinder that'd been left out on top of the coffee table. "I'm going to just pack something up. Hope you don't mind." There wasn't a question in anything he'd said so far.

"Um, okay..." Maggie said, trying not to appear awkward as she looked away from the young man. She'd represented plenty of clients over the years who'd been busted with weed. Although she didn't have a problem with the stuff, it also wasn't her thing. "This place is a mess," she finally said. "Did you just have a party?"

"Kind of." Frank offered a shrug. "I just had a group of people over last night after work."

"What do you do for work?" she asked.

"I'm a cook." Frank didn't look up as he spoke. His eyes were on his fingers while they packed green, leafy weed into a funnel-like stem that'd come out of the bong. "The Blue is a great bar here in town. It has a shit kitchen, though, one that I work in most nights of the week."

Maggie couldn't get a good read on this guy. She also couldn't tell if the young man was embarrassed by the mention of his minimum-wage job. "I waited tables all through college," she said, trying to forge a connection. "I mean, tips basically paid my rent the last few years I was at Florida."

He nodded at this. "Art used to give me shit for working at the bar."

"Yeah?"

"It's not what you think, though." Frank finished his task of packing up the bong. He looked pleased with his handiwork. "Art just wanted somebody to hang out with, you know?"

"I think so."

Frank lifted his gaze to Maggie. "See, most guys who grow up with a silver spoon in their mouth, well, they don't understand what it's like when you *have* to work. Know what I mean?"

Maggie nodded. She did know.

"And those guys are the ones who usually end up saying douchebag things from time to time when it comes to questions about money. Yet, my boy Art grew up with more cake than just about every person on this planet, and he was still pretty damn cool about anything that had to do with making money."

Maggie smiled to show she was listening.

"Art just wanted to have people around," Frank added. "But he knew my family didn't have much, so he didn't hold it against me once. I live—well, *lived*—in this house for free, but I wouldn't ever take Art's money for anything else. And my guy was beyond good about trying to understand that."

"That's probably quite the compliment for someone like Art."

"And if he were alive, he would've been celebrating with me last night, toasting the shit out of my news about Stanford."

"Stanford?" she asked.

Frank pulled a lighter out from somewhere and sparked it up. "Yeah, I got my admissions letter from Stanford University yesterday." Water gurgled as Frank took a hit from the bong. He held the smoke in for a long moment, then shot a pungent stream of it over one shoulder. "Of course, I'll wait to see who else makes an offer. Harvard doesn't usually get their letters out until March, so I'd like to see what happens there. Might pit a couple of schools against one another, see how much scholarship money I can squeeze my way."

Maggie wasn't sure what to say. "Congratulations, Frank."

He offered a glassy-eyed smile. "Thanks."

"What do you plan to study?"

"Medicine."

She grinned. "You sure you won't consider the law?"

"No way in hell, Maggie. I'd rather cook every night." He sparked the lighter once more, then leaned over to take another hit from the bong. "I mean, who *really* wants to be a lawyer? That's like signing up for a lifetime of boredom."

Maggie waited for the young man to get a good lung full of smoke, then said: "I'm a lawyer, Frank."

Frank started coughing hard right after she said this. When he finally stopped wheezing, his eyes were still watering. Maggie couldn't tell if he'd teared up from his coughing fit, or if this was just the effects of the marijuana. Once Frank regained his composure, though, he started apologizing profusely.

"That was a total dick comment, Maggie." Frank placed the bong back on the floor. "I'm very, very sorry for—"

"It's fine, Frank." Maggie could tell his flushed face and red eyes were from more than just the Mary Jane. This young man was actually embarrassed. "Really, it's okay."

"I've just been..." Frank's words seemed to trail off.

"I get it," she said. "I imagine your friend being gone hasn't been easy."

"Not one bit." Frank shook his head and looked away. "And there hasn't even been a funeral or anything. It's like they think he's sitting at a resort somewhere, soaking up the sun."

Maggie nodded. "Do you think he might still be alive?"

Frank leaned back on the couch and laced his fingers behind his head. He seemed to be thinking long and hard about this simple question. "Maybe," he finally said. "I guess if anyone was going to have something crazy happen like this—"

"Like what?" Maggie interrupted.

"Like a kidnapping or whatever." Frank wasn't looking at her as he spoke. He had his eyes on a framed movie poster, one of several that hung on the living room walls. "Art is just one of those guys, you know?"

"Not really, Frank. But I'm here because I want to find out more about him."

Frank nodded to the framed poster. "You ever seen that movie?" he asked.

Maggie turned her head to look at the poster. She recognized the shadowy faces of Liotta, De Niro, and Pesci, all hovering at the top of the frame. "Goodfellas?" she asked.

"Yeah."

"I mean, it's been a while, but I've seen it." Maggie hoped this college kid wasn't about to shoot his shot, wasn't about to ask her to watch the movie with him right now.

"You remember how Henry Hill was the only guy to make it out? He was the only one who was able to make a deal happen with the feds?"

Maggie didn't remember the storyline exactly, but she did remember Ray Liotta's character winding up in some kind of witness protection at the end. "Vaguely," she finally said. "Like I told you, it's been a while since I've seen the movie."

"Well, Art is *that* kind of guy. He may not look like it right off, but he can go in with any group of people and he'll find a way to make them love him."

Maggie pushed back a little on this idea. "Kind of hard not to make friends when you have his kind of money, right?"

"Wrong." Frank made a buzzer sound as he said this. "Art can go where people don't know him and he walks out of there being everybody's best freaking friend. The guy's one hell of an athlete, he's whip smart, and there's a secret somewhere behind his eyes that everybody wants to know. I swear, Maggie, it's all there."

"So, you do think he's alive?"

"That's not what I said. I just think if anyone can surprise us, then there's a good chance it'll be Art."

Maggie didn't get the impression that young Frank had much more to offer. She figured she could at least walk around the house, though, maybe get a better feel for who Art Mortlake was when he was living there. Maggie started offering her thanks as she stood from the couch.

"This has been..." Maggie wasn't sure how to phrase this for her host. "Well, this has been interesting."

"I'm really sorry for the messy place," Frank said, also starting to stand. "Art was a crazy neat freak, so he would've flipped his lid if the house looked like this. Didn't matter if we threw a party, everything had to be picked up."

Maggie noticed there was some guilt in those words. "Don't worry about it, Frank. I'm sure he wouldn't mind. Like you said, he would've been celebrating with you last night."

Frank only smiled at the comment. "By the way," he said, changing the subject. "You told me earlier that you met with Art's dad?"

"Yeah," Maggie said. "Clive and I had some meetings yesterday, then he flew me up here in one of his planes."

Frank paused for a moment as he seemed to consider things. "Was he the one actually doing the flying?"

Maggie was a little confused at the question. "Yep. It was just Clive at the controls."

The young man looked a little surprised at this. "Well, he must be doing better."

"I'm not so sure about that," Maggie said. "I've not spent a lot of time with the man, but I get the impression this all is still weighing heavily on him."

Frank shook his head. "I mean, can you imagine? I don't know how someone juggles losing a kid with a health problem like that."

Maggie stopped. "Health problem?"

Frank put his palm to his face. "*Oh*, shit..." he muttered. "I probably shouldn't have said anything about that."

42

Maggie found a spot on the road that ran in front of Tom Palomino's house. She sat in the car for a moment, needing to collect her thoughts and clear her head. In the passenger seat lay one of her legal pads. On it she'd scribbled some notes about her meeting with Frank King. It was a meeting that'd left her with more questions than answers, and possibly a slight contact high.

Why was Clive Mortlake hiding his cancer diagnosis? Maggie asked herself. And if the man only had a matter of months to live, what did that mean for the negotiations with Art's kidnappers? Who did Clive expect to carry the torch if he were to pass away? Certainly not her, right?

Maggie picked the canary-yellow pad up from the passenger seat, then added a few more bullet points to her list of things to consider. Although the list seemed to only be growing, Maggie hoped her next meeting might help answer some of the questions that were already on the page.

From the front seat of the car, Maggie took stock of the quiet residential street that now surrounded her. She could tell by the rows of cookie-cutter houses and well-manicured lawns that this part of town wasn't considered a neighborhood for college kids. Most of the houses had a wide driveway, a two-car garage, and a brick mailbox at the edge of the street. And *all* of the houses, of course, had a basketball hoop out front, just like the home that supposedly belonged to the college basketball star.

Maggie double-checked the address that Frank King had provided her, then hopped out of her vehicle. A thirty-something woman in spandex came running by with a dog and a stroller. She offered Maggie a polite smile and a crisp *Good morning!* as she trotted by.

Is this the right place? Maggie wondered as she offered a wave and a smile of her own to the passing jogger. Art Mortlake's little bungalow looked like it was only a step or two above a frat house, yet this Tom Palomino seemed to be living in a neighborhood that suited a made-for-TV version of the Truman Show.

Maggie turned back to face the address that she hoped belonged to Tom. It was at least a four-bedroom house, one with white shutters, board-and-batten siding, and all those little rustic details that were meant to make a new build look *farmhousy*.

The house did have a Duke Blue door though, so Maggie figured she'd at least give the doorbell a ring.

The doorbell lit up when Maggie pressed the button on it. There was a little camera at the top of the device, so Maggie figured the homeowner would be able to see her standing there on the porch, even if they chose not to come to the door. Maggie had a similar doorbell at her house in Blakeston. It'd proved useful for deliveries and such, especially since no one tended to be home on Friday mornings like this, certainly not at eleven o'clock.

But someone was at home. Maggie could see their outline through the glass on the front door. This person certainly wasn't Tom Palomino, though. They didn't have the look of a soon-to-be first-round pick in the upcoming NBA draft.

"Can I help you?" asked the twenty-something blonde who opened the door for Maggie.

"Yes, hello," Maggie started. "I think I may have the wrong house..." Her words sort of trailed off as she tried to get a look at the foyer near the front of the home. Nothing stood out from the little she could see.

The young woman wore well-coordinated workout gear that was little more than a sports bra for a top, form-fitted spandex for pants, and bright colored sneakers. It was the kind of ensemble that was fashionable for the gym girls right now, but it was the type of gear that Maggie unfortunately associated with the increasingly younger generation of women. The blonde was in excellent shape, though, so Maggie couldn't help but want to applaud the young woman for being able to rock the outfit.

A dog barked from somewhere inside the house as the young woman spoke. "Who are you looking for?" she asked. "I don't live here, but I do know quite a few of the neighbors."

"Like I said, I may have the wrong house." Maggie couldn't help but wonder if Frank King had been a little too stoned that morning to give her the correct address. "But I'm looking for Tom Palomino. Does he live here?"

The expression on the young woman's face told Maggie that this was, in fact, the correct house. "Tom isn't here right now. He's at practice. I can give you the card he uses for media inquiries. That's if you want to go about this the *right* way…"

"I'm actually not a sports journalist," Maggie quickly replied. "I'm a—"

"It doesn't matter what outlet you work for. Tom's agent pretty much asks that everyone go through their PR firm." The young woman reached over to a table just off the doorway, then picked up a business card. Thrusting the card into Maggie's hand, she continued: "The information's all on there, ma'am." Then, the door started to close.

"Hold on!" Maggie suddenly felt the urge to put this young little blonde in her place, but she decided to keep her tone in check. "I'm not with the media, okay? I'm here on behalf of the Mortlake Family. They hired me to help look into Art's, well—"

"His murder?" the young woman asked. Her tone had softened noticeably.

Maggie decided to go ahead and clarify her position on the matter. "*His disappearance*, at least that's how his family sees it."

"And by his family, you mean his father."

Maggie realized that when it came to Art's family, she didn't know much about it. It seemed that all the young man had was his father, Clive Mortlake.

"Yes." Maggie kept her tone even. "His father, Clive, is who hired me."

"And what is it you want to speak to Tom about? We've both already been interviewed several times by the investigators."

Maggie hadn't thought to look for a picture of Tom's fiancée, but she was fairly certain this was her. And it was obvious the young woman was already acting the part of gatekeeper for her soon-to-be hubby, so Maggie figured she needed to turn on the charm.

"It's a little chilly out here," Maggie said. "Would you mind if I came inside?"

"I have a Pilates class I'm trying to make. It's at noon."

"Are you the instructor?"

"Heavens no," she said with a laugh. "I'm just trying to keep up."

Maggie glanced at the time on her cell phone. It was only ten past eleven. "You sure you don't have ten minutes you can spare? You might be able to save me another trip over to meet with Tom."

The younger woman seemed to consider this.

Maggie nudged her. "I bet Tom would appreciate having to answer less questions."

"You're right." Her face looked pleasant, even welcoming as the front door opened wider. "Please come on in, ma'am."

"Great." Maggie stepped forward. "And by the way, I'm Maggie Reynolds."

"I'm Zoe."

"That's Zoe Mitchell, right?" Maggie hoped the question didn't sound too stalkerish.

"That's right," Zoe said. "But it'll be Mrs. Zoe Palomino come August."

43

Zoe Mitchell led Maggie into the living room. Other than the large flatscreen television that hung on the wall, the space could not have been more different than the one she'd left behind at Art Mortlake's little college-style bungalow. The living room in this house still looked like it belonged to a young man, but it was cleaner, tidier, and decorated with at least *some* kind of plan in mind (i.e. a design strategy with a woman's input). *Sure*, most of the decorating was the kind that belonged in an up-scale sports bar, but it all still seemed to gel. And this was mostly due to the fact that almost all the pictures were of Tom Palomino playing basketball or winning awards for playing basketball. It was a design decision that probably gave guests a helpful roadmap for how to deal with the homeowner's large ego.

Maggie took a seat at one end of the room's leather sectional, then pulled her cell phone out just to have one more check of the time. "This room is lovely, by the way."

"Thank you, Mrs.—"

"Let's just stick with Maggie, okay?"

"Yes, ma'am." Zoe paused. "I mean, sure, that works for me."

Maggie nodded. Although she'd grown up in Florida, her family hadn't stressed the same formalities that a lot of kids came to know in the South.

But her guess was that Zoe—being the daughter of an evangelical preacher—had probably grown up with the more traditional aspects of a Southern upbringing. That meant that any woman over the age of thirty automatically qualified for *missus, miss,* or *ma'am.*

"Look, I'll try to cut right to it, okay?" Maggie could tell that Zoe wasn't entirely comfortable with their unexpected meeting. "I think Tom might be able to help us find out where Art is."

"How?" Zoe looked genuinely surprised by this.

Maggie wanted to be careful with how she put things. "It's more like we think he might be able to tell us who could be involved in his—"

"No," Zoe interrupted. "I mean, *how* is it that you think Art's still alive?"

Maggie made like she needed to think about her answer. She really just wanted another few seconds to consider the face of the young woman who sat across from her. Zoe didn't look confused or intrigued. She looked more like she was genuinely shocked.

"After his blood was found all over that parking lot," Zoe added. She sounded more like she was thinking out loud. "And when they found that security guard's body...I mean, he was known to have a little bit of a temper, but I was actually worried the police were going to think Art killed the man and ran away."

"I'll admit, the thought did cross my mind at first," Maggie mused, although she didn't want to slow the young woman's rambling. "But there's no evidence of Art doing anything wrong that night."

"And there won't be." Zoe's features and tone were adamant. "Art Mortlake was a lot of things, Maggie, but he wasn't the kind of person who would do something awful like that. He was, well, mostly good."

Maggie noticed how everything about Zoe appeared to be authentic, so this made her wonder what Zoe really thought about her fiancé's family.

"I don't know how to explain it." Zoe looked like she was about to start tearing up. "I just *knew* he wouldn't have done something like that. I just knew that if Art was gone, it was because something awful happened to him."

The response from Zoe was not at all what Maggie had expected. Still, Maggie remembered her own self at twenty-two, and some of her beliefs about people were probably just as strong, certain, and baseless at times.

"What does Tom think happened?" Maggie asked.

"He was just as surprised as I was."

"About Art going missing?"

"About him being murdered."

"But has Tom accepted that's what happened?"

Zoe seemed to remember in that moment that Maggie wasn't some girl-friend she was talking to. There hadn't been any kind of rapport established between them. "I don't know, Maggie. I think we're all just grieving this thing differently. He and Art were the best of friends, but they met while playing ball together. I'm sure Tom appreciates still having basketball in his life, something he and Art both loved."

It wasn't the response of someone who had something to hide. It was more just the answer someone gave when they were wary of opening themselves up. "I know he's busy with basketball, Zoe, but would Tom be willing to help *us* find Art? That's if we can."

"What kind of question is that? Of course he'll do anything to help."

"Then, I need to talk to him, okay?"

"About what?"

"About Art being kidnapped." Maggie didn't see any reason to play hide-the-ball here. "Clive, Art's father, received a ransom note. That's part of the reason I'm here."

Zoe's voice cracked. "What?"

"He's alive." Maggie could see the tears really starting to flow from the young woman's eyes. "At least, it seems he's alive for the time being."

"Tell me what you need me to do to help?" she demanded. "I'll do anything. I'm sure Tom will too."

Maggie didn't know enough about Tom Palomino yet, but she already had her doubts as to whether he would've signed off on that last statement. "When can I come back here to sit down with Tom?" Maggie asked. "Time is of the essence, so this needs to be today."

Zoe didn't have a sleeve to wipe her tears with. She found a Kleenex, though, and dabbed her eyes with it. "We're going to have to run this by his agent and his lawyer and his dad—"

"*Please*, Zoe, let me talk to Tom before we get everyone else involved."

Zoe looked away from Maggie's gaze.

"Come on, Zoe. I'm, well, I was a lawyer, and I know how long that whole process can take. I'm not here for anyone but Art, okay?"

"His family has some rules about who Tom speaks with and they can be very, very strict."

"I'm not worried about his family," Maggie lied. "I just have a few questions about Art."

"Okay, I'll try." Zoe sniffed twice as she turned her eyes back to Maggie. "Give me your cell phone number. I'll let you know when Tom's back at the house."

44

Art Mortlake stood just beyond a tall, stone wall that surrounded one of the world's most famous courthouses. Through a stretch of iron fencing, he could see much of the main building. It was a remarkable structure, one with an interesting array of shapes and designs and colors. Although Art had never before seen the building in person, he was more than familiar with its handsome façade.

Art turned from his view of the building and looked to his right, where one of his kidnappers, Petrut Noica, stood nearby. "There's a painting of this place in one of my father's offices. It hangs right behind his desk. I used to stare at it whenever I went in there to meet with him. In fact, I used to study the painting when I was a kid, usually while I waited for my father to finish lecturing me about the things I needed to improve about myself." Art hadn't thought about his family's painting of the Peace Palace, those boyhood meetings with his father, in quite some time.

"I've also seen the painting, Arthur." Petrut wore sunglasses and a ball-cap, but Art could still tell the large man's eyes were on him. "It's in your family's home in Connecticut."

"That's right," Art confirmed. He couldn't help but be impressed by the amount of legwork that Petrut had put in ahead of their meeting one another. "The Farm is where we keep most of the artwork," he added, referring to the family's four-hundred-forty-acre property and manor they still owned in the southwestern corner of the Constitution State. "We keep a dusty art collection there, one that no one has probably cared much about in years."

"Yes and no," Petrut replied with a tilt of the head. "Your family has a dozen or so rare pieces that are currently on loan to museums around the world, and I suspect your father has placed the most valuable artwork somewhere inside the vault at your family's mountain house."

Art could only shake his head at this. Petrut knew things about the Mortlake Family that'd never once been discussed with Art. And that list of unknowable details just continued to build.

Petrut continued sharing the knowledge he'd gathered from his preliminary work-up of the family. "But the painting you referred to earlier, Arthur, the one in your father's study, that one would've been a gift to your family. It would've been a reminder of sorts."

"A reminder?"

"*Un souvenir*," Petrut replied. "A keepsake, a memory."

"What kind of memory?" Art asked.

Petrut smiled. "Arthur, come on now. You must already be catching on."

Twenty-one days had now passed since Petrut and his gang grabbed Art off the streets of Durham, North Carolina. Once the trans-Atlantic portion of their journey ended at the Port of Antwerp, Art and his captors had taken the relatively short drive over the uncontrolled border shared by Belgium and the Netherlands. Skirting the edges of the North Sea, then on through Rotterdam, their journey had eventually brought them to the city they were standing in now—The Hague.

"Why is it you think we're here, Arthur?" Petrut obviously wanted his captive audience to engage with him. "You must have some idea."

Art wasn't really in the mood to play a guessing game. "Is this supposed to be where my family took the loan out?" he finally asked. "Did my great-*great*-grandpa get in on the development project here in the Netherlands? Or wait, was *Big Arthur* the secret architect behind this masterpiece? No, I've got it now. I'm actually just another Mortlake in a long line of Dutch artists who—"

"*No*," Petrut growled, halting his hostage's increasing line of sarcasm.

"This isn't where your family executed the loan documents for the two million. But this is where the idea was conceived."

Art sighed. "What a crazy fucking idea." This was the first time he'd ever conceded an inch on the matter of the loan's existence. "But I will admit, Pete, that building does make for a beautiful courthouse."

"No, no." Petrut tutted. "This isn't just a courthouse. It's a palace, Arthur, a palace dedicated to the pursuit of world peace."

Art didn't say anything more as he turned his attention back to the magnificent building. It felt strange seeing it in person, mostly because it was an image he'd long associated with his father's study. Kids grow up seeing the images of all kinds of famous places: the Eiffel Tower, the Colosseum, Mount Rushmore, the Taj Mahal, etc. But when an individual finally gets to see one of those places in person, they are often surrounded by thousands of other people who've also come to marvel at the site.

That wasn't the case for Art on this Friday evening in January. No, Art was one of only a dozen or so people left milling around the gates to the Peace Palace. He was one of only a handful of people still peeking through the bars of fencing that surrounded the world-renowned building.

Art wondered what the other tourists were thinking as they took pictures of the grounds, wondered what they were saying to one another while they admired the monuments with quotes about peace and harmony and justice. Were they inspired by what the Palace represented? Was this multi-national commitment to peace and fairness an invigorating, refreshing concept for them? Would they leave this place thinking that world peace was *actually* possible?

Art didn't know. This place didn't prompt any questions in his mind about how wide the world was, nor did it conjure up feelings about how people were mostly good. Instead, this place made Art feel like the world was slowly closing in on him, slowly bringing everything in his family's history full circle. This place made him feel like he'd reached the end.

"Look, Pete, I get you may have your reasons for bringing me here." Art turned again to look at the big man. "But what is it that made my family ever come here in the first place?"

Petrut didn't hesitate with his answer. "Violence, Arthur. Violence is what brings everyone here."

The municipality of The Hague (officially 's-Gravenhage, a place sometimes referred to as Den Haag) is home to the Peace Palace, a building that opened its doors to the world in 1913 as a symbol of peace and international justice. The history leading up to the Peace Palace's inception, as well as its construction, is as collaborative and diverse as the designs that are found throughout the Palace buildings and grounds.

The Peace Palace is a place that began as a revolutionary idea, one founded on the people and nations' growing concerns over the horrors of war. Battles were getting messier, greater numbers of soldiers were becoming necessary to wage wars, and heads of nations were beginning to seriously consider what alternatives existed for dealing with their disputes. This was late into the Nineteenth Century, and peace organizations were forming in countries all over the world. People were taking notice of the fact that war was quickly becoming more industrialized and that massive armies would be essential in defending and fighting the conflicts of the next century.

At the same time, telegraphy and photography were beginning to bring the sheer destruction of war to the people at home. The masses who weren't yet fighting on the front lines were now able to see the horrors of battle in the photos that made it back home. They could see the suffering, see the large-scale loss of life, and many of them began calling for disarmament. And if not disarmament, maybe peace through international arbitration.

Come 1899, delegations from a number of countries gathered in The Hague for a peace conference. Meetings were held, lots of parties were had, and eventually, once the monumental idea for the Palace itself was in place, discussions began to turn to how those funds might be secured for the administrative building's construction.

This was around the turn of the Twentieth Century, of course, so there were a number of industrialists in America and abroad who had already amassed great sums of money. Although a portion of modern history paints the ultra-wealthy businesspeople of this time as *robber barons*, they were not all the same. Some of them saw the world for what it was, a violent, unfair, and competitive place, and yet a select few of those individuals still demanded more from their fellow humans.

One of those men even decided to take this idea a step further.

He was an American businessman who signed his checks E.S. Fraser.

45

With the sun beginning to set, Art and Petrut began heading away from the Peace Palace. Although Art looked free and untethered to any person who passed them by, he knew he was still being monitored by the other kidnappers from afar. He was faster than Petrut, *sure*, but Art would only be able to get so far on foot. He had no money, no cell phone, and there was always a face watching him from a passing car, a park bench, a table outside a café. Art also couldn't risk his father's life just to save his own skin, so the plan involved him continuing to wait, listen, and ask the right questions when an opportunity presented itself.

"Have you heard anything from my father?" Art asked. "It's been five days now."

Petrut was smoking a cigarette while they walked along the sidewalk together. It was something the big man seemed to do at all hours of the day. "Not yet, Arthur. But I'm confident we'll hear something soon."

"And why is that?"

"He just hired the advocate." Petrut pulled on the cigarette. "A woman who's a lawyer of some kind in your country."

Art tried to remember the last time he and his father talked about a legal matter together. Other than the few times they'd discussed the incident down in Florida, his mid-game fight that'd resulted in criminal charges in Tallahassee, Art couldn't remember another time they'd had an occasion to meet with legal counsel. The lawyers who were involved in defending Art in Florida, as well as those who helped him remain a student at Duke, had all been men.

"That's good," Art said. "What's her name?"

"It doesn't matter right now."

"I think it does."

"I'm telling you it's not important, Arthur, so don't worry about it."

"It's important to me," Art said, pushing back. "This is the person who's supposed to be helping me get home, right? I'd at least like to know her name."

"I'm helping you, Arthur." Petrut took one more drag from the cigarette, then flicked it toward the nearby street. "I'm helping you understand what's holding you back."

"No, Pete." Art didn't want to hear this crap again. "You're helping extort money from my family. That's all this is about."

Petrut stopped on the sidewalk.

"What are you doing now?" Art asked. He watched as the man pulled out his cell phone, apparently searching for something. Art waited while Petrut stood in the middle of the narrow sidewalk, blocking foot traffic. "Come on, let's go," Art said, once a couple with a dog had veered off to one side just to avoid the man. "I'm ready to get back to the flat."

Petrut looked up from the cell phone. "I'll prove to you I'm here to help."

Art actually laughed. It seemed like the big man was somehow offended by the notion that the kidnapping wasn't a service to the hostage. "Honestly, Pete, I don't give a shit about what's motivating you. I'm just trying to get back to living my life."

"No." Petrut began shaking his head. "Come on, I'll prove it to you."

It only took them ten minutes or so to get to the edge of the next neighborhood. Art had insisted several times during the walk over that Petrut tell him what was going on, but the big man simply refused to do so.

It was now dark outside, and Art could tell that the city was gearing up for Friday night. People sat outside the bars and cafés, talking and laughing, drinking together as they slipped into the first weekend of the New Year.

"Come on, man, what are we doing here?" Art asked as he followed Petrut across another road. Cycling seemed to be the primary mode of transportation in this Dutch city, so Art made sure to keep his head on a swivel whenever a bike bell went *ding!* from anywhere nearby.

"*Huygenspark* is just up here, Arthur."

Art was about to continue his protest but quickly shut his mouth once they came around the next corner. They were at the edge of what looked like another urban park, one just like the many they'd already passed throughout that day. This park had something the others didn't have, though, and Art felt a smile creep onto his face once he heard a familiar sound in the distance.

Swoosh.

As Art stepped closer to the outdoor basketball court, he didn't hesitate to offer a nod toward the group of guys who were obviously waiting on the next game. Although Art had never hooped in the Netherlands before, he figured the rules of pick-up basketball would pretty much remain the same: winners stayed on the court until they lost, losers always walked, and everybody called their own fouls.

The group of players who were already on the court had a game of four-on-four going, so Art decided to walk a little closer to the guys who were next up. "Any of you speak English?" Art asked, noticing the group only had three players. He hoped they might need a fourth to run with them during their next game.

All three men nodded back their response. The shortest of them, a guy who couldn't have been more than five years older than Art, is who decided to speak for the group. "You play basketball?" he asked.

Art hadn't dribbled a ball, hadn't shot a basket in at least two years. "Absolutely, my friend. Can I get in on the next game?"

All three of the men who were waiting on the next game were older than Art. And they all seemed a little puzzled by Art's appearance. His jeans, boots, and woolen sweater weren't part of the look someone usually brought to a basketball court.

"Yeah, okay," the short guy finally agreed. He then pointed at Petrut. "Your friend going to play too?"

The big man only shook his head as he lit up another cigarette. It seemed the former handball player wanted to watch from behind a cloud of smoke.

"Nah, it's just me," Art said, offering a handshake. "The name's *Henry*. What's yours?"

"Nick," the shorter man replied. He then pointed to his teammates who were Ruben and something that sounded like Luke. "You going to play in those boots?" one of them asked.

Art glanced down at the pair of Timberland lace ups on his feet. He smiled. "Yeah, I'll be all right."

When Art and his team stepped onto the court, the guys on both sides started jabbering back and forth in Dutch. Although Art didn't understand a word of what they were saying, he was more than familiar with the distinct pacing of trash-talk. The winners of the last game were all over six-foot, and they seemed to carry a cockiness with them that made Art decide to actually tighten up the boots on his feet.

Everyone on the court wore sweatpants or joggers, hoodies or crewneck sweatshirts, yet none of them wore sneakers made for basketball. Art recognized the brands on their feet—Kappa, Puma, Nike, Adidas—but the shoes all looked to have been designed for playing soccer. Although the NBA and other top-shelf pro leagues were littered with incredible European hoopers —*these guys weren't them*.

"You mark him," Nick said, pointing Art to the tallest player on the other team. This confident, take-ownership approach was typical of any good floor general on a basketball team. And the shortest player on the court often had to be the toughest, most vocal leader. "Baskets count two points from beyond the arc. Every other shot is one point. And we play first to fifteen."

"Sounds good," Art said, stepping closer to his man. They exchanged a fist bump. "Let's do it."

"You have a date tonight?" asked the man Art was supposed to be guarding. His accent was thick, but Art was impressed by the guy's opening volley.

"Yeah," Art replied. "It's with your sister."

The taller guy only shook his head as he offered a reply in Dutch. Everyone else on the court who heard the retort laughed at the crack back.

"Okay," Art muttered. "I see how it's going to be."

From the word *go*, Art made sure he had his way with about every player on that court. He dropped back-to-back two-pointers during the team's first couple of trips on offense, then he took it to the hole on their following drive, cutting easily between defenders for a smooth, reverse lay-up.

Art smiled as he tossed the ball to the other team. "That's five-oh, right boys?"

Nick slapped Art on the back as they turned to play a little defense. The offensive output by their opponents was pitiful, and the ball was back with Art's team after an ill-advised shot took an ugly bounce off the front of the rim. Nick got the rebound and they turned back for another trip up the court.

"Ball," Art called out, coming around from behind his point guard. The little Dutchman didn't hesitate as he sent the rock straight to his American ringer.

Art eyed the shot from where he took the ball, some seven feet from the top of the key, then zipped a no-look pass to Ruben who was already down on the block. Ruben took the pass, then clumsily turned to what was possibly his dominant hand. He let the basketball fly toward the hoop. It looked ugly, like a sort of line-drive hook shot, but the ball caught the top of the square on the backboard and fell right into the basket for another point.

"Ruuuuube," Art hollered as they all trotted back up the court. His teammate was smiling and obviously having some fun now.

"Six-oh," called out Ruben. "Let's go!"

Art could tell the other team was going to avoid bringing the ball to his side of the court, so Art left his man enough space, hoping to tempt a wayward pass. Sure enough, one of the opposing players eventually sent a lazy looper their way, one that Art picked off with ease.

Let's see if the springs in these legs still work, Art thought. Go get it…

Art rumbled down to the other end of the court, knowing good and well that no one was going to catch him from behind. His legs felt good in that moment, so he decided to showboat a little bit for whoever was watching from the park benches and cafés that surrounded the park.

"Showtime!" Art casually called out. Leaping high into the air, he pulled the basketball back as far as he could, then threw it down for a one-handed slam.

"Seven-oh!" Nick yelled as he brought up the rear.

The team was all smiles as they whooped, clapped, and offered high fives to one another. Hell, Art couldn't stop grinning himself. And when he looked over to the sideline where Petrut sat smoking on a park bench, Art was pretty sure the big man was also enjoying the show.

After all, everyone enjoyed seeing a little razzle-dazzle on the basketball court. And that's why people started to stop what they were doing in the park, started watching the little game of pick-up hoops. Someone even took their cell phone out and started filming.

46

"How good was that?" Petrut asked. He and Art were now inside a café, one that looked out on the park and outdoor basketball court. Both men stood at one end of a busy bar, sipping cold Heineken from tall glasses. It was Art's first beer since the kidnapping, and the chilled, crisp flavor of the Dutch lager tasted better than anything he'd had in years.

"That was fun." Art took another sip of his beer, then placed it down on the bar. He grabbed a nearby food menu just to give it a look. "But those guys were just weekend warriors, Pete. I probably should've taken it a little easier on them."

"That's nonsense, Arthur." Petrut also picked up a menu. It seemed the big man wasn't opposed to having dinner out that night. "They are going to go home and brag to their girlfriends about how they played a game of *real* basketball tonight."

Art nodded. "Probably so."

"You're a talented player," Petrut added. "You don't ever think about going back, trying to play again?"

Art laughed. "I think about it all the time." *Which was true.* "But thinking about doing something, and actually doing something, are completely different things."

"Well, quit thinking about it and go back and try. What's the worst that can happen to you?"

Art looked up from the menu. "I guess it can't be any worse than my last few weeks, right?"

"I'm serious, Arthur." Petrut took another large gulp from his glass. "You're no longer banned from playing university level basketball, right? Why not go play somewhere else?"

Art paused for a moment. A month ago, he probably would've answered the question with any number of excuses: there's no support from an athletic program, my left wrist and hand haven't been the same since the fight in Tallahassee, or I'm having too much fun partying right now.

But Art was tired of excuses. "Honestly, Pete, I don't want to play ball anymore. And that means I don't have what it takes, at least not to make a real go of it."

"Aren't you still good enough to compete?" Petrut wasn't leaving it alone.

Art shook his head. "No, I'm just another guy now. I met my athletic ceiling with work ethic and desire, but I'm not willing to put in the time like I used to." Art was certain he'd never said those words out loud to anyone. "So, unless it's just for fun, I'm done with playing ball."

"And you're okay with that?" Petrut asked.

"Yeah, Pete." Art nodded. "I'm just ready to go back and live my life, maybe find something else I'm passionate about."

Petrut flagged the bartender down. They ordered more beers and added some food for dinner. The subject of what Art expected to do with his life, if he ever got back to it, was something Petrut seemed unwilling to abandon.

"I thought a similar way when I was your age." Petrut didn't look at Art as he said this. "I was around twenty-two, twenty-three, when I realized I didn't have a future in my home country."

"Would that be Hungary?" Art guessed. "Ukraine?"

"Close," he replied. "I'm from Bucharest, in Romania."

"I know where Bucharest is."

"But have you been there?" he asked

Art shook his head as he picked up his fresh beer.

Petrut kept on. "Well, things are much improved now, but that wasn't the case twenty years ago. There just wasn't any work for me there."

Art recognized in that moment that this was the first time his captor had said anything remotely personal. It was a good sign. "So, what'd you do?" Art asked. "Where'd you go?"

"I packed my only bag, hopped on a bus, and made my way to France where I joined the Legion."

This part of Petrut's story actually made some sense to Art. The French Foreign Legion was a world-famous corps of mercenary soldiers, and its ranks were littered with foreigners. The Legion's regimental history was one that boasted a long line of gallant, sometimes mischievous sell swords who came to France to fight and serve a country that was not their own. Men who joined the Legion learned French out of necessity, and many of them eventually achieved their French citizenship through military service.

"Is that where you met Jetmir and the boys?" Art asked. "While serving in the Legion."

He nodded. "Marko, Jarek, and Jetmir, they all served under me at one time or another. They are good boys, all of them. That's why they work for me now."

"Why tell me this?" Art could feel himself relaxing as he got close to finishing his second beer. He wondered if Petrut had a motive behind what he was telling Art, or if the big man was just loosening up, too.

"Because the Legion is where I found my path, Arthur. I was a man when I joined, yes, but—" Petrut stopped as he seemed to search for the right turn of phrase. "But I still had growing up to do, yeah? That's what happened while I was a soldier."

Art decided not to try and test his captor's warped sense of self. The man was a criminal, for God sakes, and he expected his hostage to consider taking life advice from him. But still, there was something in Petrut's approach that Art felt he could exploit. "I'll be honest, Pete, I don't really want your advice..." Art let his words trail off when the food arrived in front of them.

"That's fine," Petrut replied. Both men began attacking the sandwiches they'd ordered. "But if your father does repay the debt, what are you going to do? Your family won't have any money."

"Let's be clear," Art said. "You're going to kill me if Clive doesn't transfer *all* of my family's assets to—"

"Yes." Petrut didn't even hesitate with the interruption. "And keep your voice down."

That's when Art decided to take his first big gamble with Petrut. "But you don't want to kill me, right?" He whispered the question. "You want me to go on and do something with my life, whether it be basketball or the military. That's what you just told me a few minutes ago."

Petrut took a big bite of sandwich and chewed for a moment while he seemed to consider the question. "My men and I *will* kill you if your father doesn't pay."

"But is that what you want to see happen?"

Petrut raised a hand to catch the bartender's attention. "I'll get the bill."

"You haven't answered my question, Pete."

"And I'm not going to."

Art had developed a theory when it came to Petrut's strategy. It was a guess, really, but it all boiled down to mind games.

See, during Art's freshman year at Duke, he took introduction to psychology. It was one of those survey courses with a hundred plus students, but Art still attended the lectures and learned enough to excel during the final exam period.

What Art remembered most about that *Psych 101* course was his professor. He was a great teacher, but he was also a guy who had a kind of nerdy passion for all things criminology. His professor had written several books on varying aspects of high-stakes hostage negotiation, and the man knew an awful lot about the bizarre things that could happen to a mind should an individual ever be left at the mercy of another violent, controlling person.

And *Stockholm Syndrome* was something that Art's professor considered very real and very possible if a person were ever held hostage. Art remembered reading case studies about people who'd been abused and taken captive, remembered reading about the awful aftereffects someone experienced when they were victimized by a person who exerted extreme control over them. What was astonishing, at least for Art, was that the case studies exploring Stockholm Syndrome always involved people who began to experience genuine sympathy for their captors. Some even developed a serious bond with their abuser.

Art was convinced that Petrut and his gang had been calculated and methodical in the way they'd gone about dealing with him. They'd physically assaulted him, threatened his life, drugged him, then isolated him to the point where he actually wanted to interact with them. And now, Petrut continued testing his hostage's attachment to him, allowing Art to toy with a false sense of freedom: passing immigration and customs enforcement alone, walking to the Peace Palace, playing basketball with strangers, and now, eating together in a crowded café.

Petrut had to be trying to develop a bond with Art, so Art couldn't help but wonder if this was a tactic that might cut both ways. "Hey Pete, do you think my father is going to transfer the funds?"

Petrut was just finishing up paying for their meal and drinks. "I don't see any reason to speculate. What happens is what happens, Arthur." He started to stand like he was ready to leave.

"Come on," Art pressed. He wanted to inject as much concern as possible into the tone of his voice. "You're here to help me, right? I need to know what you think. Is this advocate going to be the answer? Are *we* going to make this trade happen?"

Petrut looked over at the door. He seemed to be searching for someone, maybe one of his guys on the street. "Listen..." His voice was low as he turned to look back at Art. "I have my orders to do what needs to be done."

Art waited for the man to add something more.

"But..." Petrut seemed to struggle with the words. "I've also been honest in what I've told you. I want to help you. And I'll do what I can if things don't go the way they must. Understood?"

Art only nodded at this. He didn't want to push this issue an inch further.

Not yet.

As they left through the door to the café, Art couldn't help but think about another lecture his college professor had presented during that Psych 101 class his freshman year. The lecture was closely related to the one given on Stockholm Syndrome, mainly because it involved people who'd been the victims of kidnapping or hostage scenarios.

Lima Syndrome was the focus of the lecture, and Art's professor did a wonderful job explaining how the abusers or captors or *bad actors* could sometimes begin developing a strong attachment to the people they held hostage, the people they were responsible for abusing.

Lima Syndrome case studies demonstrated situations where the captors in hostage scenarios actually developed a positive connection with their hostages. In some situations, the bond was so strong that they wound up releasing the people they'd been holding captive! And it was all because of the strong sense of empathy they felt for their victims.

Art knew the game was afoot when it came to dealing with Petrut and his thugs. But he couldn't help but wonder if these mercenaries realized they were also part of the same game.

"Thanks for dinner," Art said, stepping out onto the sidewalk. He saw now that Jetmir, one of the other kidnappers, waited across the street in a parked car.

"You're welcome, Arthur."

"And thanks for getting me in on the basketball game."

Petrut nodded. "It was a good game."

Art smiled. "Yes, it certainly was. Maybe we'll do it again sometime."

47

The Peach Basket claimed to be a museum dedicated to enriching people's understanding and appreciation for the history of basketball. As Maggie Reynolds came through the front door to the museum, she hoped no one asked her for her honest opinion on the sport itself. It wasn't that she necessarily disliked basketball, she just didn't follow it. But Maggie had a feeling her stance on the sport might sound a little crazy in a city such as Durham, a place that all but worshiped the great game of roundball.

Maggie stepped into the front entryway of the museum. A young guy was tucked behind a tall desk, where he sat staring down at what was probably a cell phone in his lap. As she approached the desk, the young man didn't look up from his scrolling.

Maggie cleared her throat. "Hello," she said. "I'd like one ticket to view the museum."

The young man tore his eyes away from the screen on his phone. "The museum's free on Fridays." His tone wasn't unpleasant, just bored. "Some people do like to make a donation, though, and you'll see a kiosk to do all that when you get inside the next room."

"Okay, great." It seemed the young man's job was done because his eyes started to move back toward the cell phone. "Can I get a map from you?" she asked. "Maybe something that'll help me get to know the place."

He pointed weakly to the edge of his desk. "There's a QR code right here, and it'll take you to the museum's website. The map and other info are all on there. There's really not much to see here."

"That's surprising," she said. "I thought this town was known for being basketball crazy."

"Oh, plenty of people are around here." It wasn't clear whether he was including himself in that bunch. "But most people like to go over to campus and check things out there. The Peach Basket may be called a museum, but this place mostly just gets used by the la-di-dah folks for all their private events and such."

This kid isn't really selling the place that hard, Maggie thought. "Is anyone else here today from the museum's team? Anyone I might be able to trouble for a quick tour?" Maggie hoped this bored college student wasn't about to offer his own services in that department.

"I don't do tours, ma'am." He started reaching for a phone that was attached to his desk. "But I can check and see if our curator is in his office this afternoon."

"Thanks, that would be great."

"I'll try to reach him."

Maggie hoped the young man could manage using the land line.

Maggie stood inside a large, handsome room. It was apparently the feature space inside the museum and Maggie certainly understood why. The large glass cases that ran along the walls were filled with jerseys, photographs, old basketballs, even actual peach baskets. And comfortable looking leather chairs, along with heavy coffee tables, were positioned all throughout the space. An oak bar commanded things from the far wall. The room looked like it belonged in a big-city gentleman's club, not a museum for college basketball.

Maggie turned at the sound of a door opening. An older gentleman, maybe early sixties, stepped into the room and started making his way over to her. He was tall, well over six-foot-six, and he walked with the distinct gait of a former athlete.

"Are you one of the curators here at the museum?" Maggie asked.

"That's right." The curator slowed his pace and smiled. "Our young man at the front desk told me someone was asking about a tour. I take it that's you?"

"I'm not exactly looking for a tour." Maggie figured honesty might be the best approach here. "I was actually hoping to ask you a few questions about—"

"I understand." The man seemed to already know what she was going to say. "You're here to talk about the Mortlake boy, right?"

"Right."

"Okay." He kept his tone very polite. "Are you a reporter?"

"People keep asking me that." Maggie offered a smile. "I'm actually a lawyer, and I'm here on behalf of the Mortlake Family."

"I see," the man said. This was obviously something new. "And your name is?"

"Maggie Reynolds." She took the man's hand. "And thank you very much for speaking with me on this." Maggie hoped her appreciation might help avoid a cold shoulder from the man.

"Not a problem." He pulled a card from the inside pocket of his jacket, then handed it to her. "I'm Gerry Barnes. I've been the head curator here at The Peach Basket for the past ten years or so."

Maggie took the card from the man. It read: *Gerald T. Barnes, Curator for Basketball History, Culture, and Media.*

"We've had a lot more people come through here in the last few weeks," he added. "But I've yet to meet anyone from the young man's family."

Maggie nodded. "From what I've gathered, Mr. Barnes, there aren't very many Mortlakes left to talk to."

"That's a shame." Gerry at least seemed willing to talk. "Well, what can I do for you?"

Gerry Barnes started out by telling Maggie all he knew about the night Art went missing from The Peach Basket.

"I was out of the country when it all happened," he explained. "My son and grandkids live down in Australia, so I was actually over there for the Christmas holidays, visiting with his family."

Maggie nodded to show she was listening.

"And I didn't get back in town until New Year's Day, so I missed all the investigators coming through here, interviewing people and checking our security camera footage. I had a phone call before Christmas with a guy who told me he was with the FBI, but I didn't know anything really. I've learned most things second-hand from the employees who were here working the party."

"What'd they tell you about that night?" Maggie asked. "That is if you don't mind sharing it with me."

"We're a small museum, okay? And a lot of our funding comes from the private events we book out each year. We get corporate gigs, weddings, a college formal from time to time, and lots of community type events. But the night young Mortlake went missing was a different kind of event around here. It was a special night, mostly due to the fact that it involved a basketball player who has become a star at Duke."

"Tom Palomino."

"That's right," Gerry confirmed. "He's creeping up on the list of all-time greats around here, so it was kind of a big deal to have him use the museum for his engagement party."

Strangely enough, Maggie could tell the man didn't sound too enthused about the event. "Were you excited about having the party here?"

Gerry shrugged. "Look, I retired from the Smithsonian and my wife took a great position on campus with the English Department. I'm more like a part-time curator here, and I make it a point to have zero involvement in anything to do with the party planning."

"I understand."

"But I knew of the Mortlake boy." Gerry had more emotion in his voice now. "It actually made me sad to hear it was him who went missing. Not that you want any young person to go..." He didn't finish the sentence.

"How did you know him?"

"Art Mortlake was kind of like a flash-in-the-pan sensation around here. He was undersized, underequipped, yet he still found a way to make it onto a roster that touts some of the best college basketball players in the country."

"I take it there's more to that story."

"Are you a cynic, Maggie?" Gerry winked.

"I'm a lawyer."

He smiled. "Well, I guess there probably is more to his story. A lot of people think the Mortlake boy paid for his way onto that team, but he sure as hell found a way to get onto that basketball court when they gave him the chance. He was a pure shooter, no question about it. And he played like a hybrid of Curry and Stockton, know what I'm saying?"

"I think so." Although Maggie wasn't exactly sure what the curator meant by this. "But he was suspended from the team, right?"

"Yep. They kicked him off the team in twenty twenty-two. They probably should've booted him out of the school, too, but the kid found a way to stay in there. Which was good, because I think we all deserve a second chance, even after doing something stupid."

Maggie considered those words. It seemed everyone she spoke to always had something genuine to say about Art Mortlake. It was never anything vague, never anything lukewarm. Everyone seemed like they wanted to defend him, which only made *her* want to believe in him more.

"Have you talked to the investigators at all since you came back from visiting your son in Australia?"

"Nope, not once." Gerry then lowered his voice and leaned a little closer. "But I might have something interesting for you to look at..."

Maggie followed the curator through a heavy door, then down a hallway lined with offices. When they reached what appeared to be the curator's office, the man turned and told her to watch her step when she came inside.

"Have a seat over there," Gerry said, pointing to the only open chair in the room. It was actually a seat behind the desk. "Go ahead, don't be shy."

Maggie carefully stepped her way around the stacks of files and folders that littered the floor. "You sure?" she asked.

"Yeah, yeah, go on." Gerry fished a laptop out of a briefcase then placed it on the desk. He turned the screen so that Maggie could see it from where she was seated. "I need you to know something ahead of time, okay? I need you to know that I never expected to have this kind of thing happen in my office."

Maggie was confused by the man's disclaimer. "What happened in here?"

Gerry leaned over and pulled up a video on his laptop. Maggie could tell the still image at the beginning of the video was just a dark shot of the office she was seated in now.

She hoped this wasn't about to get weird. "What's this I'm about to watch, Gerry?"

"Look, I have a camera in my office," he began. "It's only to make sure no one comes in here while I'm away." He then made a sweeping motion with his hand as he referenced the stacks of files and folders. "As you can tell, my approach to organization is rather unorthodox, but *all* of my material is in this room. I'm researching the history of basketball during the Sixties—"

Maggie stopped him. "What's on the video, Gerry?"

"It's young Mortlake."

The curator walked around to stand behind Maggie. The video was playing, and Maggie could soon see more on the screen when Art entered the frame. The camera was positioned high in one corner of the room, so it provided a full view of everything that happened in the office.

Maggie searched for a volume key on the laptop.

"Unfortunately, there's no audio," Gerry said. "I wish there was."

"That's okay." Maggie still couldn't believe what she was seeing. "This is incredible."

The video clearly showed Art seated at the desk, snorting what was likely cocaine, and talking excitedly with someone on his cell phone. Art blew at least three rails of coke throughout the course of his phone call, then stood up from the office chair and smashed his cell phone on the floor.

"Did investigators not find a cell phone in here?" Maggie didn't take her eyes from the screen as she asked this.

"Nope. I'm not even sure how they missed the camera."

Maggie chose not to worry about that major oversight right now. The video was still running, and another person had just entered the frame. She was a person who Maggie immediately recognized as Zoe Mitchell.

"That's—"

"I know who it is," Gerry said this as he stepped away from behind Maggie. "I've already seen the video once, and I'm not comfortable rewatching it."

Maggie kept her eyes on the screen as Zoe went over to Art, wrapped her arms around his waist. The video showed everything, beginning to end. Although Maggie wasn't an expert in body language, she was willing to bet this wasn't a first-time thing for these two on the screen. They made love with a rhythm, a familiarity with one another, the kind that could only be achieved through practice.

"Have you showed this to anyone else?" Maggie asked.

"I just found it yesterday, Maggie. And I'm still not sure what to do with it."

"Law enforcement needs to see it, Gerry."

He nodded, slowly. The man had to know this would be a blow to the Duke basketball star's reputation. "I figured the investigators would need to review it."

"But I need you to do me a favor, if you can."

"What is it?"

"I need you to give me the weekend before you turn it in, okay?"

Gerry looked confused.

Maggie decided to press him. "Can you do that, please?"

"I guess it's just two more days," he eventually replied. "Do you want a copy for the family?"

"Give me two."

48

Maggie's head was still spinning when she got back to her car. She needed a moment to think, but there wasn't much time for that. Zoe Mitchell would be sending a message to her soon, letting Maggie know that Tom Palomino had returned home from basketball practice.

Did Tom know that his fiancée had been running around behind his back? Certainly not, right? But it was definitely motive, and it was also the kind of thing that investigators *had* to know about. Although Maggie didn't want to prevent law enforcement from getting the evidence, she also didn't want young Tom to lawyer up. She needed to get to him before that sexy video made the rounds, before things hit the fan.

Maggie had the video saved on two separate flash drives. She put one in her pocket, the other in the car's glove compartment.

Maggie pulled out her cell phone to make sure she'd not missed a call or text. When she glanced at the screen, she realized there were several missed calls from the number that Clive Mortlake had provided her with.

Maggie quickly called the number back.

"Hello?" answered Declan Tao.

"This is Maggie. I saw I missed a few calls from Clive."

"This isn't Mr. Mortlake's phone number. It's mine. Mr. Mortlake rarely used a mobile phone for personal calls."

Maggie jumped straight to being frustrated with Clive Mortlake. This was yet another aspect of their arrangement that he'd not communicated clearly. In her annoyance, she missed the past tense that Declan used when referring to his boss.

"Okay, Declan. Then it's you who called me. What's up?"

"It's Mr. Mortlake..." Declan seemed to stop at the edge of whatever words he was struggling to get out.

"Right," Maggie said. "I'm sure he wants to check on things. But I'm talking to people, okay? I've been working on things all day. What can I do for him?"

"He's gone, Maggie."

It took a moment for the words to register, then Maggie remembered the news Frank King had let slip to her, the news about Clive's cancer diagnosis. "Oh, Declan, that's awful. I'm so, so sorry."

The line remained silent on the other end.

Maggie continued. "Truth be told, I didn't even know he was sick. He never even mentioned anything about his health being—"

"I don't know what you're talking about, ma'am." Declan sounded stern. "I called earlier to let you know the authorities found Mr. Mortlake's plane some forty miles east of Asheville, in Pisgah National Forest."

Maggie was confused. "He dropped me off yesterday evening at a place just outside Durham. He had a car waiting for me on the banks of Falls Lake. Are you telling me he never made it back home after that?"

"I'm sorry, ma'am." Declan cleared his throat. "Mr. Mortlake never made it out of his plane last night."

Maggie wanted to get all the details about the plane crash, but she had another incoming call. She pulled the cell phone away from her ear, glanced at the screen.

The call was from Zoe Mitchell.

"Can I call you right back, Declan?"

There was a pause. The *beep!* sound notifying Maggie of the incoming call went again. "That'll be fine, ma'am. Call me at this number."

"Thanks," Maggie said. "And again, I'm sorry for your loss."

"I'm sorry too."

Maggie switched over to take the call from Zoe.

49

When Maggie pulled back up to the Palomino house, she noticed there was a new vehicle parked in the driveway. It was a shiny Dodge crew cab, one with knobby tires and plenty of chrome. Maggie knew that college athletes could profit from their personal brand (i.e. through name, image, and likeness, or *NIL*), but things weren't like this for every university kid who was on an athletic scholarship. Most weren't parking their new truck at a place in the suburbs, playing house already with their fiancée. Still, this appeared to be the way Tom Palomino wanted to spend his money, even if it did seem strange when compared to other student-athletes who played the NIL game.

But would the Palomino family really jeopardize Tom's earning potential as an NBA star? Maggie considered this while she walked from her car to the front door of the home. And even if the family of Long Island mafiosos chose to do just that, why risk putting Tom's name in the ransom note?

None of it made sense.

The front door to the house opened before Maggie reached the first step on the porch. It wasn't Zoe Mitchell who stood in the open doorway, though, nor was it the basketball star who supposedly lived in the house.

The man in the doorway was much too old to be in college, and any years he might've enjoyed as an athlete were far, far behind him now.

Maggie slowed as she took the few steps onto the front porch. "Hello," she said, making no effort to hide the suspicion in her voice. "I'm looking for Zoe. Is she in?"

"Hi there," said the man in the doorway. He offered a wide smile, one that revealed his pearly white veneers. "I'm Bedford Mitchell, Zoe's father."

Maggie accepted a handshake from the man. "Maggie Reynolds."

"Do you want to come in?" he asked.

Maggie paused for a moment, her mind working quickly to try and predict what waited for her inside. Back in Georgia, Bedford Mitchell was in the midst of a race for governor. Maggie was familiar with his political ads and had a basic understanding of his platform, but she hadn't cared to find out much more about the man himself. Bedford Mitchell's career, up to that point, had never strayed beyond the confines of his ministry and church—but Pastor Mitchell had himself a *big* church.

"Sure," Maggie finally said as she stepped inside the house. "Will you let Zoe know I'm here?"

Zoe chose the kitchen table for their second meeting together. Maggie took one end of the table. Pastor Mitchell took the other. And Zoe selected a chair that stuck her right in the middle of it all.

"Where's Tom?" Maggie asked.

"He's still at practice." It was Pastor Mitchell who answered for his daughter. "My future son-in-law is a hard charger, and he's one heck of a basketball player. God has given him a gift, but the boy still does his part by putting the hours in at the gym."

Maggie kept her gaze on Zoe.

"Have you ever seen him play?" the pastor asked. "This is his last season here at Duke."

"I'm not much of a basketball fan."

"Well, I suggest you—"

Maggie stopped the man. "Pastor Mitchell, I need to speak with your daughter about a sensitive matter. Would you mind giving us a moment together?"

From the other end of the table, the rotund pastor offered another smile. "Sweetie..." These patronizing words were being directed at his daughter. "I can step out if you'd like. I'm also happy to stay right here and help y'all discuss this whole mess."

Zoe sighed. "He can stay, Maggie."

Maggie should have known better than to fall for Zoe's little routine in their first meeting. The young woman obviously wasn't some doe in the woods. She needed to run her questions about Art's kidnapping by someone, and it seemed her father had been high on her list. And Maggie figured the man must've taken his daughter's concerns seriously, must've dropped everything and jumped on his private jet—the one funded by the congregants of his Atlanta-based megachurch.

"When will Tom be back, Zoe?"

"I'm not sure," she said. "The team has a road game against SMU tomorrow, so Tom will fly out for Dallas tonight. I'm sure he'll come by here before that."

The mention of flying made Maggie think of Clive Mortlake, made her think about his awful fate. She could only hope something similar wasn't going to happen to Art now that his father was no longer in the picture. Maggie had decided during her drive over to the house that she had to at least try and help Art. It was her entire focus now, and she wasn't even worried about getting paid for her work anymore.

Maggie leaned forward and placed her elbows on the table. "I told you earlier, Zoe, it's important I speak with him today."

Zoe shook her head. "Well, I'm not sure I'm comfortable with that."

"I'm not sure I'm comfortable with it either," the pastor added. "And I don't see what that boy can tell you that the police don't already know about the murder."

"It may not be a murder, Pastor Mitchell."

"And you have proof of this?"

Maggie could tell this wasn't going to get very far. "With all due respect, sir, I don't need any proof to speak with Tom about his friend's disappearance. And I don't appreciate you getting in the way of me helping Art's family get more information—"

"I don't care what you appreciate or don't appreciate, *young lady*." The pastor folded his arms across his chest, testing the buttons on his dress shirt. "This is my daughter right here, and she doesn't need to be mixed up in some cockamamie scheme, especially not one cooked up by a disbarred lawyer."

Maggie nodded at this. It appeared Zoe and her father had also been doing some research while she was away. "I wasn't disbarred."

He waved a hand as if he were dismissing a fact that didn't suit his narrative. "I don't want to hear it, Maggie Reynolds. Crooked is crooked, and I know everything there is to know about you. That trial you botched against our state's *fine* senator was a travesty, and I wish they'd take all you lawyers who bring politically motivated actions out to the woods and—"

"Daddy!" Zoe hissed. "I asked you to come and listen. I didn't invite you over so that you could speak for me."

"Sweetie, I just want to help—"

"No!" Zoe yelled. "Stop helping."

A silence filled the room for a moment.

"Now, I think you should leave." Zoe started to stand from her chair. "Both of you."

Maggie placed a flash drive on the table. "I'll leave after we take a look at something together."

"What's that?" asked the pastor.

"I swear to God, Daddy—" Zoe looked like she wanted to scream. "If you say another word, I'll tell Momma everything I know about you. *Everything.*"

The pastor didn't seem to like this threat from his daughter, but he also didn't open his mouth again.

"I need a laptop, Zoe." Maggie tapped the flash drive against the surface on the table. "Do you have one?"

Zoe stood and walked out of the room. When she returned, she held a black laptop in her hand. "Here," she said, handing the computer over to Maggie. "Let's look at whatever you have, then I want you to leave."

"Do you want your father to watch this with us?" Maggie asked. "Like I mentioned earlier, this is a sensitive matter."

Zoe rolled her eyes. "I don't even know what it is that—"

"It's a video, Zoe." Maggie couldn't bring herself to come right out and say it in front of the young woman's father. "It's from the night of your engagement party."

"Okay?"

"It's one that I don't think you would want anyone else to watch..."

"I don't know what you think you have." Zoe folded her arms across her chest in a way that almost mimicked the look of her father. "But I expect you to show it to me or leave."

This attitude made things easier for Maggie. "Gladly."

The video started from the beginning, and Maggie planned on letting it play all the way through to the end. It was incredibly awkward watching the events in that office unfold, especially while the young woman sat a matter of feet from her father.

"I won't watch this..." Pastor Mitchell had muttered this once it became clear from the video that Art Mortlake was removing his daughter's panties. "I'll be in the other room."

But to Zoe's credit, she just sat there in silence, watching the video of her and Art together. The desk shook, papers and folders fell to the floor, and Zoe's hands could be seen gripping Art's back all the way to the end. It was Maggie's second time watching the video through, but the experience didn't feel any less voyeuristic.

"Who else knows about this video?" Zoe asked, calmly closing the screen on the laptop.

"It's a short list right now."

Zoe nodded. "But that list is only going to grow, right?"

"Right."

Zoe sighed. "I know what you're thinking, Maggie."

"I'm not here to shame you." Maggie hoped the young woman recognized this was true. "And I didn't expect to find this when I went to visit the museum. I just stopped by there because it was the last place anyone reported seeing Art."

"And now you know I'm the last person who saw him. Art told me he was leaving, and I didn't even try and stop him. I didn't ask him where he was going. It's awful, right?"

"Beating yourself up won't help."

"And Tom doesn't know, okay?" She seemed adamant. "He can't know."

Maggie nodded.

"Because if he does find out, then he's going to freak out. And it's going to be over, all of it."

"I just need to speak with Tom."

Zoe pulled the thumb drive from the side of the laptop. She gripped it tight in her hand. "What happens with this?"

"I'm not sure. But if Tom doesn't know about it, then he eventually will. The man who found the video will turn it into law enforcement, and the investigators will no doubt want to question Tom about the cheating. They'll want to question you about the inconsistencies in your official statement."

Zoe huffed. "That's so typical."

"What is?" Maggie asked.

"He's the one who has cheated on me so many times, and I mean *so* many times. But of course, I'm the one who'll get dragged through the muck for this. I'm the one who'll get slut shamed."

Maggie didn't know what to say.

"Tom doesn't know, though. He wouldn't be able to keep something like this from me. And although he doesn't show it to very many people, Tom does have a temper."

Maggie had dealt with plenty of clients over the years who were known to be hotheads. Most of them were men, too. There were the guys who liked to brawl, liked to mix it up when they got a few drinks in their system. But those clients weren't usually the ones she worried about. No, the men who always gave her pause were the ones who acted polite, who *appeared* under control. Those were the people who could be cruel.

"But what if Tom did know?" Maggie asked. "What would he do to Art?"

"Oh, he'd want to kill him, Maggie." Zoe glanced down at her cell phone as she said this. The screen was lit up bright from a notification. "He might even think about having…" The words trailed off.

Maggie watched as Zoe picked her phone up. Her fingers worked quickly over the screen as they typed a message of some kind.

"Everything okay?" Maggie asked.

"Yeah," Zoe said. "Tom just said he'll be home in about fifteen minutes."

"Good." Maggie fixed her gaze on Zoe. "I'll speak with Tom in here, but I want your dad out of the house. Understood?"

Zoe nodded, then held out the thumb drive. "Are you going to mention any of this to Tom?"

"He won't hear it from me." Maggie couldn't guarantee Tom wouldn't hear about the racy video from someone else. "You have my word, Zoe."

50

Even in athletic gear, Tom Palomino looked like he was cover-ready. The do-it-all college basketball star was tall, wide-shouldered, and far too good looking for a young man with his kind of athletic talent. The blend of Portuguese and Italian heritage passed down from his parents had gifted him with dark eyes, dark hair, and strong olive features. It was the kind of look that would make him an advertiser's dream when he reached the NBA.

But Maggie knew that appearances weren't everything. A good reputation *still* mattered, even for the guys who seemed to have it all. And for a young man like Tom Palomino, a player who was just starting in on his professional basketball career, any threat to his spotless reputation could feel like the end of the world. At least, that's what Maggie was hoping for.

"What's all this?" Tom asked when he stepped into the kitchen.

Zoe stood from the table to greet her fiancé. "This is Maggie Reynolds," she said, the cheeriness back in her voice. "She came by earlier to talk about Art."

Tom placed his gym bag on a countertop, then stepped closer to Zoe for a kiss. "Has something happened?" His voice sounded excited, expectant. "Did they find him?"

Maggie decided to answer for Zoe. "We're still working on it."

Tom made his way over to the kitchen table, where he offered a handshake for Maggie. "I'm Tom," he said. "I didn't know you were stopping by. I would've come by the house earlier had I known you were here."

"No worries." Maggie smiled. "This was an unannounced visit."

"Cool." Tom looked comfortable as he took a seat at the table. "So, what's going on with Art's case? Anything new?"

Maggie paused. "I guess there are a few new things we could talk about."

Zoe quickly inserted herself. "Maggie here believes that Art could still be alive. I guess Art's father hired her to look into the disappearance—"

"Wait—" Tom put a hand up. "You really think he's alive?"

Maggie nodded. "I do."

Tom pumped his fist. "Finally!" he said. "I've been meeting with all these depressing investigators who keep telling me not to get my hopes up. But I told them to quit with all the blah, blah, blah, and to just get back to working on finding my friend. I guess sometimes we just need to hire people who work outside of the system, right?"

"What do you mean?" Maggie asked.

Tom looked a little confused. "I mean, you're a private dick, right? Isn't that what you do?"

"*No*, not exactly."

Maggie decided just to stick with the direct approach. The strategy lacked any real creativity to it, but sometimes a person just needed to keep hammering away until something finally broke loose.

"I'm a lawyer, Tom." Maggie hoped her words didn't cause the young man to clam up. "And I'm here because of a ransom note, one that Art's father received."

Tom's eyes widened. "Really?" he gasped. "When?"

Maggie couldn't tell if the young ball player was performing for her. If he was, it certainly felt like bad acting. "The ransom note arrived not long before the New Year," she replied. "Maybe five, six days ago."

Tom chose the obvious question next. It was the one that everyone naturally wanted to ask, yet most avoided. "How much money did they ask for?"

Maggie started to answer. "Well—"

"You know what, it doesn't matter." Tom waved a hand. "Art's family has more money than God, just don't tell Zoe's father I said that." He winked as he kept on moving the conversation. "How's Art's father taking things? I've only met old Clive twice. He's kind of a prick, if you ask me, but I remember he was the only family Art really had left."

She only nodded at this. Would news about the plane crash add an unnecessary wrinkle into the mix? Probably. "Did you ever meet his mother?" Maggie asked.

"Nope," Tom said with a shake of the head. "Art's mom died in a car wreck when he was a kid. Happened somewhere in North Georgia, not far from where the family keeps a mountain house. Some guy was coming home from a day of fishing, probably drunk, *if you ask me*, and that asshole ran Art's mom right off the road."

Although Maggie had already done some digging into Art's past, she could tell that Tom was the kind of young man who liked to hear himself talk. She decided to let him do just that.

"I remember the guy's last name was McRae," Tom added. "They convicted him of some misdemeanor offense, something that put him away for like a year, but the guy skated on the serious stuff."

Maggie layered in a compliment. "You have a good memory, Tom."

He smiled. "Well, that wreck happened a long time ago, but I kind of learned about it because of Art's more, *well*, recent history." Tom obviously wasn't a poker player because his eyes went to his fiancée as he said this. "But all that's way in the past. I'm not trying to dredge up the—"

"Go ahead, *Tommy*." It was Zoe who said this. "Tell her about all that. It might help."

———

Maggie could tell that Tom Palomino was a *saver*. He had a filing cabinet in his kitchen, one filled with newspaper articles, magazines, and promotional photos that looked to go back well before Tom's college years.

"Here," Tom said. He handed Maggie a newspaper clipping. "This happened a few years ago."

It was a front-page article from the *Tallahassee Democrat,* and it showed a picture of Art Mortlake in a basketball uniform. He was leaping over a barrier of some kind, heading right into a seating area full of fans. The other people in the photo all had varying expressions of shock and horror.

"That McRae guy I mentioned earlier," Tom began. "Well, Art whooped his ass during a game our freshman year." Tom almost sounded proud of his friend. "It probably took seven grown men to pull Art out of the first few rows of seating. There was blood everywhere, people screaming and running for the exits, yet Art gave zero fucks. He had one thing on his mind that night, and it was beating that George McRae dude senseless."

Maggie eyed the date on the article—*January 18, 2022*. "I take it this was Art's last game?"

"Yep."

"How the hell did he avoid going to jail himself after this? Sounds like what he did would've been a few felonies down in Florida."

Tom cut his eyes again toward Zoe.

What happened?" Maggie prodded.

Zoe chimed in again. "Go ahead," she said, sweetly nudging him along. "Anything you tell her might help get Art home."

51

Tom Palomino didn't come out and say what his family did to earn a living. He didn't need to. Besides, the modern mob, even at a more regional level, is far less glamorous than television and movies make it out to be. But violence hasn't completely removed itself from the dealings of organized crime, there's just less of it making the news nowadays.

Maggie decided to rephrase her question a little bit. "Do you remember if they ever charged Art after the fight in Tallahassee?"

"They hit him with a few felonies." Tom looked over at Zoe for confirmation. "There were at least three, right?"

Zoe only nodded.

"So, what happened?" Maggie asked.

"Look, I want to make it clear that I wasn't directly involved in any of it, okay?"

"We're just talking, Tom."

Tom didn't seem completely satisfied with this approach.

"Jesus, Tommy, just talk to her about what happened." Zoe reached over and grabbed his hand. "What's it matter anyway? She used to be some kind of criminal defense lawyer, so it's not like she's investigating you. She's helping the family get to Art."

"That true?" Tom asked, turning his eyes to Maggie.

Mostly true, Maggie thought. "She's right, Tom."

Tom explained how his father, Luca Palomino, sent a few guys down to South Georgia just to *talk* with the two men Art had assaulted during the Duke vs. FSU game. The Palomino Family's organization was mostly done with the past ways of doing business, or so he said, but there were still a few men on the Palomino payroll who understood how things used to be done.

"You said McRae and the other man lived in the southern half of Georgia?"

Tom nodded. "Yeah."

"Do you remember where?"

"No, not really. Like I said, I wasn't directly involved. All I remember is they had to go all the way over to the southwestern corner of the state, a place right on the Alabama line."

"What'd they do when they got there?"

Tom shrugged. "You need me to spell it out for you?"

"I'd like some kind of idea."

"They took a long car ride over to Sticksville, Georgia, and then they tuned McRae and his buddy up."

"And McRae waived prosecution after that?"

"Right," Tom replied. "A victim who refuses to testify is a *smart* witness."

Maggie could see that the family roots still ran deep in this poster boy for college sports. Still, she wondered if her next question was going to come across the wrong way. She needed to know the answer, though, and she hoped Zoe might step in to help her seal the deal. The young woman had proved to be quite the wingman throughout the course of their short conversation.

"Do you know if Art's father ever paid them anything?"

"The McRae guy? I don't think so."

"What about the men your family sent to—" Maggie considered what word might work best here.

Tom finished the sentence for her. "You mean the guys who were sent to fix the situation for Art?"

Maggie nodded. "Were they paid?"

"Not by a Mortlake."

Maggie kept tiptoeing forward with her questions. "Then, that thing your family did for Art, it was done as a favor?"

Tom smiled. It was brief, but there was something cruel that flashed in that expression of his. "I'm not sure I like what you're implying."

"I'm not implying anything—"

"No, I think you are." Tom began to stand from the kitchen table. "I'd say you're suggesting my family has something to do with this whole kidnapping scenario you've dreamt up."

"I assure you—"

Tom interrupted her again. "No, I'm pretty sure I've heard enough."

Zoe also stood from the table. "Tommy, I think you have the wrong idea—"

Tom turned to her. "Are you telling me what to think right now?" That same smile flashed again. "Is that what this is?"

Maggie only had one more card to play with Tom. "Your name was specifically mentioned in the ransom note." Maggie's words interrupted the uncomfortable staring match that was taking place between the two recently engaged lovebirds. "I wouldn't have come here if it weren't for your name—"

"Let me see the note," Tom said, turning to look down at Maggie. "Prove it."

"I don't have the ransom note on me."

"Then we don't have anything more to talk about."

"Call your father," Maggie shot back. "Ask him about it."

"Some criminal defense lawyer you are," Tom scoffed. "You expect me just to call my dad up and ask whether we're involved in a kidnapping?"

"Don't use those words."

Tom laughed. "Thanks for the free advice. Now, I need you to leave."

"Tell him I stopped by," Maggie pressed. "Just mention that Maggie Reynolds came to see you about—"

"Leave, please." Tom was walking over to where his gym bag still lay on the counter. "If not, I'll call the police."

Maggie turned from Tom to look at Zoe. She was about to say something to the young woman, to plead for just a little more assistance, but she realized that Zoe was already in the process of doing so. She had her cell phone pressed to one ear.

"Hey Luca, how are you?" Zoe's voice sounded sweet as she greeted the person on the other end of the phone. "I'm doing okay, you know, just over seeing Tom right now before he heads off for Dallas tonight. Big game, right?"

Tom seemed to realize now that Zoe was speaking with his father. "What the hell, Zoe?" he hissed. "Hang up the phone now—"

"Look, I wanted to ask you quickly about someone who stopped by to see Tom tonight."

Maggie couldn't help but smile.

"Her name's Maggie Reynolds. She's working on trying to help Clive Mortlake find his son, Art, and thought you might be able to help."

Tom cursed under his breath, then stormed out of the kitchen.

52

Maggie Reynolds sat at the airport, waiting on a flight that would carry her down to Atlanta. She needed to get back to the mountain house in North Georgia, where she'd left her Saab 900 parked. Maggie was doing her best to reach Declan Tao before she travelled all the way back there to retrieve her vehicle. She didn't want to get to the gated compound and not be able to get inside. She also *really* wanted to speak with Declan about where things were in the search for Art Mortlake.

Maggie pulled her cell phone away from her ear, the seventh call to Declan having just gone unanswered. "What the hell..." she muttered, growing more and more frustrated as the hours passed. She wanted to update the security specialist on her meetings from that day, especially the one involving Tom Palomino. She also wanted to ask him about next steps. Declan remained unavailable, though, and Maggie had a bad feeling about the bodyguard's sudden radio silence.

What do I tell Luca Palomino if he calls? Maggie asked herself. Who do I get the two million from when someone wants to make a deal? And did the kidnappers' ransom demand even matter at this point? The Mortlake money had to be going to Art, the hostage. He was the family's only surviving heir...

Although Maggie had made a quick exit from Tom Palomino's house earlier that evening, she'd at least left with a gift from Zoe Mitchell. The young woman, much to her fiancé's chagrin, had shared all of Maggie's contact details with the head of the Palomino Family. And Maggie had been assured that Luca would call her when he had something to say about Art Mortlake.

Maggie hoped that call would happen soon.

While Maggie waited at the gate for her upcoming flight, she sipped her coffee and scrolled news articles on her cell phone. She couldn't find a single article about Clive Mortlake's death. Several recent news stories made mention of a small-plane crash that took place the night before in Pisgah National Forest, but none of the articles included names or detailed information about who may have perished in the crash. North Carolina authorities were unwilling to comment on the number of persons involved in the small-plane accident. The scant findings that'd been released weren't good, though, and preliminary reports already suggested there were no crash survivors to be expected.

Maggie called Declan again.

Nothing.

The gate attendant made the first call for boarding, so Maggie started collecting the few things she'd brought with her. As she went to stuff her cell phone into her bag, the screen on the device lit up.

It was a call from Charlotte Acker back at Maggie's law firm in Blake County.

"*Hey!*" Maggie said as she answered. "I hope this isn't you calling to tell me the law firm is on fire."

"I'm doing my best to keep the flames at bay," laughed Charlotte. "But the clients here are a little crazy. Where'd you find these people?"

"The exact same place I found you!" Maggie smiled into the phone. "And those are *your* clients right now, so don't be bad mouthing them that way."

"Yeah, yeah..."

The gate attendant made her second boarding call while Maggie and

Charlotte covered the usual pleasantries. All seemed to be going fine back in Blakeston.

"Where are you?" Charlotte soon asked.

"I'm in the Raleigh-Durham Airport right now."

"North Carolina?"

"Uh-huh."

"What're you doing up there? I thought you were supposed to be relaxing in the North Georgia mountains..."

Maggie sighed. "It's a long story that I'll need to tell you about later."

"Then I'll be quick," Charlotte said. "I sent a few questions over by email and I need you to take a look at them for me. They're all things that have to do with our open cases, stuff I was unsure about."

"Of course, Charlotte." Although it was almost nine o'clock at night, Maggie thought the young lawyer sounded good. Maybe covering things for Maggie at the law firm wasn't running Charlotte into the ground. "I'll take a look at them while I'm on the plane."

"Awesome." Charlotte paused. "There's also some snail mail back at the office for you. I think the staff has been doing a good job going through the mundane, everyday stuff, but there's a few things marked *Private* and *Confidential*."

A lot of the mail Maggie received from inmates came marked that way. She wasn't in a rush to read any of it. "If they have a return address at one of the prisons, then just set it aside for me—"

The gate attendant made her third boarding call.

"It sounds like you need to go," Charlotte said. "I'll ask the team to put your mail from the inmates and Mr. Mortlake on your desk."

"Wait—" Maggie almost dropped the phone. "Mr. Mortlake? You mean Clive Mortlake, right?"

"Yep."

Maggie was curious. "When exactly did that arrive in the mail?"

"I'm not sure, but I think it was in today's mail. It has *FOR MAGGIE REYNOLDS' EYES ONLY* written on the outside of it." Charlotte chuckled at the dramatic wording. "I always like when the clients do that."

Maggie couldn't help but wonder when the envelope had been mailed. Her first meeting with Clive Mortlake had only been yesterday, and it was

New Year's Day the day before that. It was possible he overnighted something to her office after their breakfast meeting together, but that didn't make a lot of sense. Why mail something to her when Clive could've just hand-delivered it that very same day?

"Charlotte, I may need you to open that envelope for me..." Maggie tried to keep her voice even. "Did you say it's back at the office right now?"

Charlotte seemed to recognize the subtle change in Maggie's tone. "Yeah, it's on your desk, I think. Do I need to go back to the office tonight?"

"No, it's okay." Although Maggie did want the envelope opened first thing tomorrow. "You can just take a peek at it tomorrow, whenever you get there."

Charlotte promised she would open the envelope tomorrow morning, then she signed off from their call.

The flight to Atlanta must not have been very full because the gate attendant looked straight at Maggie when she made her *fourth* and *final* boarding call.

"I'm coming, sorry!" Maggie exclaimed as she started for the gate attendant's desk. The metal door behind it sat open to the jetway.

"Boarding pass?" the woman asked.

Maggie found the digital boarding pass on her cell phone, scanned it, and carried on toward the corridor that would lead her to the airplane. As Maggie hustled away, she overheard the woman at the gate speaking into her walkie-talkie. Maggie had in fact been the last person to board the flight.

When she reached the other end of the jetway, Maggie felt her cell phone start buzzing again. Hopefully it's Declan, she thought, pulling the phone from an outside pocket on her jacket. Maggie certainly wasn't planning to drive all the way to Ellijay before hearing from him.

Maggie checked the screen. The incoming call was from a blocked number. Still, she decided to answer it. "Hello?"

"Is this Maggie Reynolds?" asked a deep voice from the other end of the line. The accent sounded thick, and it was clear that English wasn't the caller's first language.

Maggie was about to end the call, then decided it was best to check and make sure this wasn't someone on Declan's security team. "This is Maggie. Who's this?" she asked.

The flight attendant who waited at the main door to the aircraft welcomed Maggie as she stepped onto the plane. Maggie smiled at the middle-aged man, her way of trying to silently communicate that she wasn't meaning to be rude.

"My name is Petrut Noica," replied the man on the other end of the line. "Is now a good time to speak with you about Arthur Mortlake?"

Maggie stopped. She was already halfway down the center aisle that ran the length of the aircraft. The heads of a dozen or so people could be seen ahead of her, and everyone was already seated and ready to leave.

"No—" Maggie paused. "I mean, yes, I can talk for a moment." Maggie turned and looked toward a flight attendant who was following her up the aisle. The young woman was checking the overhead compartments as she welcomed the other passengers who were already on board. "How long do we have until takeoff?" Maggie asked the attendant.

"The pilot is ready to push." The young woman's smile didn't do a great job hiding the fatigue in her face. "We'll be ready to go once all passengers are seated."

Maggie turned her attention back to the voice on the phone. "I'm on a plane, but I'll be landing in roughly ninety minutes. I'll be able to speak more then."

"I'll call back in two hours."

The call went dead.

53

When Art Mortlake woke for breakfast, he found all four of his kidnappers waiting for him in the kitchen. They were seated together around the room's only table, drinking coffee and discussing their plans for the day. The men switched from French to English when their hostage joined them in the room.

"Morning, boys," Art said as he made his way over to where the coffee and bread waited. "How's it hanging?"

"Good morning," Petrut offered. "How'd you sleep?"

Art found a mug beside the kitchen sink, then poured himself a cup from a glass coffee press. He'd never considered himself a morning coffee man, but the European brew was slowly bringing him around to the habit. "I slept as well as any man can who's locked in a cage. But thanks for asking, Pete."

"This is hardly a cage," Petrut replied. The man's eyes and groggy tone made him seem a little off. "But I don't have time to argue with you. We have other things to discuss this morning."

"You look like crap," Art added. He sipped from his warm coffee mug as he leaned against the kitchen counter. "You and the boys go out partying while I was asleep last night? Kind of shitty for you not to invite me along."

Petrut held Art's gaze for a long moment, and Art could tell the man had a different energy to him this morning. Something had to be up. "There've been some new developments," Petrut said. "And these changes affect our plans going forward."

Art could feel an uneasiness creeping into the room. "What's changed?" he asked. "Am I going home?"

"I think you should sit," Petrut replied. He pointed to the only open chair at the kitchen table. "It would be best."

"*No*, I'm fine right here."

Petrut lifted a hand to his forehead, began massaging the creases on it. "Arthur, please—"

"Just get on with it, Pete." Art didn't need the caffeine to wake up his senses. The eyes of the four men and the awkwardness in the room had his heartrate up and mind fully alert. "Tell me what's changed."

Petrut took a deep breath, then said, "Your father is dead."

Art considered the big man's face. The forty-something mercenary had the hardened features of a person who understood the tough things in life, and although death comes to us all, it still comes as a surprise to most. "How?" Art asked, knowing it had to be the cancer. "When?"

"He died in a plane crash." Petrut nodded to one of the men at the table. He produced a tablet, then handed it over to Art. "The reports believe his airplane went down on the night of January 2nd, somewhere over the US state you call North Carolina."

Art stared down at the news article that'd been left open on the screen of the device. The photo that accompanied the article was one that showed a burned-out, yellow airplane, one that barely resembled his father's single-engine floatplane. What the hell was the man even thinking? Art asked himself. The cancer meds probably made him sick as a dog at times, and they had to affect his concentration, his stamina. Flying was one of his father's favorite hobbies, but why take the risk?

Art placed the tablet on the counter beside him. "That's Clive Mortlake for you," Art muttered, shaking his head. "Selfish all the way to the end."

Petrut obviously had business to attend to, so he offered his condolences, then shifted their conversation toward more pressing matters.

"I have new instructions, Arthur."

Art had his eyes on the floor. "I'm listening."

"As you know, my team has done a large amount of research into your family and its assets. It's our understanding you don't have any brothers, sisters, parents, grandparents, or—"

"It's just me, Pete."

Although Petrut seemed more worn-down than was usual, this wasn't the only thing that was different from his typical demeanor. Art noticed there was now a certain amount of deference being given here, maybe a recognition that Art was no longer *just* the hostage. Art was *also* the decision-maker.

"And because you are the only heir, Arthur, that means you will need to decide how we proceed."

Art turned to look at the men at the table. He suddenly realized there was a new equilibrium at play. "I'll need to hear my options." Art took in the stares from Petrut and his three thugs. "And after that, gentlemen, I'll need to decide if we can do business."

Petrut smiled. "You want to hear your options?"

"I do."

The big man offered a tired chuckle. "There are only two options, Arthur, and both are very simple."

"Don't go acting smug with me, *Pete*." Art knew that everyone needed to be playing games now, most especially him. "You were going to kill me if my father didn't fork over the ransom money for my release."

Petrut started to speak. "And we still might—"

"Don't tell me you want to kill me and leave *all* of that money on the table—*my* money." Art pushed off the edge of the counter and took a few steps toward the kitchen table. He looked down at the four men who'd been holding him captive. "I don't know if your plan was to ever allow me to leave this place. I'm a witness, right? You can't have me walking about the world, knowing your names and faces and stories. It'd be crazy to just let the loose end walk away from all of this. You guys must think I'm stupid, right?"

"Let's not get emotional about this," Petrut replied. It was clear he understood things weren't going to be so simple anymore. "I'm sure we can find an agreement that guarantees your safety."

"I'll make things very clear, Pete." Art had some of that old cockiness back in his voice. "I'm not talking money until I'm back in the US."

"No."

"Fine." Art started to turn from the table. "There's nothing for us to talk about."

"We'll torture you, Arthur." The growl in Petrut's voice sounded menacing, familiar. "We'll hold you down, pull your fingernails back, then cut your fingers and toes and—"

Art interrupted the man with as much courage as he could muster. "I won't lie, Pete, I'm terrified of you and your thugs. And if I hadn't just found out that I'd lost the only family member I had left, then I'd probably go back into my little bedroom and cry for someone to please come get me. But no one is coming to help me, and I understand that now."

Petrut and his men only stared back at Art.

"So, here's the deal." Art could barely keep his voice from shaking. "You get me back to the US. Once I'm there, I'll do whatever I can to transfer the money over to your messed up little organization. And then I walk, yeah?"

A silence filled the room, one that hung in the air for a long moment.

"I'll consider it," Petrut finally conceded. "Now go to your room and pack your bag."

"Make it happen, *Pete.*"

Art left the room. Petrut and his men reverted back to French as they spoke with one another in hushed voices. Art couldn't make out a word, though. All he could really hear was the sound of his own heart pounding in his ears.

He would give them the money. Of course he would. Wouldn't anyone?

Art just needed to figure out how to stay alive in the process.

54

When Maggie Reynolds crossed into the northernmost parts of Blake County, it was close to three o'clock in the morning. Although she was exhausted and barely running on caffeine and fumes, Maggie wasn't on her way home yet. First, she had to stop by her law office in downtown Blakeston.

She needed to check the mail.

Of course, Declan Tao still hadn't returned any of Maggie's phone calls. But the lead kidnapper, a man called Petrut Noica, had agreed to stay in contact with Maggie. As promised, the man with the thick, foreign accent had called Maggie again to discuss the terms of Art Mortlake's release. Although Maggie had zero experience dealing in matters of hostage negotiation, she felt she was adapting quickly to the process.

Maggie would rely on what she knew best. She knew that insurance defense lawyers, along with the other black hats she often dealt with, were always more likely to cut a good deal with her when she had a client who made them nervous. Negotiations required a minimum amount of certainty to get any deal done, and Maggie liked when her clients were able to offer risky, unpredictable outcomes for whoever she needed to negotiate a deal with. The riskier the case, the more willing Maggie's opponents were to settle without ever going to court.

Negotiating Art Mortlake's life and well-being wasn't as straightforward as settling a client's personal injury case, but the rules of the game couldn't be *that* much different. So, after Maggie and the baritone-voiced kidnapper discussed Clive Mortlake's recent demise, she proceeded to imply that her job was to act as a voice of reason for those who stood to benefit from the Mortlake Family's estate.

Actually, Maggie did more than imply this fact. She lied about her role as the family's legal counsel. But it was the kind of misstatement she was willing to stand by, especially if it helped get her to the table to negotiate young Mortlake's freedom.

The kidnapper's only condition: *No law enforcement involvement whatsoever, and that included her husband.*

Maggie could live with that, at least for the time being.

Her only prayer was that Art would be able to as well.

Maggie pulled up in front of the offices of Reynolds Law, then parked her rental car at the curb. The small town's downtown streets were deserted at that time of night. Although Blakeston wasn't known for being a city with a high-crime rate, Maggie still didn't enjoy going into her own law office building in the darkness of night.

As she unlocked the front door to the office, Maggie noticed her firm's Christmas tree no longer stood in the front window. The holiday decorations had all come down along the brick streets outside, too. This reminded her that things just kept on moving without her there. That was life, right? Time still passed. Holidays still came and went. Big trials were still won and lost.

These truths about life, about *her* life in Blake County, were things she knew she could live with. She didn't have to be there in Blakeston all the time, pulling the strings, calling the shots. She didn't have to be seated at the top of the heap to claim the place as her own. And Maggie didn't *have* to redeem herself just to belong there.

People make mistakes, they move on. No matter how far Maggie roamed, though, she knew a part of her could always call Blake County home.

Maggie reminded herself to focus as she stepped inside the building and locked the door behind her. She didn't have time to worry about the past, didn't have the power to predict the future. All she could control was what happened now. And Art Mortlake, a kid she'd never met before, needed her to figure this thing out for him.

It wasn't about the money for her; it wasn't about the fame. This was about him.

His life depended on her.

55

Maggie found the stack of mail in her office. The dozen or so envelopes had been neatly placed at the edge of her desk. She flipped through the smaller pieces of mail first, recognizing a few of the names as those of past clients. Most of them were people who'd found their way to prison. But Maggie stopped when she reached the largest, thickest envelope in the bunch.

On the outside of the ten-by-thirteen manila envelope were the words: *FOR MAGGIE REYNOLDS' EYES ONLY.* The hand-written, block-printed lettering was in black ink. Printed on the other side of the envelope were the words: *Margaret A. Reynolds, Esquire*, followed by her law office's principal address. Written in the top left-hand corner of the envelope was the sender's name: *Clive F. Mortlake.* His last-known return address looked unfamiliar, a post office box in North Carolina.

Maggie continued to examine the outside of the manila envelope. The date stamp left by whoever accepted the piece of mail for the US Postal Service showed the envelope had been taken into their custody on December 30, 2024. This was *three days* before Maggie's first meeting with Clive Mortlake.

With a letter opener, Maggie carefully began working to pry open the top of the envelope. The last thing she wanted to do was destroy a dead man's end-of-life correspondence. She also wasn't sure whether this was going to be the kind of thing she'd be forced to eventually hand over as evidence to the authorities.

The optimist in her hoped for the best. The lawyer in her planned for the worst.

Carefully, Maggie pulled the papers out from inside the envelope. There looked to be two distinct sets of documents, each a few pages at most. Maggie noticed the name of a pretentious sounding law firm at the top of both sets of documents, so she placed them to one side of her desk. The other piece of paper was a single sheet.

It was a handwritten letter, one that read like a message from the grave.

Dear Maggie,

I sincerely hope we had a chance to meet one another. If not, this envelope and its paperwork will mean little to you.

If we did manage to cross paths, then I want to apologize for not telling you everything. Please know that I'm sorry for not having been more forthcoming about my health issues. Don't be offended. I told very few people in my life about my diagnosis. My family's need for discretion caused me to keep my cancer a secret, but I suspect my sense of pride made it that much easier for me to expect others to do the same.

I picked you to help my son because of your reputation. Before I had the Acker Family approach you, I spoke with people who claimed to know you well. People respect you, Maggie, for your willingness to approach risk with confidence. I asked those people who knew you what they thought about your suspension from the practice of law. Not a one believed you didn't have the capacity to come back stronger. I only ask that you bring my son home as part of your path to redemption.

With my letter, you will find my Last Will and Testament. For the last century my family has used creative lawyers for all kinds of tasks. The family's assets have been protected using different estate planning methods. I've taken the necessary steps to terminate and dissolve the various trusts that were used by the

Mortlake Family during my lifetime. My Last Will and Testament is all that remains in force.

Art is to receive everything from my estate. The men who kidnapped my son will not stop until they have what he is set to receive. Meet with my son, tell him my wishes are for him to transfer everything to these men. Explain to him that my only expectation is for him to go and live a full life.

My son took his best traits from his mother, yet his stubbornness came as a gift from me. He doesn't value money like I have, nor does he seek out power to find meaning in this life. What he has is grit, determination, and an unnatural ability to persist. He won't need wealth to find success in life.

Bring him home, Maggie. Assist with the transfer of assets. Make sure my son does what he knows is right. Handle this for me.

My best regards,
Clive

P.S. Even in winter, Pisgah is still beautiful.

Maggie walked around to the chair behind her desk, then took a seat. She couldn't decide if her mind was just playing tricks on her, a weary side effect from all the late-night travel. But her first pass through the handwritten letter read as if Clive Mortlake wanted his son to transfer *everything* that was left in his estate.

Maggie thought back to her airplane ride with Clive. The two had discussed a lot during their trip over to Durham, but it was clear the billionaire had not mentioned everything that was on his mind.

There on Maggie's desk was a letter and several estate planning documents. The penmanship in the letter looked neat and unhurried, and the other legal paperwork would've taken significant time to prepare.

High-net-worth estate planning wasn't even close to being in Maggie's wheelhouse. From time to time, she prepared the occasional will for a client, but these documents were always short, simple, and cheap. Blake County was still very much part of the Rural South, so most people didn't need to worry about the differences between revocable and irrevocable trusts, the parameters for gift exclusions, or reasons to consider transfers that skipped generations, a common tactic used to avoid the brunt of inheritance taxes.

Questions about the dreaded *death tax* came up from time to time during client consultations, but Maggie usually encouraged those people to speak with their accountant. A person's *taxable estate* needed to surpass somewhere in the neighborhood of fourteen million dollars—more if they could share the exemption of a spouse—but the majority of people just didn't have those kinds of assets. And the people who did never came to Maggie for their estate planning needs.

Clive Mortlake certainly wasn't the typical client, though, and it was no secret that his net-worth had fallen somewhere in the billions. That meant his estate would soon get hammered with taxes, the kind that probably caused Clive several arguments with his lawyers and CPA. The idea of forking over close to fifty percent of ten billion dollars, mostly in taxes, no doubt caused those professionals to shake their heads and ask: *What the hell was Clive Mortlake thinking?*

Maggie lifted the letter from her desk and examined it again. She had her qualms with Clive's decision to terminate his prior estate plan, but in that moment, she was focused more on some of the other language in that handwritten letter. The words read almost as if Clive Mortlake *knew* his death was imminent. Maggie stared at the last sentence from his note: *P.S. Even in winter, Pisgah is still beautiful.*

Was she misremembering her last conversation with Clive? Maggie tried to recall specific details from their three-hour airplane trip. *Didn't he tell me he would send me a letter the next time he visited Pisgah National Forest? Weren't those his exact words? That can't be right...*

Maggie glanced again at the ten-by-thirteen manila envelope that still lay on her desk. The return address looked strange, mainly because it was a place in North Carolina. She couldn't rule out the possibility that Clive also owned another home in North Carolina, but why include a post office box from that state on the envelope?

Once she'd opened a web browser on her cell phone, Maggie typed the North Carolina post office box's city and zip code into the search bar, then opened a tab to view its location on the map.

Maggie couldn't believe what she was looking at. "This can't be right..." she murmured, switching now to another tab on her phone. She found an article about the small-plane accident in the woods of North Carolina. The identity of the pilot had yet to be confirmed.

She then checked the crash location mentioned in the article, compared it with the one on the envelope. The return address and the place where Clive Mortlake's plane went down were only a few miles from each other.

"He knew exactly where he was going to put that plane down..." Maggie could only shake her head as she said these words out loud. "He knew exactly what he was doing."

56

When the private jet's wheels touched down on American soil, Art Mortlake felt as if an invisible weight had been lifted from his shoulders. Although his sudden return to the United States didn't necessarily solve his current predicament, this concession on the kidnappers' behalf still provided the satisfaction of a small victory.

Staring out through the small plane side window at his seat, Art studied the landscape that surrounded the little airstrip. Stands of tall pine trees, wiregrass, and a chain-link fence ran the length of the small, rural airstrip. Art finally saw a single metal hangar come into view, one flanked by a pair of Cessna 182s.

Art and Petrut sat next to one another. The two had not traded a single word during the entire trans-Atlantic flight.

Art turned to look at the big man. "Where are we?"

"Georgia."

Having spent some portion of his early years traipsing through the woods of North Georgia, Art liked to think he had a pretty good feel for the Southeast's largest state. But the terrain outside his little aircraft window looked vastly different from the setting he was used to seeing when he visited the northernmost parts of the state. His father's compound in Gilmer County sat cozied up to the Blue Ridge Mountains, a place surrounded by streams, dense woods, and apple orchards. This place looked wider, flatter, and much more like the parts of the country that were known for farming, hunting, and Friday Night Lights.

"What part of Georgia is this?" Art asked.

Petrut ignored the question as he stood from his seat to collect his things. The man wasn't happy with the recent changes to the game plan, and he seemed intent on letting Art know that this was all a mistake.

Petrut didn't even look at Art when he tossed one of the bags his way. "Let's go, Arthur."

The main door opened on the aircraft and Art started making his way down the stairs. He could barely suppress a smile when his feet touched the tarmac. Although Art loved to explore other countries, it always felt good to be back in his own. He'd been raised to keep an open mind when it came to the world around him, but he'd also been encouraged to never take his place of birth for granted.

"It's good to be back," Art said, speaking to no one in particular. "Home sweet home."

"There's our ride." Petrut pointed toward an approaching black SUV.

"Where are we going?" Art asked, feeling some of that familiar anxiety creep its way back in. He knew the four men who stood beside him at the aircraft. He didn't like them, but at least he was familiar with who they were, familiar with what they might be capable of. This SUV brought someone new.

"Where we go will be up to you now..." Petrut replied. He offered a short wave as the tinted-out SUV slowed to a stop. "I don't have any control over what happens at this point."

"Who are these people?" Art turned to look at the big man. "Aren't they with you?"

Petrut's face almost looked concerned. "I told you I reported to someone else, Arthur. It's time you meet him."

Art turned to look back at the SUV. When the driver's side door opened, Art instantly recognized the wheelman's face. "That son of a bitch…" Art muttered, watching the man step to the rear door and open it.

"Do you recognize any of these men?" Petrut asked. It was a question he obviously knew the answer to.

"Yeah," Art replied. "You could say that."

Declan Tao turned to face Art and the group of mercenaries. Beside him stood a tall, grey-haired man who wore a pinstripe designer suit. He pulled a pair of sunglasses from inside his jacket pocket, then slid them over his face. He leaned in close to Declan's ear and whispered something, then the two men started in Art's direction.

"Welcome home, Arthur." It was the older man in the suit who spoke. He stepped close and offered a handshake. "I'm Lawrence Fraser," he said. "I hope you know it's a pleasure to finally get to meet you."

Art didn't even acknowledge the man's outstretched hand. He just glared over at Declan. "What are you doing here?" Art demanded.

"Mr. Mortlake," he began, his tone even and professional. "I'm happy to see you've made it back home safely."

Art didn't even hesitate as he started to rush Declan. But Petrut and Jetmir were ready for him. They'd probably anticipated this kind of move from their hostage, so they both caught Art by the arms and held him back. "Let me get at him!" Art yelled this at Petrut as he struggled to break free from the man's hold. "Come on, Pete, let me loose. This doesn't have shit to do with you."

Declan didn't even move, didn't hardly react. Lawrence Fraser had backed away quickly, though, once it became apparent that his hostage had only one thing on the brain.

"Calm yourself, Arthur," ordered the man in the suit. "If you can't, I'll have these men do it for you."

Art relented for a moment. "Fine."

"We are gentlemen, Arthur." Lawrence had a peculiar sounding voice, especially for a grown man. It seemed like it was just an octave too high. "Take a moment to gather yourself, then I expect you to act in a civilized manner."

"You're right," Art said, letting out a breath as he relaxed his body. He felt Petrut and Jetmir loosen their hold on his shoulders.

"Of course I'm right," the man replied.

"You'll have to forgive me for that reaction." Art was still glaring at Declan. "I thought I saw a friend of the family."

"*Yes*, well..." Lawrence said this with a knowing smile. "That's the problem with help these days. It's just hard to find the right people, isn't it?"

Art stood up straight. He was beyond outnumbered. "So, Lawrence, what now?"

The man smiled again. "Now, we talk about repaying that debt of yours."

57

The *Consortium* was put together by E.S. Fraser. Although Fraser was of French descent, he started his American empire with the funds he'd received from a sizeable family inheritance. By the early Twentieth Century, Fraser was among those who commanded the upper echelons of American banking and finance. Among his closest friends were American Industrialists who had far too much money to spend. Fraser built his consortium (i.e. the Consortium) around two of the country's better-known steel magnates, as well as a coal baron who was making his name in the mountains of West Virginia.

The four men who formed equal parts of the Consortium all came from different backgrounds, and they'd all taken vastly different paths in their journey to achieving their wealth and success. What they all shared, though, was the simple fact that they'd spent their childhoods growing up without a father. They were men from different continents, from different religious denominations, yet they all shared a tragic story—they'd all lost a father to the horrors of war.

Of course, Fraser and these men weren't alone in this experience. They just formed part of a group that wanted to try and do something about the violence. They were an association of powerbrokers who shared the same radical ideal: world peace.

In 1907, when the twenty-six delegations gathered again in the Netherlands for a second Peace Conference, E.S. Fraser and his fellow peace-minded conspirators were in attendance. After all, powerful people were *their* people, and they were the perfect guests for a conference that focused on the humanization of warfare, global disarmament, and the general ideals of world peace. It was at this conference that the members of the Consortium came to meet a young man named Arthur Mortlake.

Arthur Mortlake didn't come from wealth. In fact, he spent the better part of his childhood in a single-story brick house, one that was no more than a stone's throw from Grand Traverse Bay and the northern edges of the Lower Peninsula. But Mortlake wanted a life that was larger than the one he'd come to know during his boyhood years spent in the Midwest. And young Arthur Mortlake believed that the Twentieth Century would be a new age in America.

Arthur believed it could be a new world.

The Mortlake that E.S. Fraser came to know was a cocky, brash young man who was steadily building his own small empire in the world of timber. Mortlake's modest upbringing ensured he wasn't above working hard, and his insatiable appetite for more in this world ensured he wasn't averse to risk.

Because of the productive conversations that Mortlake and Fraser had while they were abroad, E.S. agreed to meet with Arthur while they were both on trips through Atlanta, Georgia. Mortlake was in the South, cruising timber and scouting North Georgia properties for future land deals. Fraser was there doing business with the banks. The men had dinner together and Mortlake convinced Fraser that he was the perfect candidate for a sizeable loan. A two-million-dollar loan was simply unheard of for an operator like Mortlake at that time, but Fraser believed the investment might be possible so long as it remained *off the books*.

The hungry young Midwesterner found a Georgia lawyer to assist with the dealmaking, and soon the agreement between the Consortium and Mortlake became official. What was stressed to Mortlake at that time was the fact that Fraser—as well as his associates—expected to eventually recoup their *entire* investment made into Mortlake and his operation.

But what the Consortium really wanted was to carry on the ideals of good, peaceful works. Fraser's expectation was that Mortlake would earn more money from his businesses, and that he would in turn give generously to charities and other organizations that needed the support of wealthy capitalists.

Arthur Mortlake intended to do just that—until he lost his life in the First World War.

———

Art Mortlake listened as Lawrence Fraser finished telling the story about how their families came to know one another, and while they rode together in the backseat of that black, three-row SUV, Art couldn't help but feel like everything was finally coming to a head.

"We went to the Peace Palace," Art said, finally chiming in on the topic. "It's very impressive."

"I've visited several times," replied the older man. "My father used to take me there as a boy, and we enjoyed roaming the halls together during our private visits. It's a magnificent example of what people can do when they come together and work toward a common goal like peaceful—"

Art couldn't resist the temptation to interrupt the man. "Well, I went there under threat of violence, and then my father died during the time I was being held there for ransom."

To his credit, the man nodded and said, "I can appreciate the irony in your situation."

"It's not *my* situation, Lawrence. This story you told me is about a man I've never met, about a time that's so far in the past that it has nothing to do with what my family has done to yours. That story has nothing to do with the billions made by all the other Mortlake men and women."

Lawrence stayed silent for a moment. "I'm not going to argue with you."

"*No*, you're just going to threaten my life." Art folded his arms across his chest. "But let's just get this over with, okay?"

"Fine." The older man looked pleased. "We're going to meet with a woman who has agreed to hand over some legal documents that your father recently had prepared. His death makes things difficult for us to—"

"Just go to hell, man—" Art felt a hand on his shoulder, one he shook loose. "I'm sorry my father's death made things take a little longer for your scheme to unfold."

"You're right," the man replied. "That was rather crass of me to say. I apologize."

Art just shook his head as he turned to look out the window.

"But I've been keeping tabs on you for a long, long time." The man sounded like a weird stalker as he continued. "There's no question you have the fortitude and intelligence to excel, yet you squander your opportunities at every turn. You have a propensity for violence, you abuse alcohol and illicit drugs, and you're as promiscuous as those peers in your generation who share the lowest of standards."

"But I'm no criminal—"

"Ah, but you are, Arthur." Lawrence seemed to be enjoying his little lecture. "You just lean on your friends in organized crime to help you circumvent responsibility."

"See there, Lawrence, at least we have one thing in common."

After a long, awkward stretch of silence, the older man said: "Mr. Tao, how long do we have until we get to Blake County?"

"We'll be there in an hour, sir."

"Sublime."

58

Maggie Reynolds and Charlotte Acker sat together in the large conference room at Reynolds Law. It was Saturday afternoon, so the office building was closed for the weekend. They'd spent the entire morning preparing for Art Mortlake's arrival in Blakeston, and Maggie was starting to worry if this was something Charlotte didn't need to be involved in.

"Okay, Charlotte, they are less than an hour away." Maggie wanted to give the young lawyer another opportunity to simply back away. "I know I asked you to help me with this, but you can leave, okay?"

"And so can you." Charlotte was triple-checking everything in the stack of paperwork that lay in front of her. She had the Last Will and Testament of Clive F. Mortlake, a petition that would allow her to begin the process of opening his estate, and copies of several documents memorializing the termination and dissolution of the estate planning tools that had previously been in place for the Mortlake Family. "Besides, Maggie, I have a better handle on how to go about discussing this process."

Maggie knew that Charlotte was right, and she loved seeing the confidence continue to build in the young lawyer. "You're right. If I didn't already know how capable a lawyer you were, I'd think your feel for all this high-net-worth estate planning stuff just came from being a little rich girl."

Charlotte smiled at the jab. "I may have grown up as a little rich girl, but I'm a pauper when compared to Art Mortlake."

Maggie laughed. "I don't want to know what that makes me."

Maggie noticed her cell phone light up. Charlotte saw it too.

"Are they close?" Charlotte asked. "I thought we still had some time."

"No, this message is from Luca."

Charlotte only nodded as she turned her eyes back to the task in front of her.

"I'm going to the back to wait for them."

"Okay."

When Maggie initially asked Charlotte to get involved with Art's case, the first thing Charlotte wanted to know was this: *Why isn't law enforcement involved?*

It was a good question. And at first, Charlotte had not liked Maggie's reasoning for excluding anyone with a badge. But eventually, Maggie was able to assure the young lawyer they would have plenty of muscle available.

It was all courtesy of Luca Palomino.

The knock on the back door was loud. Maggie opened it and saw three men waiting outside. It was January in South Georgia, but these men were from somewhere in the Northeast. They wore dark jeans, T-shirts, and a mixture of cologne that preceded them by at least ten yards. But they acted like gentlemen as they politely came through the back door toting their small arsenal of weapons.

"I'm Tony." The man who spoke didn't offer Maggie a last name. It was clear to her that he was the lieutenant, the man responsible for the success of this little security operation. "I spoke to Luca this morning and he said you might want someone to watch the building from the street. He also mentioned you needed someone listening in on the meeting, maybe someone to make sure things don't get out of hand."

Maggie nodded in agreement. "That's right. Luca told me that was the safer way for us to do business today."

"Luca is always right." The way Tony said this made the short phrase almost sound like a corporate slogan. "The only way you can make the meeting safer is to bring one of us inside."

Maggie shook her head. "No, I don't need anything that might spook these guys. I want them to come into the office, I want them to sign the documents, then I expect them to leave. The smoother the transaction, the better."

"Let's hope so."

Maggie then gave the three men a quick tour of her offices. They stepped into the conference room and made vague introductions to Charlotte while they looked around. Then they all took their places. One man on the street. Two men in the adjacent conference space.

"Is there anything else you guys need?"

The lieutenant only shook his head.

"Okay," she said. "If you talk to Luca, please do remind him how appreciative I am. He didn't have to agree to send you guys my way. Thank you for being here, okay?"

"Don't mention it," Tony said. "You may want to pass along a *thanks* to Zoe, too. I hear she was very persistent..."

Maggie had assumed as much. "Well, Luca told me I shouldn't need to call him, and I took that to mean he doesn't want me to call him again."

Tony smiled. "He knows you appreciate the gesture."

"He should, and I'm sure I'll owe Luca a favor."

"Let's deal with today." Tony's voice provided a calming effect for Maggie, like a kind of confirmation that he'd done this kind of thing before. That everything usually ends up okay. "You text my phone if you need me, yeah?"

Maggie nodded, then pulled the door closed. She knew the men would be listening through the wall.

59

Art Mortlake thought downtown Blakeston looked like it belonged in one of those Hallmark movies. It was Saturday afternoon, the sun was shining outside, and all the little brick streets seemed to be bustling with activity. The shops, the town, the people, all of it just looked quaint, and the place itself made him feel like he was stepping into another world—a more peaceful one.

As the SUV continued to make its way over the brick cobbled streets, Art turned to look at the former Legionnaires who were seated behind him. "You guys ever watch those made-for-TV Christmas movies? A lot of them are set in little places throughout the American South."

For the entire hour-plus drive, Petrut, Marko, and Jetmir had been sitting together, three across the SUV's third-row bench seat. They looked more than ready to get out of the vehicle.

"I've seen some of those movies," Petrut replied. "They are always in—" he paused while he searched for the word. "That place called *Missy* something."

"Mississippi," Art corrected. "And you're absolutely right. I went through a string of those movies with this girl I dated over the holidays one year, and I bet half of those films were set in someplace Mississippi."

"They aren't films, Arthur." Art gave a little side-glance to the man seated inches away. It seemed Lawrence here liked to consider himself a shot caller *and* a cinephile. "Those movies are little more than silly, commercialized garbage."

"I don't know, Lawerence, that sounds a little harsh." Art got the impression that the older man had probably been the nerdy kid at his prep school, the guy who had lots of money yet still didn't have any friends. "My girlfriend and I enjoyed watching them. We didn't always make it to the end..." Art winked at Lawrence just to try and needle the guy.

But Lawrence clearly wanted to defend his high-brow taste. "The requisite standard must be met for something to be considered a film—"

"What do *you* consider a worthy film?" Art interrupted.

Art glanced over his shoulder at Petrut and his lackeys. They seemed to be enjoying the little debate, and, having spent the last twenty-plus days with Art underfoot, they were probably somewhat familiar with their hostage's penchant for sarcasm.

"Twelve Angry Men," Lawrence began. "Casablanca—"

"Come on." Art shook his head. "We're not talking about going to the *pictures*, Lawrence. I'm asking about films people actually enjoy watching. Not the ones they tell people they watched just to sound artsy."

"But I do love those films. They are *great,* wonderful works of art."

Art wasn't trying to be cruel. He never liked people who were cruel toward others. He just needed to see if he could push this man's buttons. "What about Shawshank?" Art soon asked. "The Godfather? What about freaking Goodfellas? Hell, I'll even throw some Batmans in there."

"Which Batman?" Petrut piped up from the backseat.

"It doesn't matter!" Lawrence exclaimed. He actually seemed to be getting a little worked up about this. "This is foolish conversation, so let's stop with it now."

Everyone in the SUV—except Lawrence, of course—seemed to be trying to suppress their laughter.

"*Mr. Tao*—" began the older man. The tone of his voice made clear he was still on edge. "Where is this woman's office?"

"It's right up here, sir."

When they stepped out of the SUV, Lawrence Fraser turned to look at his hostage. The man was taller than Art, and he stepped a little closer, almost to highlight this fact. Art began to turn away, but Lawrence reached over and placed a hand on Art's shoulder.

"I don't know this woman inside that office building," he began. "But I've told her exactly what I plan to do if the paperwork isn't in order."

"Are we splitting the legal fees on this?" Art asked.

Lawrence grimaced at the comment. He then reached inside his suit jacket and pulled out what looked like a small, semi-automatic revolver. "I don't want to hear another joke from you, understand?" The man held his gun in a way that made Art think old Lawrence probably knew how to use it. "I want you to go inside, sign your little papers, and I don't want to hear another smart-alecky remark."

Art made a face. "Smart-alecky?"

Lawrence didn't even hesitate. He brought the weapon up, smooth and confident, then whipped Art across the left side of his face with it. The metal smashed against the cheekbones with a force that just about knocked Art to the ground.

Calmly, Lawrence asked: "What was it that you just asked me, Arthur?"

Art was suddenly breathing hard. His system had switched into fight-or-flight mode. He steadied himself, though, and looked the man in his eyes.

"You want to hit me?" Lawrence whispered. "I bet you do. That's what you like to do when you get mad, right? Come on, hit me."

A moment of quiet passed, but soon the sounds of people talking could be heard from the nearby sidewalk. It sounded like they were coming around from the other side of the nearby buildings.

"Mr. Fraser—" Declan Tao said. "I'm ready to go inside if you are."

"Of course, Mr. Tao." Lawrence kept his eyes on Art for another few seconds, then slipped the revolver back inside his coat. He slowly turned to walk toward the lawyer's office.

Rubbing his face with one hand, Art started following the other men. He noticed Declan make a quick glance back. Art couldn't tell if the look was somehow meant for him.

When Declan looked back a second time, Art flipped his father's old friend the bird.

60

Maggie didn't know what to say when she saw Declan Tao at the back door. She'd spent very little time around the man, yet she felt betrayed by what she was now witnessing. The bodyguard had obviously decided to switch allegiances. Her only question was: *When did Declan decide to make the change?*

Declan came through the door first, followed by a grey-haired man in an expensive looking suit. After that, it was a young man with blood at the corner of his mouth and an angry looking red mark on his face. Maggie instantly knew who it was, and she almost reached out just to hug the bruised-up twenty-two-year-old kid.

Art Mortlake was in fact alive and mostly well. The sole heir to the Mortlake Family's fortune had at least made it this far.

Stilted introductions were made, then everyone took their seats at the conference table. Lawrence Fraser, Declan Tao, and Art Mortlake sat together on one side of the table. Maggie and Charlotte took the other side. There were four additional men—the kidnappers, Maggie assumed—who Lawrence Fraser had instructed to wait outside.

"I would like to see the documents." It was Lawrence Fraser who spoke first. It seemed he felt the need to make it clear to all in the room that he was *the man* at this table. "I'm familiar with Mr. Mortlake's most recent estate plan, so I expect—"

"I have the documents right here, Mr. Fraser." Charlotte Acker stood from her chair, then reached across the table to pass a thin set of documents over to the well-dressed man. "You'll note that the signature pages have each been flagged to make things easier."

Maggie started to speak, then stopped herself when Charlotte glanced her way. Something was off, Maggie told herself. *This wasn't the plan.*

"We've also prepared a number of items that will of course require Mr. Mortlake's signature." Charlotte was seated directly across from where Art sat at the table, yet she walked around to his side and placed the documents in front of him. "Please try not to get any blood on my paperwork."

Charlotte patted Art on the shoulder, then started making her way back around the conference table. She had a striking confidence to her in that very moment, the kind of energy that a person exuded when they mixed talent with careful preparation. But what are you doing? Maggie wanted to yell. What happened to everything we discussed?

"I was under the impression that Maggie Reynolds would be handling this meeting today." Fraser looked across the table at Maggie. He was probably as confused as she was. "Was I misinformed, ma'am?"

Charlotte cut in before Maggie could speak. "As you may know, Mr. Fraser, Maggie is sitting out from the practice of law at the moment." Charlotte paused, smiled. "And while she's sidelined, I've been tasked with managing *all* of her affairs here at Reynolds Law. I won't bore you with the details."

"That's cute." The older man chuckled. "I'm sure this is probably *off the books* when it comes to the matters of this little Podunk law firm—"

"Oh, there's nothing funny about this, Mr. Fraser." Charlotte fixed the older man with a power stare. "You're here today because Mr. Mortlake is being forced to transfer a portion of his assets over to you—"

"Our deal is everything, Ms.—" Fraser had obviously forgotten Charlotte's last name.

"It's Charlotte Acker, Mr. Fraser. That's *A-C-K-E-R.*"

"I'm not sure I like your tone, young lady. See, the deal is everything, Ms. Acker. Transferring a *portion* of Mr. Mortlake's assets was never discussed, not once."

"The paperwork in front of you is the deal, Mr. Fraser. It's the only deal. And you can take it or leave it."

From her seat, Maggie couldn't see what was actually on the paperwork in front of Lawrence Fraser. She was now very confused, though. Charlotte's role in this meeting was to explain the difficulties they would need to overcome due to Clive Mortlake's unanticipated death. His *new* Last Will and Testament had complicated matters, and this avenue required a lengthy probate process, one involving multiple jurisdictions. On top of that, there would be an enormous tax burden to satisfy, one that would have to be dealt with before any significant assets could be transferred out of the estate.

"Two million dollars?" Fraser laughed as he tossed the paperwork across the conference table. "This is ridiculous."

Charlotte shrugged. "Well, that's the deal, Mr. Fraser."

"We're leaving!" Fraser shouted. He began standing from the table. "Declan, grab Arthur over there by the scruff of his neck and—"

In that moment there was a loud knock on the conference room door. Everyone looked toward the sound, but no one made a move for the door.

61

Art Mortlake watched the door to the conference room open, then immediately popped to his feet. Waiting there in the doorway, leaning against a cane, stood Clive Mortlake. His face looked banged up, there was a cast around his left wrist, but the man still looked as proud as ever.

"Have you all come to an agreement?" Clive asked this as he slowly began working his way into the room. "I've notified the bank of the potential wire transfer, so you all just let me know when things are ready."

Lawrence Fraser had the frozen look of a man who'd just seen a ghost. "No, no..." he said. "This won't do, Clive—"

"Hold that thought, Lawrence." Art watched as his father shifted his eyes over to where he stood. "Hey son, you doing okay?" he asked.

Art only nodded, then began walking toward his father. The men almost never hugged one another anymore, but Art spread his arms out wide as he approached the man. "How?" he eventually asked, carefully leaning in for the hug. Art could tell his father was a little unsteady on his feet, so he supported the man while they hugged each other.

"It's a long damn story..." Clive whispered. "I'm here, though, and so are you. We're safe now."

"It's good to see you, *Dad*."

When Art turned back around to face the conference room, he noticed that Lawrence Fraser was back in his chair. The expression on his face looked to be one of resignation, and Art suspected it had something to do with the fact that Declan Tao was holding a gun on him. The revolver that belonged to Fraser now lay on the table, well out of his reach.

"Sign the document," Clive said, pointing to the thin stack of paperwork on the table. "Let's be done with this."

"You think this changes anything?" Fraser asked, picking up a pen.

"I do, Lawrence."

Fraser slowly paged through the documents, scratching his signature wherever necessary. "The Consortium isn't going anywhere, Clive."

"Maybe not."

"My men are outside right now, and they're—"

"Your men?" Clive asked. "Which ones?"

Art could almost see the gears turning in Lawrence Fraser's head. The man began chuckling softly. "I knew it was too perfect when I flipped Mr. Tao last year. How long have you known about that?"

A grin crept onto Art's father's face. "Well, Declan and I might've discussed it a time or two."

"And what about my—" Fraser stopped. "What about the men outside?"

"The mercenaries you went and hired to kidnap my son?"

"Right."

"Those men are sellswords, Fraser. I had a nice conversation with them out in the hall, bumped their compensation up another hundred thousand, *each*. It seemed they were happy to make the switch. Turned out they liked Art better than you."

Fraser remained silent for a moment.

"Who do you think they work for now?" Clive prodded.

"Bravo, Clive."

Fraser slid the paperwork back across the table, then started to stand from his seat. He still possessed the smugness of a man who didn't expect to ever really be held accountable for what he did. Art knew the look well. He himself had probably displayed it at times. Money just sometimes had that effect on people.

"I should be leaving…" Fraser began making a move for the door.

Clive tilted his head. "There are some other men out in the hall who're waiting to speak with you."

"Who?" Fraser asked.

"Well, you remember that little ransom note you sent me?"

"Oh, that."

Clive nodded. "You remember whose name you included?"

Fraser didn't have anything more to say.

"Now, I don't know Luca Palomino personally, but it seems he sent some men down here to help Maggie and Charlotte with their security today. It was only fair, right? You were bringing people with guns, so they brought some people with guns."

"I'll speak with them." There was no longer any color in Fraser's face. "I'll see if we can work something out."

"I'm sure you will, Lawrence."

Art watched the man slowly walk toward the doorway. He didn't know exactly how the Palomino Family liked to deal with people who crossed one of their own, but Art was willing to bet it wasn't good. He was willing to bet it wasn't good at all.

Art knew he didn't want to live that way. And although he wasn't sure exactly *how* he wanted to live, he planned to do some good in this life.

It was his turn to show up.

62

When Clive Mortlake heard the door to the conference room shut, he felt certain he would never see Lawrence Fraser again. It was a relief, *sure*, but Clive knew he wouldn't be around to see what impact this would have on his family down the road. He hoped there would be fewer secrets, fewer threats, and he prayed his son would find a way to forgive him someday.

"It's time we talk, Dad." This was Art who spoke. "I need to hear what this was really all about."

Clive considered his son's face. "I'm sorry, Art." It was about all he could think of to say in that moment. "I'm so, so sorry. I wanted to tell you sooner, I just..." Clive's words trailed off as he tried to acknowledge his own missteps. Although he'd attempted to do what was right for the Family, for his son's safety, Clive knew he'd abandoned Art, knew he'd allowed his son to fall right into the trap set by Fraser and the Consortium.

Art leaned forward in his chair and placed his elbows at the edge of the conference table. The young man had strong, defined features. He looked so much like his mother. "You can tell me now," Art said, his voice calm, his words encouraging. "We can be done with these secrets today."

Clive took in a deep breath as he considered his son's words, as he considered the faces of the other three people who were seated there at the table: Declan Tao, Charlotte Acker, and Maggie Reynolds. Clive knew he'd lied to everyone who sat there at the table with him, and he figured they all deserved to hear what secrets he'd been keeping stashed away.

"Would you like for us to step outside?" Declan asked. As always, the loyal bodyguard was ready to do what was needed of him: protect, cook, play the role of a turncoat. "We can leave you the room to discuss things," he added. "I imagine what you might say is going to be a private family matter—"

"*No*, Declan." Clive shook his head. "I think you all should hear what I have to say. Each of you helped get us here, helped keep Art safe, and you deserve to know what brought this on me and my family."

Clive decided to first turn his attention to Maggie.

"I know I certainly owe you an apology," Clive said. "Not to mention a long, long conversation about how much I appreciate your work on my son's kidnapping case."

Maggie hadn't said a word to anyone since Lawrence Fraser exited the room. Clive didn't know the small-town lawyer very well, and the stoic expression on her face gave him little insight into what she might be thinking in that moment. His guess was that she was still trying to process all that had taken place in her own conference space, still trying to decide what her role had been in all of this.

"Thank you for the apology, Clive." Maggie shifted her gaze over to where Art sat at the table. "And I'm truly happy to see that your son is okay. I mean that."

Clive grinned. "How about me?"

Maggie turned her eyes back to his. "My gut told me there was a good chance you might still be around."

"A good chance, huh?"

She nodded. "I think you could've been a little more explicit with what your plans were exactly, but—"

"And for that I'm sorry—"

"*Please* don't interrupt me, Clive." Maggie didn't sound offended or frustrated, she just seemed in control of the moment. "What I wanted to say was that I wish you would've told me more about your plans. I do understand, however, that you needed me to play a role in all of this. And that you needed Declan and Charlotte to serve your family in other ways, ways I couldn't at this moment in my life and career."

It wasn't the reaction Clive had expected from Maggie. "What do you want to know?" he asked.

"When did you hire Charlotte?"

Clive nodded to his left, where Charlotte Acker sat quietly. "Charlotte took me on as a client about a week after Art's disappearance."

Maggie seemed to accept this answer. "That would've been right around the time she came to work for me, right?"

"Thereabouts."

"And I suppose you instructed her to not speak of your attorney-client relationship?"

"That's right." Clive paused for a moment. He wanted Maggie to know she wasn't just another pawn on his chessboard. "But it was the only way I could trust anyone to bring the information about our meeting to you. That was our goal, okay? We wanted you to be in place for the negotiations."

Maggie didn't appear convinced. "So, you knew all along that the Long Island mobsters weren't involved?"

Clive kept his eyes on hers. "I wasn't exactly sure who it was that—"

Maggie cut him off. "What were you sure about?"

Clive could hear the tension rising in her voice. "I figured the kidnappers would be monitoring things. I wasn't sure who it was calling the shots, but my guess was that they would contact you once you went to the Palomino boy."

"Which they did."

"*But*—" Clive wanted to emphasize his gratitude here. "I never expected you to bring the Palomino Family in on this. I certainly never expected them to come all the way down to Georgia to take care of Lawrence Fraser. That was all you, Maggie."

Maggie could've responded with more frustration. Instead, she chose genuine modesty: "I had plenty of help, Clive. It was Luca Palomino and his future daughter-in-law who made this happen on such short notice."

Clive smiled. "I'll be sure to thank them as well."

"You do that."

A long moment of quiet hung over the room, then Clive heard Art ask: "But who the hell was that Lawrence Fraser guy?"

Clive looked over at his son. Whenever he stared into that face, he could see the boy, the young man, and the boy's mother, all in one. Remnants of Art's mother continued to live on in that face, and Clive hoped those shadows of Marilyn Mortlake never faded. "You know, Art, you look just like your mother..."

Art offered him a look of annoyance. "Don't change the subject on us."

"*I'm not.*" Clive tried to keep his voice calm. He was about to tell those in the room something he'd never told a soul. "I was just reminded of your mother when you asked me that question about Fraser."

"Mom knew about Lawrence Fraser?" Art seemed confused.

"Your mother and I only discussed Fraser once." Clive winced slightly as he repositioned himself in his chair. "And I explained to her that Lawrence Fraser was just a man who was trying to revive the ideals of an old, shadowy organization called the Consortium."

Art didn't offer a reply as he appeared to chew on this bit of new information.

Clive pressed on. "Now, I know you remember the day she passed away, and you probably recall the argument she and I had that afternoon before she left the mountain house in her car."

"I remember you two screaming at each other at the top of your lungs..." Art was obviously ready to make sure the record reflected exactly what he recalled about that day. "I remember her swearing to you that she was going to come back home and take me with her, that she wasn't going to let me be around you anymore."

Clive let those words marinate for a moment. His son's recollection was spot on. "*Yes,* Art, that was what she wanted."

"But what does that day have to do with my kidnapping?"

"Son, that day has everything to do with what happened to you over the past weeks." Clive felt his voice beginning to crack. "Your mother found out about the people from the Consortium. I told her they were demanding our money, threatening our lives, but I also assured her that we could handle someone like Lawrence Fraser. I promised her the best security money could buy, yet she was adamant that we just make a deal. And she told me something bad would happen to you and her and me if I didn't do something about it."

Art nodded. "And she was right, wasn't she?"

"That she was."

Another stretch of silence filled the room. Clive knew he still needed to tell his son about how this all came to be. "Art, you know that for years and years the Mortlake Family has sacrificed."

"I know all about our family's military history."

Clive nodded. "I know you do, Art. I'm not sure you appreciate the sacrifices of those people they left behind, though."

"I know it's *Big Arthur* who apparently signed for this mysterious two-million-dollar loan, and I remember you telling me about his courage in the First World War."

"*But—*" Clive needed his son to understand what happened. "I don't think you realize that it was Helen Mortlake, your great-great-grandmother, who took the reins after his death in Belgium."

"Well, did she know about this loan?"

Clive had thought about this question many times. "I'm not sure, Art, but I doubt Big Arthur ever told her about it."

"Which means she wouldn't have told your grandfather about the loan before he died in the Second World War..." Art seemed to be thinking out loud. "And that would've meant your mother and father wouldn't have known about the loan before your dad died in Vietnam."

"Exactly," Clive said. "And all the while our family's wealth continued to grow and grow and grow."

Art nodded. "Millions, hundreds of millions, then billions."

Clive didn't know what effect the money would have on Art throughout his lifetime. When Art remained focused on his goals, those like basketball or academics, he didn't allow time for their family's enormous wealth to warp his views of the world. But whenever Art strayed from purpose, the young man fell into those same unavoidable traps that all people faced when they lacked direction in life.

"How did Lawrence Fraser come to be involved?" Art asked.

"I'm not exactly sure how he came to know about the loan." Clive figured they'd probably never know the answer to that question. "But Fraser could be anyone, okay? I need you to understand this."

Art nodded to show he was listening.

"In fact, you could wind up like him one day if you're not careful..."

"That won't happen," Art scoffed.

Clive smiled. "We all say things like that when we're young, but we don't know what will happen tomorrow. And Lawrence Fraser came from immense wealth, just like you. He also convinced himself that he could pick up the charitable, peaceful cause of the Consortium, and he probably believed he could do *good* things with the wealth our family controls."

"He was obviously willing to do some terrible things to get what he wanted."

"No question." Clive glanced around the table. "You all should know that my family has always supported charities that focused on feeding the hungry, sheltering the homeless, and caring for those who don't have the means to care for themselves. But we've also provided great support to the peaceful efforts in this world."

Declan offered a nod. "I know that to be the case, Mr. Mortlake."

"Yet it's not lost on me that my family has a responsibility, one that Art will soon be tasked with carrying forward. I only have a short time left on this earth, but people like Fraser will continue to try to attack the ideals of important institutions like those housed inside the Peace Palace. They will claim that their efforts are purer, more noble, and they will come disguised as businesspeople and philanthropists and politicians."

"People like Bedford Mitchell?" Art asked.

"Yes and no." Clive set his sights squarely on his son. "You need to recognize that political ideologies and causes are always just another part of the disguise. People will grovel for your support, but they'll all have an agenda, they'll all claim to be doing what's right."

"And most will genuinely believe they're doing what's right." It was Maggie Reynolds who added this point. "You'll need to anticipate this part of their approach, Art, and you'll need to know that people often begin to believe the lies they tell themselves."

Clive smiled. "I couldn't have said it better."

Art let out a heavy sigh. "How do I know who to support? And will I just know how much I should give away?"

"That'll *all* be up to you, son."

"I'll do my best..." Art shook his head as he said this, then turned to look across the table at Maggie. "Hopefully I'll have some people around me who're willing to provide some counsel every now and then."

Clive leaned back in his seat. He watched as his son and the advocate stood from their chairs, then exchanged a handshake across the table. Art then placed a hand on Declan's shoulder and invited him to continue working with the family for as long as he was willing to serve. And Art then thanked Charlotte for her role in helping put an end to this ordeal. Clive was proud of his son, proud of Art's grit and perseverance.

What a resilient, selfless young man he'd become, Clive thought. And what an incredible person for the world to benefit from in the years to come.

63

The weeks passed slowly after that final meeting with Clive Mortlake. Maggie spent the rest of January in Blake County, but she never once went by her handsome law office in downtown Blakeston. Most of Maggie's mornings involved a long run along the banks of the Chattahoochee River, a stint of work in the new garden she'd built in her backyard, and an hour or so curled up somewhere with her nose in a book. Maggie did all of this, of course, in an attempt to keep herself from thinking about the law, to keep herself from waiting on what might come next.

Maggie was finishing up her work in the garden when the phone call came in.

It was Declan Tao.

Maggie placed the phone to her ear. "This is Maggie."

"Good morning," began the bodyguard. "It's Declan Tao."

Maggie used the back of her garden glove to wipe sweat from her brow. Gone were the spats of cold weather that'd visited South Georgia during their winter holidays. "I know, Declan, I still have your number saved in my phone. What's up?"

There was a long pause before the man spoke again, and that eerie silence brought with it a feeling of déjà vu. "I just wanted to call and let you know that..." Declan seemed to hold off on saying the words.

Maggie knew in that moment there could only be one reason for this phone call.

Declan cleared his throat, then pressed on: "I wanted to let you know that Mr. Mortlake passed away earlier this morning."

"Oh Declan, I'm *so* sorry..." Maggie stood on her porch, staring out at where her lawn stretched to the edge of the woods at the back of her house. It was early February, the sun was shining, and much of southwest Georgia was already beginning to look like spring. It would be a beautiful day for some, a hard day for others. "Were you and Art there by his side?" she asked.

"Yes, ma'am." Declan breathed a heavy sigh into his side of the call. "We were there until the end. Another friend of the family, Dr. Sarah Thompson, was right there with us. She'd monitored Mr. Mortlake in his final days and made sure he was able to pass with his privacy and dignity intact."

"I'm glad to hear he was able to go the way he wanted."

"Me too."

Maggie paused for a moment, then added: "It's strange to think how it's all so official now..."

Declan stayed on the line but didn't offer a response.

Maggie had discussed Clive's wishes at the end of their last meeting together. The billionaire had done a magnificent job concealing his where-abouts after his floatplane crashed in the mountains of western North Carolina, and his plans all along had been for him to never resurface. His intent was to instead let the investigators and appropriate authorities settle on the conclusion that Clive Mortlake had perished alone in that fiery plane crash.

"I know you're going to miss him, Declan." Maggie figured this was something the bodyguard wouldn't readily admit. "And you should take time to grieve something like this."

"I've already come to terms with what this means, ma'am."

Maggie figured the security specialist had already been questioned weeks ago about Clive Mortlake's shocking demise. In fact, two weeks had already passed since the death was ruled official, and the obituaries and articles had already run in many of the world's major newspapers. Almost all who knew Clive Mortlake believed he'd been dead for several weeks now.

"Is there something I can do for you or Art?" Maggie asked. "Was there anything more Clive asked you to tell me?"

Declan's voice regained some of its familiar professionalism now. It seemed his responsibilities had kicked back in. "He did ask me to tell you a couple of things..."

"Go on," Maggie said.

"He wanted you to know that you can continue to send any invoices directly to me. I'll make sure you get paid for any future legal work."

Maggie smiled into the phone. "I've been well paid for the work I've performed."

"Well—" Declan wasn't very good at acting nonchalant. "He believed there would be more work in the future. At least, he hoped there would be."

"Okay," Maggie said. A paying client was never something to scoff at. "What else?"

"His son."

"What about him?" Maggie asked.

"The young man will need your advice. I'm not sure when, but that day will come."

When Maggie finished her call with Declan, she couldn't help but wonder what her purpose might be in any future dealings with Art Mortlake. The young man had decided to remain in the shadows, just like his father had, and the twenty-two-year-old Duke senior had no plans to return to Durham to finish out his last semester of college. In fact, last she'd heard, the young man hadn't decided whether he would ever return to the life he once knew.

Her instructions were to tell no one he was alive. Maggie knew the investigation into his murder was still open and ongoing, but few really believed it would move forward without any new findings or evidence.

Art Mortlake was all but dead, and that seemed to be the way he wanted it.

At least for now.

Although Maggie wouldn't admit this to anyone, she'd come to be at peace with the role she'd played in the search for Art Mortlake. She didn't consider herself to be the kind of person who spent much time in the past, nor did she have much patience for matters that involved serious introspection. But Maggie had actually tried her best to decide how she *really* felt about what happened in her last meeting with Clive Mortlake.

Charlotte Acker, a person Maggie still trusted to this day, had blatantly deceived her. The young lawyer had come to Maggie with a story about this family friend who needed some advice: *a voice of reason* is how she'd put it. Charlotte had allowed Maggie to play right into the plan assembled by the late Clive Mortlake. It was an experience she wanted to be angry about, maybe even embarrassed by, but Maggie just didn't feel any of those things.

Maggie recognized that her experience working for the Mortlakes was exactly what she'd needed. Thirteen years she'd been representing clients, taking them into courtrooms, arguing on their behalf. For thirteen years she'd been telling people, as well as herself, that she deserved to be on the big stage.

The suspension of her law license had been a wake-up call, *sure*, but it hadn't caused her to stop and consider what more she needed to learn about the work itself. The six-month suspension hadn't caused her to really think long and hard about anything other than herself, about anything more than her reputation and pocketbook.

But the experience of being blindsided by a young, green lawyer like Charlotte had forced Maggie to reevaluate everything: assumptions, beliefs, process, all of it. And Maggie was willing to accept there was *always* going to be more for her to learn about her work. The practice of law was like an open book test, but Maggie had stopped going back to study and review her own materials. She'd fallen into the trap of believing she knew everything there was to know about the law.

She didn't know everything about the work—but that's why they call it *practicing* law.

Maggie smiled as she turned to head inside the house. She had a few more months to get her mind right, to reset her own expectations for the courtroom—and she knew she could be better than ever, so long as she stayed true to doing things the right way.

Her cell phone started ringing again.

This time it was Zoe Mitchell.

Maggie hesitated for just a moment, then answered. "This is Maggie."

"I wasn't sure you would take my call." From the background noise on Zoe's end of the line, it sounded like she was driving. "How's it going?" asked the young woman.

"I'm doing okay, Zoe." Maggie spoke as she continued inside her house. It felt good to be back in the air conditioning. "I've actually been meaning to call you."

"Yeah?"

Maggie wanted to kick herself for not calling the young woman sooner. "I wanted to thank you for being, well, so persuasive with your soon-to-be father-in-law. His assistance was greatly appreciated. And that's a serious understatement."

Zoe seemed to consider those words for a moment. "Well, I'm glad, Maggie. I just felt like we needed to give Art a fighting chance."

Maggie knew their conversation was heading toward a subject that Art Mortlake explicitly asked Maggie to avoid discussing with anyone.

"I waited and waited for you to call," Zoe added. "I just never heard anything back on how things went. So, I guess that's why I'm reaching out to you now..."

"Well—" Maggie knew it'd been a mistake to pick up this phone call. "I know you're not going to like my answer, Zoe, but I really can't get into how things went down. There's an NDA and some other instructions that prevent me from discussing it with anyone."

"I see..."

Maggie stayed silent for a moment, hoping the young woman might be able to just read between the lines.

"You really can't tell me anything?" Zoe asked.

Maggie deflected. "Go speak to your future father-in-law about it. Luca will talk to you, right?"

"No, that's not an option."

Maggie couldn't blame the Long Island mobster for refusing to speak with Zoe on the topic. Luca Palomino's own men probably stuffed Lawrence Fraser into the trunk of their car, and it wasn't a stretch to assume that the well-dressed older gentleman had ended up somewhere near the bottom of a lake or river, heavy cinderblock attached to his feet.

"Look, Maggie." Zoe sounded frustrated. "I wouldn't be asking you this if I didn't have a good reason."

Maggie kept quiet.

"I'm just leaving a doctor's office here in Durham." The young woman's voice sounded clear, committed. "I need to speak to Art if he's still alive. There's something he deserves to know."

"Again, Zoe, I don't know what else to say—"

"You saw the video, Maggie." Zoe wasn't giving up. "That night was a little over seven weeks ago...and, well, we didn't use protection, okay? And I realized a week ago that I was late, you know?"

Maggie did know. "And you think this—"

Zoe cut her off again. "I know it's Art's child, okay? Don't ask me how I know, I just do."

It was one of those moments Maggie wasn't prepared for.

"And before you tell me you can't help me, Maggie, I just want you to hear me out."

Maggie *did* want to help her. "I'm listening, Zoe."

There was a long pause, then Zoe said: "If Art is still alive, then I need you to tell him he's going to be a father, and I need you to tell him I'm not going to marry Tom anymore. That's *all* I'm asking you to do for me."

"If I could tell you what happened that day, I would."

"I'm not asking you to tell me anything, Maggie. I'm just asking you to tell him what I've told you. I know you'll do the right thing."

Zoe then hung up the call before Maggie could even respond.

Maggie shook her head. Now she knew what the first item of discussion would be next time she spoke with her twenty-two-year-old client.

Art Mortlake would soon have an heir to his estate.

He would no longer be the last Mortlake left.

64

Art Mortlake sat alone on a bench. His eyes were fixed on the main entryway to *Fort de Nogent*, the Paris-based recruiting center for the French Foreign Legion. The gates to the fortress stood open. *La Légion étrangère*—the famous corps of mercenary soldiers—welcomed candidates three-hundred-sixty-five days a year, and Art knew that volunteers arrived at pres-election centers across France every single day. The candidates were men who came from countries all over the world, and yet they all wished to serve the Legion for one reason or another.

Art had his own reasons, *sure*, but that didn't mean there also weren't still a few memories pulling him back toward his old life. He had friends back home, an enormous estate that would need tending to, and he also had a future there that could be molded into just about anything a man could ever want.

But his father's passing had left him with no family to speak of, and Art wasn't yet sure he was ready to make the crucial decisions that were necessary to guide the Mortlake name forward. Art needed to understand himself more, needed to test his own beliefs and limits in a world that didn't view him as the heir to billions.

To put things simply: Art still had some growing up to do.

Art lifted his backpack from the sidewalk, then stood from the bench.

He knew that once he stepped inside the walls of that historic fortress, his grit and determination would never allow him to turn back. He planned to attack this fresh start in life without quarter, and he would do so under a new name—*Henry Duke*—his *nom de guerre*.

Art knew the investigation into his disappearance still remained open, and he believed the authorities back in North Carolina would keep his investigative file on a shelf for many years to come. But contrary to popular lore, the French Foreign Legion of the modern era did not operate under a *no questions asked* policy. Although the regimental history of the Legion probably included many a man who'd joined its ranks with a questionable past, those days were gone. Proof of identity. Probing questions. Background checks. All of it was part of the modern selection process.

Except Art Mortlake wouldn't be vetted like every other run-of-the-mill candidate. He'd put in a phone call to Petrut Noica ahead of his trip to Paris. Petrut and his group of former legionnaires, the men responsible for kidnapping Art, had pulled some strings with the higher-ups in their old regiment.

The Legion would be expecting him.

As Art stepped through the fortress gates, he thought about the life he was leaving behind. *Yes*, he was running from the person he'd been, but Art wasn't set on running forever. He would hold himself to the highest standards while serving the Legion, and he would dig deep inside himself so that he could find the courage to represent his country and family with dignity. But eventually, Art did plan to return home to build a life he could take real pride in.

Art would miss his friend Frank, would miss getting to watch his buddy do big things in the next chapter of life. He would miss Zoe, too, although he knew she would be getting married later that year and would be starting in on the life she really wanted. It was a life and a marriage that would follow Tom Palomino on his path to the NBA, and it was a path that would probably lead them toward a growing family with kids and dogs and all the memories that make life truly worth living.

Art wanted those things one day.

Stopping before a large archway that stood just inside the fortress walls,

Art stared up at the words that'd been stamped high above: *Legio Patria Nostra.*

Art knew this doctrine served as a motto for legionnaires, a sort of slogan for the foreigners who joined the ranks of this famous land army. Men came to fight as mercenaries because they sought refuge and shelter in the Legion, because they were stateless fugitives, political refugees, or purposeful deserters of their own homeplace. Others came in search of adventure, a taste of the Legion's *esprit de corps*, and the opportunity to learn the craft of soldiery.

Art was there to test his own limits and to learn about the immutable laws of combat and violence. Although Art had no interest in transferring the bulk of his family's assets to any group in particular, he did recognize there was still an incalculable debt that needed to be repaid. His family had a responsibility founded on the ideals of a better, more peaceful world, and once Art had a greater understanding for what caused violent conflict, he would go in search of what solutions there were to avoid it.

This would take time. All things that truly mattered did.

But while Art was away, Declan Tao would be keeping an eye on things back home. The loyal friend and bodyguard was the only person who knew where Art was now, and Art had no doubt the man would keep his whereabouts a secret. Should an issue arise, written letters were to be the only acceptable form of communication.

The plan was simple: Art would check back in with Declan after a year.

Not a cent of Mortlake money was to move before that time.

EXHIBIT "D"
THE LETTER

March 21, 2025

Leg. Henry Duke, 852005
c/o 1er *Régiment étranger*

Mr. Duke:

I hope this letter finds you doing well.

I'm writing to inform you of a recent conversation that I had with the advocate. It appears there has been a material change insofar as your personal affairs back home. The advocate needs to discuss her findings with you as soon as it is practicable for you to do so.

Congratulations are in order, as it seems you have an heir. Your father would be proud.

Take extra care in your efforts abroad.

I'll await your response.

My best regards,
Declan Tao

JUSTICE BITES
Book 1 in the Smith and Bauer Legal Thriller Series
By James Chandler and Laura Snider

Washed-up, small-town lawyer Marko Bauer already has enough on his plate. And with his latest case, he may have bitten off more than he can chew.

Defending Allee Smith's cousin on what appear to be run-of-the-mill drug charges, Marko quickly discovers that the case is just the tip of the iceberg in their town's murky waters. The eye of the storm? The Yellow Lark restaurant, an eatery with more secrets than specials on the menu.

Allee, fresh out of the clink and trying to stitch her life back together, turns out to be the ultimate wingwoman. Dragged into the fray, she and Marko discover a thumb drive crammed with the kind of secrets that make people disappear.

They're playing with fire, and it's about to get hot.

In a town where truth is a commodity and the price of justice is steep, Marko and Allee are caught in a desperate race against time. Unraveling the town's secrets could be their path to redemption—or the road to disaster.

Get your copy today at
severnriverbooks.com

ABOUT THE AUTHOR

Joe Cargile is an American novelist, lawyer, and displaced Southerner. The pages from his books are filled with settings that have been influenced by his love for travel, sports, and the ever-evolving South. With stories inspired by his work in the courtroom—an arena he believes plays host to fearsome competitors, and often some of our world's most interesting characters—he holds deep admiration for those tireless advocates who set the standard for the trial lawyer. He lives and works in London, England, with his wife and three daughters.

Sign up for the reader list at
severnriverbooks.com

Printed in the United States
by Baker & Taylor Publisher Services